AUDREY LANE STIRS THE POT

ALEXIS HALL

sourcebooks
casablanca

Copyright © 2026 by Alexis Hall
Cover and internal design © 2026 by Sourcebooks
Cover illustration and design by Elizabeth Turner Stokes
Internal design by Laura Boren/Sourcebooks
Internal images © anna42f/Getty Images, Waehatman Waedarase/Getty Images

Published by Sourcebooks Casablanca, an imprint of Sourcebooks
1935 Brookdale RD, Naperville, IL 60563-2773
(630) 961-3900
sourcebooks.com

Cataloging-in-Publication Data is on file with the Library of Congress.

Printed and bound in the United States of America.
LB 10 9 8 7 6 5 4 3 2 1

To the team at Sourcebooks Casablanca,
without whom this book literally wouldn't have been possible

WEEK ONE

Cakes

Friday

IT WAS NATALIE'S fault. Beautiful, brilliant, ambitious Natalie, who Audrey had grown up with, fallen in love with, followed to university and to London and then, at last, been dumped by. Or, in Natalie's preferred framing, with whom she had come to the completely mutual conclusion that they'd be better off without each other.

It was Natalie's fault that she'd left Shropshire for the gleaming allure of a big-city career. And Natalie's fault she'd come *back* to Shropshire a decade later with a ton of experience in an environment she never wanted to work in again. And that she'd taken a job with a tiny local newspaper whose circulation her previous editor would have laughed at. Well, would have laughed at if he hadn't mostly reserved his laughter for sexist jokes and his rivals' failures.

It was also—somewhat indirectly—Natalie's fault that Audrey had got drunk one evening and sent in a joke application to appear on the self-described-national-favourite *Bake Expectations*. An application that had turned into an audition and then, somehow, into a place on the show. Which meant it was also—in a very real sense—Natalie's fault that Audrey was behind on work, stressed about the quality of her simnel cake, and getting called into her boss's office over what his email described as an "extremely serious issue."

The boss in question was a man named Gavin Pettiforth who had, allegedly, been quite a big deal at one point, although nobody was quite able to remember how or when. Audrey found him sitting in front of a printout of her latest article, which was normal Gavin behaviour. In a doomed effort to save paper, Audrey and Trish from Entertainment had once tried to get him to stop printing out every single email and attachment that crossed his desk. Then once they'd watched him try to read from a screen without opening the wrong document, losing his place, or accidentally deleting something, they'd got him to start again.

"Sorry." He looked up at her over half-rimmed glasses. Lisa from Advertising had once told Audrey that Gavin had been quite dashing in his day, but that had been years ago, and he'd since graduated from "dashing" to "avuncular" and was now hovering on the edge of "wizened."

"I know you've got your"—he waved a hand in distracted circles—"you know, the baking thing, and of course we're all in your corner on that front. But this couldn't wait because we're going to press soon, and I wanted to make absolutely certain that we had this piece *perfect* before you went."

Gavin, like many of the staff at the *Shropshire Echo*, had his enthusiasms. Enthusiasms that weren't necessarily directed towards ends Audrey would, personally, have hoped he'd be directing his enthusiasms towards. But he was her boss and her editor, and so it was his job to edit, sometimes bossily. "Happy to make changes before I go."

Beaming, Gavin gave Audrey an approving nod. "That's just what I wanted to hear. Remember, Audrey, we are Shropshire's second largest regional newspaper. People from Ludlow to Whitchurch are depending on us for the facts and *details matter*. Especially on a story like this. One that really impacts people's lives."

Reaching across the desk, Audrey slid the printout of her article over and turned it round to reread it. "What do you think needs doing?"

"Well, it's the headline," explained Gavin. "Headlines are very important. They're the thing that really catches somebody's eye. They're the peacock's tail. The rooster's—you know, red bit on the top of his head. It needs to entice and intrigue, but not be sensationalist. We want to *lead*"—he made a gathering motion, showing how he imagined a well-crafted header would draw the reader further into the story—"but not to *mis*lead. You see?"

It all looked fine to Audrey, but she'd got to know Gavin pretty well since joining the *Echo*. "It's too sensationalist, isn't it?"

"I think so." Concern spread across Gavin's face like marmalade over a crumpet.

"So what do you suggest?"

"Well"—he took the paper back and peered at it—"I think, to me, 'Much Wenlock Car Park Charges to Increase' might be deemed to be putting an unduly negative spin on council decisions. And media impartiality is increasingly important these days. Look what happened to Gary Lineker."

"Okay," said Audrey in her best I'm-listening-and-learning, do-go-on voice.

"The issue might be around the word *increase*." Gavin made an almost mystical gesture, as if conjuring storms or gathering teacups. "I appreciate that it is strictly speaking factual. But is that the element of the narrative we want to foreground?"

"How about," suggested Audrey, "we go to 'Much Wenlock Car Park Charges to Change'?"

Gavin thought about this for a long moment. Then for a longer moment. Then for a moment so long it slipped past the point where it could be considered a moment at all. "Change," he mused. "Change. Yes. Yes, I like it. It has sort of"—another gesticulation, like a tree growing out of a fountain—"millennial optimism to it."

"I'll get right on it."

Getting right on it consisted of Audrey going back to her desk, rebooting her computer, changing one word in a file, emailing that file to Gavin, and, in order to save time, running off a hard copy in advance so that she wouldn't have to wait for Gavin to print it himself.

In her mind, Natalie was giving her that *really* look again. And, right at that second, Audrey didn't have the energy to look back. It was, after all, true that this particular instance of this particular part of her job wasn't exactly taxing her faculties to their limits.

Three-years-ago Audrey lived in the heart of a thriving metropolis, did anything for the story, never slept, subsisted on a takeaway-only diet, had extremely infrequent but extremely intense sex with her long-term girlfriend, and was miserable. Present-day Audrey baked the occasional cake for nobody, drove to small villages in a Mini Cooper for the story, slept okay-ish, and had serious conversations about how to tackle the hot-button issue of parking charges in Much Wenlock. Sometimes, present-day Audrey wondered if she shouldn't have just stuck with the misery.

Edits made, she shut her computer down again—waiting as

she always did to be sure it was definitely off. Because if it didn't shut down properly she *would* come in on Monday to find Andy from Maintenance sitting on her desk saying, *Forgot something on Friday, did we?*—and made a dash for her car.

Reflecting on her life choices was the last thing Audrey wanted to be doing, but the long drive out of Shropshire through Wolverhampton, Birmingham, and the dreaded London to finally reach Surrey and the set of *Bake Expectations* was, unfortunately, the sort of trip that gave you plenty of time to reflect. Plenty of time to ask six-months-ago Audrey what the fuck she'd been thinking. And for six-months-ago Audrey to sit back and reply, *Oh come off it, you know perfectly well.*

And she did.

Because this was the biggest thing—so far at least—that was Natalie's fault.

Six months ago was when Natalie had won the Orwell Prize for a nuanced yet hard-hitting article she'd written in *The Guardian* about... Actually, Audrey couldn't remember the details, but something worthy: domestic terrorism or climate change or one of the many other ways the world was screwed and getting screweder. She should have known. It was petty of her *not* to know. A mature, reasonable woman in her thirties was completely capable of acknowledging that her ex-girlfriend was continuing to be brilliant and successful and celebrated without blotting out as many of the details as she could with Lidl wine and competitive baking.

Audrey had not, in that moment, been a mature, reasonable woman. She had instead decided that it was the most important thing in the world to show Natalie—or the gaping judgmental void where Natalie used to *be*—that she was more than just a technically not failed journalist working for a second-rate local paper. She was also, she could declare with the confidence of a proud LGBTQ+ role model, pretty okay at making buns, too.

It was, in retrospect, a slight point of concern for Audrey that she'd been accepted on *Bake Expectations* despite being so blitzed out of her skull that she couldn't actually remember what she'd written on her entry form. Either it meant that she was such a fantastic writer that even completely hammered she could weave an enchanting word picture about how she would be an asset to the show, or—perhaps more likely—she was this year's joke contestant: a loveable drunk who was going out in week one for putting far too much rum in her baba. Maybe she'd redeemed herself at the follow-up interview.

Or maybe she'd just cemented the idea that she was a charmingly incompetent buffoon, like Bernard from last season.

For about an hour and a half, Audrey let herself stew in insecurity like a plum in a syrup made of disappointment. Then, since an hour and a half only got her halfway to her destination and since she'd seen a lot of statistics about fatigue-related fatalities, she stopped at a service station. Checking her phone on the way to the loo, she found four messages. One was from her dad and said Good luck on BE. The other three were from her mother and said, respectively: Your father keeps telling me you're filming this week. Then But I'm sure it's next week. Followed by Good luck in case it isn't. She sent back a thanks and an actually Dad was right, gave herself ten minutes of not-driving time to grab a coffee and a croissant, and then hopped back in the car.

With the caffeine helping her feel slightly more awake and the croissant helping her feel slightly more like she'd eaten a croissant, Audrey set off on the final leg of the journey. Once she'd skirted London courtesy of the M25, she was relieved to be herself back in the countryside. Having been born in it, Audrey had an abiding fondness for rural England, although she privately felt that the South and East couldn't really compete with the Welsh borders. There was an indefinable Londonishness that radiated out from the capital and made the land for miles around seem regimented and uniform in ways the North and the West never were.

She was barely over the county line into Surrey when she spotted the first sign for Patchley House and Park, which had gone from obscure hotel in a former stately home to a semi-major tourist attraction thanks to the magic of mass media. From its iconic wrought iron gates, it was a short-for-a-road-but-long-for-a-driveway trip up to the gravelly carpark. And then it was a matter of following the CONTESTANTS THIS WAY notices that, in contrast to the homey-but-slick presentation of the on-camera parts of the show, were just A4 paper run off on a printer and taped onto whatever surfaces could support them. These led her, at last, to a bored-looking man who signed her in and told her to make her way down the hill to the Lodge. As a longtime fan of the show—albeit one who'd had to watch it alone while Natalie was out networking or otherwise living the careerist dream—Audrey was still waiting for the moment when it all started to feel *real*. Or at least to feel unreal in the way that she assumed it would. In that oh-my-God-I-can't-believe-I'm-actually-here way that other people seemed to get, rather than the "welp" way that she was currently experiencing.

She found her room fairly easily, dumped her things, and checked her phone to see if her parents had resolved their "is our

daughter on TV yet" debate. As it turned out, they both had and
hadn't, the response from her dad being see, I told her and the one
from her mum saying sorry, I was getting it mixed up with Auntie
Beryl's haemorrhoid appointment. Communication, Audrey had
always believed, was the basis of a healthy relationship. But if her
parents were anything to go by, it didn't actually have to be coherent or effective communication.

She texted back to her dad apparently she was thinking of
Auntie Beryl's haemorrhoid appointment (now that's a week next
Tuesday he replied) and to her mum do you often confuse me with
Auntie Beryl's bottom (her response was: only when you act like
an arse). Between messages, she sat on the edge of the bed, trying
not to have too many thoughts. It had been long enough since the
breakup that, theoretically, being alone was something she should
have been used to. But at home she had her work and her family
and—not to sound too materialistic—her *stuff* to keep her from
dwelling. A hotel room, especially the kind of hotel room you
got on a BBC budget, was precision engineered to make a person
regret every decision they'd ever made in their entire life.

So-called "reality" television, Natalie was explaining in her
head, *constructs false narratives that pressure people into living up
to unrealistic standards.* And Audrey tried to push back a little
by pointing out that it was just people making cakes in a nice
house, but Natalie's voice, as always, was insistent. *It's a parochial,
whitewashed—in both senses of the word—illusion of Britishness for
Brexiteers and housewives. I honestly can't believe you watch it.* And
she didn't have an answer to that, any more than she'd had one
when the conversation, or conversations very much like it, had
originally happened.

She should have brought a project. Audrey was the sort of

person who liked to have a project, even if the project was just a jigsaw on the kitchen table. The bedroom in her new flat was full of bags of yarn and piles of fabric, which were slowly being converted into scarves no one in particular wanted to wear and quilts no one in particular wanted to snuggle under.

Partly, she would be the first to admit, because they weren't very good scarves or quilts. Just like her hand-painted bowls weren't very well painted and her one attempt at kintsugi had left the broken vase looking both worse and still broken. For the first couple of years of their relationship, her fondness for crafting had driven Natalie up the wall, a conflict Audrey had resolved by… stopping. Giving up or, in Natalie's words, acknowledging there were better ways to use her time.

Sitting on the bed, staring at the wall, Audrey remained lost with her thoughts just long enough to conclude that staying in her room would definitely suck. And while wandering the grounds aimlessly might *also* suck, it would at least suck in the open air.

Besides, Audrey had always been an explorey sort. And, much as she wanted to pretend it was part of what made her an excellent—well, an adequate; well, a former—investigative journalist, mostly it just meant she'd spent a lot of her childhood increasing her mother's risk of cardiac arrest. She'd once enlivened a summer picnic by trying to climb up Wenlock Priory. And, in her defence, she'd managed it. The climbing up part, at least. Getting down had been more of a challenge and had, eventually, involved fire engines. To this day, Audrey felt guilty around a National Trust logo.

That probably wasn't going to happen at Patchley House, though. Not unless she got really, really bored. Mostly she was hoping a good, old-fashioned wander would keep the more infuriating parts of her brain quiet. With enquieting in mind, she scoped out the woodlands and, once she'd finished scoping, found her way down to the stream, locating the faux-medieval hermitage that her pre-visit research had told her was located somewhere on the grounds.

Once she'd had all the faux medievalness she could take, she looped back to the Lodge just in time to see a girl coming out of the front door. And she was definitely a *girl*, probably—if Audrey was any judge—no more than sixteen. Also probably no less than sixteen, unless the show was violating its own terms and conditions, along with a couple of child labour laws. Neither of which, given what she knew of reality TV, she would have ruled out.

"Hi," Audrey said, discovering as she got closer that, sixteen-ish as she may have been, the newcomer was still a good inch taller than Audrey. "Are you one of the other contestants?"

The girl nodded and, not being from a handshakey genera-tion, waved. "Alanis."

"Alanis?"

"Yeah. After this singer my mum likes."

The realisation that it was perfectly possible for a woman who listened to *Jagged Little Pill* at a formative age to now have a daughter old enough to be baking on national television rose up in Audrey's heart, killed a part of her, and went back to sleep. "Audrey," said Audrey. "After—"

"Audrey Hepburn?" asked Alanis.

"Honestly a bit surprised you know who that is."

"I'm really into retro stuff."

Audrey could probably have guessed that for herself, since Alanis's personal style appeared to have been culled from the greatest hits of the last two centuries: a pleated miniskirt like it was 2001, a chunky black-and-pink cable-knit like it was 2020, tube socks like it was 1974, and ribbons in her hair like she was about to get snubbed by Mr. Darcy at a country dance. "Oh," she said. "Cool. So kind of cottagecore?"

There was a certain look teenagers got when they felt an adult had been embarrassing in a way that inspired pity rather than loathing. "I don't really want to put a label on it. But I'm liking your whole thing."

"I'm not sure I have a thing."

There was another look teenagers got when they felt you were full of shit. "Sixties glasses? Fifties silhouette? That's a thing. You just don't want to admit it."

Great. Now Audrey was being called out by a child. On the other hand, the child seemed to be enjoying it. Which was probably a win on aggregate. "Fine. You got me. I'm a plus-sized stereotype."

Alanis looked immediately mortified, like she was cancelling herself. "Oh fuck, sorry. I did not mean that in, like, a shaming way."

"No, it's fine. It's just the reality of a certain height-to-girth ratio. And I'd rather own it than hide."

"You're definitely owning it."

"Okay, now you're overcompensating."

"No, no," protested Alanis, whose limited life experience had yet to teach her the benefits of quitting when you were behind. "You look really good for your age."

Audrey stared at her. Over the past thirtysomething years she'd got pretty comfortable with her body. Having to be comfortable with her age as well had snuck up on her. "Which you think is… what exactly?"

"Like maybe twenty-five?" said Alanis with complete and bewildering sincerity. "Or twenty-eight?"

This was flattering. But also not flattering. "Oh my God, Alanis. How do you think time works?"

"I don't know. I'm not Einstein."

"No, I mean, twenty-five isn't old enough to look *good for your age*. And, by similar reasoning, in no universe do I look twenty-five."

"Look"—Alanis spread her hands in a gesture of *I give up on everything*—"you seem like you're older than me and younger than my mum. I don't know what else to do here."

Tiny twinge of nostalgia aside, Audrey was pretty glad that she no longer lived in a world where the categories of people were yourself, your parents, and everybody else. "How about we leave gerontology for now and talk about baking? Because I'm beginning to sense a generation gap and I really want to get onto a topic that doesn't make me feel ancient."

"Works for me." Cheerfully, Alanis looped her arm through Audrey's and began to drag her up the hill. "Totally crepuscular."

Audrey was not falling for that one. "Crepuscular?"

"Yeah, it means *good*."

"No it doesn't. It means of or relating to twilight. This is because I said there was a generation gap, isn't it?"

"Don't be such a zymurgy."

"Study of fermentation. You're not going to get me on this. I'm old and uncool but I know a lot of weird words."

"How?" By a process of contrarian logic known only to the young, Alanis sounded almost impressed.

"I told you," said Audrey. "I'm old and uncool."

"You're not uncool. You're peripatetic."

"Wandering. Which we actually are. So I think one of us has won but I can't tell which."

Alanis flashed an Instagrammable smile. "How about both of us?"

Which—damningly—was the most mature thing Audrey had heard all week.

The lights of Patchley House were golden against the darkening sky, almost magical and, funnily enough, crepuscular. Had she not been getting yoinked along by an overenthusiastic teenager, Audrey might have stopped to take it in. The problem with living somewhere beautiful—and she'd lived in beautiful places for much of her life—was that you got inured to the specifics of it. Sure, sometimes a new, hitherto unnoticed, specific would sneak up on you, and it would be like you were seeing the world for the first time all over again. Except that feeling got rarer the longer you stuck around. And, for a while, especially living in London, Audrey thought she'd lost it entirely. That it had just faded away, like so many other things.

Coming back to Shropshire had taught her that it hadn't, and moments like this—looking up a hill at a stately home in the twilight—reinforced the lesson. But that sense of wonder still felt fragile enough that she regretted having to let it go. Unfortunately the alternative was to turn to her teenage companion and say, *Hey can we just stop and appreciate some quiet beauty because we might never see it again*, which might just have pushed her, in Alanis's eyes, from uncool into irredeemably sad.

"I'm starving," declared Alanis, substantially less concerned with the ache of the transient and ephemeral than with the buffet, which was being served al fresco outside the main dining hall.

They were making their way over to join the other contestants when a weaselly looking man with a clipboard descended on them from somewhere in the small city-state of technical vehicles and trailers that were parked on the less conspicuous side of the grounds.

"I'm terribly sorry to bother you," he began in the tones of a man who was always sorry to bother you but would never allow his sorrow to detract from his bothersomeness. "Are you the journalist?"

He was looking directly at Alanis when he said it, which Audrey tried to blame on the light but which she suspected was more to do with the fact that serious reporters weren't meant to get yanked around country estates by actual children.

"I'm the journalist," Audrey clarified.

"Jennifer wants to see you."

It had been an abrupt introduction, and Audrey wasn't sure she wanted to reward abruptness. "Sorry, who are you?"

The man winced as though he'd accidentally taken a vegan to a restaurant that served nothing but veal and foie gras. Then he held out a shaky hand and said, "Thrimp. Colin Thrimp. Jennifer's assistant. Jennifer Hallet. She's in charge of"—he made an expansive gesture—"well, everything really. And she wants to talk to you *especially* because of your…you know…"

Audrey should have seen something like this coming. Nobody trusted media people, especially other media people. "Job?"

He nodded.

"Does she think I'm going to write some kind of searing exposé?"

Alanis grinned in a way that Audrey didn't think she'd have had the confidence to grin, even at sixteen. "You should. That'd be effervescent."

"Stop it," said Audrey, trying to sound playful rather than snappish and mostly succeeding.

Colin Thrimp wrung his hands. "Can you just go to see her? She said I had to bring you to her yesterday, which normally means soon and it's already been a bit longer than soon and she'll be in a *fearful* mood if you don't go and speak to her."

"How fearful, exactly?" asked Audrey. It had been a long day and an executive in a fearful mood—or really any kind of mood—fell pretty close to last on her list of things she wanted to deal with.

"Fearfully fearful."

It wasn't the most helpful of answers, but Audrey had met several Colin Thrimps in her life and didn't think there was much point protesting further. After taking a responsible but obviously futile moment to make certain that Alanis would be okay on her own (she was, she was probably okayer than most adults would have been by a long way), Audrey set off in search of the fearfully fearful producer.

Jennifer Hallet's trailer was unmarked, which made it mildly awkward for Audrey to find, but only mildly. Her keen investigative instincts told her to try the biggest, swankiest one, and the biggest, swankiest one it was.

She knocked on the door and then stood outside waiting. When she'd been waiting for just long enough that she was about to give up, a voice from within called out, "Who the fuck is it?"

"It's Audrey?" she tried. "Audrey Lane."

There was the sound of movement and then the door was thrown open by the most intimidating woman Audrey had ever seen. Jennifer Hallet was tall and cold-eyed, with lips that curled into a permanent frown. There was something arresting about the sheer concentrated hostility of her, almost a challenge—the most undirected, universal kind of challenge, as if she was telling the entire world to come and have a go if it thought it was hard enough. And Audrey only realised she'd been staring when Jennifer asked her, quite pointedly, what she was staring at.

"Sorry, I—you wanted to see me. I'm the journalist."

"Oh *that*. Took you long enough."

"Your assistant only just found me."

"Then it took *him* long enough." Jennifer went back inside the trailer and, suspecting that waiting for an invitation would be an exercise in futility, Audrey followed her.

Inside, she found a setup that looked one step more supervillain than was strictly necessary. While the wall of constantly shifting monitors was probably a legitimate necessity of the job, and the various keyboards, microphones, and panels of miscellaneous switches likely had their uses, the enormous black swivel chair was a Persian cat away from full Blofeld. Right in the middle of the functionality to evil spectrum were the two smaller seats that had been set up at optimal bollocking distance.

"I just thought," Jennifer said in a voice as smooth and pleasant as honey over razor blades, "that we should have a nice, polite, face-to-face conversation so that we can both be crystal fucking clear how our relationship is going to work."

Settling herself onto a bollocking chair, Audrey did her best to remain composed. "If you like, but I'm not sure what there is to—"

"I've got your *number*, sunshine."

"Which number, exactly?"

"Seventy-nine thousand, four hundred and six."

To anybody else, the number would have been meaningless. But to Audrey it had a very clear, very specific meaning. It was the circulation of the *Echo*. "We get over half a million unique visits on our website as well."

"And do you know what I do with half a million unique visits?" asked Jennifer Hallet.

Audrey was pretty sure she could tell where this was going, and how this particular TV big shot liked to express herself. "Do you, perhaps, wipe your arse with them?"

"I do fucking not. Because they're a fucking ephemeral concept, and if I tried to wipe my arse with an ephemeral concept I'd wind up with shit on my fingers." Jennifer paused, definitely more for effect than for breath. "What I do is I look at them and I say, *Well gosh, what a tiny pissing number of unique visits*, then I go back to my job making one of the biggest shows on television and then I say to myself, *I hope no miserable little spunkstain—*"

"Please don't call me a spunkstain," replied Audrey with a professional calm that she was, in the circumstances, pretty fucking proud of.

"I'm sorry." Jennifer Hallet didn't even blink. "Am I being demeaning? Let's try again. *I hope no miserable little bundle of piss-drenched bedsheets comes crawling up here from fucking Shropshire to try and wank her ten minutes of relevance out of my years of back-breaking work*. But oh look, it seems Satan has jizzed in my corn-flakes again, because here you are."

Well wasn't this the beginning of a beautiful friendship? Clearly the politely-set-boundaries plan had failed, so Audrey shifted to the be-visibly-unfazed plan. "You knew where I worked when I applied."

"I did. You ticked some boxes and we needed a quirky rural one for this season so I thought I'd take the risk. But I *know* journalists"—*Here it comes*, said Audrey's inner cynic—"You're like the fucking police."

"Never off duty?" Audrey finished.

"Pricks."

"I don't suppose"—Audrey shifted slightly in a chair she was sure had been deliberately chosen to be as buttock aggravating as possible—"you have a less sweary mode of communication you could fall back on?"

"Fuck off."

"Thought so." She adjusted her position again to stop her arse from falling asleep. "In that case, let me just reassure you that I write for a local paper, about local things, and so unless you happen to have a contestant from Cleobury Mortimer, there's nothing here for me to report on."

Jennifer folded her arms like a statue of Stalin. "That's what you say. But I know what you people are like. You get one sniff of—"

Despite not having been told she could go, Audrey stood up. "Look, you've warned me not to mess with your program. I've told you I have no intention of messing with your program. I'm not sure what more you want me to say."

Clearly there was more Jennifer wanted to say, but the get-up-and-agree combo had taken the wind out of her sails.

"So I think we're on the same page?" Audrey confirmed.

Jennifer Hallet looked like she was about to nod and couldn't quite bring herself to. "Hang on, there's no *we* here."

The sensible thing to do was to get out. Because while Jennifer Hallet had a number of qualities that made sticking around a very tempting prospect—like legs for days and dark eyes that felt like they could look right through you if they didn't always seem to be looking at something else—her temperament wasn't one of them. And maybe it was the journey, or just being in a strange stately home, but Audrey wasn't in a sensible mood. So she lingered a moment, and pushed her luck. "We're having a conversation. That's a *we*."

"This isn't a conversation. This is a—"

"A what? A scolding? I've not really done anything scoldworthy, so from where I'm standing this is either a conversation or it's you inviting me onto your show—something you didn't have to do in the first place—then preemptively deciding I'm going to screw you and hauling me into your office to be a dick for no reason."

"Is that how you see it?" Unexpectedly, the producer sounded almost defensive. In fact if Audrey let herself use her optimistic ears, it might even have been defensiveness with an undertone of grudging respect.

Deciding words had done their job, Audrey nodded precisely once.

"I will admit," conceded Jennifer Hallet in a tone like she was revealing state secrets, "that I could have blocked your application if I wanted to, and I didn't."

"Because?" asked Audrey, aware that if she came across as too curious she'd confirm all of Jennifer Hallet's worst suspicions.

"Because this season needs to be perfect and you—from a certain perspective—are perfect."

Audrey knew better than to be flattered by people in positions of authority saying things that seemed superficially positive. Even if they meant it, they didn't mean what you wanted them to mean. "Perfect *how*?"

"Memorable look, interesting job, ticks a diversity box."

"The gay box or the heavy box?" asked Audrey, determined not to let Jennifer's tone affect her in any way.

"Both, but mostly body positivity. Honestly the gay thing counts against you—ginger and sparkly from last season are still looking cute all over fucking TikTok, so the *allies*"—she almost spat the word—"are in the bag. We go too queer this year and we'll lose the Middle England Tory voter market."

This was still feeling like bait. "Is that a market you want to keep?"

"Do they have money? Then yes. Plus the fuckers run the country and that includes BBC funding, so we need to reflect the rich and beautiful diversity of these islands while also pretending that we hate immigrants and are very concerned about trans people. That's public service broadcasting."

It was a deathly cynical attitude, but one Audrey recognised even if wasn't usually stated so openly. "You're meant to be apolitical, which in practice means agreeing with the home secretary?"

Jennifer Hallet nodded. "Would you look at that? She gets it. Welcome to the magical world where Brexit wasn't a shitshow, the only minorities who exist are charmingly nonthreatening, and you can only be fat if you're also pretty."

Pretty wasn't an adjective Audrey would have used to describe herself. Although that did make her fatally susceptible to its use by other people. "Fuck, am I here to be *one of the good ones?*"

To that, Jennifer Hallet offered a frankly wicked grin. "How's it feel?"

"Fine," replied Audrey, still defiantly unperturbed.

A look of genuine dismay crept across Jennifer Hallet's face. "I hope you're not going to make me like you, sunshine. I can't think of anything worse. Now if we're done, perhaps you could be so kind as to get the fuck out of my sight."

It was, Audrey thought, about the most literal example of mixed messages she could possibly imagine. And it left her with the nagging sense that this wasn't the last time she was going to run afoul of Jennifer Hallet's highly specific worldview. Along with the still more nagging suspicion that she couldn't quite tell if she was dreading their next run-in or looking forward to it.

Saturday

THE FOLLOWING MORNING, Audrey was awoken by a frantic hammering on her door.

"Aaaaauuuu-dreeeey," came Alanis's voice. "You're going to be late for breeaaak-faaaaast."

Rolling over, Audrey checked her phone, whose alarm was scheduled to go off in about twenty minutes. "I don't think I will," she called back.

"Okay not *late*, late, but come on, it's the first day. You don't want to miss the start of the first day."

This was, in a vacuum, true. Although she didn't think a little longer in bed would actually *make* her miss the start of the first day—and even if it did, she suspected that the *actual* start of the day wouldn't be anywhere near as early as Alanis thought. Audrey was used to print media, which was a very hurry-up-and-wait business, and she couldn't imagine broadcast media being any better. On the other hand, telling teenagers to fuck off was probably a job best left to Jennifer Hallet.

So Audrey got up, dragged her hair into something resembling tidiness, glad that the show would have professional hair-draggers to do the rest, dressed, and let Alanis tow her out into the dawn.

There were, she had to confess, worse places to be towed, and worse people to be towed by. The morning was bright and the sun danced across the hillside of Patchley House and Park with a joyfulness that was matched only by, well, Alanis, who—having apparently categorised Audrey as closer to the "me" box than the "my parents" box—was full of excited stories about her home ("the boring bit of London"), her friends (too numerous to count), and her planned cake-that-shows-us-who-you-are for Sunday's baketacular (chocolate and chilli, because "I'm a little bit sweet and a little bit spicy").

Breakfast, like the dinner Audrey had nearly missed because she was too busy getting dressed down for nothing by a paranoid authoritarian, was being served outside at picnic tables. Tables that were already filling up with people.

Alanis made a kind of "eek" noise. "Ohmygodtheresso -manyofus."

"Only ten."

"And there's so many *old* people."

By Audrey's count, only one of the contestants—a silver-haired woman who moved through the group with a serenity that might have been confusion—really counted as old, although a couple more were well into middle age. "Yeah," she said, "we twenty-five-year-olds get about a bit."

With a social ease that Audrey should probably have expected given how they'd met, Alanis slipped away to join the one member of the party who looked even remotely her own age—a tall, slim man with a goatee and a trilby. That left Audrey momentarily alone, which, honestly, wasn't a huge problem for her. Being on her own in an empty room would have driven her up the wall, but getting a chance to stand back and people watch was a genuine relief. A personal hobby, as well as a professional habit.

On the distaff side of the equation there was herself, Alanis, the one actually old person in the group, a graying-but-otherwise-young-looking woman who Audrey suspected was taking the role of nation's favourite mum for the season, and a tousle-haired woman Audrey's own age who was wearing a ruffled blouse and an expression of panic.

On the something-for-the-ladies side of the coin, there was the obligatory hipster baker who had already monopolised Alanis's attention, the equally obligatory blue-collar baker—complete, in this case, with a pencil tucked behind his ear—and a man who, although it was probably wrong to judge too much from his failure to eat a bacon bap without spilling ketchup on his shirt, was likely to have been recruited to be this year's "adorably hopeless one." Which, since Audrey was still half convinced she'd been cast in that role herself, came as something of a relief.

"Excuse me dear." That was the old one—the actually old one—leaning past Audrey to the cereal table. "Can you pass me one of them little things of butter?"

Obligingly, Audrey passed the little thing of butter, then introduced herself. "Audrey, by the way. Like Hepburn."

"Doris," replied the old lady. "Like Day."

An unfortunate side effect of her live-to-work years was that Audrey's brain tended to default to "interview" and it took her a second to adjust to small talk. "So," she tried, "have you just got in?"

"Oh no." Doris didn't laugh, exactly, but she had mirth in her voice. "Too old to make it this far this early. I come in last night. You?"

"Same."

"Where from?"

"Shropshire. You?" The moment she'd asked it, Audrey realised that it was a silly question.

"London," replied Doris in an accent strong enough to make the answer entirely self-evident. "Which ain't a long way when you're young but is a very long way when you're nearly a hundred."

Audrey tried and failed to stop her human-interest sensors from kicking in. "You're nearly a hundred?"

"And to think I don't look a day over ninety-three." She grinned. "That Thrimp lad says I'm the oldest contestant they've ever had."

The part of Audrey that lived permanently behind the curtain put that little factoid in her mental filing cabinet next to Alanis. Oldest Contestant And Youngest Contestant On Same Series was exactly the kind of harmless and ultimately meaningless gimmick you pulled out of the box for a season that, for some reason, had to be perfect. It was also the kind of thing that would be an amazing early scoop for the *Echo* and exactly the kind of thing she'd signed multiple contracts saying she wouldn't tell anybody about before the series went to air. "You must've seen a lot," she said.

Doris grew oddly quiet at that. "A bit but, I don't know. Sometimes you wonder where it all goes."

Despite being substantially further from her telegram from the king than Doris, Audrey could relate. She'd been wondering where it was all going since she was twenty at least. *It went to a career*, Natalie narrated from an unhelpful part of her psyche. *A career you threw away.* "Yeah."

And that *did* make Doris laugh. "And what do you know about it? I've got grandchildren your age."

"Perhaps I'm an old soul," suggested Audrey in what she hoped was a breezy tone.

"How about we swap your old soul for my old body?"

There didn't seem to be a good answer to that. A strong desire to avoid lawsuits had made other people's bodies a topic Audrey avoided on general principle. "It's seen you all right so far."

"True, I shouldn't grumble. Still, whoever decided we were going to have to stay at the bottom of a great big hill and do all our filming at the top of the great big hill…" Doris heaved an exaggeratedly weary sigh. "Well they can go take a long walk off a short pier."

Doris had said it lightly, but from Audrey's perspective making a nearly hundred-year-old woman walk up and down a hill every day was a big fucking deal. And she was about to ask Doris if she thought maybe something should be done about it when she was cut off by the sudden swarm of people with headset mics and clipboards who zoomed in to shepherd everybody off to hair and makeup.

Audrey had been right. Broadcast media was indeed even more hurry up and wait than print media. Hair and makeup had taken well over an hour, most of which was standing around doing nothing. They'd then been sent up to the ballroom where the show was to be filmed for a briefing that didn't actually begin until half an hour after everybody was assembled.

When it *did* begin, it consisted of Colin Thrimp coming in and telling them all the basic rules of filming—don't look into the camera, don't swear on camera, when people ask you a question, answer it as if you aren't answering a question — and then Jennifer Hallet coming in and telling them the exact same information, only with more swearing and threats.

"And one more thing," she added like a vulgar executive Columbo, "this is season eight. Which means a lot of people are getting bored as piss of this formula and as a result I have bent over *fucking backwards* to pick contestants who I expect to *sparkle*. And so you shower of arseholes had *better* fucking sparkle or I will personally go to each of your grannies' houses and tell them what miserable fucking disappointments their grandkids are."

"My gran died in nineteen fifty-four," said Doris from the row of otherwise-cowed-into-silence contestants.

"Oh, don't you think for one *second* that'll stop me. I'll dig her up and say it to her fucking *skull*."

Audrey had *almost* convinced herself that she could learn to like Jennifer Hallet. That she was that rarest of creatures, an authority figure who actually did respond well to pushback. But hearing her threaten personal retribution to the corpse of a nonagenarian's grandmother rather took the shine off.

Back when Audrey had been in London with Natalie and everything that entailed, she'd had a boss very much *like* Jennifer Hallet. For a while she'd let herself believe that she'd be able to earn his respect if she just ate enough shit with a big enough smile, but she'd eventually worked out that he wasn't challenging her, just bullying her. He'd been a huge part of the reason she'd decided that the run-to-the-city-and-never-look-back path that most of her school friends and *all* of her university friends had taken was supremely not for her. The breakup had been part of it too, of course, but three-years-ago Audrey insisted it wasn't the biggest part and present-day Audrey went along with it for the sake of her self-esteem.

I think you'll find, Natalie's voice was saying, *it was the other way around. We didn't work because you couldn't hack it. And I wanted so much better for you.*

Either way, what did it matter? It was only eight weeks. She could put up with a hot, shouty woman for eight weeks. Probably less than that given how stiff the competition looked and how likely it was that they were setting this season up for an oldest-versus-youngest challenge in the finale. Privately, Audrey gave herself until week five.

"So if you've got that into your tiny, squishy minds," Jennifer Hallet was finishing, "then we're ready for you to go to your stations, look confused but pretty, and act all awestruck when the—and, I use this term *very* advisedly—celebrities come in." She bent down to speak into a microphone. "Colin, send in the judges and that overpaid RADA dropout we call a presenter."

There was a brief changing of the guard as Jennifer swept out and Grace Forsythe, the long-serving host who—she took pains to inform everybody the moment she entered—did not in fact drop out of RADA, swept in. The judges followed her, and they too were, by now, long established. Wilfred Honey was the smell of fresh-baked bread given human form by a capricious wizard, while Marianne Wolvercote was to patisserie what the Queen had been to England. Which was to say, she was the queen of it. The cameras, Audrey knew, would already have started rolling, but a sad fact of the digital age was that they no longer made a satisfying clicky-whirry noise when they did. The operators just started acting a whole lot more like they were paying attention.

"Welcome, welcome, welcome," Grace Forsythe began, "viewers, young"—Audrey was ninety percent sure she could spot which camera was lingering on Alanis for that bit—"and old"—here they'd cut to Doris—"to this, the eighth season of *Bake Expectations*. We've been through a lot together—me, Marianne, Wilfred, our eighty contestants and our beautiful, beautiful audience—but this season, we're going back to basics. No frills. No sleight of hand. No tricks. All we are going to want you to do is demonstrate that you are the best amateur bakers Britain has to offer, and we're starting—as Julie Andrews would have it—at the very beginning. And so, my delightful droplets of dulce de leche, for your first blind bake of the season, we are going to ask you to make a simple, a classic, and an absolutely *perfect* Victoria sponge."

A ripple of ill-advised relief spread through the other contestants. But much as it might ruin the shot, Audrey's brain couldn't make her face play ball. There *had* to be another shoe to drop here. In the last couple of seasons, the blind bakes had grown increasingly esoteric—so esoteric that disgruntled but social-media averse fans had taken to complaining to newspapers about them. Back at work, Audrey knew for a fact that there was a file—a literal physical file because a surprising number of people, especially complaint-minded people, still wrote literal physical letters—full of people who were upset about the Saint Honoré Cake last season.

"You have one hour," Grace Forsythe concluded. "Starting from the count of three. *Three*, darlings."

Audrey turned over the recipe, and there was the other shoe.

The recipe read: *Make a Victoria sponge.*

Which was fine. It was fine. Everybody knew how to make a Victoria sponge. At least everybody who baked to a level that they'd be selected for *Bake Expectations* knew how to make a Victoria sponge. It was a test of nerve more than anything else. The secret would be to stop second-guessing, try to forget the cameras were there, and throw yourself into the recipe you knew was right.

Taking a deep breath, Audrey risked a look around the ballroom. If nothing else, the production team must have been getting exactly what they hoped for out of this little stunt, because the entire cast were emoting their backsides off. Alanis, who clearly knew what kind of meme she wanted to be, was doing a full-on reaction gif at the recipe, while behind her the resident hipster was stroking his goatee with consternation.

Seeing this much of what went on in the ballroom was distractingly interesting. At home you only got to see the edited highlights, the parts that were cool or shocking or included mild innuendoes. Having the massive multitudinous but occasionally tedious complexity of it all going on around her was, to Audrey's media-saturated brain, like being Charlie in the Chocolate Factory. Or, perhaps more accurately, like being Mike Teevee.

It was also not what she was here for. She was here for the baking, and with a strength of will she was slightly too proud to be proud of, she turned her attention back to her workstation.

They'd been given too much of everything, she was sure of that. A whole carton of eggs. A whole pint of milk. More flour and sugar than anybody could have a realistic use for. She preheated the oven to a hundred and seventy degrees. Then she greased and lined her cake tins and started measuring out what felt like—no, what she was *sure* were—realistic amounts of the various ingredients into a bowl.

The trick, she kept very firmly reminding herself, was that there *were* no tricks. It was a cake. A cake that anybody who made cakes had made a hundred times. She mixed up her batter, transferred it into the tins, whacked the tins in the ovens for twenty minutes, and moved on to her buttercream. Once the icing sugar had been smoothly beaten into the butter, she allowed herself another look around at the competition.

Doris seemed to be sailing through, as somebody who'd been doing this kind of thing for the best part of a century naturally would. Alanis was struggling slightly, probably more from nerves than from lack of skill, and Audrey wondered if it had been entirely fair to put someone quite that young through something quite this stressful. At the back of the ballroom, a man Audrey hadn't seen before was beating his own buttercream with such intense Dad energy that Audrey almost laughed. Instead, she just smiled at him, and he smiled back.

Then her timer beeped, and she had to get back to work.

In the end, as she brought her cake up to rest on the display table at the front of the hall, she thought she'd done pretty well. Trouble was, so had everybody else. Rug-pullingly terse recipe aside, the Victoria sponge *had* been an easy start. Some looked a little over, some a little under, but mostly they'd all come out okay. One particularly bold baker had topped their offering with extra buttercream rather than dusting it with icing sugar, and Audrey strongly suspected that would count against them with the judges.

It did.

"All I'm saying," Joshua with the hipster goatee explained in his post-blind-bake interview, "is that what the recipe said was *make a Victoria sponge*. It didn't say *make a Victoria sponge uncreatively*."

Despite the terrible crime of a nontraditional topping, Joshua's cake hadn't come in last. That honour had been reserved for Gerald, the man Audrey had seen spilling ketchup on himself that morning and who had proven to be exactly as ketchup spilling in the ballroom as he was at breakfast.

"Overall," he was saying in a cut-glass accent that Audrey made at least a token attempt not to judge him for, "I actually think I did pretty dashed well. There was just that teeny-tiny detail of not putting any, you know, sugar into it. I thought I had. I definitely *meant* to. Somehow. On the day." He threw his hands in the air. "You know. Is what it is."

By contrast, Audrey's sponge had been well received. Just not as well received as Doris's, which had indeed been honed to perfection over decades of mothering, grandmothering, and great-grandmothering. Still, it had been a non-embarrassing start and Audrey tentatively discarded her last concerns about being the joke contestant.

She was just wandering down the hill away from the ballroom when she spotted Alanis sitting under a tree facing determinedly away from the house. From her body language, Audrey was fifty-fifty at best on whether she just wanted to be left alone. But since in her experience even if somebody *did* want to be left alone, there was yet another fifty-fifty question to ask about whether they *should* be, she went over to check.

"Hi," she tried in her best not-intruding-just-passing voice.

Alanis looked up. She definitely wasn't crying, but she definitely had been. "Hi. How're you?"

"Okay." Deciding that in this case valour was the better part of discretion, Audrey sat down next to her, at kind of a forty-five-degree angle around the base of the tree. "Tough start?"

It seemed, briefly, like Alanis wasn't going to admit it. But then she hugged her knees to her chest and said, "It was just so *hard*. I didn't expect it to be that hard. And I've been baking since I was a kid—"

"You know you're kind of still a kid?"

In a paradoxical attempt to protest the accusation of kid-dishness, Alanis stuck her tongue out. "All right then, I've been baking since I was *really small*. So I thought I'd at least be fine on week one, but then they didn't give us any instructions and I didn't know what to do and…"

Shuffling closer, Audrey put an arm around Alanis's shoulder and let her have another little cry. "And you did fine."

"Only because other people did worse."

This felt like a moment that called for wisdom, for Audrey to reach deep into her well of stored experiences and pluck out some pearls of advice that Alanis could treasure for the rest of her life. "I think," she tried, "that other people doing worse is often what success looks like."

Alanis seemed unpearled by this wisdom. "Mr. Reynolds would say that's not very growth mindset of you."

"From context, I'm assuming not-very-growth-mindset is something I *don't* want to be?"

"*You don't have to be better than other people*," Alanis seemed to be quoting, "*you have to be better than you were yesterday*."

Audrey considered this. It was the kind of advice she saw the value in but felt was less universal than its peddlers claimed. "I don't think that applies in a literal competition."

"I just wanted to do well."

"And you will. You've got eight whole weeks ahead of you. You can pull it back tomorrow."

Having not yet had the optimism knocked out of her by life, Alanis took that at face value and perked up considerably. So considerably, in fact, that she was soon hugging Audrey with such a well-practiced combination of gratitude and dismissal that she suspected she was sliding back from the "me" box into the "my parents" box. Which at least meant she could go back to her room without worrying that she'd abandoned a child to despair beneath an ironically picturesque tree.

It was a pleasant walk down to the Lodge, almost an amble. And putting thoughts of baking aside—probably too far aside, given she was on a baking competition—Audrey wound her way through the grounds, stopping now and then to look back up at the Patchley House. It was partly just a fan instinct; she'd been watching the show since season one and it always, always opened with the same panning shot of the manor, and so there was a strange sense of reality-unreality to seeing it in the flesh.

But on another level, it had nothing to do with the show at all. Since long before Audrey had made her parents call 999 to get her rescued from the walls of Wenlock Priory, she'd been fascinated by the past. Or perhaps not by the past, exactly, so much as the things that called back to it. Those out-of-place relics and incomplete bridges; ruins that let you imagine all the stories in the world through the holes in their sides. Of course sometimes, for some people, the holes were all you had.

She wasn't a historian, so she had no idea how old Patchley House actually was—it could have been anything from Tudor to Edwardian and she'd have put it in that same category of long-time-ago-but-not-so-long-ago-they-had-jesters. Still, there was something strange about the thought that this was a place people had built, that people had lived in, that was now being used for a purpose none of those people could possibly have imagined.

It was like nostalgia, only for things that had happened to somebody else. There was a sense of loss to the feeling, in some ways—although Audrey wasn't quite such a romantic that she could say she pined for the days of domestic service and tugging forelocks—and gain in others. What had once been the exclusive purview of the landed gentry was now creating something for everybody. Well, for everybody who watched *Bake Expectations*. And, she supposed, really to make money for a largely amoral media company.

But if you ignored the whole capitalism angle, it was rather a beautiful thought.

There was a story she remembered, although she couldn't recall where she'd heard it or from whom, about somebody who'd met an old man at a dinner party in the 1980s, and the old man had shaken his hand and then said, "You have just met a man who once met a woman who once danced with Napoleon." Audrey had no idea if it had really happened, or even if the numbers added up—it would need to have involved some lucky overlaps of some very old people with some very young people. But, as a journalist, she was keenly aware of the difference between *factual* and *true*. And it *did* capture something true, something about the way that people and places and things formed this strange, tangled chain across time. Something that, if you looked hard enough and went far enough, connected everybody to everybody else.

Theoretically anyway. But in practice those dances through time tended to go boy-girl-boy-girl unless you looked really hard. And even if you *did* look really hard, you'd get people telling you that you were making shit up. After all, what with the world being what it was, you were extremely unlikely to meet a man at dinner and have him say, "You've just shaken hands with a man who once fucked a guy who was once one of Oscar Wilde's rent boys." Which was ironic in a way because Bosie's boyfriend probably banged more people than Napoleon danced with.

Sighing, Audrey stared up at the house and tried to imagine

it as it used to be, when it was a house instead of a hotel, and then whatever it was before that—probably a different sort of stately home. Or a monastery. Or a Roman fort. Or an empty hillside where long ago druids gathered to greet the twilight and the dawn. And then, as she always did, she tried to imagine herself there. Or someone like her.

Except that just made her feel sad. Because while she'd done the research and knew the talking points—blah, blah molly houses; blah, blah ladies of Llangollen; blah, blah Alexander; blah, blah Sappho—it didn't actually help. It was like trying to get drunk on other people's empties. Or build a jigsaw from pieces of other jigsaws. What stories could she tell when that was all she had? How could anyone find belonging in fragments?

About halfway up the hill between the Lodge and the house proper was a log that had been placed to give people somewhere to sit that married artificial convenience with a natural aesthetic. And when Audrey trudged back to the hotel for dinner, it was occupied by Doris. She was sitting gazing up at the stars and, if Audrey was any judge, breathing a little heavily.

"Are you okay?" she asked.

It took a moment for Doris to register her. "Fine, fine. Just giving the old plates a rest."

Audrey had never actually heard somebody using cockney rhyming slang in the wild, but she adjusted. "Going for dinner?"

"In a bit."

Looking down the hill back to the Lodge and then up the hill back to the house, Audrey did a quick mental calculation of the distance. Well, not calculation, so much as estimate. Well, not estimate so much as blind guess. "It's a trek, isn't it?"

"Nothing wrong with a long walk."

"I mean, there *can* be, if it's long enough."

With a stifled *oomph*, Doris raised herself off the log. "Now, now dear, there's no need to be silly about things. I've been slogging up and down hills my whole life and it's never done me any harm."

Audrey was no expert, but she suspected that at least seven of the nine most harmful things in the world were things that people insisted had never done them any harm. "Maybe not, but there's a first time for everything."

"Oh hush." Doris gave her what she thought was a playfully stern look. "We'll be late for supper if we don't hoof it."

So they hoofed it. Or at least they came as close to hoofing it as they could while going up a relatively steep incline when one of them was nearly a hundred years old. Which was to say, they progressed slowly but cheerfully, with Doris chatting away in the manner of somebody used to having to fill long walks.

"She's a pretty thing, isn't she?"

"Who?" asked Audrey, a little confused.

"Patchley. One of the prettiest houses in England I've always thought. I wish my Bobby could be around to see her."

"Bobby?" A mix of professional training and basic humaning had taught Audrey that people opened up more when you echoed at them.

"My husband."

"Fan of the show?"

Doris laughed, sadly. "No. Never watched it. He's been gone more than twenty years."

There it was again, that eerie sense of echoes across time. Audrey was just old enough that she could meaningfully *remember* twenty years ago. But to have lived a whole life with somebody, had children and grandchildren and great-grandchildren, and for that to have still ended so long ago… It was almost unencompassable. "I'm sorry."

"He had a good innings. What about you? Got one of your own?"

"A husband?"

Doris nodded.

"No." This had the potential to be awkward. "I'm sort of single. And also sort of entirely gay."

"Oh." Doris went quiet for a moment. Then said, "Good for you."

As reactions from the over-eighties went, it was one of the better ones. "Thanks. Neither of them are by choice though, really."

Doris nodded again. "Fair enough, fair enough. Still, maybe you'll find a nice girl on the show."

This seemed very unlikely. Audrey began running down the options on her fingers. "Well, you're a bit too old—no offence—and Alanis is *way* too young; Meera's very, very married; and Linda—I've not really talked to her, but I think I wouldn't be her type."

"Look at you having everybody's name down." Doris was smiling again. There was something warm in her smile, something that reminded Audrey of her own grandparents, and possibly also of a kind of cosmic meta-grandparent that spoke to her soul. The same Jungian archetype that Wilfred Honey had made his career by embodying. Possibly since the age of forty. "I still just remember people by what colour top they were wearing and how tall they are."

At last they arrived at the main hotel, or at least at the hurry-up-and-feed-yourselves bit of the hotel that was the designated dining area for contestants. Honestly, Audrey wasn't entirely hungry and so, having picked at some lukewarm spaghetti bolognese, she made her excuses and set off back to her room. About a quarter of the way down the hill, though, she stopped, looked back up the slope, and changed her mind.

"What part," said a loud, irate voice from inside the trailer on whose door Audrey had been banging for what felt like six minutes, "of *I don't want to fucking hear it* do you not understand?"

"You don't even know what it *is* yet," Audrey pointed out. "Or who I am."

"It's almost like neither of those things make a difference. Now fuck off."

Audrey banged again.

"I'm sorry," said the voice. "Were you taking that as a request?"

"Since you're not actually allowed to give me orders, yes."

There was a very brief silence. "Excuse me, sunshine, I can give you all the orders I like."

"And I can ignore them. I don't work for you."

"Everybody on this fucking *set* works for me."

The part of Audrey that had never learned to quit while it was ahead dug its heels in hard. The fact that she *wasn't* especially ahead made that easier. "No, I'm a contestant on a show you're running, and I have some concerns I want to raise with you, and I'll be out of your hair much faster if you just listen to them."

A sound of angry despair emanated from behind the door. "Fine. Come in. But this had better be really, really fucking good because I have sixty different things to be doing right now and you are none of them."

"I wasn't planning on doing you today either," retorted Audrey.

Stepping inside, she found Jennifer Hallet was sitting in her supervillain chair, frowning at footage. "So you say. But I've met you once and I'm already willing to bet you've found some way to fuck me mightily."

Audrey couldn't allow herself to get sidetracked by thoughts of fucking Jennifer Hallet, mightily or otherwise. "I wanted to talk about Doris. In a non-fucking way."

Jennifer rotated just far enough to shoot a baleful look across the room. "This is about the granny?"

"The granny has a name."

"Not to me she doesn't. Now tell me what was so important that you had to hammer on my door at this time of the evening and bother me about it."

"I walked up to dinner with her today, and it's a *very* long way up the hill for somebody her age."

Jennifer Hallet's eyes narrowed. "You know what I hate?"

"I'm going to go out on a limb and say…everything?"

"I hate clichés. Which is why I'm so fucking furious that you're forcing me to tell you to go cry me a fucking river."

The *Echo* was not, Audrey knew, the *Guardian* or the *Times* or even the *Mail*, but she was still a professional reporter and that meant knowing how to deal with bullshit. "I'm not forcing you to do anything. I'm telling you that it's not okay to make a woman in her nineties trek up and down that hill three times a day just so the BBC can save a couple of quid on hotel rooms."

"She hasn't complained."

"Her generation was raised not to."

That didn't impress Jennifer. And few people, Audrey was realising, could signal their not-impressed-ness with as much silent eloquence. "Her generation w—"

"If you're about to say her generation won the war, I will laugh in your face."

The barely perceptible tip of Jennifer's tongue ran across her lips. "I wouldn't, sunshine. I'm not in the mood to have anyone get cute with me, least of all you."

"I'm not being cute. I'm being concerned about an old woman's well-being."

"And I'm being concerned with my fucking show not being a fucking disaster."

Given that Jennifer Hallet had been smashing this show out of the park for seven years solid, Audrey didn't quite buy that. "Why, did we not sparkle enough for you?"

Jennifer was glaring now, but Audrey thought she could see genuine frustration in that glare. A sense that she really did feel an intense need to go back to work or else some grand unspecified Bad Thing would happen. "Well of course you didn't. The contestants never fucking do. We add the sparkles in postproduction. That's why the bumbling one is loveable instead of just begging for a smack in the teeth. It's why the insecure one makes you hope she'll see how good she is deep down. It's why the granny feels like *your* granny and the mum feels like *your* mum even though they're really just two fuckers you've never met. And if they weren't on TV, they could both die slowly of a rectal prolapse and you wouldn't know or care." She swivelled her chair around fully. "And none of that, sunshine, none of that happens unless I *make* it happen, so I would be *unbelievably* grateful if we could wrap this up before we both develop age-related incontinence."

Probably the right thing to do was to leave it there. Audrey didn't leave it there. "Alanis had a rough time today as well."

"Oh boo fucking hoo."

"She's sixteen, Jennifer. She's basically a child."

Jennifer Hallet sat back looking, for a moment, like a grimier, more technologically up-to-date version of the wicked queen in a Disney movie. Which, for someone whose first crush was Maleficent, was a bad comparison to be making. "Not according to the law."

"Yes, according to the law. According to the law she's still a child for another two years."

"And yet the law also says she's old enough to join the army or get fucked wherever she wants to be fucked by anybody she wants to get fucked by if that's what she wants to do. It's a funny old world, but I don't make the rules."

Audrey tried very, very hard not to lose it, and mostly succeeded. "Okay, one: I *really* don't think you should be talking about Alanis like that and two—actually I'm not sure there *is* a two. Because one is already quite important."

"And that's the best you've got?" The look on Jennifer's face was exasperation commingled with…with something Audrey couldn't readily identify. "The bad woman said a bad thing and I'm outraged. Fuck off."

"I'm not outraged I'm—"

"If you're about to play the *I'm not angry I'm just disappointed* card I'll remind you that you're not my fucking primary school headmistress. And, for the record, I didn't give a fuck what she said either."

Audrey had, in fact, been about to play exactly that card. Except it wasn't a card. It was just *true*. Working in media—new, old, or whatever—you got very used to the fact that almost anything that made any sort of money was, if you dug deep enough, controlled by the same three straight white men. And *Bake Expectations* being one of its genre's heaviest hitters and being entirely woman-run was something that got regularly brought up as a bright light in an otherwise dark industry. So yes, in a lot of ways, encountering Jennifer Hallet was becoming disappointing. Even if the image of a tiny, foul-mouthed Jennifer telling her school where it could stick its rice pudding was ever-so-slightly adorable.

"Okay." Audrey put the complex reality of Jennifer Hallet aside and took a deep breath. "Let's look at it like this. I'm aware that people don't normally come to you about these kinds of issues, and maybe I'm a bit out of line, so I'm making some allowances. But I don't believe you'd let anybody treat you the way you treat the contestants on this show."

"And?"

Audrey wilted slightly beneath Jennifer Hallet's precisely raised eyebrow. "And—I don't know. Think about that maybe?"

"Sure," said Jennifer Hallet, in a tone so sarcastic that if it tried to enter a most sarcastic tone contest, its application would be rejected because the judges would assume it was sarcastic. "I'll go away and reflect and grow as a person. Now have you quite finished wasting my fucking time?"

It had probably been foolish to expect better. Whatever Audrey thought she'd seen in Jennifer Hallet the night before had been an illusion brought on by overexposure to televisual nostalgia. And it

made sense. You didn't get to be at the top of a competitive industry without basically turning, in one way or another, into a colossal
piece of shit. She'd seen it happen to so many people in her old job,
and the ones it didn't happen to had breakdowns or…well, they
ran home to get jobs writing about parking fees in Much Wenlock.
Still, it was a little sad-making to realise that the woman who created the nation's favourite celebration of all that was wholesome
and comforting was just as willing to put profits above people as
every other macho prick in the industry.

Trying not to deflate like any soufflé she tried to make while
sober, Audrey decided to give it one more go. "You know," she
tried, "I really hoped you'd be better."

The disdain on Jennifer Hallet's face was all the answer she
needed to give, but she gave a verbal one regardless. "Oh no, disapproval, my one weakness. Just get out."

"Yeah." Audrey gave a resigned nod. "Guess we've been wasting each other's time after all."

She left quietly, because Jennifer was clearly the kind of person
who took storming out as a win. Then she very sensibly decided it
was a good idea to get an early night before the next day's competition. And then somewhat less sensibly stayed up until well after
midnight having imaginary arguments with an imaginary Jennifer
Hallet.

Some of which she even won.

Sunday

THE NEXT MORNING, Alanis woke Audrey slightly later than she had the previous day, although still fundamentally too early for comfort, and hauled her up the hill to breakfast. Once Audrey had actually got to sleep, she'd slept well, but she'd woken up ravenous and was, therefore, very disappointed by the watery sausages, flabby bacon, and undercooked hash browns that she was offered. Although she counted herself lucky that she wasn't vegetarian since then her options would have been cereal, a fry-up minus any of the interesting parts, or an involuntary fast day.

Since she was focusing more on getting herself fed than paying attention to social cues, Audrey was already sitting down and deciding which of the congealed breakfast products on her plate looked least unappetising when she realised she'd inadvertently sat directly between Alanis and Joshua. Who now seemed to be trying to flirt across her.

"You did well yesterday," Joshua was saying over his cereal and under his trilby.

"Thanks." Alanis wasn't quite looking at him and wasn't quite looking at her breakfast. And across more years than she cared to remember, Audrey recognised the awkwardness of a teenager trying to seem like a twentysomething. "You did—yours was good too. They shouldn't have marked you down for using buttercream."

"They asked for a Victoria sponge," Joshua agreed, "and they got a Victoria sponge."

The conversation continued in this not-exactly-about-anything-but-also-not-really-inviting-Audrey-to-participate vein for long enough that she began to feel acutely uncomfortable but also that she couldn't leave because she'd somehow positioned herself as unofficial chaperone. Audrey was, therefore, immensely relieved when Gerald rolled up with a plate of nothing but hash browns, sat down uninvited, and immediately butted in.

"Hello, hello, hello." He speared a hash brown with a fork and took a nibble. "Bright new day and everything. Hope you are all, each of you, shaped like ships and fashioned like Bristol."

Wordlessly, Alanis looked to Audrey for help.

"We're all good," she said. "Just getting ready for the next challenge."

Gerald nodded enthusiastically and started his second hash brown. "Ah yes." He adopted an expression of utmost seriousness. Or at least as much seriousness as one could adopt when one still had a notable ketchup stain on one's shirt. "*A cake that shows who you are.*"

"I'm making chocolate and chilli," Alanis volunteered in the exact tone she'd used to explain her bake to Audrey the day before, "because I'm a little bit sweet and a little bit spicy."

Joshua's comment was "Like it" in a tone that Audrey tried hard not to cringe at.

"I was going to make something that included my Somali

heritage," Alanis continued, "but that's all on my dad's side and he doesn't actually cook. So I spoke to his mum—my grandmother—and she was, like, so happy I'd asked that I felt bad saying *actually I just need a cake for TV*. So now we do this whole weekly family cooking thing, which is great but doesn't help with the show." She took a spoonful of cereal. "Still, might do sambusa if I make it to pastry week."

The moment Alanis had finished, Joshua stepped in like he'd spent the whole time nodding and waiting for his turn to talk. "I'm going to do"—he put his hands out in a gesture that might, if interpreted generously, indicate something vaguely cake-shaped—"it's hard to put into *words*."

Gerald fixed Joshua with a look of genuine awe. "Are you making an *ineffable cake*?"

It took Joshua a moment to acknowledge the question, but when he did he nodded, laughed, and said "Like it" again. Followed by, "And kind of. But it's actually more"—he swirled his hands—"cupcakes."

"That doesn't sound *very* ineffable," Audrey pointed out. "I mean I'm pretty sure you could eff a cupcake."

Alanis punched her on the arm. "*Audrey*, don't talk about effing cupcakes over breakfast."

Audrey hadn't actually intended to eff in the euphemistic sense. "I just meant," she said, aware that she was drifting back into Alanis's "me" box, but possibly as *that* friend, "they're, you know, comprehensible."

"What I wanted to do"—Joshua's hands were still spiralling—"was, like, it's supposed to be a cake that shows *who you are* but, like, *who are any of us*?"

Alanis was giving him the *you're so deep* nod that Audrey

remembered giving a few girls herself down the years, Natalie among them. It was not a nod that ever ended well.

"So," Joshua went on—he was a terminal wenter onner. "I'm doing a range of cupcakes in a range of styles and flavours because I just don't think one cake can, you know, really encapsulate a whole person."

"I can see you've given this a lot of thought," Audrey told him. It was how she avoided telling people they were full of shit.

Joshua nodded appreciatively. "How about you?"

Although Audrey privately didn't think "I'm making ten different cakes because I refuse to be categorised, man" was a great response to the brief, she was starting to wonder if her own was any better. "Simnel cake."

Gerald's sincere tell-me-more look searchlighted from Joshua to Audrey. "I've heard of that. It's French, isn't it?"

"Not really. More Shropshire."

"Ah." He nodded. "Sort of chocolatey?"

"Fruit."

"And it has a distinctive decorative style?"

Audrey nodded. "Yes it's—"

"Sort of a fleur-de-lis in sugar work?"

"Balls of marzipan."

Gerald smiled. "That's the bugger. Knew I'd heard of it."

"And how does it show who you are?" asked Alanis with the devastating innocence of a young boy asking whether the emperor might not be a bit chilly with his dick out.

"Well…" Audrey squirmed in her seat. It felt a bit pathetic to say *Because it's from Shropshire and I'm also from Shropshire*. But what else did she have? "It's traditional, where I'm from. I used to make one for my mum every Mother's Day."

Joshua laid a gentle hand on Audrey's arm. "I'm sorry. How did she die?"

Since parsing potentially ambiguous headlines was a major part of Audrey's job, it didn't take her long to work out where the confusion had crept in. "Oh, no, I mean I used to make them, but I stopped. She's fine. She lives in Much Wenlock."

"That's not a real place," Alanis protested, oddly insistent for somebody in no position to actually know. "You're refabulating us."

"That's not real slang," replied Audrey. And then, used to having to prove the reality of her hometown, she pulled out her phone and brought up Much Wenlock on Google maps. "See, here it is."

Snatching the phone, Alanis dragged and dropped the little streetview figure into the middle of Much Wenlock. "Oh, it's *so cute*. I didn't think people really lived in places like this."

"What did you think all the houses were for? Instagram?"

Alanis was still staring somewhat entranced at the chocolate-box wonders of Much Wenlock. "I just…it's super pretty and I don't, I don't know, I suppose it would be nice to live there? Your parents are very lucky."

They were. For a start they'd been lucky enough to buy a house in Much Wenlock before property prices went through the roof. Which meant that when Audrey had come slinking back from London with her tail between her legs, her choice had been to live in her childhood bedroom for the rest of her life or move somewhere comparatively normal. Like Bridgnorth.

"So why did you stop?" asked Gerald. "Making the cake, I mean. Seems a very fine tradition to have if you ask me."

"I moved away." It was a technically correct answer but an

uninformative one, so Audrey continued. "To London. And, well, I was busy and my girlfriend wasn't one for baking."

Alanis blinked like Bambi's cottagecore sister. "That's really sad. What happened with the girlfriend?"

"We broke up."

"Probably for the best." Alanis shot a shy glance at Joshua. "I wouldn't want to date somebody who wasn't into baking."

"Welcome," Grace Forsythe was saying, her hands clasped in front of her like she was trying to crush a mouse to death, "to the *first* baketacular of the *eighth* season of *Bake Expectations*. And in keeping with this season's back-to-basics theme, we're going to ask you to make a cake. No particular kind of cake—any cake you like."

Audrey had watched enough episodes of the show to suspect that this was about to launch into one of the host's famously long, whimsically alliterative lists. That suspicion was about to prove founded.

"It could be," continued Grace Forsythe, "chocolate or cherry, madeira or matcha; you could make cupcakes, bundt cakes, upside-down cakes, or right-side-up cakes. It could be tiered or layered; you could top it with ganache, or just with panache. If you wanted to be trendy, you could even make it naked, although then we *might* have to broadcast after the watershed."

There was a brief pause for people to give suitably amused reactions, during which Colin Thrimp managed to sneak in a "Jennifer says please wrap it up before Christmas."

"Just as long," Grace Forsythe kept right on talking as if nobody else had spoken—which, in Audrey's limited experience, was pretty usual for celebrities, "as it shows"—she clapped—"us"—she clapped again—"who"—clap—"you"—clap—"are. You have three hours, starting on three. *Three*, darlings."

Audrey had barely started sieving her flour when the judges and camera crew descended on her station. The part of her that paid attention to technicalities wondered if they'd picked her first out of kindness to the other contestants, assuming that her media background would make her more comfortable and give the rest of them time to settle into things. The part of her that had met Jennifer Hallet, however, suspected that people's comfort wasn't a high priority for the production team.

"So, lass," Wilfred Honey was asking, "what're you making, and what does it say about you?"

More used to being interviewer than interviewee, Audrey took a moment to gather her thoughts. "Well, I'm making a traditional Shropshire simnel cake."

"Ooh, now that's interesting is that." Wilfred Honey didn't seem excited exactly—more sort of in his element. If there was one thing that the nation's grandfather loved, it was a slightly obscure heritage cake from a British region. "It's an Easter bake, isn't it?"

Audrey nodded in what she hoped was an appropriately yes-anding way. "That's right. Once it's done it'll be decorated with eleven little marzipan balls to represent the disciples."

From the other end of the counter, Grace Forsythe leaned in with a hang-on-a-second expression. "*Eleven* balls? I admit I never paid a tremendous amount of attention in Sunday school, but—"

"They don't count Judas," Wilfred Honey explained. "On account of his being a wrong'un."

Marianne Wolvercote, however, had other concerns. "I assume you're making your marzipan from scratch?"

"Yes." There had been a brief window on Tuesday when Audrey had been considering not and just using store-bought like she usually did when she made simnel cake in contexts that were neither competitive nor televised. But she'd decided against it and was now sending Tuesday-Audrey heartfelt thanks. "The cake needs two hours in the oven so I should just be able to make it within the time."

The mention of time hadn't been a hint, but they'd taken it as one anyway. "Then," Grace Forsythe told her, "we shall leave you to it."

Audrey went back to her sieving immediately because while it was probably more polite to watch the judges walk away, she had timing to think about. With her flour and spices mixed, she turned her attention to her butter and sugar, digging her fingers in and rubbing them together into a delicious coarse yellow mixture. And for just a moment, she let herself forget the lights and the cameras and that she was in a very real sense about to be judged for this, and just enjoy herself. And it turned out to be surprisingly easy, because for a part of Audrey this—wrist deep in cake sugar and eggs—was what happiness felt like.

Natalie had never approved, but Audrey had always liked making things. Cakes, scarves, newspaper articles, or TV shows—it wasn't the final product that mattered, not really. It was seeing something—feeling something—coming together in front of you. Getting it as right as possible and then putting it out, for better or worse, into the world.

But you could, Natalie reminded her, *be making history*.

"Ah yes, so, well," Gerald was saying on the other side of the ballroom. "This is my, well, it's my show-you-who-I-am cake."

Audrey knew she should be focusing on her own bake, but it

was hard to take her eyes off Gerald's bench now that it had drawn her attention. His mixing bowl had overspilled and a measuring jug entirely too full of mascarpone was looming ominously close to his elbow.

"Is it not…" Grace Forsythe was doing her best to be tactful. "That is to say, is there not rather a *lot* of it?"

"That *was* intentional," Gerald looked down at his bowl with a look that edged very close to a grimace. The spoon was slowly vanishing into the batter like a TV cowboy sinking into quicksand. "Trying to convey that there's rather a lot of *me*. In the personality sense, I mean, not the physical. Turns out I *may* have slightly miscalculated. I wanted it to be twice as big as normal, you see, but then I remembered from school that twice the"—-he held his hands out to indicate length—"means four times the"—he indicated a square—"and then eight times the"—a cube—"Now I look at it, though, I'm starting to think that might have been the tiniest bit of an overcorrection."

Grace Forsythe patted him on the arm. "Well, good luck. Might want to nab that spoon before you lose it completely."

Turning her attention reluctantly back to her own workstation, Audrey began adding the spice-and-flour mix to the butter-and-sugar mix. While she worked, snatches of other people's interviews drifted towards her and, although she tried to block them out, she couldn't help making mental notes in case they came in handy.

I just feel like this has gone really wrong. That was Linda—about Audrey's age and permanently harried—working on a fruit cake with royal icing, intricate details picked out by hand. It hadn't gone wrong at all from where Audrey was standing, but Linda had exacting standards.

...and a little bit spicy. That, of course, was Alanis. She'd been practising the line all day, but while that was obvious to Audrey, it would probably come across well on camera.

"And you're actually our youngest *ever* contestant, aren't you?" Grace Forsythe was saying as Audrey put her cake mix aside and started on her marzipan.

"That's right." Audrey wasn't looking but she could imagine Alanis's enthusiastic nod anyway. "I'm sixteen."

Grace Forsythe gave a gasp of faux shock. "You realise that means I've been presenting this show for half your life?" She sighed. "I need to lie down."

She didn't, of course. It was a bit. Setup for the next part. Audrey half-followed her with her eyes while she was adding the egg to her ground-almond-and-sugar-mix.

"Hello, dear." Doris greeted Grace Forsythe as if she was a wayward grandchild rather than a B-list celebrity with A-list pretensions. "I suppose you want to know what I'm baking."

Ever the professional, Grace Forsythe rolled with it. "You're going to do me out of a job, Doris."

"Well, I'm making a carrot cake. This is the recipe my old mum used during the war and I thought it'd fit." There was a pause, and although Audrey was trying to keep her mind on her marzipan, she wasn't trying very successfully. And frankly she was far less interested in her batter than in the trace of melancholy she could hear in Doris's voice. "Bit obvious really, isn't it?"

"Darling," replied Grace Forsythe who, for all her faults, never let a contestant run themselves down, "this is a cooking show with a tenuous baking pun in its name. Obvious is very much the order of the day."

Once again, Audrey tried to make herself focus on the job at

hand and, once again, she didn't try particularly hard. She told herself it was because it was more difficult to concentrate under studio
lights and surrounded by other people than in a silent kitchen in a
flat in Bridgnorth that you shared with nobody. Except she could
see so many stories here, stories Jennifer Hallet had probably seen
from the beginning, and would draw out expertly over the course
of the next eight weeks.

You ran away from your story, Natalie told her. *You couldn't take
the heat so you went into the kitchen.*

✦ ✦ ━━━ ✦ ✦

"So this is a simnel cake," Audrey explained when the judges called
on her at last. "It's a traditional cake made at Easter in Shropshire."
It had come out okay in the end, though it was quite an austere
offering, all told. Then again, most traditional cakes were. It had
caught a little on top but she hoped the marzipan would cover it.

Wilfred Honey looked down at it approvingly. "Well it looks
lovely. I used to have these myself when I were a lad. We used the
Yorkshire recipe, obviously, but I'll not mark you down on that
score."

While Wilfred was making friendly noises, Marianne
Wolvercote was slicing into the cake with icy precision. "It seems
to have caught a little here." Using her knife, she indicated just
under the marzipan layer. "And while you've covered it adequately,
it *was* a little incautious of you." She stood up. "Still it *is* the first
week and we can overlook the *occasional* imperfection."

"Especially," Wilfred Honey added, "if the taste is right."

Although on one level—several levels, probably—Audrey
was aware that this was a very silly thing to be doing and that an

old man liking or not liking her simnel cake was going to have no meaningful effect on her life whatsoever, it was still a weirdly heart-stopping, stomach-clenching moment.

Wilfred Honey dug a healthy forkful out of the simnel cake and popped it into his mouth. For a moment he just chewed contemplatively, and Audrey tried not to worry that he was finding it too dry or too solid.

"It's good is that," he said at last. "Very traditional. I like traditional."

Marianne Wolvercote wasn't quite so kind. "Perhaps a touch *too* traditional for me. I appreciate that this is a home baking competition, and that the brief was to give us something personal, but I think you've been a little casual here. The marzipan is slightly uneven and the little spheres you've made for decoration aren't quite the same size."

Casual was a difficult word from Marianne Wolvercote. It was a step harsher than *rustic* but not quite as bad as *Don't eat that, Wilfred.*

"Oh, you're being too hard on her," replied Wilfred Honey, riding to Audrey's defence like a knight in tweed armour. "It's a lovely cake, exactly what we asked for, and it's got a really *homey* feeling to it, and that's not something you can buy."

"It's not, but that doesn't excuse a lack of precision." Marianne Wolvercote momentarily permitted her expression to soften. "Although Wilfred's right. It's the first week and we asked for authenticity rather than accuracy, and in that regard you've delivered."

Not quite sure what to make from such a mixed review, Audrey nodded the politest thanks she could muster and returned to her place. It hadn't been the *worst* feedback so far. Alanis had been the first up to the plate and while they'd been kind to her on account of her age, the chilli hadn't come through in her chocolate and chilli cake. The two who'd come after that—Jim and Reggie, Audrey told herself; getting names down fast was a point of professional pride—had received similarly equivocating feedback, but Linda's intricate icing work had won her high praise and set her up as the one to beat.

Neither of the next two contestants (John and Meera, Audrey name-checked) showed much chance of beating Linda and neither did Doris, whose carrot cake was praised for its story but was a little plain. That just left Gerald and Joshua, and Gerald, from what Audrey was seeing, did not seem likely to be taking the week one crown.

He was staggering forward with a platter full of something that could—on a good day, in the right light—just about be called cake. Having started life overflowing its bowl, it had overflown its tin as well, which meant it was now an uneven splurge of half-burned rivulets running down from an almost certainly raw centre. He'd iced it somewhat hastily, making the whole thing look like the monster of the week from a seventies science fiction series.

"So this," Gerald explained as he set his slightly wobbly creation down before the judges, "is a giant sponge cake."

"Well it's certainly giant," agreed Wilfred Honey, who was always the show's designated good cop.

"But as for whether it's a sponge cake…" Marianne Wolvercote stabbed at it gently. "That remains to be seen."

Eventually a slice was cut out of the cake and laid on a plate for inspection. Audrey didn't have a good angle, but the fact that the judges were hesitating to taste it implied that things had gone about as badly wrong as they possibly could.

"Don't eat that, Wilfred," said Marianne Wolvercote, inspiring gasps of dismay from the other contestants.

Gerald gave a nervous hop. "Oh my."

"It isn't baked," Marianne Wolvercote continued. "I understand what you were trying to do here, Gerald, but it hasn't *remotely* worked."

"You do seem to have had a bit of a day," Wilfred Honey agreed, "don't you, lad?"

Gerald nodded. "Looks like. But you know what they say: you win some, you lose some."

He seemed oddly chipper as he made his way back to his station, but then he'd been oddly chipper ever since Audrey had first seen him and from what she knew of Jennifer Hallet he'd probably been cast precisely for that odd chipperness. *We need a quirky weird one to go out in the first week*, she'd have said. *And that prick looks the part.*

Joshua was already coming forward, his I-can't-be-defined-by-a-single-item-of-confectionary cupcakes arranged rather prettily on a stand that also looked handmade.

"Now, I was worried about this," Marriane Wolvercote began, examining the display with the eye of a connoisseur. "But it seems to have come together remarkably well. My concern was that you'd either do too little—cupcakes are rather simple, after all—or too much. But you've actually done wonderfully."

Wilfred Honey reached out and grabbed a cake. "Tell us what flavours you've got."

"Well"—suddenly, Joshua was coming across a lot more sincerely than he had earlier in the day—"the one you're holding is red velvet, these ones here are lemon, those are chocolate, those are vanilla, that's pumpkin and cinnamon, and those ones are *also* vanilla but they have strawberries on top."

"I think it's a very clever interpretation of the brief." From Audrey's experience watching the show, this was one of the highest forms of praise Marianne Wolvercote ever gave. "And it took real discipline to get this number of different flavours done in the time."

Wilfred Honey had tried the red velvet and was moving on to the pumpkin and cinnamon. "And each one's worked nicely," he added. "You've done well here, lad. Very well. Reminds me a bit of myself at your age." Since Wilfred Honey was considerably quicker with the praise than Marianne Wolvercote, this didn't land quite as hard as *clever interpretation of the brief*, but it was still pretty good going.

When they all gathered on their stools for the results, it was clearly down to Linda or Joshua, and Audrey—if she was honest with herself—was rooting for Linda. While she was sure Joshua was a perfectly nice young man, she couldn't quite bring herself to cheer for a guy in a trilby.

After more time deliberating than seemed at all reasonable when the question was "Whose cakes were nicest?" the judges returned and Grace Forsythe took up her customary position at the front of the ballroom.

"And so, my little gateaux chocolates, we reach the end of the first week of the new season and we begin with the joyful task of selecting this week's winner. Wilfred and Marianne debated long and hard, but in the end they decided that while his Victoria sponge was a touch *unconventional*, he really turned it around with his baketacular cupcake display. Congratulations"—she gave a totally unnecessary pause—"Joshua."

There was a sequence of congratulations and back pats, and Alanis beamed like she'd won herself, which the part of Audrey that still thought whatever Natalie would think judged harshly and the rest of Audrey tried not to.

"But of course, with every cake there must be crumbs," Grace Forsythe went on, "and with every victory, there must be loss. And so today, we say goodbye to our first contestant." It was pretty obvious who this was going to be—so obvious that despite her classically trained tendency to try to build everything up like it was the state opening of Parliament, even Grace Forsythe kept it relatively succinct. "In the short time he was here he made a mark, a Victoria sponge, and a gigantic mess of the kitchen. Gerald, we're sorry to see you go."

This time the sequence was of goodbyes and commiserations. Although since Gerald had been so patently inept for the whole weekend, everybody had been expecting it. Everybody, in this context, including Gerald himself, who bore it with the same grace he had borne his ketchup-related travails of the previous day.

"Well, I messed that one up," he explained to the camera afterwards. "I suppose I should really apologise to all the thousands of people who applied and didn't make the cut. I *promise* I was better in auditions."

Audrey's own interview was relatively perfunctory, which was to be expected given that she had so far failed to distinguish herself either positively or negatively. Just a quick "Well, I think that went okay but I need to make sure I stand out more next week" and then off to pick up her things.

It was a pleasant summer's afternoon as she strolled back down to the Lodge, and since she had—now she thought about it—precisely nothing to be hurrying back for, she took a moment to linger in the woods. There was a river nearby, and taking little walks by rivers was one of the small things she liked doing, which she'd been meaning to do more of when she got the time. *It's easy to have time*, Natalie reminded her, *when you're not actually doing anything with your life. I hope your pursuit of the bucolic idyll makes up for all the things you threw away.*

Blocking her ex-girlfriend out as best she could, Audrey took a stroll. She hadn't originally meant it to be a long stroll, but with the sun dappling through the trees and across the water she went further than she'd intended, down to the faux-medieval hermitage she'd seen the previous day. It felt…not odd, exactly, but sort of nonspecifically disorienting to look closely at something designed to feel old-fashioned to people who had long since passed into old-fashioned themselves. She'd heard that sometimes landowners would hire faux hermits to live in their faux hermitages, and while that had stopped being the kind of thing you could get away with sometime in the eighteenth century, there *was* somebody inside it now.

"Doris?" Audrey poked her head through the archway, hoping none of the loosely piled stones would fall on her head. "What're you doing here?"

"What're you?" she replied, pricklier than Audrey had expected.

"Going for a walk."

"Same."

"And…" It wasn't her place to pry. But she was a professional pryer with a strong interest in extracurricular prying, so she pried anyway. "You chose here to sit down?"

"There's a seat." Doris, who was resting on a slab that might have been intended to represent a bed or a bench, patted the space beside her.

"Well, yes," Audrey conceded, "but—"

"But it smells like piss?"

Audrey nodded.

"I've smelled worse."

It was hard to think of a good response to a ninety-six-year-old woman reassuring you about her ability to tolerate the scent of urine, but Audrey gave it a go anyway. "And you don't want to come out here where it *doesn't* smell of piss?"

Doris sat for a moment, gazing at the walls of the hermitage. "Probably should. Just thought it'd be…I don't know."

"It'd be what?" In moments of doubt, Audrey had a tendency to fall back on open questions.

"Different."

"Different in what way?"

Doris gave a little shrug, got up off the slab, and left the piss-smelling hermitage. To Audrey's relief, the smell of piss did not follow her out. "Just different."

And sometimes open questions weren't the thing you needed. Sometimes you needed to put two and two together and hope you got a nice tutu out of it. There were a number of possible explanations for an elderly woman to have specific expectations about an eighteenth-century folly in a stately home, but they all pointed in roughly the same direction. "Have you…have you been here before?"

Doris didn't answer immediately. She had an almost wistful look about her, and it was a look Audrey recognised. She'd had it herself when she first came back to Shropshire—that mix of nostalgia and whatever the opposite of nostalgia was, the realisation that some bits of the past were gone forever.

"In the war," she said at last. "Lifetime ago. And I come back after, back when I was a domestic."

Audrey did not especially like the part of her brain that was constantly dissecting other people's lives to see if they'd make good human interest pieces. If she was honest, she'd always had it. Even now she was only half sure which of her childhood stories were things she actually remembered and which were things she'd told herself over and over again until it felt like remembering.

"So"—Audrey tried to convince herself she was taking a friendly interest, not an intrusive one—"were you evacuated here?"

Doris's eyes grew sharper and warier. "No flies on you, are there? That's right. I come off the train in thirty-nine, got picked up, brung out to Patchley, and stuck in one of them rooms like the ones we're in right now." She pointed up the hill towards the Lodge. "They was put up for us, originally. Meant to be temporary but it would've cost more to take 'em down. Used as servants' quarters for a bit they was too."

Audrey was trying extremely hard to stop her auto-narrativiser from piecing this woman's scattered recollections into a Timeless Tale Of How Far We Have Come and was failing, hard. "You must have some stories."

"A few. But not as the likes of you would care for I'm sure."

"The likes of me?" Doris had been okay with Audrey telling her she was gay, so she *probably* didn't mean it homophobically. But the phrase had such connotations that Audrey's mind went there anyway.

Doris smiled in what Audrey was pretty sure was a non-homophobic way. "Young folk have better things to do than listen to an old woman talk about rationing."

"I really don't." The sad thing was it wasn't even a lie.

"Well, you should."

This seemed like a good time to deflect. Admitting her social life was so limited that anecdotes about doodlebugs and painting your stockings on with gravy browning looked good by comparison felt like a personal low. "It's heritage," said Audrey instead. "Heritage is important. Like the recipe you made today—that's part of where we come from, and it was good to have it on the show."

"I just thought Wilfred'd like it." Doris looked almost embarrassed. "And the judges was right, him-in-the-hat did better this week."

"Joshua," Audrey filled in instinctively.

"Why don't men wear hats no more? I used to like a man in a hat."

Audrey took Doris gently by the arm and started leading her back up the hill towards the Lodge. "I don't want to be dismissive of Joshua's preferences or yours, but I think a big part of it is that they make you look like a wanker."

"Didn't make you look like a wanker in my day. Made you look very dashing."

"I'm not sure I'd be the one to judge," Audrey admitted. "Not really how my bread's buttered."

Doris gave a wistful smile. "Reckon girls can look dashing in hats, too. Some girls, anyway."

"Some, maybe," Audrey agreed, trying not to think about Natalie, who had been known to rock a hat or two when she was feeling particularly *His Girl Friday* about things.

Slowly, they walked back to their rooms. And as they walked, as if to nobody in particular, Doris started talking.

SEPTEMBER 1939

I HAD A carrot cake with me then, as it happens (Doris was saying). My mum and dad walked me to school and when I got there we all lined up to get took to Paddington by the volunteers. You've probably seen the pictures—not of me, like, but of some of us from them days. All lined up in our warm coats with our bags or boxes or what-have-you, ready to start new lives away from the bombs.

We was being sent all over, some nearby, some as far off as Devon. Some even went up north, though that was mostly folks from closer-to, Manchester and that. I was lucky to get Surrey, it meant it weren't far to go. And I sat on the train with my carrot cake on my knees wrapped in paper. There was this boy sitting opposite me. I don't remember his name or much of what he looked like, but I gave him a bit, broke it off in my fingers and handed it to him, and he swallowed it down like he'd not eaten in a week. I remember that alright, though it's been near on eighty years.

As a kid I'd barely been outside Stepney so it was odd to see all

the trees and grass and fields and such going by the train window.
And when we got to Tapworth the ten of us as was going to Patchley
got out in a big mob and the marshals met us at the other end to
walk us up the hill to the big house. It weren't a hotel in them days
of course. Family owned it, name of Branningham—I don't think
they was the ones what built it, that would've been some bugger
named Patchley I suppose. But it was the Branninghams when I
got here in thirty-nine.

It looked the same, mostly. These kinds of places always do—
you ain't allowed to do much to the main house, and the grounds
don't change much neither. Course it looked bigger to me, because
I was smaller then. Not by much, mind. Twelve I must have been,
perhaps thirteen. One of the older girls, though I was the youngest at home. Anyhow I'd been put in sort of charge on account of
that, and I had to help lead the others up that long drive, what you
probably saw on your way in, and then line them all up in front of
the house so Mr. Branningham—Sir Arthur Branningham, he was
actually, been a big deal in the last war but sitting this one out—
could inspect us.

So there we was, me and nine others, all lined up by height
like *The Sound of Music* and Sir Arthur comes down with his whole
family. It's not big, just him, the missus, two sons and the little girl.
My age, she was, standing just apart from the rest, wrapped in this
long blue coat with fur trim, hat pulled down over her ears. And
her eyes—like she was looking at the whole world all at once and
seeing things you'd never see.

I remember Sir Arthur walked up to us and did his welcome
bit. "You've come a long way," he said, "and you'll find we do things
very differently here from what you're used to, but keep your backs
straight and your heads down, and I'm sure you'll fit in all right."

Then he told us where we was going to be staying—that place they call the Lodge now—and how we wasn't to bother the family or the staff, but we was to have meals provided for us and could have the run of the grounds so long as we stayed out the flower-beds and didn't drown ourselves in the river.

And that was that. Me and this boy called Tom—nice lad, we stayed in touch 'til he died in ninety-two—got the other eight together and took them back down to our rooms. And they was cosy. Not as cosy as they is now—things have come on a bit since the war—but better than a lot of us was used to. I'd never had my own room in my life. I slept like a dead horse that first night and most nights after. Missed my mum and dad of course. And my sisters. My brothers had both gone off to fight, though one had lied about his age, which made Mum upset. But they was good times all in all and I kept busy.

Most days we went to a little school in the village—it's not there anymore and it was mostly your three Rs, not like now where you learn all kinds of stuff. And we had church on Sundays of course—the church *is* there, I saw it when I come up for the contest—and Saturdays we had to ourselves.

Day after we arrived was a Saturday, as it happens. And I took the time to explore these woods and the river—there's a bridge down that way if you ever fancy the walk, least there was in my day—and that afternoon I was taking a wander when I saw her again. The daughter. Her with the eyes.

She was sitting on the bank in a yellow dress just one shade too summery for the weather, 'cause there was a nip in the air though it hadn't fully turned yet. Her hair was down, all chestnut-brown and wavy. And she was throwing rocks at frogs.

"What you doing?" I asked her.

"Throwing rocks at frogs," she replied.

"Why?"

She looked up at me. Some things get foggy, but I remember the look on her face like it was a week last Thursday. Like she didn't know whether to laugh or spit. "It's very rude, you know, sneaking up on a person when they're throwing rocks at frogs."

"I weren't sneaking."

"Wasn't."

"Right, I weren't."

"No, I mean you wasn't sneaking. I mean I wasn't sneaking. I mean—look, who are you?"

I didn't know what to make of that. "I'm an evacuee."

"I know that, bumblewit. I mean what's your name?"

I didn't know what a bumblewit was neither, but I thought I could work it out. "Doris."

"Really? How peculiar."

"What's wrong with Doris?"

"She's a nymph. You don't look like a nymph."

I weren't sure what to make of that. "What do nymphs look like then?"

"Touché."

I weren't sure what to make of that, neither.

"You don't know what that means, do you?"

"No."

She laughed, then. And I remember that, too. Remember how it sounded there by the river. Like water itself running over me and through me. "Don't know much, do you?"

"Guess not."

"It's French," the girl explained. "It means *you got me*. I have no idea what a nymph should look like, I only know you aren't one."

She'd distracted me. I tried to stop her distracting me. "Why you throwing rocks at frogs?"

"I like to see them jump."

"Ain't that a bit cruel?"

Most girls, I reckon, wouldn't have smiled at that, but she did. She smiled at me. "Daddy says it's a cruel world, and I think he's probably right."

"My old man says you shouldn't pick on anything smaller than you."

She thought about that. But she didn't like it. "Really? It seems a lot safer than picking on things that are bigger than you."

Getting tired of standing, I sat down next to her, and she looked at me like I'd broke some rule I didn't know about.

"Excuse me, did I invite you to come sit with me?"

"Your dad said we had the run of the grounds."

"My father isn't here." She turned around, going from sitting to kneeling. "This is my riverbank. If you want to share it with me, you have to pay a toll."

I didn't have much, but I'd brung what was left of my carrot cake with me. I took it out my satchel and showed it to her. "This do?"

She looked down, more pleased than I'd expected. "It looks very crumbly. Did you make it yourself?"

I had, and I said as much. Though my mum had helped.

"Oh how nice. Very well, your toll is accepted."

I'd expected her to hold out her hand, but she opened her mouth instead. Not wanting to upset her, I broke off a piece and fed it to her. She took it, and her lips brushed over my fingers like a breeze over leaves.

"I think I shall enjoy you, Doris," she said. And then she got up and left.

It weren't 'til she were gone that I realised she hadn't told me her name.

Sunday Evening

ON THE WAY back to her car, Audrey tried to maintain a sensible, mature mindset. Yes, she'd met a nice old woman, and yes, maybe something about that nice old woman had pinged very slightly on Audrey's gaydar, and yes, that nice old woman had just told Audrey a story with sapphic overtones so blatant that a certain kind of shitty ally would think it was unsuitable for children. But maybe she was projecting. Maybe if Doris had continued the story, the next words out of her mouth would have been "But anyway we never spoke much after that and I've only remembered that meeting with crystal clarity a literal lifetime later because I have an eidetic memory."

Maybe.

And even if Audrey wasn't projecting, what did it matter? It was just an old woman telling a story. The world was full of old women telling stories and—and somehow Jennifer Hallet was standing by Audrey's car.

"Slow getting away, Lane?" she asked, arms folded and lips so close to smiling that it seemed like it would be less effort to just give up and smile. There was a studied air about her that gave Audrey the infuriating suspicion that Jennifer Hallet knew *exactly* how hot she could be if she put her mind to it and chose the most inconvenient times to make the effort.

Audrey did her best not to look flustered or, for that matter, flushed. "Got caught up."

"Caught up talking to one of my contestants is what I'm told."

It was Jennifer's job to know everything that happened on her set, so Audrey didn't really have the right to feel spied on. But she still felt spied on. "Oh my God. You really do watch everything, don't you?"

"It may shock you to realise this," replied Jennifer Hallet in a tone that Audrey suspected was her second least withering, "but when one of my crew spots a woman in her nineties wandering off into the woods, I do actually get somebody to check on her. But apparently you decided to do that little bit of my job for me."

Despite Jennifer's earlier instructions, or perhaps because of them, Audrey felt an overwhelming compulsion to get cute. "Glad I could help."

Cuteness didn't work. "If you were telling her to make a fuss about the hill I swear to whatever gods you're stupid enough to believe in that I will—"

"I wasn't," replied Audrey, who wasn't especially in the mood to know what Jennifer would have done if she had. "She was just telling me a story."

It would be wrong to say Jennifer looked sceptical. A sceptic could be convinced to change their mind. "A story?"

"She's had an interesting life."

Jennifer's lips, which had been flirting with smiling since the start, finally curved into a grin. "She fucking well has not."

"She fucking well has," replied Audrey, figuring the is-not, is-too school of debate was at least worth a shot.

The shot missed. "I've had you lot vetted so thoroughly I can tell you the shape of your most recent shit. Doris is a boring old woman with a boring old family who lived a life so boring I'm actually boring myself telling you how boring she is."

"Then," said Audrey cheerily, "there's no harm in me listening to her talk about herself, is there?"

And now Jennifer Hallet was glaring again. If Audrey tried really, really hard she could almost believe it was a glare of grudging respect. Almost. "I told you, Lane, I know journalists."

"Yes, yes, we're all pricks."

"And there's always an angle."

Smiling sweetly, Audrey eased past Jennifer and into her car. "Don't be silly"—*silly*, she had to admit, was a risk—"if there was, you'd have found it already."

Apparently unused to having her own competence weaponised against her, Jennifer was stuck momentarily for an answer. But only momentarily. "I've already told you, Lane, it's a bad idea to fuck with me."

"And I've already told you: I have no intention of fucking with you."

"Are you sure? Because you keep acting like you have every fucking intention of fucking with me."

"I have no fucking intention of fucking you." Audrey paused, definitely extremely composed and in control. "With you."

The grin was back, just for a second. Like a wolf that had just realised the brick house had a spare key under the doormat. And then, Jennifer Hallet stood aside with a kind of mock gallantry that made Audrey want to do something physical to her. From a short list of viable physical somethings.

"Take care, Lane." Her eyes gleamed wickedly. "I've a feeling you'll need it."

WEEK TWO

Bread

Monday

IT WAS, AUDREY knew, technically a violation of her contract with the BBC and a vindication of every single negative thought Jennifer had expressed about her, her integrity, and her profession, but she couldn't help herself. All thoughts of simnel cake were forgotten and all thoughts of the show's frustratingly charismatic producer were not forgotten but were, for a while, rigorously suppressed. She'd typed up her notes on Doris's story as soon as she got home, her brain borderline fizzing with the possibilities. Some of those possibilities—and this really was going to confirm Jennifer's worst suspicions—were commercial. War nostalgia sold. Stuff with TV tie-ins sold. This could be a real scoop for the *Echo*. Then again the *Echo*'s last big scoop had been about a series of vicious goose attacks in High Ercall.

But salability aside, even if you cut out the extremely lucrative connection to a very popular television show, the story itself wasn't letting Audrey go. Which was foolish in a lot of ways, because all she really knew was that Doris had come to Patchley House more than seventy years ago and had met another girl who, honestly, had been kind of shitty to her. What this said about Audrey's own issues she didn't want to interrogate too closely.

Nevertheless, she'd arranged a pitch meeting with Gavin as soon as she got into work. And while the more relaxed atmosphere at the *Echo* sometimes gave Audrey a nebulous sense that she was doing it wrong (*You're not doing it wrong*, said Natalie, *because you're not doing it. This isn't journalism.*) it did mean that a pitch meeting was more likely to be a pleasant cup of tea after lunch than a three-minute conversation in a lift with a guy who'd try to put his hand up her skirt.

"Biscuit?" said Gavin, pushing a plate of hobnobs and pink wafers across the desk as he perused Audrey's printed proposal.

"Not right now." She was slightly too nervous for a biscuit. Although, given how incredibly low the stakes were, she wasn't sure why.

Gavin read. He wasn't a slow reader, but he was a meticulous one. It was, in abstract, a good quality for an editor. Just not when you were sitting in front of him, trying not to dwell on how much you were about to piss off a woman whose default state of being already involved a certain level of pissed-offness.

"You've got to admit," she said, as Gavin was starting his third reread, "it's a strong human-interest piece."

"Yes"—he pushed his glasses back up the bridge of his nose—"but…"

"But you're worried what the BBC will say?"

Gavin gave the most sheepish of nods. "The producer lady has quite the reputation."

"Her name's Jennifer, and she's not that bad." Audrey knew for a fact that she was *exactly* that bad, but this was very much the wrong time to point that out. "I really think if we reach out to her she'll go for this."

"Do you?" It was only two words, but the look in Gavin's eyes provided the rest.

"Yes?" Audrey tried to restrict her voice to rising one octave rather than several. "I think she can actually be pretty reasonable?"

"Do you?" Gavin repeated.

"Look at it this way." Who was she trying to convince here? "The absolute worst *possible* outcome is she says no."

"Is it?"

Audrey considered this. "Okay, the worst *possible* outcome is that she says no, kicks me off the show, and vindictively sues the *Echo* every time we so much as mention baking from now until the BBC goes bankrupt from underfunding."

Gavin drummed an anxious pattern with a single fingertip. "That does sound like quite a bad outcome. Possibly an extremely bad outcome."

"Not if the BBC goes bankrupt from underfunding really *quickly*. Which seems increasingly likely."

"Even then I think they'll probably outlast local newspapers," Gavin observed, still drumming.

"Yeah, fair point. But"—Audrey smiled; she had sometimes been told she had a nice smile and she knew how to employ it, if not disarmingly then at least in a way that signalled commitment to a series of ongoing talks about nonproliferation—"given what readership's been like, might it not be worth taking the *tiniest* little swing for the fences?"

Looking down at the printout, Gavin further adjusted his glasses. You could tell how concerned Gavin was about something from how frequently he repositioned his eyewear. "I suppose journalism *is* about taking risks."

"It is," Audrey agreed.

"And it'd show the bloody *Star*."

"It would."

"See how *they* like being Shropshire's second biggest regional newspaper."

This was going well. "Right."

"I mean, obviously they'd like it quite a lot. Nothing wrong with being Shropshire's second biggest regional newspaper. I think we do rather well here at the *Echo* all things considered."

Okay, maybe that had been optimistic. "We do, but wouldn't it be nice to be Shropshire's biggest regional newspaper just for a *bit*?"

Gavin was fiddling with his glasses again. "It'd be a lot of pressure."

"Gavin"—Audrey gave him her most supportive and sincere look—"I really believe we're up to the challenge."

Gavin fell into a mulling-things-over silence and Audrey decided to let him mull. Because sometimes the right thing to say was nothing.

Once appropriate mulling time had passed, Gavin settled his glasses into their most decisive position. "Very well," he said. "I'll reach out to Inveterate Productions."

Not entirely convinced that Jennifer Hallet was a bus she wanted to throw Gavin under, Audrey had hoped he'd leave it to her. "I can do it for you if you'd—"

"No, no. This is my decision and I should take responsibility for it."

Now Audrey thought about it, maybe it would be best if the initial approach came from someone who hadn't personally argued with Jennifer multiple times in a single weekend. "If you're sure."

Gavin just nodded. "I'm sure. But listen, Audrey. Even though this is an exciting opportunity, you can't let it distract you from the core work we do here at the *Shropshire Echo*."

"Of course not," said Audrey.

"Seventy-nine thousand four hundred and six people are relying on us to keep them informed about the things that really matter to the real lives of the real people of Shropshire."

"Absolutely," said Audrey.

"So what I really need from you right now is for you to leave this with me." Gavin slid his glasses up his nose and, fleetingly, he looked like the journalist he'd probably been in his younger days. "I'm serious, Audrey, we need to do this properly or it could cause the *Echo* a lot of trouble. Put your energy into the ghost barge story."

In her heart of hearts, Audrey did not want to focus all or indeed any of her energy on the ghost barge story. Nor, if she was being one hundred percent honest, was she convinced that the ghost barge story counted as something that really mattered to the real lives of the real people of Shropshire. But now was not the time to bring that up. Especially since she'd just asked Gavin to go out on a limb for her. A limb that ran under a sewage outflow pipe.

She mustered her most team-playerey voice. Which, honestly, wasn't that different from her normal voice because Audrey was kind of a team player. Or, as Natalie had put it during an argument once, had a subservient mindset. "You got it."

Grabbing her things, she hurried out of Gavin's office and down to the car park where Eddie, the *Echo*'s best and only photographer, was waiting for her. He had an enormous grin on his face, camera around his neck, suspiciously new-looking black bag over his shoulder.

Audrey always tried very hard not to pretend that she didn't want to know things she blatantly wanted to know. With Eddie, that policy was occasionally a liability. "What's that?" she asked.

Still grinning, Eddie opened a Velcro pouch on the suspiciously new-looking black bag and pulled out—Audrey wasn't really sure what he'd pulled out—some kind of plastic box with red lights all over it and an ergonomic grip. "I'm glad you asked, because—"

"No."

"You haven't—"

"It's a ghost-hunting kit, isn't it?"

Eddie nodded. "I thought since we were investigating a haunting, it would be best to be prepared."

"We're not investigating a haunting," Audrey reminded him. "We're interviewing an amateur historian from Ironbridge about a local legend."

"A local legend about a"—Eddie's voice fell into that deep, trembly tone that's the universal code for supernatural—"*ghoooooost baaaaaarge.*"

"And you think we're going to see this ghost barge at two thirty on a Monday in June?"

Not willing to let go of a good thing, Eddie waggled his ghost detector. "*Ghooooost baaaaaarge.*"

Sometimes you just had to let people have things. And, when you got right down to it, who was Audrey Lane to take a ghost barge away from a perfectly nice man who she was beginning to suspect was really a fourteen-year-old boy in elaborate cosplay.

Accepting her ghostly fate, she unlocked the car door and got into the driver's seat, leaving Eddie to pile in beside her with his overpriced collection of EMF meters and EVP recorders, each of which he insisted on explaining to Audrey during the eleven-minute drive to Ironbridge. Or at least he insisted on explaining them as well as he was able, which wasn't very, possibly because their function was intentionally vague to stop people demanding refunds.

The most significant landmark in Ironbridge was—and every time Audrey mentioned this to somebody who wasn't from Shropshire, they thought it was a joke—the Iron Bridge. It was, she would then explain to them, an iron bridge of genuine historical significance, the first of its kind in the world. Except today she would instead be explaining to them that it was *also*, allegedly, the best spot from which to see the terrible Ghost Barge of the Severn Valley.

They'd arranged to meet their contact at the north end of the bridge, which was where they often arranged to meet people when they came to Ironbridge. It was, however, somewhere Audrey was beginning to think they should *stop* meeting people, because the north end of the bridge was also home to a shop that specialised in hand-raised pork pies, and Eddie tended to find that distracting.

So Audrey waited on a bench overlooking the gorge while Eddie grabbed himself a selection of pies, pasties, sausage rolls, and pork scratchings. To her relief, this time at least he managed to get back before the interviewee arrived.

Her name was Melissa Pope and she was a sensible, tweedy woman in her mid-forties who turned out to be a folklorist rather than a ghost hunter. Which to Audrey was a blessed relief, and to Eddie a crushing disappointment.

"So you've never actually seen a ghost?" he asked while inelegantly cutting himself a slice of pork pie.

"No."

"Or a ghoul?"

"No."

"Goblin? Spectre? Poltergeist?"

Melissa Pope was, in Audrey's estimation, handling this rather well. "No. And I think poltergeists are meant to be invisible."

"Banshee? Barghest? Bandersnatch."

"No, no, and that's from 'Jabberwocky.' Now, shall we talk about the barge?"

It was, in the end, a better interview than Audrey had been fearing, despite the supernatural theme and the pie crumbs. They got some interesting quotes about the ghost barge itself, about its journey up the Severn ending in Jackfield, where there was some evidence of plague bodies having been buried at the end of the seventeenth century.

"I think for me," Melissa Pope concluded, "that's what makes ghost stories so fascinating. It's not the ghost, it's—well, it's the story. The plague hit Shropshire extremely hard and that must have been this huge traumatic event for people back then, and today we still get…I suppose we get echoes and memories of it. That's what legends like this are, when you get right down to it."

Eddie was looking at his EVP recorder, bitterly disappointed. "So there isn't really a ghost barge?"

"There might be." From her tone, Melissa probably had this conversation a lot and was used to being diplomatic. "I'm not saying people are wrong for believing in mysterious things if they want to. Just that…to me it doesn't matter if it's real or not. It doesn't even matter if there really were plague barges running up the Severn in those days, although I think there probably were. What matters is the connection. Come up onto the bridge at night, look down into the gorge, and you'll see ghosts. Even if you don't believe in an afterlife."

"Wait." Eddie looked briefly thrilled. "So there *are* ghosts?"

Then abruptly unthrilled. "Oh. You mean metaphorically, don't you?"

Melissa Pope gave an enigmatic smile.

But Eddie was continuing to dethrill. "This is like when I was little and my dad said my mum was coming home from hospital with a present for me and it turned out to be my brother." He rummaged disconsolately in his bag of pork scratchings. "Like, he's an okay guy. But I really wanted a PlayStation."

They wrapped the interview there, and after making Audrey swear to look after what was left of his pies, Eddie went out onto the bridge to take some shots of the gorge that they could use to illustrate where the nonexistent-but-possibly-metaphorically-resonant-ghost-barge might be seen if you showed up at the right time of night. Mostly it was just an opportunity to get some pretty pictures of the view that would give locals a warm glow of recognition and, if they were lucky, inspire outsiders to drop by and visit the village.

While she was waiting, Audrey let the parts of her brain that did this sort of thing automatically unpick the story and look for its heart. Given how little she'd wanted to be involved with it, she'd found it surprisingly moving in the end. Ghosts she had no time for, but there were some kinds of magic she definitely did believe in. The magic of places and people. The way they worked upon each other and time worked upon them.

How you weren't just what you were now. You were everything you'd ever been.

Tuesday

"WHAT ARE YOU doing here?" asked Audrey.

The *you* in question was Jennifer Hallet. The *here* was the doorstep outside Audrey's flat. She'd have said it was the last thing she was expecting, but who was she kidding? This was exactly the kind of shit you would pull if you were exactly the kind of person that Jennifer exactly was.

Arms folded, mouth tight, she was leaning against Audrey's front door like she owned it. "Making an entrance."

Audrey had spent the whole day chasing a group of firefighters who were chasing a greyhound that had briefly been trapped between a gate and gatepost and had celebrated its release by bolting across the fields almost like it had been specifically bred to move at high speeds across open country. Right now, she needed a cup of tea and a buttered crumpet, not a television producer and an argument.

Not quite sure whether pushing past Jennifer was any more rude than just letting her stand in the street, and even less sure whether she cared about being rude in the first place, Audrey fished her keys out of her pocket. "Did you really come all this way just to stand there like"—she waved her hands in frustration—"like that?"

"I can tell you're a journalist, you have such a way with words. And yes, I came all this way just to stand here. Because I wanted you to know how seriously I take it when people *fuck with me*."

With a speed she was sneakily proud of, Audrey gamed out the rest of this conversation: *I didn't fuck with you / Yes you did, you [vulgarity]ed my [vulgarity] so now I'm going to [vulgarity] on your mum's [vulgarity] / okay but… / [vulgarity]* and decided, as a result, it was a discussion she didn't want to have in front of her neighbours. "Would you like to come up?"

Jennifer sneered. "Sweet of you."

Letting Jennifer Hallet into her flat was a little self-conscious-making. The flat Audrey'd shared with Natalie for over a decade had been chic to the point of hostile (*minimalist*, Natalie corrected her) and looking at the flat she'd moved to directly afterwards with fresh company-coming-around eyes there…might have been an overcorrection.

She liked to think it was still tasteful. The cushions matched the sofa and the rug, and since she'd got most of her furniture off Freecycle, that had been a major interior design win. The flowers, which she changed weekly, were chosen to complement the curtains, the fairy lights framed the fireplace just like she wanted, and she'd specifically crafted the lampshades to…fuck, it was twee. She was twee. She lived in a twee little flat in a twee little town in a twee little county that only an incredibly twee person would ever go anywhere near.

To Audrey's dread and relief, Jennifer settled herself into the only armchair without comment, even though in sitting down she'd had to remove the cuddly tortoise that child-Audrey, with a contrariness that Audrey remembered having once and feared she might have lost, had chosen to name Lion. Lion the tortoise had been Audrey's constant companion for the first fifteen and past two years of her life, and held very strong preferences for which seat he sat in.

"What," Jennifer asked in a tone that made it very clear the question was rhetorical, "was the *one thing* I said you weren't supposed to do?"

The main advantage of getting bollocked in your own house instead of Jennifer's trailer was that you could sit somewhere comfortable. Taking off the bolero she'd been wearing over her checked sundress, Audrey defiantly claimed her own sofa. "If I could—"

"One thing." Jennifer was holding up a single finger to indicate the single thing. "What was it?"

Sighing, Audrey decided compliance was faster than resistance. "Not to write anything about the show, bu—"

"No. It was *don't write anything about the show, no buts about it.*"

"Bu—"

"No."

"You came a long way to say a short word."

Jennifer leaned forwards with an air of menace only slightly marred by the fact that she was cradling a fluffy tortoise. "I wanted to remind you I know where you live."

This was definitely a not-taking-your-shit moment. "I told you where I lived when I applied for the show. Rocking up here isn't some huge power play or baffling magic trick, it's just…mildly annoying."

She might have been imagining it, but Audrey thought she saw the glimmer of a smile on Jennifer's usually very unsmiley lips.

"You did *not* just call me mildly annoying." For a moment, she sounded almost amused. Then she remembered herself and finished, "You diminutive rural hack."

Of the three words in that sentence, only one was really insulting. "I think you'll find I did. Look, I'm sorry Gavin reached out to you, but I really do believe—"

"That you know what's best for my show?"

"That I know a good story when I hear one."

The contempt on Jennifer's face was palpable to the point of parody. "Oh yes, because if there's one thing this country needs it's more dewy-eyed pap about blitz spirit and how great it was to live in a world with rationing, conscription, and the constant threat of death by bombing."

A tiny upside to having spent a decade with a miserable job and an opinionated girlfriend was that Audrey had come out with a very, very high tolerance for disapproval. And if her goal had been to win the argument, she'd have told Jennifer that. Well, not *that* that. But something kind of like it. Something cool and cocky like, "Babe, you ain't got shit on my issues." Unfortunately, Audrey wasn't cool or cocky. She was earnest and embarrassing. And, more to the point, she wanted the story more than she wanted Jennifer Hallet. Wanted *to get one over on* Jennifer Hallet.

"And you don't think"—she leaned forward, earnest and embarrassing to the last—"it's even a *little* bit interesting that one of your contestants lived at the house your show is filmed in more than eighty years ago? When it was owned by different people, used for a different purpose, when it was almost a different *world*?"

Jennifer didn't even blink. "No."

"You're not just shooting this down because it comes from me?"

"Oh, I'm completely shooting this down because it comes

from you. You. Are. Not. Using. My. Show. To. Boost. Your. Career. Not how it works."

Audrey was less good at withering expressions than Jennifer Hallet, but she tried one anyway. "You really think a lot of yourself, don't you?"

"Yes." Another moment of Jennifer Hallet not blinking. "Sorry, was that meant to make me have a harsh moment of self-reflection? I'm good at what I do and I know it. And you aren't, which is why you work at the *Shropshire* fucking *Echo*."

The sad thing is, said Natalie, *that's not even true—you were good, Really good.* "I *like* working at the *Shropshire* fucking *Echo*," Audrey replied. *And that,* Natalie added, *is even sadder.*

Jennifer gave the kind of incredulous laugh Audrey had once been too used to hearing. "You like writing about carpark fees, closed swimming pools, and rail delays."

"Yes," said Audrey, only belatedly realising that those weren't random topics, they were the specific topics of her last three published articles. "Hang on, are you stalking me?"

"I'm monitoring you. I monitor every one of you fuckers." Something almost tired had crept into Jennifer's voice. "I know what you write in your little hack rag, I know what Joshua says to his followers when he Instagrams his breakfast, I know if Meera's got in a barney at the PTA. That's my *job*."

"And my job"—Audrey decided a new strategy was in order—"is to look for things that the diminutive, rural people of Shropshire—"

"Don't be an idiot, you can't all be diminutive. *You're* fucking diminutive—don't go passing it off on the whole county."

Audrey refused to be distracted. "Is to look for things that people in Shropshire will find interesting. And yes, often those things are small. But small things matter. And stories matter. And I think Doris's story matters, and she should have the chance to tell it, and the fact that you don't want her to because you think I'm trying to get one over on you is honestly…honestly, it's petty."

"Petty?" It wasn't designed to get a rise, but a rise it got. "I am not fucking petty. I just have an eye for detail and a zero-tolerance policy for time-wasting bullshit."

Daring, inasmuch as she ever could where Jennifer Hallet was concerned, to hope she was getting somewhere, Audrey decided to press her objectively minimal advantage. "Nobody would be wasting your time. All I want is your permission to talk to another contestant, make some notes, and not publish a single word until I've run everything past you and got your go ahead."

"And if you change your mind and decide to go behind my back?"

Audrey threw her hands up in a gesture of frustrated submission. "Then I guess you—I don't know, sue my tits off or litigate me until I have an anal prolapse or whatever inappropriate threat you want to make this week."

There was a slight pause, in which Audrey sincerely hoped Jennifer was thinking about the proposal and not just of mean things to say.

Finally, she sighed. "You are being an unbelievable pain in my urethra."

"I'd get that looked at. Might be an infection."

For a moment, Audrey was worried she'd pushed it too far. But Jennifer seemed almost to relax. "You're going to keep on at this until I say yes, aren't you?"

It would have been convenient to pretend she was. But Audrey had given up pretending a long time ago. "Honestly? No. If I was going to keep bugging you about anything, it'd be putting Doris in the main hotel."

Jennifer's eyes narrowed. "What if I let you do the story and in return you *don't* bug me about that?"

That was…that was an unexpected win. Unless it was a trap. "Are you just trying to prove that I'll choose my career over an old woman's health? Because if you are, then I'll choose the old woman's health."

"No, I'm just trying whatever I can to get you off my fucking back."

"You're the one that showed up on my doorstep."

There was a moment's silence in which Audrey and Jennifer just looked at each other. Audrey tried to pretend it was a moment of mutual respect, but it might just have been a moment of mutual exhaustion.

"How about," Audrey tried, "you let me do the story, and we'll accept that moving Doris is a different conversation."

To Audrey's surprise, Jennifer Hallet actually laughed. It wasn't a transformative laugh that lit her face with joy and made Audrey see her in a whole new light. It was one missed invitation to a Christening from being a full-on cackle. "Audrey Lane, you canny little fucker. That is some heads-I-win-tails-you-lose bullshit."

"I don't know what you mean," said Audrey, who knew exactly what she meant, and normally got away with it.

"You realise"—Jennifer gave a provocative smile—"I could also solve both these problems by kicking you off the show."

"Ah yes. Because journalists famously stop being annoying when you give up all your leverage."

Jennifer's gaze was caught in a weird space between glaring and smouldering, and Audrey was caught in an even weirder space between irritated and into it. "I hope," Jennifer went on, "you're not mistaking me for the sort of uncreative, management-book-reading, self-help-believing *arsehole* who respects people that stand up to me. Because if so, you are in for a rude awakening. All of this"—she waved a hand in a way that indicated Audrey's entire person and demeanour—"is just pissing me off."

It was, Audrey reflected, wrong to be enjoying this quite as much as she was. Especially because part of it had another person's health on the line. But the thing about being a local journalist asking a reality TV producer if she could run a heartwarming story about the-war-and-maybe-some-lesbians-unless-Audrey-was-projecting was that it had *way* lower stakes than she'd been used to in her old job. And that made it much easier to roll the dice on things. "Is it though?" she asked. "Because the door is right there, and you could have walked out of it at any time."

"You'd follow me."

"This is my house. The following has already occurred. I am the followee in this relationship."

"You fucking are not." Strangely, Jennifer Hallet showed very little sign of moving from Audrey's armchair. "You sent your boss to pitch me a story like you were sending your better-looking friend to ask a girl to dance at a disco."

"Excuse me," said Audrey, stung. "I have always done my own…girl-disco-dancing-asking, thank you very much. Also, who goes to discos anymore?"

"Long answer: Gen Zers on roller skates with AirPods in their ears. It's this whole big trend. Short answer: fuck off."

This was getting further and further from the point and taking Audrey further and further away from her story. And since this was basically a question with a one-word answer, that meant Jennifer was spinning it out deliberately, either for the joy of fucking with Audrey specifically or because a little light conflict was Jennifer's general idea of a fun Tuesday evening.

"I went to my boss"—Audrey eased off her shoes and tucked her feet under a cushion—"because it was the professional thing to do. Just like the professional thing for you to do is give me a straight answer. Can I keep working on this?"

Something thwarted flickered in Jennifer's eyes like a cat whose mouse had stopped running and given it a very disappointed look. "Fine. But you put every fucking word past me. And if I don't like what I read, I'll club this whole thing to death like a baby seal."

Audrey elected not to rise to dead-baby-seal bait. "Thanks."

Silence seemed unlikely in a room with Jennifer Hallet. But there it was. And there also was Jennifer Hallet herself, still enarmchaired despite definitely now having no reason to be there.

"Are we done?" asked Audrey. "Do you want a cup of tea?"

Jennifer gave a look of disgust. "Of course I don't want a fucking cup of tea."

"Then, um, why aren't you leaving?"

"I'm establishing dominance."

"Okay, I know you're a highly successful woman. But if you'll take a tiny bit of advice, it's hard to establish dominance when you're holding a cuddly tortoise."

There was a brief moment where Audrey feared a dominance-challenged and outraged Jennifer Hallet was going to fling Lion the tortoise across the room. But she seemed to have run up against the limits of her own capacity to grandstand. Instead, she stood, crossed to the sofa, and settled Lion the tortoise very gently next to Audrey. "Fuck you both," she said.

"He felt that," Audrey replied. "He really felt that."

"Good. He should. The chelonian prick."

"Anything else in my home you want to insult?" Audrey asked. "I can get my teapot or my sponge. Or here you are." Bundling up the quilt that was lying next to her, she basketballed it at Jennifer. "Have a go at this."

Jennifer managed to catch the quilt before it flopped into her face. "Excuse me, you don't get to choose which bits of this living Pinterest board I mock you for."

She shook the quilt out and looked at it. It wasn't one of Audrey's best. But then, none of them were. You needed more time than Audrey could spare and more skill than Audrey could manage to be a decent quilter. In this case, she'd taken on a pattern she wasn't ready for, so the stars had come out crooked and the borders were all wonky.

"What the fuck's there to have a go at with this, anyway?" Jennifer demanded.

"I mean, everything? It's just sort of…not a very good quilt? Because I'm not very good at quilting? And…and…" *And yet*, said Natalie, *you wasted hours trying to learn a skill that the patriarchy forced on our grandmothers.*

Jennifer shrugged. "It's a fucking quilt. It's for keeping your tits warm. Who the fuck cares?"

"Is this you telling me you like the quilt?"

Jennifer shrugged, even more aggressively somehow. "I work in a trailer. I get very fucking cold."

Six minutes ago Audrey had been convinced this conversation couldn't get weirder. She had been very wrong. "You can have it if you want," she said. "You know, for your tits. Or, um, any other part of your body."

For what felt like a very long time, Jennifer Hallet just stared at her. "I should never have let you on the show."

Then she left.

With the quilt.

Saturday

"WELCOME BACK," GRACE Forsythe was saying. "It's week two and I'm going to be brief. I won't beat about the bush. It's bread. It's back to basics. It's baguettes. Wilfred and Marianne have given you four ingredients, they want you to make four perfect, identical loaves, and you have four hours starting—well for consistency, what do you say this time we start on four? *Four*, darlings."

Audrey turned over her recipe. She was unsurprised to discover that in addition to the four ingredients, four loaves, and four hours, there were also four lines of instructions. Helpful lines like "Make a shaggy dough using flour, salt, water, and dissolved yeast" and "Once it's rested for an appropriate amount of time, turn out onto a floured work surface and press into a rectangle."

So far, Audrey was enjoying the do-simple-things-well nature of the competition. Of course, she wasn't necessarily that *good* at doing simple things well, at least not relative to some of the other contestants, but aesthetically it appealed. Part of the *point* of baking, as far as Audrey was concerned, was that it was simple. She felt like a gigantic millennial cliché being all *Ooh, modern life is too complex, let me cling to the trappings of a simpler time*. But the fact was, you knew where you were with a baguette. It didn't ask you difficult ethical questions or force you to confront your complicity in an unjust system. It just sat in the oven and browned.

Well, for the moment it was sitting in a bowl, gently expanding, but soon it would be sitting in the oven, and she'd be watching it brown and there'd be a calm to that. A little window where she didn't have to think about deadlines or what the hell she was doing with her life, and she could just enjoy the wholesome-to-the-point-of-parody smell of bread baking.

Making baguettes, Audrey could vaguely remember from the few times she'd done it, was mostly downtime, and she had a feeling that the real test in this challenge was going to be having the confidence to leave the dough proving for long enough. The rule was almost always to let it double in size and when an hour had passed and Audrey's dough had definitely *not* doubled in size, she began to worry that this was a test she would fail.

But they'd been given four hours, and if she'd worked out her timings right—which wasn't guaranteed—she'd only need about thirty to forty minutes for the final bake, so it was okay to give it a bit longer—maybe a lot longer if need be.

Thirty minutes later, things weren't looking much better, and Audrey decided to go for it. The dough was meant to make four loaves, each of a good size, but there only seemed to be enough of it to fulfill one of those criteria. Probably best, Audrey decided, to make the requested number and accept the dimensions being a bit off. As she was working on her third loaf of four, Grace Forsythe appeared at the end of her bench with a glint in her eye that said she wasn't going to let a baguette challenge pass without giving *somebody* a full run of penis jokes, and it seemed like Audrey was first in the firing line.

"I must say you handle that very well," said Grace Forsythe, smirking.

Audrey wasn't really sure how to play this one. *Actually I'm a lesbian* sounded both dismissive and implicitly transphobic, but anything along the lines of *whoar I love cock, me* would be both inauthentic and kind of squicky. All in all, best to play ignorant. "Well I do make a lot of bread."

"No risk of working it too roughly, then," Grace continued. "Getting it too stiff."

Still massaging her bag into a guette, Audrey did her best to think of a response that came across as suitably demure yet witty. Then, when she couldn't, tried a different tack. "Are we…are we still doing this, in the twenty-first century? The French-bread-looks-like-a-willy thing?"

With the dramatic instincts of a woman who had literally been trained to have dramatic instincts at a school of revered dramatic-instinct trainers, Grace Forsythe pressed a hand to her chest in mock-aghastitude. "Why *Audrey* you *wound* me. Here I am asking perfectly innocuous questions about the technical details of your approach to baking, and you somehow decide that I'm talking about willies."

This was a run-with-it situation. "So sorry. Don't know what came over me. I'm sure as a beloved television presenter you've never alluded to a willy in your life."

"Quite so." Grace Forsythe took a deep, theatrical breath. "Nary a willy have I spoken of in all my days, and with God as my witness I shall go to my grave with my body of work untainted by willies. A willyless legacy shall I leave, and should ever a willy inveigle its way into my life I shall not hesitate to whip it out again."

Colin Thrimp sidled up to the far end of Audrey's bench and raised a hand. "Grace? Jennifer says that if you don't shut the fucking fuck up with the fucking willy shit right fucking now she will cut off *my* willy, stretch out the foreskin over a large teapot, and make you wear it as a hat."

"Understood." Grace Forsythe gave Colin Thrimp a look of almost sympathy. "Got to say, though, I think you actually came out of that one worse than I did, old boy."

Wincing, Colin Thrimp nodded.

"I suppose she's right." There was an almost melancholy tone in Grace Forsythe's voice. "All this willy talk is a bit immature, isn't it?"

Hoping she hadn't offended a relatively major celebrity, Audrey gave a reassuring smile. "A bit, but if you can't be immature on the BBC where *can* you be immature?"

"You see?" Grace Forsythe gave Audrey a chummy pat on the shoulder that just about managed to avoid messing up her fourth loaf. "I knew I liked you. Good luck with your willies."

Unable, now, to think of her loaves as anything but pleasant-smelling squishy phalli, Audrey transferred them to a towel, covered them with oiled plastic wrap, and left them for a final rise. None of which were thoughts that followed well from the willy conversation.

At the judging, Audrey kicked herself when the judges tried her baguettes and found the crumb too tight.

"Not proved long enough," Wilfred Honey explained to the camera. "You can see here it's just too dense. Didn't need much longer, maybe twenty minutes, but even though it's only week two, we're holding you to a very high standard."

"Yes, the thing about these bakes," Marianne Wolvercote added, although Audrey sincerely wished she wouldn't, "is that there's nowhere to *hide*."

Doris didn't do so well this time, presumably not having made quite as many baguettes down the years as she'd made Victoria sponges, but Alanis surprised herself by coming out on top while last place went to the man with the extreme dad energy, who Audrey's inner Rolodex had finally managed to file as "John."

"I will admit," he said to the camera afterwards, "I make a lot of cakes at home for the family, but I don't *quite* have the commitment to bake my own bread. So this might not be my week."

Audrey finished up her own interview, but, while she was trying very hard to focus on the competition, the part of her brain that couldn't stop working and wouldn't have wanted to even if it could, was gaming out the question of how she'd approach Doris about the whole can-I-formally-write-up-your-life-story plan.

The sun was dipping lower in the sky and the contestants were splitting off into little groups, some headed barwards, some back to the Lodge, some just going to wander the grounds. Doris was walking back down the hill with Alanis, whose ability to move confidently from social group to social group Audrey envied, not because she couldn't do it but because it was always annoying if a skill you'd work hard to develop came easily to someone else.

"…during the war," Doris was saying as Audrey caught up with them.

"Audrey"—Alanis looked way happier than she had the

previous week, but time went quickly for teenagers and nothing bolstered confidence like a win—"did you know Doris was evacuated during the war?"

"I did, yeah." It wasn't nice, Audrey reflected, to wish a young woman would stop chatting with an elderly woman about said elderly woman's personal history for fear of being scooped by a child, but journalism wasn't a nice profession. "Congratulations, by the way."

Alanis, high on her baguettey triumph, half-nodded. "It's just really weird, you know?"

"Weird?" Hoping that Doris wasn't going to take that the wrong way, Audrey gave her a *kids-will-be-kids* look that Doris singularly failed to reciprocate. Probably, Audrey reflected, because from her perspective *kids* meant anybody under sixty.

"Yeah." In an effort to keep both older women in the conversation, Alanis was walking backwards at a slight distance, which made Audrey really worry she'd trip. "Like, I grew up hearing a lot of stories about what my dad and grandparents went through—well, mostly my grandparents to be honest; Dad was pretty young and doesn't talk about it much—but it's weird meeting somebody who had to escape a war in this country."

Doris gave a contemplative nod. "Reckon I had it easier. Your dad's family had to come halfway across the world. I just got on a train to Surrey."

Hopping nimbly over a divot in the grass that Audrey had been sure she'd fall over, Alanis made a kind of *hold-it* gesture. "Not a competition. Just saying it was interesting is all."

"You close, then?" Doris asked. "With your grandparents?"

"Fairly. I was when I was little but then we drifted apart a bit. I don't know why. I think I was just, y'know, busy." An expression of almost wistful melancholy floated across Alanis's face. The nostalgic yearning of the very young for the life they had when they were very slightly younger. "But I'm making up for it now."

Together, they walked on a little, Doris sharing fragments of her recollections about Patchley House in wartime and Alanis spinning off from them into anecdotes of her own. Audrey, meanwhile, trailed a little behind them just listening, which was another professional habit she probably needed to shake off. The trouble was she found it so much more interesting to listen to a story she hadn't heard than to talk about one she'd been over too many times.

"Umm," Audrey tried to break out of the fly-on-the-wall space, "on the subject of, you know, the evacuation thing?"

"Yes, love?" The look in Doris's eyes was the very definition of grandmotherly.

"How would you, I mean—look, I know it's pretty intrusive and you don't have to, but, well, I've been speaking to Jennifer and—"

"Are you okay, Audrey?" asked Alanis, looking more concerned than a sixteen-year-old should be looking about an adult woman with an interesting career. "You sound like you're choking on a Cadbury Button."

"Can I write you up for my paper?" asked Audrey very fast.

The fact that Doris didn't react with immediate betrayal struck Audrey as a good sign. "What paper?"

"I write for the *Shropshire Echo*." Audrey didn't expect that to mean very much so she followed it up, as she always did with, "We're the second biggest regional newspaper in Shropshire."

Alanis went straight to the obvious question. "Who's the biggest?"

"We don't like to talk about it." Hoping that her credentials would be solid enough to be reassuring but also small enough to be nonthreatening, Audrey turned back to Doris. "Anyway, what do you think?"

Doris gave the slightest shake of her head. "I don't know, love, I think people are probably a bit tired of war stories."

They probably were. But what they weren't tired of was tie-in stories about popular TV shows. Although having articulated it in her head, it seemed gauche to say out loud. Besides, there were other reasons that Doris's story mattered. Or at least, Audrey was pretty sure there were. Although it seemed gauche to mention them out loud, too, since Doris hadn't. "Right," she tried instead, "but your story is actually *here*." She put her arms out and rotated in a circle to indicate as much of the grounds as possible, which got her some funny looks from her companions. "Isn't that... I don't know, it feels like *something* to me. Maybe it's not a big important exposé about, I don't know, corruption at the highest levels of whateverthehell, but I think it's sweet and interesting and people do like things that are sweet and interesting."

"It *does* seem like they might, actually," said Alanis. "My mum loves this show and I think she'd think it was cool to hear that one of the contestants used to live here."

"Would she now?" Doris seemed to be considering it, but Audrey had been in this game too long not to be able to spot reservations. "Well, I'll give it a think." They were approaching the sitting-down log, and Doris took the opportunity to sit down on it. "You two go on without me, I'll be fine."

Audrey really, really hoped she hadn't blown it, but since worrying that you'd blown something—or more precisely acting on the worry that you'd blown something—was often the best way to ensure that blowing definitely occurred, she walked on.

Beside her, Alanis followed along talking about the next day's challenge.

"I'm doing salted honey for sweet," Alanis was saying. The task, in keeping with the back-to-basics theme of the series, was the classic *twelve sweet and twelve savoury rolls*. "And sun-dried tomato and herb for savoury. They're pretty simple, but I figure simple's what the season's about."

It was a good call. At least Audrey hoped it was a good call because it was the call she'd made, too. Even if, privately, she was beginning to worry that her choices of "blueberry jam" and "seeded" might have gone through *simple* and into *basic*. "Feeling prepared?" she asked instead.

"Yeah, actually. I like bread. It's got a sort of"—Alanis made a cheerful kneading gesture—"plus it's got this, like, you know—*making your own bread*."

Audrey nodded. "I know what you mean. There's that *this-is-something-my-great-grandmother-would-have-done* feeling." *Because your great grandmother*, began Natalie, *didn't*—

"Right? When I've finished university I'm going to have a little house with a garden and I'm going to bake all my own bread, and people'll come round and I'll be all, *Would you like some bread?* and it'll be a whole big thing."

"That"—Audrey scrunched her face into a look of confusion—"is a very specific ambition."

"I mean, I also want a good job and everything, but I've still not worked that bit out so much. Bread though, you know where you are with bread, and it's not like I'm ever going to not need it."

"True."

"Compare that to, say, SOHCAHTOA."

"Bless you?" The moment she'd said it Audrey wished she'd

picked any other joke. But Alanis laughed anyway. It was a bit of an indulging-the-old-person laugh, but Audrey was willing to take it.

"Seriously though, teach a girl to bake, you feed her for life. Teach a girl the cosine rule, you just make her quite bored."

The walk to the Lodge was short once they were no longer walking at Doris's pace, and when they got to their rooms Audrey realised that, since she'd only been heading that way to raise the *can-I-ask-you-a-bunch-of-intrusive-questions-about-your-personal-history* topic with an elderly woman, she didn't actually have much reason to be there. So after about ninety seconds sitting down staring at a wall, she got up again and made her way back up the hill towards the bar.

On the way she crossed paths with Doris, just getting up from the sitting-down log and beginning the second phase of her walk to the Lodge. Not wanting to crowd a potential interviewee, Audrey gave her a polite nod, walked past, walked a little further, caught herself looking over her shoulder for the third time, and then paused.

In an absolute sense, it was none of her business. And there did come a point at which helping people who didn't want to be helped was obnoxious. Especially if the specific form of help you'd chosen to offer happened to also give you an excuse to see someone who you, at the very minimum, liked looking at. And maybe kind of liked arguing with.

Definitely nothing to interrogate there. Moving on.

+ ✦ ▬▬▬ ✦ +

"No," Jennifer said loudly and clearly through a closed door.

"I've not said anything yet." And since Audrey *hadn't* said any-thing, another thought occurred. "Also how did you know it was me?"

"Playing the odds. I'd gone nearly a full day without Audrey pissing Lane showing up at my door to—"

"Yes, yes, I'm shitting in your coffee or wanking over your favourite teddy bear or something—can you just come out here?"

There was a silence, followed by, "Wanking over my favourite teddy bear?"

"Or something?"

"You are fucking twisted. How the fuck did you get to fucking teddy bear wanking?"

Conversations through doors weren't exactly the thing Audrey liked best in the world, but given how talking to Jennifer usu-ally went, she rolled with it. "By listening to you speak for fifteen seconds?"

"I have *never* suggested *anybody* wank over a teddy bear. I told a guy to go wank over a picture of his mum once, but he had it fucking coming."

"I feel this is getting off topic." Audrey was really beginning to wish she'd picked a different opener.

Another silence. "Did you mean *over* as in *physically onto* or *over* as in *while imagining*?"

"I hadn't given it that much thought?"

"And I'm not even sure which would be worse. The idea of you—"

"Okay, stop." On some level, Audrey suspected, this was a game of vulgarity chicken, but *playing* vulgarity chicken was prob-ably just giving Jennifer an intense home-field advantage. "Will you just please come out here?"

"No."

And now it was a different game. One Audrey hoped she was substantially better at than Jennifer Hallet, on account of it requiring patience. Then again, Jennifer Hallet had stood glaring on her doorstep while Audrey had been stuck in traffic coming out of Telford so maybe she was underestimating her.

She waited. And waited.

Finally, "You're still there, aren't you?"

"Yup."

There were sounds of movement from inside the trailer, and the door opened, revealing an irate-looking Jennifer. Not that there was really any other sort. "You…you know you fucking suck? Just as a person."

Not for the first time in her life, Audrey wondered if she needed therapy. Because being told she fucking sucked shouldn't be that reassuring. She half-shrugged. "I can live with that. Come on."

Jennifer reared back like a pissed-off lamia. "Don't you fucking come on me. What do you think I am? Your fucking teddy bear?"

"Look"—Audrey made a gesture of despair—"I'm sorry. I drew a line between soft toys and ejaculation that I should never have drawn. Can we let it go?"

"Never," said Jennifer Hallet. "Now, what's this about?"

"I want to show you something."

"I bet you say that to all the girls."

"No," protested Audrey, her gestures still somewhat despair adjacent. "What I say to all the girls is *Hi, you look nice. Would you like to get a coffee?* Because I'm not a grandstanding swear demon."

The corner of Jennifer Hallet's mean but irritatingly tempting mouth kicked up slightly. "Word of advice, Lane. You catch more flies with honey, but you get more pussy with vinegar."

This was getting further and further from the elderly lady on the hill. Which was ironic because they were actually pretty close to the elderly lady on the hill. "Can you *please* just humour me?"

Jennifer heaved a sigh so theatrical Grace Forsythe would have been proud. "I suppose I'll get no fucking peace 'til I do, will I?"

"None whatsoever."

Audrey led Jennifer back from the trailers to the steps outside the ballroom and stood looking towards the woods, the river, and the Lodge. And between the Lodge and the steps, Doris was still struggling down the hill, about three-quarters of the way along now, the rapidly diminishing sunlight casting a long shadow beside her.

As a print journalist, Audrey wasn't normally inclined to emphasise the power of visual storytelling over the written word, but there were times when she had to admit that a striking image really added something to an argument.

"And?" Jennifer sounded beyond unimpressed.

"And," said Audrey, "she does this every day. Twice a day, really, if you count both ways. Four times if she needs to go back to her room for anything."

There was no trace of a reaction on Jennifer's face, but she wasn't looking away. She was just watching Doris's steady progress down the hill with the cool impassivity of, well, of a professional television executive, if Audrey was honest. "You've already told me about this. And I've already said we're not doing anything."

"I thought it might help to see it."

This *was* enough to break Jennifer's focus. She turned to Audrey with an expression that was probably meant to be withering. Although Audrey was mostly struck by her eyes, which were flecked hazel in the half light. "Oh did you? Because apparently she's Tiny Tim now, and I'm going to get all upset because you've shown me a sad picture of a sick frog."

Despite everything, despite Doris still working her way down the hill and Jennifer *definitely* not being worth the time or the energy, Audrey couldn't quite let that go. "You know Tiny Tim isn't a frog in the book, right?"

"Muppet version of that story's the best version. Including the original."

Was that cause for hope? Somebody with opinions about the Muppets couldn't be totally unfeeling. "Okay, but she's not a puppet, she's a person. She's a person you could help, and pretty easily, if you'd just stop being an arse."

"Do you think maybe calling me an arse isn't the best way to get me to do what you want?"

Audrey made a play of considering the question. "Not really. I think you've got pretty thick skin, and I think you also know that this is the right thing to do."

"How about you stop calling me an arse, *and* stop telling me what I know?"

"How about you stop making Doris spend two hours a day walking up and down a hill?"

"She does not—" If Jennifer's instinct had been to quibble about the timing, that instinct faded as her gaze turned, not totally unsympathetically, back to the hill. "Fuck, she is fucking slow isn't she?"

Seeing Jennifer Hallet, even for a moment, acknowledge that another person was a human being instead of a bundle of story beats and performance metrics was a bit like having a butterfly land right next to your face. Slightly magical. But also liable to poke you in the eye. "Would it help," Audrey tried, "to think of it as being about production schedules? Isn't it extremely inconvenient?"

"Not if she gets out of bed early enough." For all the cynicism in Jennifer's voice, Audrey was beginning to think she was cracking. This was sounding more like spite-by-numbers.

"And what about insurance? What if she has a fall?"

"Check y—"

"Yes, yes, we've all signed a bunch of waivers. And I'm sure if a ninety-something-year-old woman breaks a hip on the set of your family-friendly baking show, that won't reflect badly on you *at all*."

For once, Jennifer Hallet didn't have a reply. Or at least, she didn't have a reply beyond, "You are a fucking piece of work."

"You know," said Audrey sweetly, "I think I'll take that as a compliment."

Because, in a strange way, she did.

In place of an answer, Jennifer made an incoherent noise of frustration, then stormed off back to her trailer muttering a stream of mostly inaudible invective. Audrey just about caught the words "manipulatively tenacious."

Which, again, from Jennifer, felt like a compliment.

Sunday

"WELCOME," GRACE FORSYTHE was saying, "to the second baketacular of the season. In keeping with our back to basics, or should I say *bake* to basics"—she waggled her eyebrows—"theme, we're asking for something as simple as it is sumptuous. As austere as it is au…ncredible. There'll be no bells or whistles to hide behind here. Wilfred and Marianne want you to make rolls. Twenty-four beautiful rolls of which half should be *sweet* and half should be *savoury*. Which means, yes my lovelies, we want you to spend the next four hours showing us all your buns and your baps." She turned her head slightly to camera. "And to think this goes out before the watershed. As always, your time starts on three. *Three*, darlings."

Still a little—a little what exactly? Triumphant? On edge? Flushed?—a little whatever from her apparently successful confrontation with Jennifer Hallet the night before, Audrey took a beat or two to get her focus back on the competition.

The tricky thing with this kind of challenge was multitasking. Neither bake by itself was that complex, but the two of them together made for some fiddly questions of timing. The sweet rolls were harder to make, but the savoury dough required a longer rise, so that was where she started, mixing a blend of white and wholemeal bread flour in a bowl and rubbing through butter and salt.

While getting distracted by all the interesting things other people were doing hadn't exactly served Audrey well so far, she still took advantage of the current, relatively mindless, step in the bake to…get distracted by all the interesting things other people were doing. On one side of the ballroom, the man she remembered as *Reggie* had taken a pencil out from behind his ear and was making some very complex notes on a sheet of paper. On another, the woman Audrey had filed as Linda—about Audrey's age, permanently harried expression—was expositing her concerns to the camera.

"I'm doing cinnamon rolls," she was saying, "and I know that's really too simple and probably I'll get marked down for it, but I'm also making spinach and cheese rolls and those need two separate proofs and I think that'll probably be fine, but the lights make it hotter and that might mess things up and—"

Grace Forsythe swept in from out of shot. "Well this looks *fascinating.*" It wasn't especially, but Audrey had a glimmering suspicion that she was just saying something, anything, to keep Linda from spiralling. "And I'm so sorry, I missed what you were telling us." A pause, just long enough that the prompt could be edited out to make for a smoother, less humiliating piece of television. "What're you making for sweet?"

"Cinnamon rolls."

"Wonderful." Although having said *wonderful,* Grace made an exaggerated grimace. "But am I right in thinking that *cinnamon roll* is some kind of awful *meme* thing that I'm far too old and past it to understand?"

Linda nodded and blinked back what had been the beginnings of tears. "It sort of means *very nice person*. I'm not sure where it comes from, though."

"Darling I assure you, *none* of us are sure where *anything* comes from, so in that regard you are in the *very* best company."

A little concerned that at least one contestant was making something notably more complex than she was, even discounting whatever Reggie was doing that apparently involved a slide rule, Audrey returned to her bake. She added yeast, sugar, and warm water, and began kneading the mixture into dough.

She could probably have used a dough hook, but the time they'd been given was generous and Alanis had been right, there was something satisfying about making your own bread. Something you could get lost in.

And so Audrey let herself get lost.

Despite having worked in a very time-hungry medium for a decade now, Audrey was still a bit surprised at how quickly four hours turned into zero hours. She took her rolls out of the oven and then stepped away so that the professional making-food-look-good people could film her creations from flattering angles. Privately, it was one of the things she was looking forward to the most: watching the series back with her mum and dad and getting to see something she'd baked herself put under lighting that made it look TV good instead of pretty-decent-home-cooking good.

Outside, everybody was gathered on the steps leading down to the garden. It was one of those awkward filming breaks, too short to do anything useful, too long to not be annoying. There was something of a generational split, with the older contestants standing around making polite small talk about yeast and the younger generation taking the opportunity to catch up on whatever social media they'd been missing out on while wrist deep in sweet dough. Every so often Alanis and Joshua would exchange a glance, which Audrey was just online enough to recognise as the *you've sent me something I think is cool* look.

Watching the little exchange took enough of Audrey's attention that when Doris popped up behind her and said, "So I've given it a think," she gave a frankly embarrassing jump.

"And?" She turned, trying not to sound too eager or anxious.

"And I figure why not. Might be nice to talk about the old days."

For something that had been, on some level, a whim of the moment, Audrey felt surprisingly relieved. Perhaps it was just that it would have been really embarrassing to fuck up something as basic as "convince an old lady to talk about the blitz." Only, talking to Doris had been—well, honestly, she wasn't sure what it had been. Intriguing? Interesting? Nice? *Stop calling things* nice, *Audrey*, said Natalie. *It's a meaningless word and you know better.*

The thing was, Audrey wouldn't exactly have said she was lonely. She had her family, her coworkers, a less-active-than-when-she-was-at-university-or-in-London-for-that-matter-but-still-probably-fine social life. But when she'd been listening to Doris, she'd felt something more. A sense of connection maybe that she hadn't realised how badly she was missing.

"Thanks," she replied, hoping she sounded mostly professional. "Can I catch up with you after the judging?"

"Seems like that'd be best. Perhaps you can buy me a cup of tea."

It seemed a fair exchange. There'd be more formal paperwork to sign at some point, probably some quite fiddly paperwork since there was a TV production company in the mix as well. But for now Audrey preferred to think in terms of conversation. Of one person telling a story to another. In a lot of ways that was why she'd gone into journalism in the first place.

Bakes filmed, the contestants were herded back in to their places where they waited to come up one at a time and have their rolls assessed on the basis of sweetness, crustiness, and simple-thing-flawlessly-executedness.

The first few contestants—Meera with her chilli cheese rolls and lemon buns, Joshua with his playing-it-surprisingly-safe combination of stilton-and-walnut mini-loaves and blueberry and white chocolate finger buns, and Jim-the-dad with a straightforward fruit-in-one-spinach-in-the-other combo—did fine. None of them had excelled but nobody got a frown and a *This was a straightforward bake, so we expected perfection* either.

Alanis was next, approaching the judges' table with a confidence that Audrey wished she could borrow about ten percent of. "So these," she said, "are salted honey sweet rolls and sun-dried tomato and herb savoury rolls."

Marianne Wolvercote and Wilfred Honey scrutinised Alanis's bready offerings. "They're well finished," Marianne conceded, never wanting to give too much praise too early in case it compromised her position as the mean judge.

"Aye," agreed Wilfred Honey. "The glaze on them buns is smashing. Clear and bright and even. You know, they look so tasty, I might even not mind you've put salt on them."

With the confidence of eight years of stage rivalry, Marianne Wolvercote turned to her co-judge. "Putting salt in sweet pastries is quite common, Wilfred."

"I know it's common, I just miss the days when sweet was sweet and savoury was savoury." Despite his protestations, he took a large bite of one of the salted honey rolls, and when he'd finished chewing, gave an approving nod. "But I'll tell you what, when that's the result, I see the point of it. I think sometimes these things are just trendy, but I really feel you've made a strong choice there."

Marianne Wolvercote was nodding along with him. "I agree with Wilfred. This is top-notch. The balance of flavours is just right. Subtle but really comes through."

"And the savoury's lovely, too," added Wilfred Honey. "Good crunch to the crust, and even with the flavours it still tastes like bread."

"As opposed to what?" asked Grace Forsythe, from the sidelines.

"Takes a lot of work to make bread taste like bread," explained Wilfred Honey, sagely.

Secure in the knowledge that her bread tasted like bread, Alanis returned to her station, to be replaced by blue-collar John, whose rolls had come out perfectly adequately but whose buns had caught a bit. Then Audrey was up, yesterday's fears that she'd erred too close to basic flooding back as she placed her sweet and savoury rolls in front of the judges.

"The jam's homemade?" she offered, apologetically.

"Well I am a fan of blueberry," Wilfred Honey said, taking a nibble. "And these have come out well. They're very simple, but we *wanted* simple."

"Yes." Marianne Wolvercote was doing one of those slow

nods. "The seeded rolls in particular are…well on the one hand I can't fault them but on the other hand I think you could have been just *this much*"—she held her fingers so close together they were practically touching—"more ambitious."

"You've got real skill," Wilfred Honey followed up. "And more importantly, you can taste that these were made with heart."

"Metaphorically," added Grace Forsythe from the back row.

It was still more praise than Audrey had expected. She replied with a "thanks" and a wide smile, and almost floated back to her workbench.

Next up was Reggie, still with a pencil behind his ear even though he had a perfectly good breast pocket. He was carrying two platters that looked more like traybakes than rolls, irregular lumps forming two neat rectangles overall.

"So these," he said with a mix of pride and awareness that he'd gone out on a bit of a limb, "are my tangram rolls."

Wilfred Honey shook his head. "Sorry lad, you've lost me."

"Those"—Reggie indicated the first rectangle, golden-brown rolls in a variety of different shapes and sizes—"are olive bread, and those"—he indicated the second—"are Chelsea buns."

Marianne Wolvercote was looking decidedly unimpressed. "They're not very uniform."

"They're not meant to be."

Somehow, Marianne Wolvercote managed to glare at Reggie over the top of a pair of glasses she wasn't wearing. "I think you'll find they *are*."

"They're not." For a man who seemed to have an engineering background, Reggie seemed surprisingly confused about the efficacy of digging as a hole-exiting strategy. "Because they're tangrams."

Either out of mercy, or a terrible realisation that she'd been off camera for fourteen seconds, Grace Forsythe stepped forwards. "Perhaps I can help. You see, as I explained in my three-part docu-series about the history of geometry, *The Shape of Things*, tangrams are a kind of puzzle in which you have seven different polygons that can be rearranged into a variety of different patterns."

Wilfred Honey looked down. "And you made your rolls into one of these?"

"Yes." Reggie's initial look of confidence was fading. "I made two sets for each, so there's actually fourteen rolls total because you asked for twelve."

"Fourteen isn't twelve," pointed out Marianne.

Grace Forsythe waved a hand. "It's a baker's twelve."

"It's not." Wilfred Honey was looking sceptical, but he'd cut a piece off the corner of two triangles, one exactly twice as large as the other, and was inspecting them closely. "Mind you, it's a surprisingly even bake. Did you need to do them for different times?"

Reggie nodded. "Yeah, took some trial and error at home."

"The flavours," Marianne Wolvercote announced, having turned her attention instead to the Chelsea buns, "are excellent. Which means I'm torn. Because on the one hand this was a highly technical bake, executed well and actually *mostly* on brief, but on the *other* hand I can't help thinking you're taking the mickey just a little bit."

Grace Forsythe pressed a hand to her bosom. "Marianne, darling, I have been watching this dear man all day, and I swear to you he has been resolutely mickeyless."

Reggie returned to his place with that aura of coming-first-or-going-out that you sometimes saw when somebody took a swing for the fences. And once the remaining contenders had faced the music—all doing fine, none so polarising as Reggie nor generally well-received as Alanis—the judges retired to deliberate.

They didn't take long in the end. Just long enough for everybody to share a few nervous glances and to agree privately amongst themselves that if Reggie didn't win this one, then it was probably going to be his last week but that at least he'd be going out in style.

The presenters returned, and Grace Forsythe took up her place of honour in front of the contestants. "We will start, as ever, with the good news. Our winner this week delivered baguettes that were ba—hang on, I had something." She waved a hand at the camera. "Let me have that one again—delivered baguettes that were absolute bally bangers, and a range of rolls so exquisitely crafted"— Audrey shot a look at Alanis, who was trying not to look excited; *exquisitely crafted* wasn't the language Grace Forsythe would use for tangrams—"that you could stick the word *Royce* on the end of them and sell them in a high-end car showroom."

Across the ballroom, Colin Thrimp put his hand to his ear. "Jennifer says *who the fuck do you think you are, noted Dadaist Marcel Duchamp?*" And Audrey's brain not so helpfully offered her a very clear mental image of Jennifer saying it, her lips half smiling as they dripped that slightly-trying-too-hard sarcasm.

"I actually did a BBC special on Duchamp years back," replied Grace Forsythe, ever unperturbable. "Fascinating fellow. Now where were we? Ah yes. *In a high-end car showroom.* That's right, our winner this week is the wonderful Alanis. Now isn't that ironi—"

"Jennifer says don't you dare," shouted Colin Thrimp in a great hurry.

While Grace and Jennifer-by-proxy were debating the validity or otherwise of nineties music references in a contemporary work of reality television, the contestants passed congratulatory hugs to Alanis and early commiseratory hugs to Reggie.

"But now"—Grace Forsythe's RADA training took her from joy to sorrow in a heartbeat—"it's time to say goodbye to our second contestant. Yes, it's that heartbreaking point in bread week when we have to reveal which of our perfectly risen bakers is actually *toast*. And this week, I'm sorry to say…"

Reggie was already wincing.

"It's John."

John was nice about it. From what little Audrey had seen, he seemed a nice-about-it sort of guy. And while the group consensus was that, despite straying from the brief, Reggie did definitely deserve a second chance. Audrey couldn't help wondering if John had been doomed from day one by the fact that a wholesome stay-at-home dad with two kids had won the *last* season.

"Just over the moon to have made it this far," John was saying in his exit interview, "and looking forward to getting back home to my family."

Meanwhile in a slightly different filming location, Reggie was making an exaggerated *phew* gesture and trying one more time to explain what tangrams were.

Audrey finished up her own interview and, with a big-sisterly impulse she was increasingly worried might be patronising, had a quick look around for Alanis, who she found perfectly happy giving an interview of her own.

Which just left Doris. She'd already been debriefed and was now sitting on a bench a little way from the entrance to the ballroom, looking out over the garden with a quiet smile on her face.

"Are you…?" Audrey began. "I mean shall we…?"

"No rush, is there?" asked Doris, looking distinctly unrushing.

"No, I suppose not." Audrey sat down beside her putative interviewee at a comfortable *I am interested but not crowding you* distance. "Whenever you're ready."

Whenever Doris was ready, it turned out, wouldn't be for a while. She sat quite contentedly people watching, saying the occasional hello or goodbye as contestants filed away to the carpark and standing up to give John a kiss on the cheek as he left since they wouldn't be seeing each other again.

It wasn't until they were alone that Doris finally turned to Audrey and said, "Right, about that cup of tea."

JUNE 1940

I'D BEEN THERE near on a year (Doris was saying over tea). And it had been good, all told. I missed my mum and dad of course, and my brothers and sisters, but we got to be like family amongst ourselves, living so close by each other as we was.

Me and Emily—that's the daughter from the big house, her as was throwing rocks at frogs as you might recall—had got to be…well we wasn't exactly friends. Hard to be friends with somebody when they're from money and you're not, when they spend their days in dresses the colour of summer throwing rocks at frogs and you have to darn your own stockings and clean up after the younger kids.

Still, we talked a fair bit. Most days actually. I weren't allowed up to the house much, 'cept on special occasions or if Sir Arthur had something he wanted to tell us, which he didn't often. But she'd be down in the woods a lot, down by the hermitage and that. And we'd chat, like. Though I think she was laughing at me a lot of the time. Maybe all of the time.

"Hullo, nymph," she'd say to me, when she saw me down by

the river, and I'd say "hullo" back and then she'd tell me about something she'd read about in her father's big library or learned about from one of her tutors and I'd say, "I don't know about that," and she'd say, "Don't you? How queer," or words to that effect.

I remember I was sitting by the riverbank one day, end of June it was, and suddenly this pair of hands come down over my eyes and I hear Emily's voice in my ear saying, "Guess who, nymph."

And I said "Emily" because she was the only girl on the estate what talked posh and because nobody else called me that 'cept her.

"You could have played along," she said, taking her hands away. "A guessing game is no fun if you guess on the first try."

I turned around to look at her. The sun was lighting her up from behind, and she looked like everything. Like freedom. Like an angel. Like the sort of thing the likes of me only sees in pictures. "Umm," I said, "King George?"

"Better." She smiled at me then. She often did but that day it was different. More for me less at me, if you get what I'm saying. "But no, it's *me*. Aren't you shocked?"

"Yeah," I told her, doing my best to play along. "Shocked as arse."

I'd heard her say worse, but she covered her mouth with her hands. "Doris, how *dare* you say such things. But you'll be even more shocked when I tell you why I'm here."

I wanted to think of something clever. Some kind of guess that would make her laugh. But I couldn't so I just said, "Why're you here?"

"Because I have a *surprise* for you," she told me, "for your *birthday*."

I'd forgotten. She'd got the day out of me months before, I'd thought just because we'd run out of other things to talk about. "You didn't have to."

"Don't be silly. I want to."

I sat there a bit. She didn't give me nothing. "Well?"

"Impatient. I told you it was a surprise. Now I'm going to need to cover your eyes again."

So she did. And she made me get to my feet and walk all the way up that hill with her guiding me. It was further than she thought, I reckon, because we fell a couple of times on the way up, all tangled together like string and honestly if I'd had my way I'd have been happy to stay there. But she got me to my feet and covered my eyes again and took me all the way up until I heard my shoes crunching on the gravel and then she put me up a step and into a chair and when she took her hands away I was sitting in the passenger seat of Sir Arthur's Cadillac V 16.

"What's this?" I asked, which even then I knew was a stupid question.

She got in the driver's side, looked over at me, and grinned. "An adventure."

I will say that what happened next was technically a crime. Because it weren't my car and it weren't hers and what with us both being fourteen—me only *just* fourteen—we didn't neither of us have much of an idea what we was doing with it. But that was the thing with Emily. She was—nothing stopped her, no one said no to her. If she wanted to drive, she'd drive.

Honestly I've never been so scared in my life. I mean, you've seen the roads round here and they was worse back in them days. Rougher and narrower and we was going so fast round some of them bends that swear to God I thought she'd wrap us round a tree and kill us both. Though looking back I think I'd have gone happy.

We drove for miles, which the rate Emily was going didn't take us that long, until we got to Tapworth and then she parked up outside this old pub, got out and come round to my side to open the door for me, almost like we was courting.

I was going to ask her what we was doing in Tapworth, but I'd had enough of feeling stupid so I just let her lead me through the village to the little cinema they had there in them days. "I thought," she said as if it were the most natural thing in the world, "we could see a movie."

"Don't got no money," I told her, hoping she wouldn't insist on paying for me.

"Don't need any. Nobody *pays* to see movies. Follow me."

So I followed her. The picture house was a run-down little thing, and it had a back door what didn't lock.

"Ain't you rich?" I asked her as we was creeping in the shadows that led into the theatre. "Couldn't you just buy a ticket out front?"

"Could," she whispered. "Shan't. How do you think rich people get that way?"

I shrugged. "I don't know. God?"

"Generations of never paying for anything we don't have to. Come on, quickly."

She darted away then, into the dark, and I followed after her half certain I was going to get nabbed and sent to prison for skipping a movie ticket, but nobody spotted us and nobody cared. She took me through this little service door, what I reckon the pianist used back when pictures was silent, and we slipped into some seats what nobody wanted and nobody would see.

"What film is it?" I asked her as the lights was going down.

"New Hitchcock," she told me. "*Rebecca*."

I'd heard of Hitchcock, of course. Everyone had heard of

Hitchcock. Never heard of *Rebecca*. Not then I hadn't anyway. Now—well, now I've had it on tape and DVD and them Blu-rays, what was big for a while. My grandson set me up with that Amazon thing, and I've got it on there and all.

It's a good film. One of the best I reckon. Joan Fontaine and Laurence Olivier and that. And it brings back memories.

Emily didn't take her eyes off the screen the whole time. But she held my hand, and I didn't take my eyes off her.

After the show we grabbed some bread and some cheese from a shop in Taplow and Emily drove us out to a field not far from Patchley. We lay next to each other on the grass and ripped chunks off the loaf and fed them to each other.

"He kills her in the book, you know," Emily told me.

"That seems a bit rough. They've only just got married."

She laughed again. "Not the girl, nymph. Rebecca. But you're not allowed to kill your wife in a movie so she had to kill herself."

"Oh." I chewed on a piece of cheese and gave it a think. "Good film, though."

Emily was lying right beside me, her head next to mine. Our hair was all spilling together in the grass. "One day," she said to the sky, or maybe to me, "I'm going to have a life like that."

"What, marry a rich man with a dead wife?"

And she laughed at me. Of course she laughed at me. "Not like the girl—poor silly thing who doesn't even get her own name. No, when I grow up I'm going to be *Rebecca*."

"And get shot?"

I felt her nodding where her head was touching mine. "Go where I want. Do what I want. Love who I want. Die how I want."

"You're so—I dunno. Why're you talking about dying?"

"Morbid."

"You what?"

She shifted, rolling around and coming to her knees so she was kneeling over me, looking down. "The word for somebody who is fixated with dark things. With death and dying and the like. It's *morbid*."

"Then you're morbid."

And there was the laugh again. "I thought I should be. I believe it looks rather well on me."

"You're daft."

That didn't please her. "I'm not daft. I'm actually rather precocious."

She tore a piece of bread from the loaf and worked it between her fingers. Crumbs from its crust were drifting down onto me like little brown snowflakes.

"We should have bought some honey," she said, not really to me. "I'm in the mood for something sweet."

I propped myself up on my elbows and tried to shrug, but it was hard with my weight all funny. "What we've got's good enough."

"I suppose it is," she said.

And then, for the first time, she kissed me.

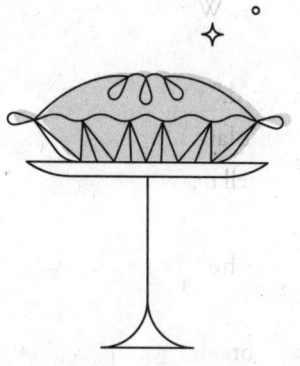

WEEK THREE

Pies

Wednesday

AS IT TURNED out, trying to convince a reality TV producer to let you do something that you were contractually obliged to not do wasn't just difficult, it was complex. Complex enough that it was forcing Audrey to visit Jennifer Hallet at her office. Rationally, of course, Audrey knew that she did not live full-time in a trailer on the grounds of a stately home, but emotionally it was weird to be heading back to London after years of resolutely having shit all to do with London, just so she could have a meeting with a woman whose career-defining project sold itself as quintessentially rural.

She also knew, rationally, that Jennifer hadn't chosen to base her production company in the city where everybody bases every production company just to personally annoy Audrey by making her drive three hours out of her way on a Wednesday, but that was emotionally hard to accept as well.

In fact, by the time she'd driven around Holborn for forty minutes looking for somewhere to park her damned car, Audrey was pretty close to blaming Jennifer for London existing at all, as if she'd built a time machine and said to the Romans, "Now you listen to me you pack of toga-wearing imperialist fucks, you'd better start building a city on an inconvenient bit of the Thames or I'll come down on you so hard you'll think the Visigoths are a band of fucking tourists."

There was a slight chance Audrey's imagination was running away with her.

Jennifer's offices were in a fairly nondescript redbrick building on a narrow street only a few minutes' walk from the carpark that Audrey had, eventually, managed to find. She buzzed at the door and recognised the voice of Colin Thrimp on the intercom.

"Ah, Audrey. So lovely to see you—well not see you, I can't see you—let me buzz you up."

Buzz he did, and Audrey made her way upstairs to the offices of Inveterate Productions, the company that Jennifer Hallet cofounded and had, for eight years, run more or less solo.

She'd sort of expected it to be more impressive, what with it making one of the nation's favourite TV shows, but she supposed offices were offices, especially in London, where square footage was at such a premium you were often lucky to get square inchage.

"Come in," called Jennifer's voice from behind a resolutely closed door, and then when Audrey came in, added, "Oh, it's you."

"You knew I was coming."

"I did. I was being dismissive to keep you on your toes."

Having learned the futility of waiting to be asked, Audrey sat down in front of Jennifer Hallet's desk. "You really are always on, aren't you?"

"Yes, yes, I have a thin facade of hostility that you alone can see through or call me on. Fuck off. Now can we talk about"— Jennifer lifted a tablet that was lying in front of her—"this?"

It hadn't been an encouraging *this*. It had been at best an ambiguous *this* and at worst the *this* in *What is this shit?*

"Is there a problem?" Audrey asked in her best I-suspect-I-know-what-the-problem-is-but-don't-want-to-admit-it voice.

"Yes." Jennifer Hallet gave a slow nod. "Yes I think there might be the tiniest bit of a problem."

"I can redraft?" suggested Audrey. "If you can point me to the parts that aren't working for you."

Although the angle of the screen made it impossible for Audrey to see the text, Jennifer waved her hand over it anyway. "All the parts, sunshine. This is very much *not* what I thought I was signing up for."

"No?" Audrey tried her best to sound innocent.

"No. What you pitched me was an in-this-together story about the blitz spirit. Something that the flag-waving, royal-watching, bunting-fucking, VE-day obsessed, middle England NIMBY pricks who *very* much keep my lights on would be able to read and think, *Ooh, that makes me feel all warm and patriotic and in no way confronts me with anything I might disagree with.* What you've given me is a story about two teenage lesbians stealing cars."

There was that. "One car. And they brought it back."

Jennifer Hallet made no reply. She just glowered. It was a good look on her, in a lot of ways.

"Also, they might not be lesbians. One or both of them might be bi."

"Oh, well that changes everything."

One of the nice things about working on a local paper with extremely limited distribution where virtually all your articles were about parking prices and hypothetical ghost barges was that you normally didn't need to have this kind of conversation. "I hope," said Audrey cautiously, "I'm just misunderstanding you, because it sounds to me like you're saying you don't want me to run this story because it has an LGBTQ+ element."

"It's not just an LGBTQ+ element, it's a *be gay do crimes* element. And there's no sounds like. That's exactly what I'm saying. This is the BBC, my girl—"

"Don't call me *my girl*—I'm not your girl." *Friday or otherwise*, a more whimsical Audrey added.

"I'm so sorry. This is the BBC, *sunshine*. And that means being neutral on controversial topics."

Audrey couldn't quite believe where this was going. "Are you really saying that a story where two girls kiss once is a *controversial topic?*"

"Have you read a newspaper lately? Other than the one you work for I mean."

Much as Audrey hated to admit it, she understood where Jennifer was coming from. She just didn't agree with it. "You're not going to get kicked off the BBC because of one article, and it's not as if there have never been gay people on this show. Aren't Tariq and…you know, thingy, the tall one nobody liked…aren't they dating now?"

Jennifer rested her forehead on her fist like *The Thinker*. If what *The Thinker* was thinking was, *I cannot be fucked with this*. "When will people stop thinking they know *my show* better than I do."

"Sorry, been a fan for a long time."

"The point is," Jennifer went on, still not looking up, "is that there's a difference between two photogenic young men giving an interview, after the show has gone out, where they happen to mention they're together now, and you running a long-form story, while the show is airing, that goes in-depth on Doris and her tragic but gay as balls childhood romance."

It wasn't quite the point, but something in Audrey felt the need to protest. "You don't know it was tragic."

"Well in 1953 she married a man named Bobby Rice and they were together until he died in 2002…"

Journalist-Audrey couldn't help filling in *one year before their golden wedding anniversary.*

"So unless they were reunited *very* late in life or she spent fifty years fucking some posh tart behind her husband's back, I'm going to go out on a limb and say that this"—Jennifer waggled her fingers over Audrey's article like she was warding off the evil eye—"Mills and Boon historical romance you're trying to conjure up for them did *not* end happily."

On some level, Audrey had known that. Which meant that being confronted with it now didn't do much to change her mind. "Okay." She put her hands up in a balancing kind of way. "A lot to unpack there. Firstly, I don't think a story isn't worth telling just because it has a sad ending. Secondly, I think that's doubly true for stories about gay people in the *forties* because those often ended badly for very specific and obvious reasons."

With a groan of frustration, Jennifer Hallet looked up at Audrey. Her eyes said, *You are boring my tits off,* more eloquently than words ever could. "And that's what you think people—the people of Shropshire, mind, a county where sixty percent of the population vote Tory and fifty-seven percent voted for Brexit—want to hear when they're tuning in to their favourite baking show is it? You think they want to look at the relatable granny and say, *You know, she was sticking it to a posh bird all through the war, but then they had to break up because of institutionalised homophobia.*"

"Can you…" Audrey shook her head plaintively. "Can you just stop being deliberately awful for three minutes?"

"No."

Sighing, Audrey got up. "Then I guess we're done here."

"Looks like. Sorry it didn't work out."

Her hand was just on the door when, despite everything rational-Audrey and for that matter remotely-professional-Audrey was telling her, she turned back. "I'll admit I'm disappointed."

Jennifer didn't even blink. "Not surprised. It would have been a good opportunity for you."

"No, I mean, when I applied to the show I looked into you and, well…"

Jennifer blinked now. Her lips tightened and she jabbed a finger across the room at where Audrey was standing. "Oh no you fucking don't."

"I just thought maybe as—"

"I swear if you say *as a queer woman* you will be off my set so fast, scientists in Geneva will be detecting anomalous readings on their—their things scientists detect readings on."

Audrey backed very slightly off. On this one, specific point, Jennifer was maybe not being completely unreasonable. It had been a pretty shitty card to play. "Okay, okay. You're right. I shouldn't be…you've not got an obligation to be visible. It's just—I mean, leaving aside what all the, all the bunting-wearing king-fucking whoevers will say, what did you think about it as, you know, as a story?"

The look on Jennifer Hallet's face was far from encouraging. "You really want to know?"

"I mean I think you're probably just going to say something needlessly cruel, but yeah, I do."

For a moment, Jennifer looked back down at her tablet, scrolled through a few lines of the article, then said: "What I mostly think, looking back at it is, *This rich bitch is going to break that poor girl's heart.*"

It wasn't the answer Audrey had been expecting. At least it mostly wasn't. "You know you could have expressed that without using a gendered insult."

"Oh fuck off."

There was a very, very narrow window here to turn this around. "Okay. But taking my fucking off as read, it sounds like you do care a *bit*. About what happens next at least."

"I know what happened next. She got old, got boring, and went on a baking show, the end."

Jennifer's overall vibe of Jenniferness was increasingly easy for Audrey to ignore. And what that said about either of them, Audrey didn't quite like to contemplate. "The thing is, I don't actually believe you mean that. I think you want to know what happened between them."

"And why do you think that?"

A hundred reasons. Although the chances were Jennifer Hallet wouldn't accept ninety-four of them. "Because connection matters? Because this is—I mean, it's sort of our heritage, isn't it? Everybody's heritage really."

When Audrey looked, Jennifer was wearing a look of scorn so obvious it felt like a misdirect. "That's the most sentimental pile of—"

"Just let me carry on talking to her. We've already agreed nothing gets published until broadcast anyway, so you have plenty of time to torpedo this if it's not working for you."

A different sort of hardness crept into Jennifer's eyes and tightened her mouth. "No."

"What do you mean, *no*?"

"Not a question you should be asking in a post #MeToo world."

"Oh…oh…" Audrey flailed. "Fuck off. No to what?"

"No to the whole fucking thing."

Technically, this was well within Jennifer's rights. And getting shot down or told something wouldn't work was a huge part of being a journalist. As was not taking it personally. Only Audrey was. She really, *really* was. "Why?" she demanded, far more demandingly than she'd intended to demand it. "You lose nothing by letting me—"

"I do, and you're smart enough to know I do."

This was the second time Jennifer had caught Audrey in what she politely liked to think of as a gambit. And the thing about being called on your bullshit was that it made you feel seen, but not in a good way. "I realise," said Audrey, trying to do a hand-brake turn into conciliation, "the story isn't going exactly the way I pitched. But I really think I can tell it in a way that leaves everyone looking good at the end."

There was a long silence, in which Audrey braced for a salvo of vulgarity that never came.

"You know I was joking earlier," Jennifer Hallet said finally. "But you really do need to learn to take no for an answer."

"Professionally"—Audrey offered her most winsome smile—"I kind of don't."

But it turned out that you win some, you lose some. Not only did Jennifer not smile back, she coasted straight through pissed off into a tranquil fury. "Listen very carefully, Lane. This is my show and I will decide what happens to it, what happens on it, and what stories get told about it. If I need the granny to be a comforting icon of good old days that never existed, then that is what she will be, and you will not stop me or change that or give anybody else ideas about changing that."

Clearly the thing to do now was to back off, give Jennifer time to cool down and try again at a better moment. Alternatively: "Why though? Why does she have to be that? Or why can't she be that but also super gay? This show has been running for eight seasons. You could do something different. Or take a risk or—"

"Have you considered that not approaching every situation the exact way you'd approach it isn't a moral failure?"

That was… Not something Audrey was expecting. Or ready to hear. Or ready to think about. "I'm not like that," she said, far less forcefully than she would have wished.

And for whatever mercurial reason, Jennifer Hallet backed off. "Maybe not. But you came in here and took a giant shit all over the way I do my job. I don't need to explain myself to you. I don't need to justify myself to you. Kill the fucking story."

Better ways to handle this were still sort of floating past Audrey like Poohsticks. Unfortunately, she'd degenerated into a state of mess: hurt and vulnerable and confused and increasingly worried that maybe Jennifer had a point and even more worried that she'd lost the ability to judge. So in a panic she reached for the hardest ball she had. "And if I don't?"

"Then you will be in breach of contract, and I will sue you, and your pissant little paper, until you are both nothing more than skid marks on the arse of Shropshire."

The problem with hard balls was that they bounced back at you really fast so you had to keep whacking them back harder. "You know" six-years-ago Audrey took the wheel—"I think I might actually like to see you try. I'm not a teenager or stay-at-home dad or any of the other randos you're used to pushing around. I've played this game and I've won it. Suing journalists for telling the truth is a bad look for a fast-fashion brand. It's an even worse look for a family-friendly show about buns."

"Well." Jennifer Hallet didn't flinch. "This has been interesting. Always nice to see a new side to somebody."

Six-years-ago Audrey had left the wheel, abandoned the vehicle, and stolen the keys. "I didn't mean… I was just pointing out… All I was saying…"

"You know the difference between us, Audrey?"

There was no way the answer to this was going to be good. "What?" she asked, suddenly exhausted. "You're great, I suck? I'm not sure I care."

"I don't pretend that I'm not a piece of shit."

The words settled heavily like a bad kebab.

"Okay," said Audrey. "Thanks." Later on, quite a while later on, Audrey decided that, actually, the difference between her and Jennifer Hallet was probably that Jennifer hadn't immediately gone to sit in her car and cry.

Typical, said Natalie.

Saturday

"BONJOUR," GRACE FORSYTHE was saying as the remaining contestants gathered on the Saturday morning. "And it's one of the bonnest jours we can expect all season because this week is a personal favourite of mine. It's the week you're breaking out your sweetest, shortest, or hotwateriest crusts, indulging in deep, rich, luscious fillings that we can't *wait* to plunge into—"

"Jennifer says," Colin Thrimp directed from the sidelines, "that you need to sound about ten percent less like you want to fuck the bakes."

The mention of Jennifer knocked Audrey's never-terribly-fixed internal chronometer back to Wednesday and to the bitter taste the whole confrontation had left in her mouth for days afterwards.

"That's right," Grace Forsythe went on, oblivious to both Colin's instructions and Audrey's inner turmoil, "it's pie week."

A moment's pause for reaction shots, although honestly Audrey wasn't sure how she was supposed to be reacting. Partly because she was still adrift in nasty Wednesday feelings but mostly because she'd always found pie week blah in general. Bread and patisserie had reputations for being tough and technical, cakes and biscuits for being relaxed and homey. Pies she always felt, as a fan with a media background, were sort of a filler week. Something you put in to space the more iconic episodes out a bit.

"And we're starting you off with something warm, wholesome, and sumptuous—Colin, Jennifer cannot *possibly* object to my saying *wholesome and sumptuous*."

"She says it's the way you say it."

"Tell her she's projecting. Now where was I?" Grace Forsythe found her spot, cast a wicked glimpse at the camera—one that Audrey felt pretty sure was meant to signal that *wholesome and sumptuous* was absolutely intended to be read as suggestive even if it wasn't entirely clear what it was meant to be suggestive *of*. "Ah yes, the perfect dish for a balmy evening in whatever month this winds up going out in. Wilfred has obligingly provided you with his finest recipe for a summer vegetable pie, and all you need to do is follow it."

There was something ominous about the way Grace Forsythe had said *follow it*. Like the instructions were going to be in code or mirror writing or something.

"You have five hours, starting on three. *Three*, darlings."

Five hours wasn't a good sign either. Both in terms of what that implied about the bake and in terms of how long it meant Audrey would have to keep her game face on for the cameras. She turned over the recipe and began reading through it. For the blind bake, the instructions were surprisingly detailed. *Halve the tomatoes*, normal, *preheat the oven*, normal and they'd even specified temperature and timing. *Lay out the filo*.

Ah.

Audrey checked the recipe again, then checked the ingredients arrayed in front of her on the bench. So that was the trick. They'd been given a recipe that assumed premade or store-bought filo pastry but hadn't actually been given any.

What they *had* been given was a carefully measured allotment of plain flour, salt, warm water, and olive oil.

Well this was going to be fun.

And since making unnecessary fuckups on national television would be a particularly shitty ending to a particularly shitty week, Audrey made a concerted effort to focus on baking and only baking. Having double-checked in case the production team had somehow tucked the "this is how you make filo pastry if you've forgotten" instructions into the fine print somewhere and concluded that no, they definitely hadn't, Audrey bit the bullet and started trying to make a famously fiddly pastry from memory.

The first part was easy enough, mixing flour, salt, and water—the show had even provided a dough hook and mixer as a little extra clue in case anybody hadn't realised what the game was here. The second bit, though, that was going to be trickier.

"I never buy filo pastry," Meera was saying to camera from two benches over. "I always make it from scratch. I just hope the recipe I'm used to is the one the judges expect."

"And how about you?" an anonymously black-shirted producer was asking Audrey all of a sudden. "Normally buy in or make your own?"

In her mind's eye and ear, Audrey could already see how the two bits would go together on television. And out of a kind of semi-professional semi-solidarity that she still felt for the crew, if not for the producer, she decided to go with it. "It's been a while since I've done this," she said as if the thought had just occurred to her. "I've got to be honest, if a recipe calls for filo, I usually just grab some from Sainsbury's."

As if conjured by some primordial incantation, Grace Forsythe appeared at Audrey's shoulder to say, "Other supermarket pastry brands are available," before vanishing into the ether.

"Got everything you need?" Audrey asked the producer, hoping the answer would be yes because she actually had quite a lot to be getting on with.

The producer nodded. "Yeah. Just wanted to get a bit of contrast, y'know?"

"You mean between me and the one who actually knows what she's doing?" replied Audrey with what she hoped was an in-on-the-joke smile. And when the producer, without replying, followed Grace etherwards, Audrey shrugged and turned her attention back to baking. Once her dough was prepared, she separated it into nice round balls on a baking tray and covered them with a damp tea towel. And then froze. Because she knew it had to stand, but had no idea how long it had to stand *for*.

Fortunately, from a brief glance around the ballroom, it seemed like nobody else did either. Well, almost nobody else. Meera seemed pretty confident, and so did Reggie, but the rest of them were just giving each other mutually supportive *I'm-as-in-the-dark-as-you-are* looks. They were in a pastry standoff, sizing each other up like filo-based gunslingers. Eventually somebody would crack and start rolling out, and then everybody would be racing to be as neither first nor last as they possibly could.

As the minutes ticked by, it became clearer and clearer to Audrey that, much as she'd been dreading the idea of having to bake for five hours, having to bake for maybe two hours and sit in silence staring at a mixing bowl for the other three was way worse.

Nothing quite encouraged you to stew in your own thoughts like staring at a mixing bowl.

Was Jennifer right? Had Audrey become the kind of person who assumed her way was the only way? Of course, part of her job was guiding people to the conclusions she wanted them guided to, but there were some places you didn't go and some lines you didn't cross.

Sometimes, said Natalie, *you're right and other people are wrong, and they just have to live with that.*

The problem was—and this was also something Natalie had frequently reminded her—Audrey didn't have that confidence. At least, as one of the people just living with being wrong, she'd always thought it was confidence. From the other side, she wasn't so sure.

In the end it was Linda who broke the filo stalemate, only managing to wait an hour and a half before the mounting pressure to do something, anything, other than sitting down waiting for the seconds to drain away overwhelmed her and she started frantically rolling her pastry into sheets. Most of the rest of them went at around the two-hour mark, which seemed comfortable, leaving them enough time to finish up their pastry without cutting too much into the pie-making window.

For a while, at least, assembling her pie gave Audrey something to do other than dwelling. But once it was in the oven, her choices were another round of unwelcome introspection or intrusively spying on the other contestants. She chose spying. But, unfortunately, there was very little to spy on. Alanis and Joshua were still giving each other looks that Audrey really hoped didn't qualify as flirty, Doris was stacking all her things up neatly to make life easier for the techs who came and did the washing up, and Reggie was doodling something with that pencil he always carried.

Despite what Natalie had said about her reality-TV-viewing habits, Audrey had always been deeply aware of the artificiality of the medium. And one thing that had struck her as particularly artificial was the sense of companionship you typically saw contestants displaying. The way people would be declaring that they'd made friends for life after one or two weekends making cakes in vague proximity and breaking down in tears at being parted from somebody that Audrey, watching from home, barely remembered was on the show. Except now she was here, she was realising that it was way less fake than she'd thought.

She was…*invested* in these people, and not how you were when you watched from home. They were part of her life. Well, part of part of her life. And it really did feel that there was a bond between them, forged by the whiplash mix of tedium and intensity that you got with filming. She was weirdly going to miss them: Reggie's pencil and Meera's quiet confidence and Linda's nervous energy. And, of course, Alanis and Doris whose lives, in their own way, had drawn her in.

After what seemed at once far more and far less than five hours, the bakes came out of the oven—some looking sorrier for themselves than others and Audrey's, to her relief, not looking especially sorry at all—and were set down at the front of the ballroom. And that was it. There was nothing to do now but wait for judging.

In the framing that Inveterate Productions had apparently chosen for the series, "a summer vegetable pie" was meant to be another simple task that the contestants were required to execute well. In reality it had involved making filo pastry from both scratch and memory, making it quite technically complex, and not especially about nailing the basics.

This, Audrey suspected, would be quietly elided in editing. But it didn't change the reality that it had been a tough challenge, and that performances had been decidedly mixed.

"Now this one," Wilfred Honey was saying, looking at Linda's pie with an air of sympathetic disappointment. "You can see that the pastry wasn't let sit long enough, and that's thrown the texture off. Which is a shame because it's otherwise lovely. Whoever this was they just needed to have a little bit more nerve."

Linda gave a perfect reaction. A shot that said, *This is my arc for this season and I know it.*

"This one," Marianne Wolvercote took over narration, with much more disappointment and much less sympathy. "It's too thin, so it's fallen apart, and I don't know quite how but the filling's come out too moist."

To Audrey's relief, that wasn't hers, although the next one, which was "too thick, just a touch, mind, but a touch matters" was, placing her firmly in the middle.

Doris, Joshua, and Alanis had all done well, although Reggie had just pipped them, which was about what Audrey would have expected from a man with his sense of precision. Meera's never-using-store-bought-filo strategy, however, had paid off and put her comfortably at the top of the pack.

Afterwards, the remaining contestants gathered around the picnic benches either celebrating or lamenting their success or failure. Audrey's little group, on this occasion, consisted of Alanis, Joshua, and a deeply despondent Linda.

"So," Alanis was asking in a keeping-people's-spirits-up kind of tone, "who do we think's going all the way?"

"You," said Joshua immediately, and apparently sincerely. "And I reckon you're in with a chance as well," he added to Linda.

Linda looked glum. "Not after today. I messed up really badly."

"Your nerve went," Joshua told her. "Happens to everybody."

She looked unconvinced. "Didn't happen to you."

"Well, I think," offered Alanis, with an encouraging smile, "that we're all in with a good chance of making the final."

Audrey—whose head was still twelve percent elsewhere—gave something a bit like a laugh. "That's very diplomatic of you, since there's only three people can be in it."

"Which is why I said *chance*." Turning to Audrey, Alanis gave her a playfully challenging look. "But okay then. If you're going to be like that. Who are your *exactly three* choices?"

To be fair, Audrey had sort of brought this one on herself. She shuffled slightly uncomfortably. "I do have some thoughts but, fair warning, they're probably a bit unfun."

Alanis blinked at her. "Wow, you're really selling this."

"Sorry. It's my inner journalist. It tends to make me think about things from a very specific perspective."

For the first time in three weeks, Joshua looked almost respectful. "Nothing wrong with thinking about things differently."

"Yeah." Alanis nodded her agreement. "Thinking about things differently is *good*."

Audrey shrugged. This wasn't exactly a trade secret. It was something pretty much anyone could work out from watching enough YouTube videos. But it still got a bit laws and sausages—knowing how they were made kind of ruined it. "Well I used to hang out with a lot of media people and the thing about this type of show is that… It's not that they're *rigged* exactly."

"Knew it." Joshua threw his hands in the air. "That's why I came bottom of the blind first week."

"No." A half lifetime of interviewing difficult subjects kept Audrey's tone as non-patronising as she could make it. "There you genuinely did just miss the brief. But it's why I think you're not *likely* to make the final if I'm honest."

Alanis had gone from cheerful to distressed in an eighth of a second. "But he's *great*."

"We're *all* great," Audrey pointed out, though she privately felt she was the least great at the table. "But this is a TV show and TV is about storytelling. *Your* story"—she nodded at Alanis—"is that you're the youngest contestant ever to be on the show. *Yours*"—she indicated Linda—"is that you're good but you don't have faith in yourself. You and me"—she waved her hands between herself and Joshua—"we're sort of filler."

Aren't you always, said a voice that sounded like Natalie. Except Natalie would never have said that. In some ways, it might have been easier if she had.

"Filler?" repeated Joshua, with as much outrage as he could muster without breaking his lifelong commitment to ironic detachment.

Audrey nod-winced. "Maybe that's not quite the right word? We're there to be recognisable characters, but nobody's rooting for us and nobody's going to tune in to see if we win or—"

"You're making it worse," cried Alanis. "This is horrible. You're not characters. You're *people*."

"To us we're people." Audrey's nod-wince was progressing down her body and had just reached her knees. "But to the audience, and kind of the crew because it's their job, I'm the quirky chubby one—"

"You're not," began Joshua predicably.

And that, Audrey waved aside. "Joshua, I know what my body looks like and I'm fine with it. Anyway, I'm the quirky chubby one, you're the obligatory hipster. Neither of those characters win."

"I'm not sure"—Joshua extended his forefingers like he was making half a picture frame—"I like *hipster.*"

"I'm not sure anybody likes being reduced to a reality TV archetype." Audrey shrugged. "But that's what we signed up for."

"Still not comfortable with it," said Joshua.

It shouldn't have surprised Audrey that a man who refused to be pinned down to a single cake didn't like the idea of being reduced to an elevator pitch, even if that pitch was essentially *the kind of man who refuses to be pinned down.* "Didn't say you had to be. But look at it this way, people are going to think about *you* the exact way you thought about the contestants from last season."

The other three shared a series of crestfallen looks.

"Fuck," said Linda, "am I the Paris?"

Audrey made an I'm-afraid-so face. "Assuming he was the tall one with the hair, yes."

"Fuck."

Despite the length of this particular tangent, Audrey had singularly failed to distract Alanis from the who-will-win question. "You still haven't told us who you actually think is making the final."

Honestly, it was pretty simple. Well, as simple as these things got. "There *are* regulations here," she said carefully, "so it can't be completely set in stone. And besides, production wouldn't want it to be because that would kill the spontaneity."

"You're still hedging," Alanis pressed her.

"Fine. It'll be you, Doris, and Meera. They won't be able to resist the"—Audrey bit her lip; this was likely to land even worse than *hipster*—"old lady versus mum versus young girl hook. It practically pitches itself." And now she'd said it aloud, she had to admit it was going to make one hell of a season. No wonder Jennifer was protective of it.

The expression on Alanis's face, however, suggested she wasn't appreciating the artistry. "But that's so…*basic*."

"It's reality TV. It's a basic medium."

Joshua was staring in the middle distance, which made him look either contemplative or constipated. "This is depressing."

"I wouldn't go that far," said Audrey. "It's just that TV magic is like all other magic. Mirrors and hidden wires."

"Um." To give Audrey credit, she'd successfully distracted Linda from one set of worries. If only by giving her a new set. "I'm not sure *magic isn't real* is as undepressing as you think it is, Audrey."

They seemed to be taking this harder than Audrey had expected. "Yeah. But. We all knew that, right?"

"We *know* it," complained Linda. "But we don't like to say it out loud. I mean, if we took you to see a movie, would you be sitting there going, *Oh, it's all just CGI and pretending*?"

"Not in those terms." Audrey was used to asking herself if she was weird, but she'd really hoped that it would stop when she left London. "But I might want to talk about what was done with physical effects or whether the acting was any good or if the story beats landed."

Linda, using only her eyes, managed to flawlessly communicate the sentiment, *Remind me never to go and see a film with you.* "You wouldn't want to talk about, I don't know, if you enjoyed it? Or who your favourite character was? Or if the ending made you sad?"

And because she didn't want to be a dick, Audrey said, "Well that, too, obviously."

"You know"—Joshua got to his feet abruptly—"I think I need a drink."

In the end Audrey didn't quite fancy the bar. She'd killed enough joy for one day, especially given her normal quota of joys killed per day was zero. Of course, reminding reality TV contestants that reality TV could occasionally be the tiniest bit artificial shouldn't have been a big deal. And probably wouldn't be. But it made Audrey feel off her game. Which was a pisser because she'd worked really hard over the last couple of years to reestablish what her game actually was. Without London and Natalie to decide for her.

In any case, whatever Audrey's game might have been, it *definitely* wasn't half-arsing filo or dropping trite truth bombs on children, neurotics, and hipsters. And it *definitely, definitely* wasn't telling other queer women they were doing their jobs wrong and then threatening to force them into mutually disastrous legal action to try and make herself feel better.

The only thing to do was to apologise.

Two minutes later, a shaky but determined Audrey was knocking on Jennifer Hallet's trailer door.

There was no answer. Not even a *fuck off*.

She knocked again. Then she listened very, very carefully. Jennifer was in there. She could tell.

"Jennifer?" she tried.

Still no answer.

"Jennifer, it's Audrey."

Nothing.

"Jennifer, it's Audrey, and I'm sorry."

The level of nothing, if anything, intensified.

"I shouldn't have said what I said."

Yet grander and deeper nothings answered.

"Really."

In many ways, Jennifer's silence was worse than her swearing. It felt more hostile somehow.

"Jennifer?"

Still nothing.

Audrey's sense of contrition didn't waver. Her patience, however, was beginning to. "You know you're being kind of stubborn here."

If the devastating allegation of stubbornness moved Jennifer to repentance, her closed door showed no signs of it.

"Actually, check that. You're not even being stubborn. You're being childish."

The door bore that accusation with similar equanimity.

"I'm trying to do the right thing here."

Nothing.

"But you won't give an inch, will you?"

A temptation was building inside her to say something, anything, to bait a response. It would have been better than the silence. Except that would also have defeated the point of apologising and, in a perverse way, would have felt like letting Jennifer win. And how had she gone from *I have hurt this person and must make amends* to *This is a competition in which somebody must lose* in less than three minutes?

"Fine," Audrey said instead in a desperate bid to showcase her maturity. Which she promptly ruined by adding, "be that way then."

Because this was so typical of Jennifer Hallet. Here was Audrey, doing her best, making the first move, like you were meant to, admitting responsibility and generally being *great*. Meanwhile Jennifer was sulking like a…like a dick. Probably under Audrey's quilt. And, yes, if you wanted to get all *reasonable* about it, Audrey *had* fucked up and Jennifer *was* entitled to her privacy. Just like she was entitled to stop Audrey publishing Doris's story. But she wasn't entitled to stop Audrey speaking to a fellow contestant. Just on her own time. For her own reasons.

Defiantly, Audrey went to look for Doris.

AUGUST 1947

THINGS WAS...SIMPLE for a bit (Doris was saying, sitting next to Audrey on the sitting-down log as the sunlight was fading over Patchley House and Park). Me and Emily, we wasn't—we was young and we was friends more than anything. Not even that really. Sometimes we'd go a day or a week and she'd not come looking for me at all. But she'd kiss me when she were in the mood, and each time she did, it was like a gift. Like something she'd saved up just for me.

They started winding up evacuation in forty-four, and since I was eighteen by then I was one of the first ones back. It was good to see the family again, though only one of my brothers made it home from the front. Still, it's not that you want to hear about, is it? It's this house.

(It was not, Audrey had long since suspected, really the house that was interesting to her, but she let Doris talk.)

I missed it, you know, when I first got home. I'd not been as young as some of the others but I'd still grown into a bit of a country girl. Got used to the trees and the grass and having sheep and cows and horses just a little ways off from when you wake up in the morning. We wasn't far from the Thames, where I come from, but—well—walking by the river at Patchley and walking by the river in Wapping ain't the same thing now are they?

And I missed…I suppose I missed the house, and everything that came with the house.

Which is why when I was twenty-one, I come back.

Service was good work in them days. Not so good as it used to be, of course. The Downton Abbey days was gone and we'd not see that world again, but folk still needed maids, and I was a good one. A good enough one that they took me on at Patchley.

The train ride down was different than the one from thirty-nine. I was bigger for a start, and the trains had been nationalised so it was British Rail that took me to Tapworth this time, and there was no little evacuee boy sitting opposite me. There was just me, on me tod, with a suitcase not much different from the one I'd had with me the first time around.

There was no little line of us neither, no welcome from the master of the house. Just the housekeeper—Mrs. Loris her name was, she'd been there while I was a kid and all, and she'd liked me well enough back then. Remembered me when I come back, too. Said as I'd always been a good girl and that she knew I'd do well.

Got to sleep in the big house, then. Below stairs. The room weren't that much better than I'd had in the Lodge but it felt different. Closer to the heart of things.

And I *was* close. Not touching close—I weren't a lady's maid, just a housemaid—but I'd set the family's tables and turn down their beds. I'd be there in the background—seen but not heard was the rule for children when I were a girl and it was the rule for servants when I were a young woman, and I don't think it's changed much since.

It was hard, them first few weeks, because I knew my place and my duties, but every now and then—maybe more often than that now I look back—I'd be in the room with her, with Emily, and she'd look at me. Though there was normally company of one sort or another, she'd look at me with those knowing-too-much eyes of hers, and she'd smile.

Of course, she smiled at everybody.

I remember it was shooting season. A devil for the shooting was Sir Arthur, and Emily was no slouch with a shotgun herself. A party was up from, well I think it was London, though if I'm honest they didn't tell the likes of us, and we was all of us working double time to look after them. They'd go out in the morning, come back with the kills, and dine on game in the evening. 'Course what with meat needing to hang that weren't normally the *same* game, but most sportsmen don't know much about cooking so they didn't seem to mind the difference.

They was having a game pie that evening. Nice thing about a pie is it's basically a stew in a crust so you can use birds as hasn't been hung for so long, or the ones what's been gut-shot that you wouldn't want to leave around anyway. I didn't cook it, didn't even help to cook it—that was the cook and the kitchen-maids' jobs—but I set the table ready so's there'd be a centrepiece when the guests came in.

And that's when I heard her.

"Hello, nymph."

I'd just got time to put the pie down nice like before I dropped it. And when I turned around I saw her—really saw her, not just cross-the-room saw her. She was dressed in tweeds for the hunt and she'd got a brace of birds over one arm. I reckon they was grouse, though I weren't so good at telling one bird from the other in them days. Gone too city in my time at home. "Hullo," I said, like I were fourteen again and I'd just caught her throwing rocks at frogs.

"I *thought* it was you." She came closer. There was a swagger to her. She'd always had a swagger, but it'd grown with her. Spilled off her like the sea off a mermaid. "My God you've barely changed."

"Neither've you," I said. And it was true. In a way. But also not true. She was everything she'd been and more. And I remember wondering if this was what the first Mrs. de Winter had been like when she were alive. This picture of everything a woman could ever want to be.

"The uniform suits you. Do something with these, will you?" She tossed me the birds underarm and I caught them. They'd not been dead long—I could feel they were still warm under my hands, and the blood was still wet where she'd shot them out the sky.

I nodded. "Yes ma'am."

"Oh don't *yes ma'am* me, nymph." She was closer now. Closer than was normal for a servant and mistress, though not so close as I'd have wanted. "We used to be friends, didn't we?"

There was something about the way she said the word *friends* that made me feel queer. "Yes m—yes Miss Branningham."

"Please, call me Emily."

I looked down, not wanting to make eye contact. Or not wanting to want to. It weren't my place, though her eyes were beautiful and terrible, like the first storm of a hot summer. "Don't seem right, miss."

And she was closer again, taking the birds back out of my hands. "Of course, how thoughtless of me. And I've made you get blood all over your fingers. You must think me quite boorish."

"No, miss."

Without much care, she set the grouse aside, which meant now they were bleeding onto the white tablecloth and it'd need to be reset, though I reckoned Mrs. Loris'd understand. I'd only been there a little while and she'd already told me many times to watch out for the young mistress's fancies.

"Still, won't do to have you go about your duties dishevelled."

She took my hand then, turned it palm up. There weren't that much blood on it to be honest, but she was looking down on it like it was a wounded mouse.

"It's not a worry, miss," I told her. "Really."

"Even so." She began to smooth the blood from my palm with her thumb. She was wearing these soft leather gloves, and her touch sent a shiver through me. "It's the least I can do."

If that was the least she could do, I was a little worried what the most was. "My hands is easier to clean than your clothes."

"Pish." She shook her head dismissively. "This is my shooting getup anyway. Made to get dirty. Whereas *you*"—she raised my hand to her lips, smeared just a touch of blood across her mouth—"you should be taken care of."

"I'm meant to be taking care of you, miss." It weren't exactly true. I was mostly meant to be taking care of the table, though that was shot to buggery if you'll pardon my language, what with the dead birds and everything.

"When we were girls we took care of each other."

I didn't think that was really how she saw it. But I liked the idea. "That was years ago."

"And you've never thought of me since?"

The right thing to do, I knew, was not to look up at her. But I did. And then I had nothing. "Every day."

She smiled again. Blood mingling with her lipstick. "I think I would rather like to kiss you again."

And I'd got no words. I never did when I was with her. I just nodded, and maybe smiled back, just a little.

So she kissed me. And it wasn't like the first time, when we was barely more than kids. Nor even like the last, when it was her way to say goodbye as I went off to London. There was a fire in it that I'd always known was part of her but that'd got stronger in the years between, turned into something that melted me. That near broke me.

She was pulling me to her with a strength I'd not expected and I felt myself doing the same, and some little voice at the back of my mind was reminding me that I had work to do and that she was the master's daughter and that no good would come of it. But a much louder one at the front was telling it to shut up and just let me have this.

I mean, don't get me wrong, I've had a good life. I've had my joys and my tears and my in-betweens. But where I come from you don't think you'll get the magic, and that's what Emily was giving me, what she was pouring into me. What made me feel like I really could be some nymph out the ocean what walked ashore and took a human girl away with her.

Somewhere I lost my balance and letting go of her—though I'd've given anything to *not* let go of her—I reached back to steady myself and I knocked the stand what I'd put the pie on, and it toppled over with this awful crash. The pie split open, though it was so dense that the filling stayed mostly inside. She used to make a great pie, did cook.

"Ah," Emily looked down at the mess, then at me. "That might take some explaining. Don't worry, Daddy will understand."

I weren't sure what to say. My lips were still almost stinging from kissing her so hard, and I couldn't quite think of anything except kissing her again.

She reached past me and broke off a piece of the pie and popped it into her mouth. "Waste not, want not," she told me. And then she left.

I had to tell Mrs. Loris what happened. Parts of what happened, at least. That the young mistress had come in with a brace of birds while I was setting the table, and that she'd startled me and that'd led to the pie getting knocked but that I was very sorry and that I hoped how she wouldn't dismiss me though I'd understand if she did.

She took me through to the pantry and sat me on a stool.

"What happened?" she asked again.

"I told you," I told her. "And Miss'll back me up, I swear."

"No, I know that." She looked grave. And she had a good line in grave looks, did Mrs. Loris. "But how did she—how did she startle you, exactly?"

"I just wasn't expecting her."

She didn't say anything. Didn't move. She just waited.

"I swear."

"Very well." She pulled up a stool of her own and sat opposite me. "And you don't have to say anything else. But please listen."

So I listened. Though in the end I didn't much like what I was listening to.

"I have known Miss Emily all her life," Mrs. Loris said, "and she has always been a girl with certain…qualities. She can be very charming and very persuasive. But if she had"—and she took a deep breath here—"if she had persuaded you into anything, you should know that you would not be the first and that you will certainly not be the last."

The little voice in the back of my head said it'd told me so, but the bigger voice at the front didn't want to hear it. "She didn't persuade me of anything," I told her. "Honest."

I don't think she believed me. But she was a kind woman so she left it there. She just said, "As you say." And then she got up to go.

Except before she did, she had one more question. Though not one she expected me to answer.

"Are you in love with her?" she asked me. "You don't have to decide right now, just—know it will be much harder, in the end, if you are."

Then she left me. And I sat there on my stool, thinking about what she'd said, wondering if I was.

Which was a silly thing to wonder. Because I always had been.

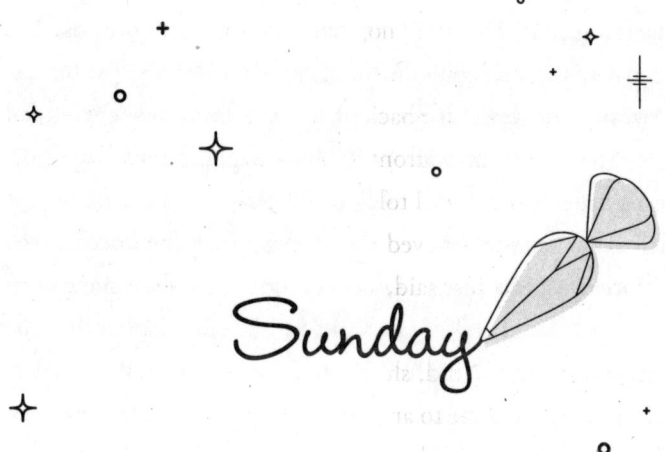

Sunday

LOOKING BACK OVER her notes, Audrey was—and this was a total pisser—starting to see Jennifer's point. This would make a good story. It was a story that she badly wanted to tell. But it was not a story that overlapped well with the narratives *Bake Expectations* tended to build around its contestants. There was a reason that, when Grace Forsythe did the voice-overs explaining who everybody was she wound up saying things like *Rosaline is a twenty-seven-year-old full-time mum, and her daughter Amelie loves shortbread* and not *Doris is a ninety-six-year-old former car thief who once had a deeply erotically charged relationship with a rich disaster lesbian in the 1940s.*

And that was total pisser number two. Because the other thing Jennifer might—and Audrey was only willing to go as far as might—have been right about was… Well. The more Doris had told her, the more likely it seemed to Audrey that things were going in a heartbreaky direction. A heartbreaky direction with deeply entrenched class inequalities and power imbalances. All of which was slightly too much to deal with in a short human-interest piece in Shropshire's second largest regional newspaper.

Leaving that, and the fact that the story was supposed to be dead anyway, as problems for an inevitably resentful future-Audrey, present-day-Audrey went to breakfast. As she tromped towards the hotel, she was caught by a nagging sense of…not-quite-rightness. A not-quite-rightness that she was finally able to identify when she reached the sitting-down-log and realised that Doris was nowhere to be seen. Ordinarily she'd have been up early and already taking her mid-hill-climb breather, but the log was empty. The thought crept fleetingly into Audrey's mind that if she wasn't taking a breather, perhaps she wasn't breathing at all.

She'd seemed fine yesterday. Maybe a little melancholy, on account of talking about her complicated ex. But not more fragile or more tired or more likely to drop dead of a heart attack than usual. Oh God. Audrey made it another half dozen paces before "dropped dead of a heart attack" settled over her mind like a damp flannel and would not de-settle. It was, in fact, settling deeper with every second that passed. She had to do something.

Turning, she pelted back down the hill and into the Lodge, where she knocked on Doris's door. When there was no answer, she hammered on it. When there was still no answer, she tried hammering and yelling together, and when that didn't work she dashed out of the Lodge again and sprinted up the hill.

Well, sprinted to start off with. Then jogged. Then stopped for a second because she was getting a stitch and it was a really long way and running was so much harder when you were an adult with boobs. Finally, she urgent-walked the rest of the way, hoping she'd be able to find someone at the house with a key and that the person with a key would be able to get help. And that they wouldn't be too late.

She wasn't too late, in the end. In fact, she arrived just in time to see Doris sitting down with a plate of bacon and eggs.

Trying not to look too betrayed and/or winded, Audrey hobbled over to her. "Hi," she wheezed. "Didn't see you on the hill."

"Got moved." Doris dipped a corner of toast into a pool of runny yolk. "Said it was an insurance thing."

It was kind of a relief for Audrey to learn that not everything she'd tried recently had ended in abject failure. Even if it had been liability that had swayed Jennifer Hallet rather than—oh what did it matter? "I'm glad."

"It's nice," agreed Doris. "Though I'm still not sure I like the fuss."

Linda, who was sitting opposite and seeming slightly less despondent than she had the day before, gave Doris a reproving look. "It's not a fuss. It's just doing what's right."

"It can be both," Doris pointed out.

While Doris and Linda debated the fussiness or otherwise of not requiring elderly people to climb hills, Audrey made a somewhat belated, somewhat exhausted play for the breakfast table. She was, unfortunately, really very sweaty, and while she was sure hair and makeup would be able to cover *some* of her sins, she wasn't convinced they'd get the whole multitude.

But there wasn't much she could do about it now. And since there'd just been a brief period of time where she'd been convinced that running about like an extremely neurotic bluebottle had been necessary to save somebody's life, she felt her priorities were in the right place.

+ ✧ ━━━ ✧ +

The challenge for their third baketacular was—yet again—a simple one. Of course, that simplicity didn't make Grace Forsythe any less loquacious.

"…two pies," she was saying, "that would sate the appetites of the most gluttonous gourmand, one hearty and wholesome as a hug from an aggressive grandmother, the other as sweet and luxurious as a jacuzzi full of marshmallows. You have four hours, starting on three. *Three*, darlings."

Right. Time to focus. No more obsessing about postwar lesbians. No more obsessing about Jennifer Hallet. It was week three. And just because Audrey was a filler contestant, that didn't mean she had to act like one. A single really good bake was all it would take for her to go down in history as… *Y'know, thingy, from season eight, the one that did that really good pie.* Instead of *Oh yeah, she was in it, too.* It wasn't the loftiest ambition, sure. But it was hers, she was owning it, and she was up for it. Not in a sex way. Up for the challenge.

When Audrey had first received the brief, she'd seen immediately that the trap was making two pies with the same type of crust. It was the sort of choice that would result in Marianne Wolvercote saying, "I just think you could have pushed yourself a little more." Which was code for "You half-arsed this."

At the same time, it had also occurred to Audrey that the *other* trap was doing two different kinds of pastry, meaning you had to work at two different oven temperatures, and therefore make things too complicated for yourself. That was the sort of choice that would result in Wilfred Honey saying, "I like what you've tried to do here, but I don't think it's worked."

Audrey had gone for trap number two.

She started on the sweet pastry for her blackberry and ginger pie first, because that would need to chill for a good couple of hours before it was actually usable whereas the hot water crust, for her savoury, would just need to stand for a while.

As she mixed sugar and salt, butter and flour, she tried to stay true to the promise she'd made herself all of eighteen seconds earlier. To be in the moment instead of somewhere that wasn't the moment or was someone else's moment. The only thing she had to do now was bake. And, ideally, bake well.

Except that never worked. While here-and-now-Audrey was trying to mix vinegar-water into her dough, five-years-ago-Audrey was standing in a kitchenette in silence while Natalie glared her disapproval, and last-night-Audrey was listening to an old woman spin a story about a girl she'd loved more than seventy years earlier.

For a moment, Audrey shut her eyes and it was 1947. It was right now. It was yesterday. It was five years ago.

"So what have you got for us, pet?" asked Wilfred Honey, who had appeared with Marianne Wolvercote and Grace Forsythe beside him while Audrey had been distracted with the decades tangling into each other.

"Oh"—Audrey shook the history out of her head and looked at what was in front of her—"well I'm making a traditional cheese and potato pie with a hot water crust pastry for my savoury option. And for the sweet I'm making blackberry and ginger."

Marianne Wolvercote was looking at the potatoes with an air that hovered between worry and disdain. "Are you not concerned that a potato pie might be a little *too* traditional? You *are* supposed to be demonstrating what you're capable of."

This was another two traps issue: Wilfred liked simple and homey, Marianne liked basil on strawberries. "I'm hoping the flavours will come through," said Audrey, which she was well aware meant nothing but gave her time to make a prepared answer sound spontaneous. "I know it's not exactly flashy, but we'd have this on picnics when I was younger." Time to let twenty-years-ago-Audrey take the reins. "I remember my mum and dad used to take me to the gardens by the priory, and we'd bring a hamper, and we'd have a cheese and potato pie and, well, I suppose it always tasted like summer to me."

"And to me too, lass." Wilfred Honey gave his trademark approving nod. "There's nowt wrong wi' traditional, Marianne."

"No, but a potato pie will need to be very special *indeed* to be of the quality we expect in this competition."

With an avuncular expression, Grace Forsythe leaned forwards. "You'll forgive Marianne, I'm afraid she's being especially mean today."

And yesterday-Audrey, in the middle of getting her apology rejected, who'd been tempted to say whatever it took to get a rise out of Jennifer Hallet, replied, "Did somebody jizz in her cornflakes?"

Grace Forsythe burst out laughing, Marianne Wolvercote raised a devastating eyebrow, and Wilfred Honey actually covered his mouth with his hands and said, "Ooh, I say." From the other side of the ballroom, Colin Thrimp's profanitidar pinged and he bounded over waving his hands. "No," he squeaked. "No, no, no. No jizz cornflakes. Unusable. For, I hope, very obvious reasons."

"Yes," agreed Grace Forsythe. "I'm sure it'd curdle the milk."

Wilfred Honey looked as serious as Audrey had ever seen him. "Oh no, that's not right at all. You see Grace, milk curdles when it becomes acidic enough that the proteins start clumping together. But semen is neutral, or slightly alkaline, so it'd have the opposite effect."

"Could you please," pleaded Colin Thrimp, "stop talking about semen, euphemistically or otherwise."

Marianne Wolvercote gave the tiniest of smiles. "Yes that's probably for the best. You know, Audrey, you should be careful. Jennifer's clearly been a bad influence on you."

Yesterday-Audrey was unrepentant. Today-Audrey was deeply embarrassed. "Sorry. I don't know what happened. It just slipped out."

"I understand jizz will do that on occasion," offered Grace Forsythe, apparently in no mood to take instructions from Colin or to stop talking about bodily fluids. "Tell you what, how about we wrap this bit up from Marianne's last comment?"

Marianne Wolvercote cocked her head to one side. "About Jennifer being a bad influence?"

"About a potato pie not being special something, something." Grace Forsythe was making a rolling-things-back gesture with her hands. "They'll want it for continuity."

"A potato pie," Marianne Wolvercote repeated, any trace of mirth gone from her voice, "will need to be very well-executed indeed if it's going to reach the quality we expect from this competition."

And yet again, Grace Forsythe leaned forwards supportively. "Don't worry about Marianne dear," she said. And then, with a grin, added, "Somebody poured salt on her cornflakes."

Time, the various Audreys from across history agreed, could get fucked. Four hours had gone like nothing, and while she'd more or less got everything to work, it had been touch-and-go in places.

And it turned out that forbidding yourself from getting distracted was extremely distracting. While she'd managed not to lose herself in other people's dramas, Marianne's admonition about the dangers of potato had been nestling in Audrey's head like a toad in a bucket. Which, in turn, had made it all too easy to remember every bad decision she'd ever made.

And then she was called up first for judging.

"So these are a traditional"—she hoped emphasising the word *traditional* would help, though she wasn't sure how—"cheese and potato pie savoury. And for my sweet I've made blackberry and ginger."

"Now, I *love* a potato pie, me," said Wilfred Honey, cutting into it with gusto and a carving knife. "Though I know it's a bit rustic for Marianne."

"I don't have a problem with rustic," Marianne Wolvercote lied, "as long as it's well baked and the flavours come through properly."

Audrey held her breath and bit her lip in that order. The flavours, she suspected, were not going to come through properly.

"You see, *I* like it," Wilfred Honey said after he'd finished his mouthful. And the way he emphasised *I* didn't exactly fill Audrey with confidence. "But I'm not sure it's to Marianne's tastes."

All eyes turned to Marianne Wolvercote. "Actually, I'm pleasantly surprised."

Audrey let out the breath she completely knew she'd been holding. "Oh, good."

"It's not my favourite, and I do think you could have done more in the time."

The part of Audrey that was still in jizz cornflakes mode wanted to say "Really, because I felt pretty fucking rushed as it happens." But she didn't because it would be a total dick move and require a reshoot.

"I can taste the rosemary," Marianne Wolvercote went on. "The cheese isn't overwhelming, and the potatoes have a good texture."

Wilfred Honey, by this stage, had moved on to the blackberry and ginger. "I like this, too," he said. "The first one was summery, but the ginger makes this one a bit more warming, and I like a warming pudding."

Leaning in from just behind the judges, Grace Forsythe put up a hand. "Translator's note, *pudding* in this context is regional slang for *dessert in general* as opposed to the puddings we sometimes ask contestants to make in this competition, which are *dessert in particular*."

"Yes, thank you Grace." Wilfred Honey did not look especially thankful.

Marianne, who had been sampling the blackberry and ginger while all this had been going on, agreed that the flavours were good but, with her usual attention to detail, noted the uneven latticework on the lid.

Still sorting through that jumble of mixed feedback and faint praise, Audrey thanked the judges, collected her pies, and went back to her spot.

Doris was next, followed by Joshua, and they'd both done fine. Their bakes were well chosen but not spectacular, and their feedback had ultimately been similar to Audrey's, albeit with less emphasis on potato.

Next up was Meera, and from where Audrey was standing she seemed notably confident. Having done well on the blind bake she clearly knew her way around pastry, and the judges were apparently expecting something interesting.

"So this," she said, "is a sweet rhubarb and strawberry pie with balsamic vinegar and thyme." The judges made acknowledging noises. "And this is a chicken jalfrezi pie for savoury."

This time Wilfred and Marianne went for the sweet pie first, which Marianne enjoyed and Wilfred appreciated on its technical merits, although his famous disapproval of putting savoury flavours in sweet dishes kicked in just slightly. When they were done with that, they moved on to the savoury.

"By 'eck," Wilfred Honey said, all thoughts of misplaced vinegar forgotten, "it's gorgeous."

"It *is* good," Marianne Wolvercote agreed. "I think this was a really interesting way to use Asian flavours. There's—there's something in the pastry, isn't there?"

Meera nodded. "It's made with a lime pickle."

"Very clever choice." Marianne Wolvercote sounded more approving than Audrey had heard all season. "Well done."

The rest of the contestants came and went quickly. Reggie had designed his pies to stack on top of each other, but for that to work he'd needed to make the bottom one—a sausage and leek pie with hot water crust pastry—extremely dense, which had worked structurally but which Marianne Wolvercote felt harmed the eating experience. Wilfred Honey had disagreed, insisting that he enjoyed having something to sink his teeth into, and between the two of them Audrey judged that he was safe but not quite in a position to win it.

After that was Jim, whose job Audrey kept forgetting but who seemed to be filling the blue-collar-worker-you-wouldn't-expect-to-bake role, like the carpenter lady from the last season or the electrician from the one before that. He'd done okay, and Audrey was beginning to feel distinctly bottom-of-the-packish. Even

Linda, who earlier had been convinced that she'd screwed every-thing up beyond recognition, had received good feedback for her venison-and-stout savoury, though her apple, pear, and hazelnut sweet had come out just a touch overdone.

"Which is a shame," Marianne Wolvercote had said, "because with just a little more attention to detail it could have been excellent."

Linda, being this season's one-who-took-everything-incredibly-to-heart, took that feedback like a drawing pin to the paw, but she nodded gratefully, made a well-intentioned stab at mastering her emotions, and returned to her place looking only slightly like she thought she was garbage.

That left Alanis for last. Though she'd seemed fairly happy earlier in the day, as she came forward now with her pies she looked a lot more, well, a lot more *sixteen* than Audrey remembered her looking.

"This," she said with a slight tremor in her voice, "is a beef bourguignon savoury pie, and a summer apple sweet pie."

"Puff pastry was a risk in the time," Marianne Wolvercote told her, cracking the pastry lid of the beef bourguignon and then peering at it like a coroner at an autopsy. "And I don't think it's entirely worked. I'd have expected better lamination and it's a *little* underbaked."

Audrey didn't have the best view from her bench, but from the tone she suspected that "a little underbaked" was an understatement.

With an unerring instinct for the right time to good-cop, Wilfred Honey dug in and chewed. "Although I think Marianne *is* right about your pastry," he said gently, "your filling has cooked well, and it's got a real richness of flavour to it that I like a lot."

"And the apple pie is much better executed," Marianne

Wolvercote added. "Although it is *very* simple, it's well baked and"—she took a forkful—"it has a pleasing tartness, but we are looking for a *little* more from you, even this early."

"I think it caught a bit," Alanis admitted, looking shame-facedly at a corner of singed crust that she'd made an obvious-now-she-pointed-it-out attempt to cover up with icing sugar.

"Word to the wise, darling," volunteered Grace Forsythe from the sidelines. "They already know, and if they've not mentioned it, you probably shouldn't either."

Alanis nodded, by now visibly shaky.

Wilfred Honey had gone full grandfather-to-the-nation. "Well, I think they're both smashing. There's a couple of mistakes, but I'm a straightforward man and a beef and mushroom pie followed by an apple pie is my idea of a proper dinner."

His tone was gentle but reading between the lines—and also, for that matter, reading a few of the actual lines—it was pretty clear that Alanis hadn't done well that week, and she walked back to her bench looking somewhere between downcast and devastated.

When the judges retired to deliberate, the contestants gathered around to share their congratulations, commiserations, and fears.

"You'll be okay," Linda was saying to Alanis. "I did badly, too, and, well"—she glanced up at Audrey—"I think she's right about them wanting you for the final."

This, Audrey felt, had dropped her right in it. Everybody was turning to her now with looks of nervous confusion.

"What do you know?" asked Jim, a little warily.

"Nothing."

This didn't convince anybody.

"I've just"—Audrey made a frantic attempt to de-escalate—"watched a lot of reality TV."

Alanis was looking at Audrey with unhelpful faith. "She's in media. She understands how these things work."

"I'm in local journalism," explained Audrey. "I'm not an expert."

"No, but…" Linda looked so sheepish that she was at serious risk of winding up in a traditional roast dinner. "What you said yesterday. It made sense."

"What made sense?" This was Jim, still more warily.

"It's not big a deal," said Audrey. "Obviously a show like this needs characters and arcs, and one of the more obvious arcs they *could* be going for is oldest contestant versus youngest contestant."

Meera frowned. "Now you've said it, that does make sense. Although it also makes the whole competition feel a bit pointless."

De-escalation had spectacularly failed. "It's not pointless," said Audrey, as firmly as she could. "Mostly the judges *will* be basing their decisions on how well you do. It's just there's, you know, wiggle room."

"Wiggle room?" It sounded worse when Jim said it.

"Only in the sense"—help—"that there's no objective criteria that the judges are actually held to. They're the only people who taste the bakes. They get to decide what's too simple and what's too ambitious, if the flavours compensate for the appearance, things like that."

Everyone was nodding. But not in a we-get-that-this-is-complex way. More in a we've-just-learned-about-the-doomsday-planes way.

"So really"—double help—"the only rule is that what the judges say goes. Which means *if* there happened to be a situation where, say, two bakes were mostly even and it made a better story for them to pick one over the other, then they'd be able to... wiggle?"

There was a long, long silence.

Then Linda straightened her spine and put a reassuring hand on Alanis's shoulder. "There you go. It's going to be me, not you."

"But that's not fair." Alanis was tearing up now. "It should be about who makes the best pies, not who makes the best television."

"Suppose it depends how you look at it," said Jim, with the air of somebody who had been quietly looking at it for a while now. "Like there's always that couple on *Strictly* what can't actually dance but they stay in because the audience loves them."

"I just really think"—Alanis's mascara was beginning to run— "that Linda deserves it more than I do."

From his position just behind her, Joshua leaned forwards. "Don't say that. You've earned your place here just like the rest of us. And it's okay for them to make decisions based on the whole contest, not just on the day."

Although she was ever-so-slightly suspicious of his motivations, Audrey did think Joshua had hit on the right strategy. "Exactly. Don't think of it as them going easy on you, think of it as them taking a...a holistic approach."

"Also," Doris added, "they might kick you out anyway." She nudged Audrey. "No offence, love. I'm sure you know what you're talking about, but I'm also sure smarter people'n you've been wrong about bigger things."

That much was definitely true. Although in this *specific* case Audrey was ninety-nine percent certain that it was Linda who was getting the chop. If the judges had been building up to send Alanis home, they'd have mentioned that her pastry had caught, and they'd probably have played up the very-good-for-your-age angle.

The little gathering shared a round of sympathetic noises, which were marred only slightly by the fact that consoling one person had to come with the implicit reaffirmation that the other person was definitely screwed. And then, after a relatively short period of debate, the judges returned with Grace Forsythe leading them.

"Once more," Grace Forsythe was saying, "we come to the happiest, and the saddest, part of the show. The part where we celebrate one baker's floury triumph while another, unfortunately, bites the crust."

There was a pause. Then Colin Thrimp raised a hand. "Jennifer says that doesn't make sense."

"It makes perfect sense." Grace Forsythe was still standing immaculate on her spot, facing the cameras. "It's *bites the dust* but with a more pie-appropriate substitution for the last word."

"Jennifer says it's awful."

"Well I'm not reshooting." And without waiting for a reply, Grace Forsythe went straight into the rest of her endgame speech. "We begin, as always, with the joyous task of naming this week's winner. And it was a close one, because we saw some remarkable baking, but our winner is somebody whose filo filo-ed us with joy, whose pastry was perfection, and who, most importantly, also served us a banger of a curry." She paused in the place where she always paused. "That's right, it's Meera."

And Audrey was happy for her. Unsurprised, since she'd got the first *by 'eck it's gorgeous* of the series, but happy for her. So hugs were hugged and smiles were shared and then Grace Forsythe's face fell theatrically.

"But now," she said, "we come to the sad part of the week. Though Wilfred, Marianne, and I wish with all our hearts that we could take every single one of you home and keep you on little doilies on our mantelpiece—"

"Jennifer says she's warned you about being surreal," interrupted Colin Thrimp.

"On our mantelpiece," Grace Forsythe continued. "Sadly, we must regift one of you to the aunt we dislike. And today, though it grieves me deeply, we are saying goodbye to Audrey."

Audrey blinked.

And then, out of nowhere, started crying.

"What the fuck," Audrey was shouting to Jennifer Hallet's still closed door. "What the actual fuck. This was personal. You know it was personal."

The door snapped open to reveal a somewhat rumpled Jennifer Hallet, sleeves rolled up, hair half-tumbled down. "And you know it was complicated."

Audrey had been gearing up for a was not/was too shouting match, so getting a tacit admission that, at the very least, personalness had been involved was a little disorienting. Although not so disorienting that she couldn't preserve the essence of the not-too strategy.

"It was *not* complicated. You kicked me off the show for annoying you, just like you kept threatening but which I foolishly didn't believe you were petty enough to actually do."

Jennifer looked down. She was a fair bit taller than Audrey anyway but standing at the top of a small staircase made her positively loom. "You had a bad week. Linda still has a story to tell. You were only ever set dressing."

"Set dressing you were pissed off with."

"I will admit, that didn't help."

Folding her arms, Audrey tried to look unintimidated. "That's flagrantly unethical."

"Whereas you've been a picture of journalistic integrity."

"Oh my God, I have." Audrey folded her arms even tighter. "You just don't like what I'm doing."

"No," agreed Jennifer. "I don't like what you're doing. On my show. From which I am fully entitled to remove you. If you, for example, carry on chasing a story I told you to drop."

"Are you spying on me?"

"Nothing happens on my set I don't know about."

"I was talking to Doris because I'm interested." And why was Audrey on the defensive all of a sudden? "I'm allowed to talk to the other contestants."

"So you didn't make any notes then?"

Audrey opened her mouth and shut it again. "I…it was… habit. And besides"—she tried to reverse the polarity of the argument—"I still did better than Linda."

"Not in the edit you won't."

"You…" began Audrey explosively.

But Jennifer just sneered. "I *what*, Lane?"

"You…"

"Interfering, micromanaging harridan with a god complex?" suggested Jennifer Hallet.

"Y-yes but also…"

"Performatively cynical foul-mouthed hack?"

"I mean—"

"Callous, belittling needlessly hostile she-demon?"

"Now you're—"

"Bitch?" finished Jennifer. "I've heard it all before, sunshine."

"And you don't think"—Audrey's arms unfolded themselves like they were on springs—"any of that feedback might have been leading you somewhere?"

"It led me to the conclusion that I don't give a fuck what people think of me."

"Clearly not." Audrey's anger was beginning to cool and congeal like gravy in yesterday's pie. It was still there; just not as appealing as it used to be. Her whole body slumped. "But you didn't have to do this."

"I did. You were a walking conflict of interest."

"I tried to apologise, Jennifer. And I really was going to drop the story."

"It's cute you believe that."

"If you'd said no—"

"Were you not fucking listening? I did. Several times."

Shit, they were back here again. And Audrey knew where that ended: with her saying things she didn't want to say and being someone she didn't want to be. "I just thought," she said carefully, "that if I finished the story and you saw how good it was, you might change your mind. But I would never run it unless you said I could."

An expression that Audrey couldn't read—or perhaps didn't dare to—crossed Jennifer's face. "Just because something's amazing," she said, "doesn't mean it's what I need in my life."

The evenings could be sharp in the summer. And it was probably just the chill that raised goose bumps on Audrey's arms. "What are you—"

"Oh come on, Lane."

Audrey's anger gravy was getting reheated in the microwave. "You better not be implying that you wrote me off the show because you fancy me."

"I wrote you off the show because you spent the last three weeks doing everything in your power to get in my fucking head."

Of this, Audrey had to admit that she was profoundly guilty. So naturally she didn't. "I have not."

"You have, and you know you have."

"So it *was* personal," said Audrey in a tone of triumph she didn't feel.

"I never said it wasn't. But it was also the right call. You're disrupting my show and I can't have that."

"You realise you aren't the show?"

"That's where you're wrong, sunshine."

Audrey was, she felt certain, just about to come back with the most devastating and appropriate retort ever retorted by a living human. But Jennifer slammed the door in her face before she got the chance. And so she was left standing there, the last dregs of sunlight draining over the horizon, wishing she was still angry.

Angry would have been a whole lot less confusing.

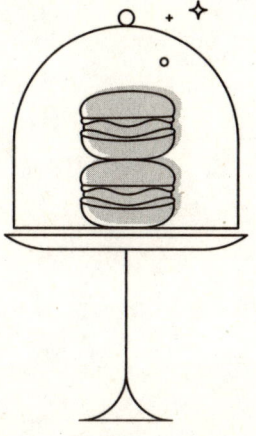

WEEK FOUR

Biscuits

Saturday

IT WAS STRANGE, not being at Patchley. Although given how things had gone with Jennifer, being there would have been massively worse.

That week at work had gone by quickly, Audrey letting Gavin know that she'd probably have to shelve the uplifting story about the nice old lady in the war because it had got weirdly steamy and run past VE Day. And now it was the weekend and Audrey was, for the first time in a month—more than a month, really, what with the anticipation and derustifying her baking skills before the competition even started—at a complete loose end.

She tried to tell herself that it was fine. That it was nice to have her time back. And in a way it was. Journalism—even not-especially-prestigious local journalism—was demanding enough without also trying to bake at a televised level and to use the access you got from baking at a televised level to dig into the personal history of one of the other contestants. And without the tension caused by your digging into the personal history of one of the other contestants creating a weird foe yay situation with the producer of the televised show on which you were attempting to bake competitively.

In an absolute, objective sense, it really was good to have a free Saturday.

It was also kind of not.

Audrey had, she would be the first to admit, many faults, but she wasn't a wallower. At least not a sit-around-your-house-not-knowing-what-to-do-with-yourself wallower. So on this particular loose-endy Saturday, she did what she always did when she felt herself sliding in a wallowy direction, and went for a walk.

Actually she went for a drive first, because while there were perfectly nice places to walk around Bridgnorth—that was the thing about Shropshire, it was perfectly nice all the way down—she had a nagging but sharply embedded desire to go back to Much Wenlock. To spend a while wandering around the fields and lanes she remembered from her childhood. To go back to Wenlock Priory and, this time, maybe not try to climb up it.

There was a strange timelessness to the British countryside. To all countryside, Audrey suspected. A time traveller from a hundred years ago, or two hundred, might notice a couple of things that were unfamiliar—if you looked in the right direction through the right set of trees you'd spot power lines, and the little roads that snaked between the fields had modern tarmac surfaces, although Audrey was pretty sure even they wouldn't stand out to a visitor from, say, 1923.

But the more prosaic kind of temporal voyager, the kind who, like Audrey, had got here by the inevitable process of waiting while the past ticked by at a rate of one second per second into the future, could see barely anything different. The aggressive *Private Property KEEP OUT* signs had certainly been replaced and updated in the past couple of years to ensure they'd stay appropriately red and noticeable but they weren't really any different than they'd always been. Than they'd been a decade and a half ago when Audrey and Natalie had cheerfully ignored them to go and lie down in whatever fields they fancied and talk about how they were going to fix the world.

"The thing is," fifteen-years-ago-Natalie was saying, "we can't stay in Much Wenlock forever. People just *don't*."

And fifteen-years-ago-Audrey was trying to summon up the courage to say that she didn't see anything so very wrong with staying in a lovely little village and being happy, although all she'd been able to manage was, "I think people do okay here, don't they?"

And fifteen-years-ago-Natalie had come back with something like, "I swear, Aur, sometimes it's like I don't even know you."

It still stung. A decade and a half later.

Strolling up to the priory proper, present-day-Audrey and fifteen-years-ago-Audrey walked hand in hand. It was still, she thought, one of her favourite places in the world. A garden in a ruin—bushes clipped into neat little shapes alongside wells that had long since run dry and walls that sheltered nothing any longer.

They'd fucked here, of course. She and Natalie. When they were seventeen and you had to pretend—at least Audrey had been pretending, though in retrospect she suspected Natalie had meant every word—that places like this were only interesting if you could have orgasms in them. And since fifteen-years-ago-Audrey had been every bit as sentimental as present-day-Audrey, there had been a kind of magic to it, for her at least. Feeling all at once so connected to a person and a place and a time.

She'd said as much to Natalie, and Natalie had laughed and

called her an idiot, and then kissed her more sweetly than anybody ever had.

With her eyes closed, present-day-Audrey could still remember every detail. The taste of Natalie, the feel of her skin beneath her fingertips. The conviction that had been in Natalie's voice even then that had eventually come to sound more like cruelty.

In those days, Audrey would have done anything for her. And she had.

On the Saturday of the fourth week of filming the eighth season of *Bake Expectations*, Audrey Lane was leaning by a stone wall at Wenlock Priory, her face turned to the sun. On the day of her A-level results she was tangled with Natalie in an alcove in the same ruin and learning what it was to love somebody who would always be just a little beyond you. In 1947 Doris and Emily were meeting for the first time in three years, and in 680 Merewalh, king of Magonseate, was ordering the construction of a monastery that in 1080 Roger de Montgomery was refounding and in 1540 Henry the Eighth was dissolving. And for all those thousand years, families and friends and monks and nuns and puritans and lovers were walking under these stones and looking up at this sunlight and standing on this ground and—it was a carrying away feeling, an anywhere-but-here feeling, and if she'd wanted to, Audrey could have stayed lost in it all day.

To some extent, she *did* want to. It would stop her thinking about the show, about Doris and Alanis (were they both doing okay?), about Jennifer Hallet (what the fuck was going on there? with both of them?), about the enigmatic Emily Branningham, and about bloody Natalie. But spending the whole of Saturday absorbing the melancholic immensity of everywhen was probably a touch on the self-indulgent side. Besides, she was back home—in the where-she-was-born sense rather than the where-she-lived-now sense—and if her parents found out she'd been in Much Wenlock without stopping by, there'd be hell to pay.

Well, okay, maybe not hell. Her parents weren't really the hell-to-pay type.

"Audrey, love, you've come at the worst time," said Audrey's mum as she was opening the door. It was a pretty standard greeting in their household.

And the standard response was to sigh and say, "What's he done now?"

From a little way into the house, her father's voice echoed from up, under, or inside something. "Downstairs loo."

"What *about* the downstairs loo?" Audrey asked in an I-dread-to-ask tone.

"Painting it."

"Eleven years," Audrey's mum said between furrowed brows and folded arms. "He's been saying he was going to do it for *eleven years* and what's the weekend he picks? The weekend our only daughter was kicked off the telly. He won't learn."

"She wasn't kicked off this weekend," argued Audrey's dad from the loo-ey depths. "She was kicked off last weekend. And we said then that we'd be here if she wanted to come by, and she didn't, so I thought, well, why don't I use the time to do something useful…" His voice grew momentarily muffled then louder as he came to join the rest of the family in the hallway.

"And will you look at him?" added Audrey's mum.

Audrey did, and the sight was a reassuringly typical one. Her father was a short man, balding, and usually covered in something. In this case, the something was paint in an unfortunately lavatorial shade of dark brown.

Audrey shook her head at the mess that was apparently her father. "What have you been *doing*?"

"Painting." On the one hand, it was a materially correct answer. On the other, it didn't quite explain why he'd looked like he'd been dipped in…for comfort's sake, Audrey went with chocolate.

"And"—Audrey tried to phrase the next part as delicately as she could because insulting her parents' decorative choices wasn't necessarily what she was here to do—"is it *all* that colour?"

"It's what your mother wanted," explained her father.

"It bloody well was not," replied her mother.

"Taupe, you said."

"I said *teal*."

"Ooh, you never did."

Eventually, the parental instinct to avoid leaving their child standing on a doorstep overrode the Lanes' matrimonial instinct to bicker about paint colours, and they ushered Audrey inside to the sitting room where Audrey's mum sat down while Audrey's dad went off to make tea.

"Are you very disappointed?" her mum asked with that slight excess of concern that Audrey had always found strangely comforting.

"Honestly, not really?" It felt almost like a confession. "At least not about the competition. I think I could have made it a couple more weeks, but I don't think I'd have ever got near the final."

Audrey's mum leaned forward to give her an encouraging pat. "I'm sure you would, love, you're very good."

It was nice to hear but not, Audrey felt, remotely true. "Not compared to some of the other contestants. There's a girl there who's only sixteen and already well out of my league."

"I won't hear it." Audrey's mum was holding up her hand in that highly specific way that suggested you should talk to it because of the face's relative disinterest.

"Won't hear what?" asked Audrey's dad, who came in still empaintened but now at least bearing teacups on a little tray.

"She says that there's a sixteen-year-old girl on the show who's a better baker than she is."

Setting the cups down, Audrey's dad gave an apologetic smile. "Well I suppose she'd know. And that girl *is* still in the competition."

Audrey's mum didn't seem to think that was an acceptable response. "Whose side are you on? This is our daughter and if we can't believe in her, who else is going to?"

"I *think*"—Audrey gently picked up a teacup and transferred it to her lap—"that believing in me when I've already been knocked out is probably going from supportive to delusional."

"We're your parents," insisted Audrey's mother, "it's our job to be delusional."

Although Audrey wasn't quite sure that actually was their job, it was true that her parents had always been in her corner to an almost comical degree. When she'd been with Natalie it had been a frequent source of tension. "It's a form of gaslighting, really"—ten-years-ago-Natalie would say—"they *perform* being on your side but they really aren't."

Some days, Audrey had let herself believe that. Like she'd let herself believe that wanting to stay in Shropshire instead of moving to London was wrong and selling herself short. Like she'd let herself believe that a life where you weren't burning all your candles at all their ends at once and making yourself sick with the stress of it was a life half lived. Like she'd let herself be another person's shadow.

"It's okay," she said aloud. "It really is. I don't have to be the best amateur baker in the country. And even going out in week three, I'm still the seventh best amateur baker in the country, which I think is pretty good going."

Audrey's dad took a triumphant sip of tea. There was a special technique to sipping tea triumphantly, and her dad had mastered it. "You see. She's completely fine."

But Audrey's mum wasn't buying it. "If she was completely fine she wouldn't be here."

"Wouldn't I?" It probably hadn't been meant as a dig, but part of Audrey took it as one. "That makes it sound like I only come to see you when I'm upset about something."

And now Audrey's mum and Audrey's dad were both giving her the same affectionate but reproving look.

"I visited last month," Audrey protested. "I visited last month just to see how you were because I'm a good daughter."

There was a short silence.

"What?" Audrey demanded.

"*And* to borrow a flathead screwdriver," her dad reminded her.

Setting her tea down, Audrey adopted a posture of defiance that she hoped didn't come across as teenagery but probably did. "It wasn't really about the flathead screwdriver."

"You were quite insistent at the time, love," observed Audrey's mum.

Since nothing about this day had been planned, Audrey couldn't quite say it hadn't gone according to one, but when she'd woken up that morning she hadn't expected screwdrivers to be a major factor in her evening. "I just said, *Oh by the way, while I'm here, you wouldn't have a flathead screwdriver I can borrow.* If you hadn't, I'd have bought one. There's a B&Q in Telford."

This prompted diametrically opposite parental reactions, with Audrey's mum going at once to "Oh there's no need to do that, we're happy to help" while her dad opted instead for "You probably should anyway, it's a useful thing to have."

"The point is," Audrey's mum continued, "that *generally* if you're here it's because you need your old mum and dad for something. And that's nice, isn't it?" She nodded at her husband, who echoed back that it was. "So why don't you just tell us?"

Normally, Audrey wasn't proud about this kind of thing. But normally she had a better sense of what this kind of thing was. When Natalie had dumped her (*When we'd agreed that our relationship had run its course,* Natalie reminded her) she'd sat on her parents' sofa crying into a cup of cold tea for four straight hours.

When she'd decided, shortly afterwards, to jack in her fancy London job and move back to Shropshire, she'd sat on their sofa not crying but feeling like she wanted to, and also a little bit like she wanted to vomit, for three hours. But this was different. All she'd really lost was a never-really-there chance at ten thousand pounds and a nebulous sense of…of something like belonging.

"I just…" she began, then stopped because the *just* was going to sound incredibly pathetic. But these were her parents and they'd seen her in tears over straight girls, B grades on homework, and the opening sequence of *Watership Down.* "I just think I'll really miss everybody."

Audrey's mum nodded sagely. "Well that's natural. You've probably made friends. You were always good at making friends."

In point of fact, Audrey *wasn't* always good at making friends.

At least, she hadn't been in a long time. "Am I? I mean it's Saturday night and even though I'm moderately young, relatively free, and extremely single, I'm sitting on my mum and dad's sofa getting upset about some people I met three times on a TV show."

"Sometimes," said Audrey's dad with an air that Audrey knew from experience suggested what he was about to say wouldn't necessarily sound as wise as he was expecting it to, "it's the people we know the least that affect us the strongest."

"Really?" Audrey asked. "Because I think the opposite might be true actually."

"What about Tom and Carol?" said Audrey's mum, sounding very much like she'd just laid the trump card.

There was that. But it seemed very much like an isolated incident. "Hang on, you can't cite your weird obsession with Tom and Carol—"

Audrey's dad seemed genuinely offended. "It is *not* a weird obsession. They were very interesting people. Your mum and I talk about them all the time."

"You met them *once* in Torbay while you were waiting for a bus," Audrey reminded him.

"But we got on—" began Audrey's mum.

"—so well that you decided to have dinner together at a Thai restaurant in Paignton and it was like you'd known each other your whole lives," Audrey finished for her. "I know the story. You've been telling the story for years. I just don't think it's particularly typical."

"Lovely couple, though," said Audrey's dad. "And she was *so* funny—what was that thing she said…about windscreen wipers? It'll come back to me. Anyway, point is, it's natural to feel strongly about people. It's good. It shows you're not a robot."

For a moment Audrey let this faith in her not-a-robotness sit. And while it was sitting, her mum said, "Is there a girl?"

In theory, Audrey felt, there had to be a window in which she would be able to answer "no" to that question without her mother interpreting either the hastiness or the hesitancy of her reply as confirmation. But she hadn't managed to find it yet, so instead she said, "Maybe. Yes. Kind of."

"It's not…" Her father looked concerned. "It's not the sixteen-year-old is it?"

That one, on the other hand, could be denied instantly without any problems. "No, definitely not. I'm not a vampire with self-esteem issues. It's…she's…I *may* have a thing for the showrunner."

"And does she have a thing for you?" asked Audrey's mum.

Audrey shrugged. "Hard to tell. I think she might? She keeps dropping hints that she thinks I'm hot, which is nice. But she tends to do it while swearing at me, which isn't."

"You know"—a thought had occurred to Audrey's dad—"if her fancying you was part of why you got knocked out, you could sue her for…"

"For what?" asked Audrey, trying to sound genuinely curious even though her dad had this kind of half idea all the time.

"Well, for something," he finished. "There's bound to be *something*. You can't go around kicking people off TV shows because you fancy them."

"Of course," Audrey's mum added, "you can't keep them around because you fancy them either. That's what people said about the tall ginger one last season—that he only stayed in so long because Marianne Wolvercote wanted to do him."

"Well, they won't say that about me, because I didn't stay in long at all." Audrey's intent had genuinely been to reassure her mother that she'd be fine, but as an admission of failure it also made Audrey feel a little hollow. She really should have done better.

Audrey's dad still seemed to be chasing his inner monologue. "Are you going to see her again?"

"Jennifer? Honestly, I don't know. Probably not."

"Do you want to?" asked Audrey's mum.

"I think so?" Audrey admitted. "But it's hard to tell because we spent most of our time arguing. And not like"—she waved a hand—"the way you and dad argue—"

"We do not," put in her mum.

"We do, love," replied her dad.

"Ooh, we never do."

This gave every sign that it could go on a while. So Audrey—having learned from experience—kept on talking like it wasn't happening. "It's more me annoying her and her calling me a miserable interfering prosefucker or something."

Her mum's eyes widened. "A what, love?"

"I don't know. The thing about Jennifer is that she's extremely articulate within a very narrow set of parameters."

"I don't want to be funny"—Audrey's mum was wearing an unmistakably parental expression—"but have you ever considered trying to get with a girl who isn't completely horrible?"

Five-years-ago-Audrey burned to defend the woman she loved. Present-day-Audrey was all dying embers and falling ashes, but some long-ingrained habit made her say, "Natalie wasn't completely horrible. She just—she was very driven."

"She drove you all the way to London," fauxgreed Audrey's dad.

"And made you stop speaking to your family," added Audrey's mum.

"No she didn't," protested Audrey weakly. "She...we were very busy and she..."

There was nothing after *she* really. Natalie's reasons were Natalie's and always would be. They made sense when you were in her orbit, but once you got outside it they turned to leaves like fairy gold.

"I just think you should be with somebody nice," Audrey's mum explained. "There's that lesbian book group in Shrewsbury. Why don't you try that?"

"And what? Say, 'Hi, I've got a thing for extremely controlling women, will any of you be kind to me?'"

Audrey's dad scratched a flake of paint from his nose. It fell into his tea and began dissolving. "Maybe you could say, 'Hello, my name's Audrey'?"

It was a thought. But for reasons Audrey couldn't quite pin down it seemed an impossible thought. To walk up to somebody, anybody, and say, "Hey, I'm just me, is that enough for you?"

Who'd be fool enough to go for that?

Back at her flat, Audrey was just making herself a probably-ill-advised-if-she-wanted-to-sleep-that-night cup of coffee when her phone rang. And since she was the kind of person who kept her contacts meticulously up to date, she could see at once that it was Jennifer Hallet.

A tiny, silly, forever-sixteen part of Audrey wondered if... well. Since she was no longer on the show maybe. Actually. No. That was absurd.

She answered anyway—mainly out of curiosity—and was treated to a "fuck you" instead of a greeting.

"Hi, Jennifer," she replied.

"Don't you *Hi, Jennifer*, me. Do you have any idea how thoroughly you have shat in my toothpaste?"

It was probably wrong to find *shat in my toothpaste* endearing. But apparently a week without Jennifer swearing at her had given Audrey profanity withdrawal. "How would that work?"

"What do you mean how would it fucking work?"

"I mean how do you shit in somebody's toothpaste? If there's one thing toothpaste tubes are famous for it's being hard to get stuff into. Like, you can't even get toothpaste back into them. There's a saying about it."

"Are you taking the piss?"

"You killed my story, threw me off your show, then called me up at"—Audrey checked the time on the corner of her phone—"thirteen minutes past seven on a Saturday to tell me to fuck off and treat me to a vulgar but poorly thought out metaphor. I'm not sure you've got the high ground here."

A noise of barely coherent rage echoed down the line. "You. Have. Made. My. Job. Difficult."

"Sorry, I didn't understand that because it wasn't expressed in terms of bodily fluids in inappropriate places."

The coherentness of Jennifer's next noise dropped from "barely" into "not." "Alanis wants to drop out."

Audrey's stomach lurched. "I'm sorry, I think I must have misheard?"

"No, you heard fine. I said the jailbait baking minx wants to chuck in the most interesting thing she'll do in her shitty—"

"*Please* don't talk that way about Alanis. You know it makes me uncomfortable."

That got a laugh. Not a sincere laugh, but a loud one. "Uncomfortable? How *comfortable* do you think I am right now?"

"Oh I don't know"—her mum had been right, Audrey reflected, she really needed to start being attracted to women who weren't horrible—"probably about as comfortable as if you'd got something you don't want lodged in a place where you don't want things lodged."

"If this is your twisted parochial attempt at flirting, save it for your cousins."

"That's Norfolk."

For a moment Jennifer was silent. "What?"

"The county that gets the tired jokes about inbreeding is Norfolk," Audrey explained. "The stereotype for Shropshire is that it's so boring we don't have a stereotype. Though if you absolutely *must* accuse us of something sexual and untrue, we're close enough to Wales you could borrow the one about fucking sheep."

"God I hope that rod up your arse is turning you on."

Jizz-in-cornflakes-Audrey rose like Venus to the occasion and just replied, "Immensely," before handing the reins back to regular-Audrey. "So go on. How am I making your job more difficult *this time*? And why should it remotely be my problem?"

"Let me put it this way," said Jennifer. "Remember when you told my entire cast of contestants that the show was rigged and that nobody who wasn't either the maiden, the mother, or the crone had a wanker's chance in hell of actually winning?"

Ah yes. Audrey *had* done that, hadn't she? "I was just—"

"I don't care what you *thought* you were just. What you actually *just* was you *just* got in everybody's heads and made morale on set drop faster than the knickers of a strong, well-educated, independent woman who chooses to enjoy a very sexually active lifestyle."

It didn't take much to make Audrey feel guilty. And potentially ruining a teenage girl's life was decidedly *much*. "I didn't mean to."

"And I'm sure that prick on Pudding Lane didn't mean to start the Great Fire of London, but here we are. My fucking show is burning down and it's your fucking fault and you're fucking well going to be the one to fix it."

"Are you sure I'm actually the right—"

"No, I'm not sure at all. I called up out of the blue because I missed your sexy voice and sunny disposition."

"I just mean—"

"Get here. Now."

It was late and, since she'd officially been kicked off the show, any contractual obligation Audrey might have had to Inveterate Productions, or to *Bake Expectations*, or to Jennifer was basically over, bar the come-back-for-the-spinoff / don't-talk-shit-about-us bits. "Look, I…"

"Lane." Something not quite vulnerable but slightly less acerbic than usual crept into Jennifer's tone. "Seriously. I need you."

Audrey did not melt. Not even a little bit. Nor did any part of her brain start imagining those words being said in that voice in any context other than the totally appropriate and professional one they were currently being spoken in.

But she did get in her car very, very quickly.

It was well after ten when Audrey arrived at Patchley House. She was met in the carpark by an even-more-stressed-looking-than-normal Colin Thrimp.

"Thank goodness you're here." Without waiting he grabbed Audrey by the hand and started dragging her in the direction of the hotel. "Things have got very peculiar and we need you to talk to Doris."

"Doris?" Audrey had, ultimately, not been super clear on what she was being invited down to do but she'd been working on the assumption that it was mostly about Alanis.

"Yes. She's having a bit of an altercation with the manager and Jennifer insists—I mean, well, she insists…"

"That it's all my fault and I need to sort it out immediately or she'll do something unpleasant to a part of my body that a person in a position of authority shouldn't be talking about?"

Colin Thrimp nodded.

Jennifer herself was in reception pacing a hole in the carpet. The manager was with her as, for reasons Audrey didn't want to speculate about, was an irate woman in a dressing gown. Doris, however, was notably absent.

"Ah." Jennifer greeted Audrey with all the warmth and enthusiasm of a shark with a chainsaw. "Audrey, so glad you could make it. Now perhaps you can explain to these fine people"—she indicated the manager and the woman Audrey had to assume was a guest—"how you managed to fuck me so hard that your strap-on ripped through the back of my uterus and wound up going up both of their arses."

The manager, the guest, and Colin Thrimp all winced at various elements of the image, but Audrey just said, "Happy to, only I have no idea what's going on."

"There's…" The guest sounded hesitant in the way people tended to be once Jennifer broke out the uterus talk. "There's an old woman in my bedroom, and she won't leave."

"She's saying she needs to think," explained the manager. "And since she's a contestant, I asked Jennifer to handle it, but she said, well…"

"That the interfering sack of chaos vomit responsible would be here soon enough, and that this was entirely on her," finished Jennifer.

Normally Audrey tried to resist her instinct to build stories out of limited information. It was bad journalism and worse social interaction, but this time she had a pretty good idea what was going on. "Which room?" she asked.

"214," the guest and the manager said at once. Then the manager followed up with, "But I'd really appreciate being told what's happening."

From Audrey's perspective, he could appreciate it while walking, and so she set off for the lifts with the guest and the manager trailing after her. Jennifer Hallet and Colin Thrimp stayed behind. Audrey would have taken it as a sign of trust if she'd thought Jennifer capable of trusting anyone or anything.

"I *might*," Audrey explained to her two new companions, "have accidentally started a sequence of events that *might* have resulted in an elderly woman getting your bedroom mixed up with a bedroom that…" She struggled for a moment to find the words. "That meant a lot to her when she was younger."

"Did she used to live here?" asked the manager. "Before it was a hotel."

"No," Audrey replied. And then because that wasn't accurate, "Well, yes. Sort of. I'm guessing a bit."

The lift stopped at the second floor and the little group made their way up the corridor to room 214. The manager opened the door to reveal a pretty little bedroom, still decorated in vintage style, with Doris sitting morosely on the end of the double bed. "Oh," she said as Audrey entered, "it's you."

Audrey waved an apologetic wave. "It's me."

"Wasn't sure you'd be coming."

"I am. I mean I did. I mean I'm here."

The guest, who was still wrapped in a robe and thus had good reason to want things resolved quickly peered over Audrey's shoulder. "Look can you just get her out?"

"Her's in the room," Doris replied dryly.

"But can you, though?" asked Audrey, striking the best balance she could between compassionate and patronising. "I get why you're here—at least I *think* I get why you're here. Was this her room?"

Doris nodded. "Sort of. They've knocked a bit through"—she pointed at one wall—"and blocked a bit off"—she pointed at another—"and the furniture's all changed of course but it's still… well I suppose it's like him with the boat isn't it?"

"If you…you didn't do this for the story, did you? Because you didn't need—"

But Doris was already shaking her head. "No, love. This was for me. I've not talked about this in so long it was—I could feel it slipping. And I didn't want it to slip, not none of it."

"Not none of what?" asked the guest, who seemed to be drifting now from irate towards intrigued.

Audrey was about to explain that it was private, that Doris hadn't meant to upset anybody but that she was going through something personal and would be out of everybody's hair immediately, but before she could Doris said, "I can explain if you want, but it's a long story."

And then everyone was speaking at once, Audrey and the manager both coming down heavily on the side of "that won't be necessary" while the guest went instead to "go on then."

It was the *go on then* that Doris chose to listen to.

DECEMBER 1951

I WERE IN service at Patchley (Doris explained for the benefit of those who hadn't already heard that part). Before that I'd been evacuated here and all and when I was I'd met this girl. Emily her name was, daughter of the family what owned the place back then. Back before it was sold off to be a hotel. (The Branninghams, the manager clarified.)

Me and Emily, we'd been close when we was young. Then when I'd started working at the house we'd been close again. Least we'd been as close as you could be when one of you was in service and the other was the young mistress. I'd started as a housemaid but when Miss Emily's lady's maid had gone off to get married, she'd put a request in for me special, like. And it were a bit irregular because I weren't that experienced, but Sir Arthur—that's the one it was back then, though Master James took over after he died in sixty-two—didn't kick up a fuss.

Mrs. Loris did, though (the housekeeper, Audrey explained to the other listeners).

I was angry about it at the time because I heard some of what

she said to the master. "Highly irregular," she said, "cause problems below stairs," she said. But to be fair, she were right. Other
servants as had been there longer didn't much like having to call
me *miss* like I were better than them. Because I weren't, really. I was
just me.

They tried not to whisper too much when I was around,
because even then they was nice folks in general and there's solidar-
ity in the servants' quarters, but I heard things. Couldn't not. "You
know how she got it," I remember one of them saying when she
didn't realise I was there, "what she had to do." And I remember
another saying back, "Well better her than me then." And some
of the other girls looked at me with pity, or with fear, and that felt
dark and sick in a way that never quite left me, for all I loved my
new position.

And I did love it. The duties were lighter, for a start; taking
care of the mistress was a sight easier than taking care of whatever
needed taking care of that day in a big, messy house. But what I
really loved was that it kept me close to Emily. And I think she
liked that it kept her close to me and all.

Each morning I'd bring her breakfast in bed, which she
wouldn't eat, though she'd drink the coffee, sitting up in her silk
nightdress with her hair all mussed from the night before and spilling around her head like a halo. Only her hair weren't gold, it was
brown like oak and beautiful as the autumn.

And some days—not every day, but often enough—she'd pat
the bed and I'd sit beside her and then she'd pick something from
the plate she'd otherwise not have touched—bread dipped in egg,
perhaps, or a single slice of thick bacon—and she'd feed it me. And
her fingers would stay on my lips and then her lips would follow
them, and she'd lay me down and call me her beautiful, wayward

nymph, and in them moments when it was just her and me and the morning I was happier than I'd ever been. Than I've ever been since, in a way—though that's an unkind thing to say because I've had a wonderful life. But nobody's ever made me feel how she made me feel, when she took the time to make me feel it.

When we was done I'd turn down the bed so as not to make too much extra work for the other girls, and fix my uniform so as not to make too much of a scandal. And then I'd dress my lady and do her hair and that, and then she'd nod and say *very good, Cooper,* on account of that was my name back then, and she'd be off to face the world. And I'd take a bundle of sheets that still smelled of her and of us down to be washed, and then I'd wait until the next time she needed me.

I lived like that all the way through fifty into fifty-one, and though there were parts that were hard, and though Mrs. Loris would take me aside regular to tell me to be careful, I was swept up in it all. In this place, and in Emily.

Back in them days the gentry was still the classy sort what cared about community, so Patchley was forever hosting fairs and fetes and big events for folk from Crinkley Furze and the like. And Christmas was always a big time of year, with people coming in from as far as Tapworth to celebrate the season with the family. Some of the lower rooms was opened up—the ballroom what we does the baking in now, for example—and the grounds was all decorated and set with tents and stalls and games for the kiddies.

It was round that time in fifty-one, and I'd just finished setting the mistress's hair. We was standing by the window (Doris had gone to the window herself at this point and was gazing out over the grounds where the TV crew were still running their cables and rigging their gear) looking down at the fete setting up beneath us.

It weren't snowing. But in my mind, it feels like it was snowing. That's the thing about getting old—memory plays tricks on you. How it was gets all tangled up with how you wish it was, how it should have been.

We stood there watching as the villagers and the house staff was getting ready and I got this, like this ball of sort of wanting inside me. Because down in the grounds, that was a community coming together. And though the house was a community of a sort, being where I was and how I was and what with the way things were between me and Emily, I was apart from it. Hard to gossip with the other maids when they think you only got your place because you let the mistress put her hands up your skirt.

Back home, though—and I mean home as it was when I were young, before I went to Patchley the first time or the second—I'd had family and I'd had neighbours, and this was when neighbours knew each other and did things with each other. In forty-seven a bunch of us from all over Stepney had a Christmas fair on an old bomb site and a right old time of it we got to having. For all I loved my life at Patchley, I missed things like that.

As we stood there watching, I remember my hand come to rest, natural-like, on the small of Emily's back, like we was the regular sort of lovers, and when she noticed she shook me away almost violent.

"What are you *doing*, nymph?" she asked, and her voice was cold and cautious.

"Sorry ma'am." I looked down. Whatever else we was to each other, I was in service.

Emily was still staring out the window. "God, look at them."

I was looking. But I don't think we was seeing the same things.

"Can you imagine anything more dreary?" she asked. I don't

think she was asking me exactly—Emily was like that, she'd ask questions but she wouldn't expect answers.

But this time I answered anyway. "I think it's nice," I told her.

"You would."

I didn't ask her to explain what that meant because I knew.

But she told me anyway. She turned to face me, tilting my chin up with two fingers and looking into my eyes. "You're such a romantic, aren't you? It's one of the things I—" She cut herself off there. And I've never quite had it in me to believe she was going to say what I wanted her to say. "It's one of the reasons I keep you around."

She was a fickle thing, was my mistress. So often I'd seen the worst thing she could imagine turn on a sixpence into the only thing she wanted. And now a smile was on her lips, wicked and scheming and enticing.

"Very well," she said. "If that's what you want, I shall take you to the fair. We can rub shoulders with the hoi polloi and I can— oh, I don't know—win you a fruitcake or something."

"Not sure that would be proper, miss," I told her.

And then she put her hands on my shoulders, all stern like. "My dear sweet nymph, you've just had your—" Actually there she said some things I'd probably best not repeat in company. Point was she made a strong case as how I were in no position to worry about things being proper.

So I didn't. Not for then, at least.

The fete was a three-day thing, and Sir Arthur was kind enough to give each of the staff a half day while it was running so we could go visit if we liked. Standoffish he might have been, but a proper gent of the old school was Sir Arthur and sore missed.

The first day and the start of the second I was working, and since about a third of the staff was off on account of the reasons we've established, I was working double hard to cover for them as was enjoying themselves. After tending to my mistress in the morning I was called down to help in the kitchen, because while most of the food at the fete come from the village, Sir Arthur were always keen to send something down from the house to show that the family was still part of it. And over the years, that had settled into a tradition of making gingerbread. And so we made a lot. Hundreds and hundreds of rounds over days.

It were beneath me, technically, not work for a lady's maid, but the house was short and I didn't want to give myself airs. Besides, as far as Mrs. Loris and Cook was concerned, I weren't a proper lady's maid anyway.

So I made gingerbread. It was an old recipe. Victorian, Cook said, and the house had been serving it at Christmastime for nigh on a hundred years. It was more a cake than a biscuit in some ways, soft and sticky and still a little wonderful. When I come off-shift at last my hands smelled of ginger and my hair smelled of rum and my fingers were sore from stirring. But I was happy, because I'd been part of something, and because I'd arranged with Miss Emily to meet her in the grounds and play, just for a little while, at being regular folk.

I didn't have Sunday best to get into, not exactly. But I had my own clothes as well as the uniform, so I did myself up in this knee-length dress in navy blue under a little jacket with sharp shoulders and a fitted waist. Fashions was simple in them days what with rationing, but I thought the cut worked well on me and with my barnet set and a touch of makeup I thought I looked nice enough.

Emily and me wouldn't be going down together, of course. That would have raised eyebrows even on a day off. Especially on a day off, when I'd no call to be attending on her. So I went down with some of the girls and a couple of the lads. We was a gaggle, mostly, but there was pairs among us. Tall quiet Sam had been sweet on young Vera for months and now they was holding hands shyly as they weaved in between stalls.

It didn't take long for me to shake the crowd. Since I'd moved half upstairs the other girls hadn't had much time for me, and if any of the young men were paying attention I'd not noticed. I remember walking on my own for a long time, watching little kids dashing about playing in the—not in the snow, I keep thinking there was snow but there weren't.

But I remember the kids still. And I remember thinking even back then that if there was any way that me and Emily, that me and the mistress…well there'd be choices to make. If I'd ever get to make them.

Not that I would.

I made sure to keep in sight of the steps—right round where we do the interviews now—and so I saw Emily coming down at last with her brother, Master James that is, the one as took the place over in sixty-two and sold it in eighty-nine.

She looked impossible, like always. A long black coat that went to her knees with light-grey piping around the lapels. A hat in a matching colour, warm enough to fit the season but set for fashion more than comfort.

They were talking to each other in low voices, and I only got snatches of what they were saying. But snatches were enough.

"—dy *knows*, Em. You're not half so clever as you think you are. And even if you were, *she* certainly isn't."

And then Emily's laughter, bell-bright and fearless. "You worry too much, Jimmy."

"Easy for you to say."

I don't think Master James saw me, but Emily did. She saw me and she smiled, and her eyes told me to wait.

So I waited. And when her brother had left to go and do heir-to-the-estate things amongst the common folk, she wandered all careless-like to my side.

"Hello, stranger."

"Reckon you don't have to pretend we don't know each other, miss," I told her. Though I'd not curtseyed as I would have normally. "Folks understand."

Emily looked almost upset, like she'd wanted me to play along. "What they'll understand is that you're an ordinary girl who the lady from the big house has kindly chosen to show around the fete. Come on."

She reached out a gloved hand, and I took it. There was something electric about that, for usually when I touched her it was private, just us, with all the doors closed and the curtains drawn and the unspoken understanding that it never happened.

But now she took me by the hand and just for a moment we were no different from Vera and tall quiet Sam. No different from any other young couple.

We was, of course. Even then. Even at Christmas. Even on a half-day off with me in what passed for my best and her not giving a damn like always, we was different. When we stood to listen to the carollers, she couldn't hold me, she could only stand by my side with a half an inch of air blowing cold between us. And when she bought me a bundle of gingerbread for luck, we had to eat it separate, just staring at each other in a crowd. I had to be content knowing that the spice and the sweetness that was on my lips was on hers as well. Even if that was all we could share while there was eyes on us.

The fete spread over most of the grounds, and we wandered out of sight of the house, down towards the river and then along it, past the bridge to the hermitage (and here Doris looked around at Audrey). You remember the one? Didn't smell so bad of piss in them days. Or if it did, I didn't care. Maybe it was just 'cause I was with her.

She sat me down on that hard stone bed and buried her fingers in my hair.

"Fuck," she said—sorry, but she did, though; if it bothers you I can just say *eff*, "I wish I didn't have to hide you."

Well I didn't know how to take that. Because as I saw it there was no sense wishing for things that would never happen, and though it had its costs and its pains, right then I'd not have changed what we had for anything.

So I just begged for her to kiss me. And she did. And when I could speak again I begged her for more besides, and though there'd been times when she was cruel—because she liked to withhold things, did Emily, just in general, just because she could—on that day, she gave me everything I asked for.

I think I told her I loved her. I don't think she was listening.

But her brother was.

He stepped into the door of the grotto like a wolf eating the sun. And all I can remember him saying was, "Em."

I wanted to die then. From the shame of it, and from the knowing it was over.

I'd expected the news to come from Mrs. Loris. And it did, in a way. But all she said to me was, "Sir Arthur will see you now."

I'd known the Branninghams on and off for a decade and I think I'd said maybe a hundred words to Sir Arthur. Less if you didn't count *sir* and *yes*. So it was strange to be shown through now to his study, a place I'd cleaned dozens of times before I made lady's maid but never really *been* in, and sat down opposite him like I was being interviewed in a newspaper.

"I want you to know," he said, "that I don't hold you responsible."

I kept my eyes low. I remember he had this fountain pen in front of him, marbled blue with the name of the maker engraved on the nib. "Thank you, sir."

"My daughter is a troubled young woman."

"As you say, sir."

Looking down, I couldn't see his face clearly, but I think he frowned. "However, you understand that my family has a reputation to maintain. That should you make any accusations…"

"I won't, sir." The word *accusations* stung. As I saw it, Emily had done nothing to be accused of. Leastways not as he meant it.

"Mrs. Loris will see to it that you are provided with an excellent reference."

"Although"—Mrs. Loris spoke up here—"for your work as a housemaid only. Your services as a lady's maid are, I think, best left undiscussed."

That seemed right enough. And even if it hadn't, I'd not have had much choice in the matter.

"But this is contingent," Sir Arthur was saying, "on your complete discretion. Should I find that you have been spreading any kind of rumours about my daughter or my household—"

"I wouldn't," I blurted out. "I wouldn't do nothing to hurt Miss Emily. Not never."

There was a kind of sorrow in Mrs. Loris's eyes then. "On that much, at least," she told Sir Arthur, "I believe we can trust her."

And that was that. I packed my things at once, and that evening I was on the last train back to Stepney.

I never got to say goodbye to Emily. Never got to take nothing to remind me of her, 'cept a half-ate, half-wrapped bundle of gingerbread. And I carried that all the way back to my mum and dad's house in Stepney. Stuck it in a box under my bed.

Never could bring myself to finish it.

Midnight

IT CAME AS no surprise to Audrey that the lights were still on in Jennifer's trailer, nor did it come as any surprise that the response she received when she knocked on the door was a clear, "Fuck off, Audrey."

"I thought you'd want to know that I got the Doris situation sorted."

"And in less than two hours. How blisteringly efficient of you."

Audrey stood on the steps facing a blank expanse of caravan with a-not-taking-this-shit expression that, as an inanimate object, it was in no place to appreciate. "If you're going to insult me, could you at least do me the courtesy of not doing it through a door?"

"Best way to insult somebody. It means you don't have to put up with their sulky faces."

"I do not have a sulky face."

"Sweetheart, you're *all* sulky face." Jennifer's voice was a little louder now, as if she was moving about inside. "You did nothing in your mercifully short tenure on my show except whine about things. Oh boo hoo, you're sexualising a teenager. Boo hoo, an old woman has to go for a bit of a walk. Boo hoo, you won't let me publish my affirming story about two hot lesbians in the forties."

Audrey knew when she was being baited, but she hoped that like the wily octopus, she'd learned to hook the bait out of the trap without actually getting caught by it. "Firstly, at least two of those were actually very bad things you did need to stop doing, and the last one I'm at peace with even though I still think it's a good story. Anyway, I just came to tell you I'd done what you asked, and I have so"—she gave a kind of flustered exhalation that was part sigh part general yargh—"so good night I guess. Sleep well. I'll talk to Alanis in the morning."

Having said her piece and not wanting to stand around like a fool, Audrey turned and walked slowly away. Very slowly. Hopefully slowly.

"You know if you were really leaving, you'd have got much further by now," said Jennifer's voice from behind her.

Turning back, Audrey saw a very awake, somewhat dishevelled, mildly irate Jennifer Hallet standing in the now-open doorway. There was, she thought, something about Jennifer that was *made* to be seen the wrong side of midnight. Something about the way her hair, normally pulled into a severe ponytail, spilled loose over her shoulders. The way the shadows fell across her eyes and cheekbones like she was some kind of highly caffeinated vampire. She danced that line between *overworked* and *wanton*, and if Audrey'd had more energy she would have pretended she wasn't into it.

"If you were really going to let me," Audrey replied after just *slightly* too long a pause, "you wouldn't have looked."

"Maybe I was just going for a walk."

Honestly, Audrey had expected better. Or at least more vulgar. "That seems unlikely. You don't seem like the moonlit-stroll type."

"Then maybe I just wanted to remind you, to your smug face, that you don't actually have anywhere to sleep because you're not on the show anymore, so you don't have a room assigned."

"Well, if you were," retorted Audrey, "that would make you both a dick and bad at your job. And I'm pretty sure you're only one of those."

"You're right," Jennifer grudgingly admitted. "Colin'll sort you out."

Which resolved the question of sleeping arrangements. Which left Audrey with no other reason to stay. But she hovered anyway. And so did Jennifer. "Unless…" Audrey began.

Jennifer sneered in a way Audrey was at least hoping constituted protesting too much. "Unless what—unless I wanted to make you a better offer? Sorry to disappoint, sugartits, I don't shit where I eat or fuck where I work."

That was the thing about midnight. It wasn't just Jennifer Hallet it was kind to. Audrey didn't believe in magic, but there was something about this witching hour that made bad ideas look like good ideas. She took a step forwards. "You say that, but you called me up to solve a problem you could perfectly well have solved yourself."

"I delegated."

"And I could have said, 'No, go fuck yourself,' but instead I drove for nearly three hours to come and help you out."

"So you're either a soft touch or you've got a crush on me. Not sure why either of those are my problem."

That *almost* stung. Because there was a grim chance that yes this whole thing was one-sided. And she'd been in enough one-sided relationships to know that they stopped being fun long, long before they just stopped being. Although in this case "enough" was actually "one".

But this did feel different. Sure, Jennifer was a horrible, driven, objectively gorgeous woman with a high-end media job, and that did look the tiniest bit like a pattern, but Natalie had always swept Audrey along, never pushed her back. Which meant towards the end she'd almost given up trying to work out what she wanted on her own account and what was just the echo of somebody more remarkable than she was.

Jennifer, she was bitterly, resentfully certain she wanted entirely on her own terms.

"You know what," she said, "fine. Yeah. I'll cop to that. I've got a weird, probably deeply ill-advised crush on you that somehow didn't go away when you kicked me off a TV show for ethically dubious reasons."

"If you didn't want to get kicked off a TV show for ethically dubious reasons, you should have baked a better pie."

"Right. And you didn't in any way imply that part of the reason you got rid of me was that you secretly want to get all up on this."

"In my defence, who wouldn't?"

"Well…" Audrey looked down at herself. The thing was, you could have all the positive self-image you liked—and she worked hard to maintain a positive self-image—but that didn't actually change what anyone else thought. Or mean that normative beauty standards weren't, like, a thing. "Quite a few people honestly."

Jennifer was giving her a flat stare.

"Oh come on. I look like a young Dawn French."

"Fuck me." Jennifer Hallet took a deep breath. "I knew you were a mess, Lane, but I didn't realise you were *that* much of a mess. Also, Dawn French is a very attractive woman."

Audrey could put up with a lot of shit about a lot of things, but this was straying into areas where she had a no bullshit policy. "Don't, that's beneath you."

Now it was Jennifer's turn to step forwards. "Sorry, are you really suggesting that you think the only reason why you're not over my desk with your legs in the air and my tongue where it counts is because you trend slightly more Penelope Featherington than Daphne Bridgerton?"

The words *legs* and *tongue* circled Audrey's head like cartoon birds. "Okay"—she opted to focus on the other half of the sentence—"that wasn't the cultural touchstone I was expecting from you."

"Because you think an important part of my job is *not* knowing what key demographics are watching on television?"

Audrey shuffled, still very much caught in legs/tongue/desk space. "Just didn't have you pegged for a fan."

"I've got hidden depths."

That seemed like as good a time as any to reset the conversation. "Nice to know. So…umm…I guess just forget that I made a colossal prat of myself if that's okay?"

Jennifer Hallet probably wasn't capable of looking kind, but for a moment she looked less like she actively wanted to disembowel everybody around her. "You didn't make a prat of yourself."

"Thanks, but—hang on, why are you being nice to me? Why aren't you calling me a rancid sack of fox vomit or something?"

"I didn't say you *weren't* a rancid sack of fox vomit. Just that I didn't think you'd made a prat of yourself. About this anyway."

This was very slightly messing with Audrey's head. "Is this just you being contrarian? Are you so stubborn that your first instinct to somebody talking themselves down is to tell them they're wrong about that *as well*?"

"Why do you think I get such good results out of Colin?"

This was feeling a lot like a *gah* situation. But Audrey was fresh out of *gah*. "How do you *ever* get laid?"

"I'm hot, successful, and emotionally withholding. It's not difficult."

"Well," Audrey pointed out in exasperation, "for someone who insists she doesn't find me unattractive, you're making it quite difficult at the moment."

"You're not unattractive. You're just not my type."

"That's code for unattractive."

"Oh for fuck's sake." Jennifer turned her eyes skywards. "You're not my type because you're a quilt-making, nose-poking, heart-bleeding pile of feelings and teddy bears. You'll want to talk about shit and snuggle afterwards."

As assessments of Audrey's character went, this was depressingly fair. "Right now, I mainly want you to shut up."

"And can you maintain that focus for a twenty-minute fuck session?"

Audrey glared up at her. "I can maintain it for a *forty-minute* fuck session."

"Well, okay then," said Jennifer Hallet. "Get in and get your pants off."

She was bluffing. She was clearly bluffing. And Audrey always resented people for thinking they could bluff her. It was fairly dark in the carpark and there was no one around. So if, hypothetically, she wanted to whip her knickers off, just to prove the point, she totally could. She totally did. "All right." She waved her cute-but-not-entirely-sexy stripy briefs in Jennifer's direction. "They're off."

Jennifer glanced from Audrey to the pants and back to Audrey. "You're a fucking madwoman."

"This was your idea."

"I said inside. Not in a field surrounded by bored techs who are professionally required to carry recording equipment."

"Nobody is filming. All that's happening here is that you're stalling. Because you, Jennifer-Whatever-Your-Middle-Name-Is-Hallet, are all talk."

Reaching down from the top step, Jennifer hooked her fingers around the strap of Audrey's sundress. "Get the fuck in here."

So Audrey got the fuck in, still holding her pants, still not entirely certain what was going on.

"Ground rules." Jennifer kicked the door shut with her heel. "No conversation. No cuddling. No staying the night. No catching feelings. I get to keep your pants."

"What? To hang on your dorm wall?"

"That was a joke, Lane."

"Oh, so we're allowed to do jokes then?"

"You're allowed to do anything that's not on the list."

"Aren't jokes," asked Audrey, "technically conversation?"

Stalking from the cluttered office section of the trailer to the, if anything, more cluttered living area at the back, Jennifer *foomphed* down a folding bed and then *foomphed* onto it. "I knew this was a mistake."

Holding her own pants while Jennifer half-scowled, half-smouldered at her from a semi-supine position was throwing off Audrey's game. She folded them neatly and left them on Jennifer's desk. "Assuming *I knew this was a mistake* is code for *You're annoying me but I still want to do you,* what's your dream version of how this plays out?"

"You shut the fuck up and sit on my face."

"You realise that mainly ensures *you* shut the fuck up."

"Not if I do it properly."

Audrey couldn't quite tell who was winning here. Which meant she had two choices: leave now or go through with it and find out. "Okay," she said. "Here I come. Ready or not."

"New rule: no adorable bullshit."

By now, Audrey was partially straddling Jennifer, who'd dropped to her elbows. It felt…unexpectedly dangerous, like trying to get a fork out of a food mixer. Except also quite a lot sexier. Because, beneath her, Jennifer was all heat and taut muscles and erotic hostility.

"I was keeping you informed," Audrey explained. "Next time I'll just slap my labia on your head."

"Which part of shut the fuck up do you not understand?"

"The part"—Audrey crawled her way up Jennifer Hallet in dress-destroying, sheet-displacing tangle—"where you have any power to make me."

"We'll see about that sun—"

Truthfully, Audrey had positioned herself with more confidence than she was actually feeling. Because this was, undeniably, an exposing thing to be doing. Even if she was kind of in control of it. Then again, *exposed and only slightly in control* was a pretty good summary of her relationship with Jennifer Hallet in general. It was therefore slightly surprising when Jennifer's hands slid up Audrey's thighs, almost like she was cradling her. And that the first touches of her tongue were exploratory rather than aggressive, as if she was more interested in discovering what Audrey liked than shoving her towards orgasm to prove a point.

Not that Audrey was going to take much shoving.

Because Jennifer Hallet was annoyingly, inescapably, predicably good at this. And went at it with the same Machiavellian focus she brought to, well, everything else. It made staying self-conscious almost impossible—that and the fact they were both almost fully clothed still, Audrey's dress flaring around them like the petals of a very suggestive flower. Of course, being a quilt-making, nose-poking, heart-bleeding pile of feelings and teddy bears, Audrey would have preferred to see Jennifer's face somehow while all this was going on. But—while she'd insisted there would be no conversation and wouldn't have been particularly able to have one anyway—Jennifer contrived to be…communicative.

The clutch of her fingers. The restless arching of her body. The, admittedly slightly muffled, sounds she was making. Breathless and appreciative and lewd. And everything tilting into this *Alice in Wonderland* unreality, because this was still Jennifer Hallet. The sweary Byronic telly goddess. A nightmarish razor-edged puzzle box of woman. Currently going down on Audrey like it was her whole to-do list.

It was flattering and bewildering and more than enough to undo a girl.

"Um," Audrey told the wall breathlessly, "I might be getting quite close."

Jennifer made an irritated sound, which, from context, Audrey took to mean, *Do we need to revisit the shutting up part of this agreement?*

Deliciously heavy shudders were running down Audrey's spine. Tensing her legs. Curling her toes. "I just thought you might want to know."

With another irritated sound, Jennifer partially extricated herself, flipping up Audrey's skirt in order to glare better. "I can fucking tell. Would it shock you to know I've done this before?"

Audrey tried to glare back. Which she was finding difficult

because her body was in the middle of dissolving into rainbows and orgasms. "I've done this before, too. And it's polite to tell people."

"Are you going to write me a thank-you card as well?"

"I'm trying"—Audrey was beginning to wish she'd stuck to the *don't talk* rule—"to…to be considerate. You might not want to be…exactly there…when I…you know."

"Jesus, Lane," snapped Jennifer Hallet. "Just come on my fucking face."

"It might get…quite messy."

"Been there. Done that. Soiled the T-shirt."

The prospect of Jennifer Hallet's mouth re-busying itself with something that wasn't bickering with Audrey hovered tantalisingly. The part of her that was bold and decisive and took her pleasure where she found it was very ready to pass Go, collecting two hundred pounds as she went. Unfortunately, there was another part of Audrey that somewhere down the line had learned to second-guess itself. That expected every good thing to come with a *but*. "And this is okay for you?" she asked. "You wouldn't prefer—"

"No," interrupted Jennifer, sounding marginally more sincere than she sounded annoyed, although it was touch-and-go. "I want to be doing this. Here. Now. With you. Which is why I'm doing this. Here. Now. With you."

"Oh," said Audrey, trying not to break the *no feelings* rule as hard as she'd broken the *no talking* rule.

At the very least, she managed to not break it visibly or verbally. But it was always the feelings that got you. Like, sex was great and everything. But it got better when you liked someone and even better when you knew they liked you. And, for all of Jennifer's obstreperousness, Audrey felt very liked just then. Which, in turn, made her feel pretty damn sexy as she vigorously rode the face of a hot irascible television executive, until she came hard and triumphantly, with a trailer-rattling whoop.

"Hang on," she said afterwards. "Is this my quilt?"

Jennifer, looking about as bedraggled and debauched as you could while fully dressed, rolled her eyes. "It's fine. I'll get it dry-cleaned."

"So. Um." Audrey made a Jennifer-encompassing gesture. "Can I do anything for you?"

"You just did, sunshine. Now, fuck off."

Well, that was exactly as advertised. Audrey sat up reluctantly. "I know you said there'd be no cuddling. But I've barely got my breath back."

"So walk slowly."

"Seriously? You know there's a middle ground between *hold me for the rest of my life* and *don't let the door hit you in the arse*?"

"I told you how this was going to be." Jennifer got up, went to the front of the trailer and switched on her computer. "And I really want to remember this as fantastic sex with a journalist who avoided pissing me off. Don't ruin that for me."

Audrey was just slightly too afterglowy to call that for the bullshit it was. She just readjusted her dress, gathered her dignity, her shoes, and her sunglasses, and—with a weaponisedly polite "See you tomorrow, Jennifer"—let herself out the trailer.

All things considered, she thought she'd handled that pretty well. She'd been mature, she'd been confident, she'd got laid, and she'd left with her head held high.

Then she remembered that she'd also left her pants on Jennifer's desk.

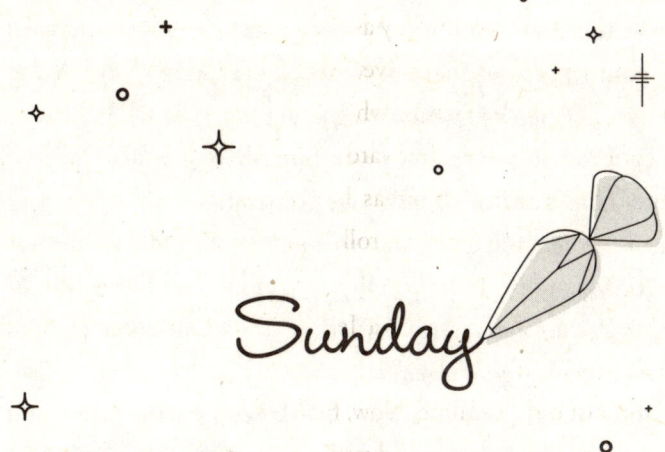

Sunday

AUDREY SLEPT BADLY and woke up early. And the thought that awoke her was, *fuck Jennifer fucking Hallet.*

Fuck Jennifer fucking Hallet and her smug face and her swearier-than-thou, I-think-aggression-is-confidence attitude.

Fuck her and her fantastic oral dexterity and her fucking show.

It wasn't so much that she objected to being asked, or more accurately told, to leave. She had, after all, agreed to Jennifer's rules. Shit rules though they may have been. But there were ways. You could say, "That was great, but I've got an early start and I'm sure you'll need to be getting home," or, "That was great, but I've got serious emotional problems that mean I'm not cool with being around people after we've fucked," or basically anything as long as it began "That was great, but."

You had to really work to get as abrupt and dismissive as "You just did, sunshine, now, fuck off." The only way Audrey could imagine it being more abrupt and dismissive would be if Jennifer had texted for an Uber while she still had her face in Audrey's muff.

In theory, at least, Audrey knew that it was pointless to get angry at somebody who was *trying* to make her angry and even more pointless to get angry at somebody for *successfully* making her angry. She had half a mind to get up early, get back in her car, drive back to Shropshire, and never think about Jennifer Hallet or Patchley House or *Bake Expectations* ever again.

Except there was still Alanis to consider. Not that Alanis was technically Audrey's responsibility, any more than Doris was, or anybody else for that matter. And in fact the whole damned lot of them were explicitly *Jennifer's* responsibility in the actual, formal, legal, duty-of-care sense. Because if Audrey was being picky (and she was increasingly in a mood to be picky), whacking a sixteen-year-old-girl on national television and then leaving her emotional well-being entirely in the hands of a fellow contestant was what Ofcom standards would describe as a *dick move*.

None of which stopped Audrey from feeling very strongly that she had to help anyway.

And in the end, the decision was rather made for her when, very slightly after she would normally have got up for breakfast, she heard a hammering at her bedroom door and Alanis's voice calling from outside.

"Audrey?"

"Yes?"

"I heard you were back but I didn't believe it."

This was going to take some explaining. "I'm not really."

"You sound back."

"I mean, I'm here, but I'm not back on the show. I'm—actually I don't know what I'm doing. Jennifer said you were thinking of quitting."

There was a moment of quiet that Audrey didn't find reassuring. Then another moment of even more quiet, which she found still less reassuring. She opened the door and found Alanis looking very small and very uncertain.

"Do you want to come in?"

Alanis nodded.

So a few minutes later they were sitting on Audrey's bed because there wasn't really anywhere else to sit in the still-relatively-small rooms that the BBC provided for the contestants.

"It's just that," Alanis began at the exact same time that Audrey was saying, "Look, you shouldn't," and then they both fell silent again.

Being the adult in the room, Audrey eventually psyched herself up to take something resembling charge. "I know I said that they'd want to keep you around for the story," she managed, "but that doesn't mean you aren't really good."

"I wasn't last week." Alanis looked intensely glum.

"You made some mistakes," Audrey began, but Alanis immediately checked her.

"Don't say, 'But you're young.' I shouldn't be here if I'm not good enough. It's not like Meera gets special treatment because she has kids to look after, or you got a pass because you were busy being a journalist."

"I wasn't going to," Audrey replied, and she genuinely hadn't been. "I was just going to say that people can have bad weeks."

Unfortunately, Alanis didn't seem convinced. "But they can't, though, can they? If you have a bad week, you go out. That's what happens. So why didn't it happen to *me*?"

Audrey bit her lip. The last time she'd tried to explain why "this whole thing is rigged" didn't necessarily mean the whole thing was rigged it had gone... well it had left her with a sad teenager, an angry producer, and an old lady breaking into other people's rooms. Still, just because it had gone disastrously before, that was no reason not to try again.

"It didn't happen to you," Audrey said, slowly, "because the judges thought that you'd do better next week. And they were probably right. But I…" Reflecting on why you completely deserved to lose something you'd shouted at someone for taking away from you was, it turned out, kind of a crappy thing to have to do, and the crappiness of it took Audrey aback for a moment. "I probably wouldn't. I think…honestly I think I was plateauing already. I was never going to win a week, I was only ever going to do fine. And that's okay. The series needs people to do fine. It needs people who get to about week three and who you immediately forget were in it."

Looking up, Alanis smiled at Audrey. She hadn't quite been crying but there was still an air of vulnerability about her, like she was choosing very determinedly to be cheerful despite strong temptation to the contrary. "People won't forget you were in it, Audrey."

"You won't. But the audience totally will. They'll get to week five and they'll be, 'Who was that boring one who never really did anything special, I think she was a lawyer or something.'"

It seemed like Alanis was about to protest, but then an expression crossed her face that Audrey suspected was her trying to remember the early eliminated candidates from previous seasons and coming up blank. So instead of reassuring Audrey of her definite unforgettability, she changed the subject. "I still feel like I don't belong here, though."

"Did you ever?" asked Audrey.

When she'd said it, Audrey hadn't known what reaction she'd expected. Maybe a slow nod and a *good point*. Instead, Alanis just looked perplexed. "Well, yeah. Obviously."

Which was awkward. "Right"—Audrey reached out and patted Alanis on the shoulder—"then congratulations. You've just discovered imposter syndrome. If you're lucky or much better adjusted than most people, this'll be the only time you get it."

Alanis winced. "It sucks."

"I know. And this probably won't help, but I'm pretty sure if you'd gone home, whoever stayed in your place would have been feeling the exact same way. Also, some of us had been feeling that way the whole time." Audrey thought about this for a moment. "Actually some of us have been feeling that way for most of our lives."

Alanis flopped back on the bed. "You make being a grown-up sound really shit."

"Honestly"—Audrey shuffled around to keep facing her companion—"I don't think that's a being-a-grown-up problem. I think that's a being-me problem. Although I also reckon most grown-ups are pretty bad at telling those two things apart."

Alanis nodded, only slightly ruefully. "Yeah, I reckon you are."

Deciding that joining them was in this case decidedly better than beating them, Audrey flopped back next to Alanis and let herself just stare at the ceiling. It felt like a strangely teenagery position to be in, and if present-day-Audrey had let her, fifteen-years-ago-Audrey would have taken the wheel completely and suggested they go buy cider from a store with a lax ID policy and then hang out talking about girls.

"It honestly really scares me," Alanis said into space. She didn't elaborate or explain what scared her.

"Being a grown-up?"

"That being a grown-up will suck. Because being me *kind of* sucks sometimes, and if being an actual proper adult will suck worse, that's *really* upsetting."

"I think"—present-day-Audrey and fifteen-years-ago-Audrey compared notes behind her eyelids and came to a rapid conclusion—"I think it sort of sucks *differently*?"

"Thanks. I'm going to put that on my wall." Alanis stretched her hands upwards as if framing an imaginary banner. "*Everything sucks, but sometimes it sucks differently*. Real inspirational stuff."

"Sorry."

"It's cool. I'm beginning to accept it," replied Alanis with apparent sincerity. "*Everything sucks, but sometimes it sucks differently*. I think I can work with that."

"I really didn't mean—"

"No, no, that's my philosophy now. I'm like a...a kind of a happy nihilist."

Still not entirely sure if she was being humoured, mocked, or genuinely witnessing the birth of a philosophical movement, Audrey lay still for a while.

And when it became clear that happy nihilism wasn't a great conversation starter, Alanis asked, "So you really feel like you don't belong *all the time*?"

"Sort of?"

"*All the time*, all the time?"

It was hard to squirm lying down, and a bit embarrassing to be squirming in any position when you were talking to a sixteen-year-old whose emotional health you were supposed to be supporting. "Not so much anymore. In my old job, yes. Constantly."

"What was your old job?"

"Journalist."

For a moment Alanis was silent, then she asked the obvious question. "I thought that was your regular job."

"Different sort of journalist."

"How?"

And wasn't that going to take some unpacking? "Well, what I do now is very… I mean I love local news but it's very…it's small. Whereas what I did before was very…very not small. I got into it with a friend of mine. More than friend. Girlfriend. We had this whole…we were going to set the world on fire and she sort of did and I sort of didn't and so most of our relationship was just me following her around trying to keep my fingers warm."

"That must have…"

"Sucked?"

"Yeah."

Audrey nodded. "It did. And it was—I don't think it was her fault really."

"It sounds like you were kind of doing what she wanted and not what you wanted."

That was probably true, but even that, Audrey didn't really feel Natalie could be blamed for. "If we'd done what I wanted, we'd have never left Shropshire."

"So?"

"What do you mean, so?"

For a second or two, Alanis just gathered her thoughts. "Well, I don't know but from what you've shown me, you come from this pretty little village that lots of people would love to live in, and I don't really see what's wrong with wanting to stay there."

That was silly. "Would *you* want to stay where you were born your whole life?"

"I think that'd depend on where I was born. And even if I don't want to stay in London forever, that doesn't mean it'd be wrong if I did."

"Right, but that's London. *Everything's* in London."

Alanis took a contemplative sort of breath. "Maybe, but I've been talking to my dad's family more recently and I don't think being able to stay in the place you grew up in is something you should take for granted either. No matter where it is."

"Even if it's Shropshire?"

"*Especially* if it's Shropshire. I mean, I've never been, but I've told you, when I'm old and rich I'm moving to a little village *exactly* like the one you grew up in. Getting a little cottage with roses around the door."

"You know," Audrey said to the ceiling, "door roses are actually a bit of a pain to look after."

"I'll be rich. I'll pay somebody."

They lapsed back into silence for just long enough that Audrey started to feel like she'd done a terrible job of whatever it was her job was actually supposed to have been. "Sorry," she said. "My plan was honestly just to get you to stay on the show. I didn't mean to dump my extremely boring adult baggage on you."

Alanis waved a dismissive hand. "It's fine. I think it helps to realise that grown-ups are just as screwed up as we are." She sat up. "Come on, we're going to be late for breakfast."

The *we* in *we're going to be late for breakfast* was a bit awkward because Audrey absolutely did need to eat, but at the same time she didn't really feel comfortable eating with the contestants on account of no longer, strictly speaking, being one. Of course since she also wasn't crew that meant eating with *them* didn't feel right either. Also, she probably wasn't technically entitled to eat anything so having breakfast at the show's expense would be stealing.

Alanis, of course, had been very keen for her to come join her former peers and screw the consequences, but Audrey decided against it. There'd just be too many questions to answer, and while Audrey wasn't sure of much, she was sure she didn't want to answer them.

So instead she mooched, hovering on the periphery of the production and trying not to feel like she'd lost something irreplaceable. It turned out, however, that melancholy mooching got dull fast, and so with a strong sense of anticlimax, Audrey made her way towards the carpark and settled into her car.

Then she sat there feeling like a pillock.

Deciding that doing something was a good deal better than doing nothing, and that at the very least she needed to eat, Audrey took a short jaunt up to Crinkley Furze and then, because literally everything was still closed, a rather longer jaunt into Tapworth. She arrived just in time to catch the opening of the local Co-op and without quite being able to explain why, she decided that what she really wanted for breakfast was a loaf of crusty bread and a jar of honey.

Tapworth was big enough that finding a decently picturesque sitting-around-and-eating space involved a long walk or a short drive, but eventually Audrey found one. A little field that was probably private property (check that, definitely private property, there was a sign) commanding pretty views over Surrey. Out of deference to the rights of the landowner, Audrey didn't go into the field, but she leaned on the gate overlooking it and let herself savour the rustic simplicity of her bread-and-honey breakfast.

Not that it really *was* rustic simplicity, of course. Even if the bread had been baked in-store, which the little tag had said it was, the honey was pure off-the-shelf, and while the co-op tended to be okay-ish on its sourcing, it still wasn't quite the same as a girl in a white dress squeezing a honeycomb with her own fingers as the sun set over the hills.

Where the girl in the white dress had come from, Audrey couldn't say.

Having made it as far as Tapworth, the logical thing for her to do now would be to go home. It was a Sunday after all, and having a nice, quiet, relaxing day would be good for her. She might even be able to get an early night, which would leave her well set up to go into work on Monday and crack on with—she checked her email to remind herself what the next big story was—ah yes, interviewing a woman whose social media account was documenting abandoned shopping trolleys in Bagley Brook.

It didn't seem like the *most* exciting plan, if she was honest.

And it also felt like running away.

Of course, if she was being totally objective, it *wasn't*. It was being told quite firmly to go away, and then being told to come back for a specific purpose, coming back for the purpose, making a probably ill-advised sexual decision in the middle of it, being told to leave again, finally fulfilling the original purpose, then leaving.

Her whimsical desire to eat bread and honey while leaning on a gate and absorbing the timelessness of everything satisfied, Audrey got back in her Mini and set off towards the M25. With Sunday traffic, if she got a good start, she'd be able to make it home before noon.

She did not get a good start. She was only about two minutes out of Tapworth when she stopped, did a probably illegal U-turn, and began driving back towards Patchley House. Because sure, the mature thing was to put all of this behind her and never think about *Bake Expectations*, or any of the contestants, or Jennifer fucking Hallet ever again. But sometimes being mature could go fuck itself.

So twenty minutes later she was parking again, just as the

people who were still actually competing on this season were filing out of hair and makeup and heading into the ballroom. As Audrey strode with more purpose than she really felt past the house itself and towards Jennifer's trailer, she saw Grace Forsythe and the judges coming the other way. With no cameras around, each of them looked slightly different—Wilfred Honey a little less warm, Marianne Wolvercote a little more relaxed. Even Grace Forsythe, who Audrey suspected was one of those performers who was *on* 24/7 seemed to be having a moment of being merely effusive rather than ebullient.

"She's in a foul mood this morning," Grace Forsythe warned her as they crossed paths.

A more on-the-ball Audrey—not necessarily a version of Audrey that had ever actually existed—might have taken the moment to pretend that she didn't know which *she* Grace Forsythe was talking about, or at least to pretend that her assumptions regarding the *she* Audrey was looking for were unfounded. But she didn't. She just pivoted mid-stomp and said, "Isn't she in a foul mood *every* morning?"

"When you've known her as long as we have," explained Wilfred Honey, "you'll learn that there's a lot of different flavours of foul."

Marianne Wolvercote nodded. "And in case you were wondering, this very much *isn't* a blasted heath situation."

"Come again?" Audrey was not, all told, in the mood for riddling.

"Where Jennifer is concerned," clarified Marianne Wolvercote, "foul is most definitely not fair."

The three more famous people continued on their way to the ballroom, but, as Audrey was getting back to her own journey,

Grace Forsythe broke off from the group and tapped her on the shoulder.

"By the way, old thing," Grace Forsythe was saying before Audrey had even managed to turn around. "I've told Jennifer that she should *definitely* keep fucking you."

"What?" It wasn't the *last* thing Audrey had been expecting. The last thing she'd been expecting was probably something like *I've been working undercover for the CIA this whole time and now I need your help to save the president.* But it was pretty near the bottom of the list, expectation-wise.

"If you want her to. Obviously." Grace Forsythe put her hands into the mea culpa pose. "Not suggesting anything untoward. It's just that the impression I got from her was that you'd given her indications and that you'd, y'know, like her to and that she'd blown it as usual."

There were several things to unpack here. "So…first of all, I'm not sure I like that she was discussing this with you."

"It wasn't a professional conversation, darling. It's just that as it turns out I'm the closest thing young Jennifer has to a friend. Which must be pretty miserable for her, now I think about it."

Filing that away under *too complex to deal with at the moment*, Audrey pressed on. "Okay, but I'm also not super comfortable talking about…"

"Or you could fuck her, of course," Grace Forsythe continued with the blithe insouciance of a woman who has made a career out of insouciant blitheness. "Whichever works for you. Actually, might work even better that way around because honestly Jennifer is carrying a *lot* of tension."

There were many things that could have gone wrong banging Jennifer Hallet. Audrey had known that. She'd never quite realised that being gossiped about by a beloved eighties television person-ality was on the list. "Oh my God, this is not—"

"She also told me that she kicked you out immediately afterwards."

Audrey covered her face with her hands. She should have just gone home. This was getting beyond humiliating. "Please, just stop."

"I told her she was being an arse, if it helps."

It didn't, especially. "And how did she take that?"

"About as well as you'd imagine."

Looking up, Audrey treated Grace Forsythe to her most inter-rogative expression. "So why are you so keen for us to keep, um, fucking each other in whatever configuration suits us?"

"Partly, I just think Jennifer needs to get laid really rather badly, but I've also got a sneaking suspicion you'd be good for her."

"But would she be good for me?" Audrey wondered out loud.

Grace Forsythe shrugged. "I think she could if she'd let herself. Although I admit that's a very big *if*." She grimaced. "Thinking about it, probably not what you're looking for in a girlfriend. Forget I said anything."

Before Audrey could reply, Grace Forsythe had set off deter-minedly for the ballroom, spitting obnoxiously loud vocal exer-cises as she went.

Now that she'd been interrupted, Audrey couldn't quite say what she was intending to do once she got to Jennifer's trailer. She'd started with the intent of having a vaguely self-righteous storm, something in the vein of "I won't be treated like this," which would inevitably fail as hard as it had every other time she'd tried it. On the other hand, she didn't think there was much mile-age in showing up with "An interfering boomer who works for you thinks we should bang" either. It had the virtue of honesty, but the not-a-virtue of being absolutely mortifying.

Storming, on the whole, was probably safer.

"Fuck off, Audrey," called Jennifer Hallet when Audrey banged on her door.

"No."

It was a little surprising to Audrey that the door opened immediately, rather than after a lot of frustrating back-and-forth. Jennifer looked like she'd slept so badly she'd crossed the line from *interestingly raddled* to *babe, are you okay?* "You understand we're filming?"

"I've been on set. I know how much waiting around there is."

Looking down, Jennifer scrutinised Audrey like she was an application from a prospective contestant with questionable credentials. "I suppose you're why Grace is late?"

"Pretty sure Grace is why Grace is late."

With the barest shrug of acknowledgment, Jennifer vanished into her trailer and sat down in front of a bank of monitors, each showing the feed from a different camera.

She hadn't strictly been invited inside, but adjusting for the Jennifer factor, an open door combined with only being told to fuck off *once* was practically a welcome mat, so Audrey followed her in and then hovered behind her, just watching her work. If she'd come to say anything, it stayed unsaid while Jennifer switched from feed to feed, channel to channel, keeping her eyes on everything.

On one of the screens, Grace Forsythe was launching into her opening monologue. It was odd, seeing it tiny and silent. So odd that Audrey didn't notice that Jennifer was holding up a headset.

"Since you're here."

And Audrey took it. She felt almost like she was in a dream, with the lights down and the screens glowing and Jennifer for once focusing on something that wasn't swearing creatively.

"—traditional," Grace Forsythe was saying in the ballroom, "but exceptional. For this week's baketacular we want you to make your finest, fanciest, child-luring-into-the-woodsiest—"

Jennifer pushed a button. "Colin, get her to can the paedo talk."

The way the microphones were arranged, it was hard to know what Colin was actually saying, but Grace Forsythe's reply came through clearly enough. "It's a fairy-tale reference, Jennifer; everybody will understand."

"Just tell that glorified Fringe show we call a host to redo it."

There was a little more from Colin. Then, "Finest, fanciest, Hansel-and-Gretel ensnaringest—really, Jennifer, I think we're pandering—gingerbread house. It can be tall or short, classic or contemporary, as long as it has four walls, a roof, and stands up by itself. You have five hours, starting on three. *Three*, darlings."

Jennifer Hallet slid her headset down for a moment. "I fucking hate it when she says that."

Not wanting to be the only one getting audio, Audrey reciprocally de-headphoned. "Really? Isn't it sort of iconic?"

"It's so twee, though." Jennifer gave an audible sigh and a visible shudder. "*Starts on three: three.* Every single episode. For eight fucking years."

"Isn't twee the point?" asked Audrey, slightly confused by this not-currently-raging version of Jennifer and not wanting to ruin it. "I mean, it's supposed to be a comforting show."

"There's comforting, and there's kicking off every week with a dad joke." The look in Jennifer Hallet's eyes was one of weirdly sincere pain. "But apparently that's what the public demands. Because the public are a giant fucking nest of baby birds with their beaks open screaming for people to come and vomit entertainment into their lazy gaping mouths."

This was beginning to sound more like the Jennifer Audrey knew. "Do you really have that much contempt for your audience?"

"Every week, we get at least one letter of complaint from somebody who burned themselves trying to make something they saw on the show. Or from somebody who put something they were allergic to in a cake and then ate the cake, and now think it's my fault that they're feeling poorly. So no, I don't think I have too much contempt for my audience. I think I show them too much fucking respect."

"Isn't that a small and unrepresentative minority?" suggested Audrey, not really expecting the suggestion to be taken.

"True. Then there's the hipsters who watch ironically but never miss an episode. And the housewives who watch because they want to fuck the one with the nice arms. And their husbands who watch because they want to fuck the one with the nice tits. And the kids who watch because they don't realise their parents are only watching because they want to fuck some of the contestants."

"That feels reduc—"

"And then of course there's people like you. Who watch because you so *desperately* want to believe that this chocolate-box fantasy we're spinning out of sugar and bullshit is real."

Jennifer had said some pretty vile things to, about, or just generally *around* Audrey, but for some reason, this one landed harder. She could feel herself beginning to tear up, which was absurd. More than absurd, it was humiliating. "Nice things exist," she said.

"Quite the philosopher, aren't you," replied Jennifer, though her tone was less acerbic than Audrey might have expected. It was almost defensive. Without waiting to see if Audrey had a response, Jennifer slipped her headphones on like they were armour.

And Audrey...Audrey just hung. Like she was buffering. It seemed like a really good time to leave, but also it seemed like a really terrible time to leave. Because *quite the philosopher, aren't you* was such a fucking condescending line to go out on.

Of course waiting for Jennifer Hallet to apologise for anything was the platonic ideal of a waste of time so...

And then Jennifer Hallet glanced upwards. Just for a second.

It wasn't *sorry*. Nothing in her expression said *sorry*.

Almost nothing.

But sometimes, almost was enough.

Or maybe it was just that some deep and primal part of Audrey had to follow any story to its conclusion. Even one she'd been written out of. She put her headphones back on.

"Honestly," Doris was saying to Wilfred Honey, "this might not be my week."

"You must've made a fair bit of gingerbread in your time, though," he replied, walking the fine line between acknowledging Doris's seniority and just straight up calling her old. "I'm sure you've got a great recipe."

Watching Doris and Wilfred Honey interact was like watching a competitive grandparent-off. She nodded warmly. "I do, love, I do. But it's the piping." She held out a hand, which, from what Audrey could see through the monitors, was still steady as a rock. "Old fingers."

While Wilfred Honey was making small talk, Marianne Wolvercote was poking at Doris's ingredients. "Am I right in thinking you're using a heritage recipe?"

Doris nodded and didn't elaborate.

"Well that's lovely," said Wilfred, who couldn't hear the word *heritage* without going into at least a bit of a reverie. "It's interesting you see, Marianne, how gingerbread has changed through history. Because it used to be a lot more like a cake and a lot less like a biscuit."

Marianne seemed to find it less lovely. "That's what I'm concerned about. Isn't structural integrity going to be an issue?"

"I'm just using it for the floor," Doris explained. "The walls'll be something else. It's the decorating I'm concerned about."

Wilfred Honey gave an encouraging grin. "I wouldn't worry, pet, there's life in us old dogs yet."

"Less of the us"—Doris grinned back—"you're young enough to be my son."

Audrey followed from monitor to monitor as the presenter and judges went about their rounds and Jennifer flipped from camera to camera, keeping track of the whole complex business.

It was remarkable, in a way, how quickly the hours passed. Not as quickly as they would have if she'd still been competing, of course, but quickly none the less. There was something voyeuristically calming about the producer's-eye view. About being able to watch each contestant attacking the bake in their different ways—Linda staring at her ingredients like they were about to bite her, Reggie measuring twice and cutting once, Joshua very much doing the opposite, and Alanis, after her conversation with Audrey that morning, looking more confident than Audrey had feared she would be.

"You talked her round, then," said Jennifer, her eyes meeting Audrey's as they both glanced at Alanis's monitor.

"We talked. I think she brought herself around, to be honest."

Jennifer nodded, only half paying attention.

But perhaps half was exactly the right amount. "You could have been nicer, you know."

"Nicer about what?" asked Jennifer, just distracted enough that it seemed like a sincere question, rather than a burn.

"Kicking me out. I'd have gone anyway. I only needed, like, five minutes."

Reaching up, Jennifer slipped her headset off again. "Are we having this conversation now?"

"No?" Audrey tried to keep her tone light. "I mean, we don't have to. I just…I wanted to say it."

For a moment Jennifer looked like she wasn't registering a word Audrey said—then she let her head flop back, made a garbled sound of frustration, lifted her mic to her mouth and said, "Colin, tell Grace I'm going to fucking kill her." Finally she turned back to Audrey. "What did she say to you?"

"She seems to want us to get together," explained Audrey only slightly sheepishly.

"That talentless interfering hack."

The instinct that made Audrey defend more or less anybody Jennifer was having a go at stepped up once again. "I don't think her interest in your love life has much to do with her ability as a presenter."

"Don't you believe it. She's just trying to get in my head so I don't fire her."

Even for one of Jennifer's blasts of drive-by cynicism, that seemed unconvincing. "She said you were friends."

"Grace doesn't have friends. She just has bits that flake off her ego."

Audrey did her best to look sardonic, but it wasn't an expression she'd had much practice with. "Whereas you're surrounded by well-wishers and loved ones?"

"Excuse me, for all you know I have a thriving social life."

"True. But *do you, actually*?"

Jennifer glowered. She had a good glower. "I get by."

"We all get by, Jennifer. But don't you want...I don't know?"

"To date an annoying journalist? Not especially."

Standing up, Audrey took off her headset and put it down on the desk next to Jennifer. "Fine. I tried. See you, I don't know, next time you're threatening to sue the *Echo* I suppose."

Jennifer was silent until Audrey had her hand on the door and then she said, very softly, "Just sit down."

"Pardon?"

"You heard."

"I really don't think I did."

From where she was standing, Audrey could just make out the tension in Jennifer's jaw. "I said, will you please sit down. You've come all this way. You might as well see the day out."

"Might I?" Audrey was still of half a mind to leave. Well, a third of a mind. "Because if you think you're doing me a favour..."

"I would *like* you to stay," clarified Jennifer through clenched teeth.

It would have been churlish to make her say it again, and while Audrey sometimes saw the appeal of churlishness, she didn't want to risk a good thing. So she returned to her seat and wasn't too surprised when Jennifer went straight back to work without saying another word.

+ ✦ ▬▬ ✦ +

Audrey had seen the judging of *Bake Expectations* from two directions already, as a viewer and as a contestant. Seeing it as…whatever she was now, a sort of unofficial adjunct to Jennifer Hallet, was a different experience again.

Here, as in both of her previous perspectives, the process still began with each baker bringing their bake up to the judges to receive their feedback, and then from the contestant's-eye-view there was another round of interminable waiting while the judges made a decision. But from the viewer's position there was a seamless transition to Wilfred, Marianne, and Grace sitting around a table in a lovely, sunny—or sometimes slightly drizzly; this was still England, after all—gazebo talking about how everybody had done and who was safe and who was in danger, which would cut away coyly before they actually reached a conclusion.

Rationally, of course, Audrey knew that the conclusion was going to have been reached long before that spot was filmed. But it was weird seeing it. Especially because they *were* on the cosy table set, just with Jennifer Hallet leaning by a wall glaring and calling the shots.

"I don't care which," she was saying, "just lose a disposable and give me a win for somebody who needs one."

The disposables, it turned out, were Jim, Joshua, Reggie, and either Linda or Meera, because apparently production didn't really need them both.

"Linda did genuinely well this week," Marianne Wolvercote said, "but I don't think she'll make it all the way."

Jennifer frowned. "We can't have the good-but-insecure one going out in the semi though—we did that last year."

"I think"—even off-camera Wilfred Honey didn't quite lose his grandfatherly edge—"that she'll either plateau or crash next week. Might be nice to give her a win before she's out."

That got a nod from Grace Forsythe. "And it'll look like classic winner's curse. I think this week we probably need to give Jim the *We needed to see more* or to give Reggie the *One experiment too many*."

"Did he do one experiment too many?" asked Marianne. "I thought he actually played it fairly safe this week."

"Then he gets the *This should have been your week but you got complacent*?" suggested Audrey, who only realised she probably shouldn't be speaking when it was already substantially too late to stop.

Wilfred Honey looked around. "Sorry, pet, can I just check why you're here?"

To spare Audrey from having to explain herself, but most certainly not to spare her from several different kinds of embarrassment, Grace Forsythe stepped in. "Jennifer wants to get into her pants."

"You are so fucking fired," said Jennifer in a tone that suggested it wasn't the first time she'd said it that series or, indeed, that afternoon.

"Face of the show, darling. Besides you know I'm right. As, for that matter, is our lovely guest—*Sorry you got complacent* works perfectly well as an arc finisher. Although I think it's probably more of a *Drag Race* beat than an *Expectations* one if I'm honest."

Marianne Wolvercote had been nodding along quietly with the discussion. "I think on balance we lose Jim? I don't think he's shown us much." She looked up. "Jennifer, no plans?"

"Nope, can the fucker. And give the win to Linda. I agree with Wilfred that she needs the old"—she mimed something going up, exploding, and crashing. "And make sure you emphasise that Doris has been coming close every week because if she makes it to the final without a win we'll get letters."

"We could give her this week," Wilfred Honey suggested. "She'd deserve it. She made two kinds of gingerbread, and her decoration was good."

Jennifer seemed to be thinking about it, but in the end she shook her head. "No, she might wind up peaking too early. She and the teen need two more wins between them, but we've got space to make that happen. Everybody good?"

Everybody was. Well, everybody with the slight exception of Audrey, who was feeling a little awkward at quite how disillusioning this view of the show was turning out to be.

"Great," said Jennifer. "Action."

And as if it was the most natural thing in the world, Wilfred Honey, Marianne Wolvercote, and Grace Forsythe turned to each other over the little gingham-covered tablecloth and smiled. "Well," said Grace Forsythe, "the contestants have given you a lot to think about this week."

Wilfred Honey gave a deep, knowing nod. "That they have, that they have. Some of them did very well, but there's one or two I've got my concerns about. What do you think, Marianne?"

And so they went on, dancing around a conclusion that everybody present knew they'd already reached. It was sad in a way, being behind the curtain. It was like seeing how a magic trick was done. And, yes, as she'd told Linda, on some level you knew it was all mirrors and wires. That the lady in the box wasn't really sawn in half. That the card wasn't really lost in the pack. But having it confirmed still kind of marred the experience, especially when you weren't quite close enough to appreciate the artistry involved.

With the decision made and the segment in which the decision was meant to be made filmed, Audrey followed Jennifer back to her trailer to monitor the endgame.

Having already watched the baking from a distance, Audrey thought she'd be prepared for watching the elimination, too, but she wasn't. The baking, for all it was a tactile experience, was also a solitary one, so observing everybody from a monitoring station outside the building wasn't that different from observing them from across the ballroom. But the elimination was shared, a joint tension of thinking, *Will it be me?* and *Thank God it wasn't me, Fuck it was me,* or *Sorry, it was you.* And now it felt isolating. Like she'd switched sides.

A week ago, she'd been in the same boat as these people. Today everybody else was still tossing about on the sea while she was safe and warm in some fancy club hanging out with retired admirals.

When Jim was eliminated, everybody hugged him goodbye and trooped outside to do their exit interviews. So for a while Audrey was just left staring at a live feed of an empty ballroom. And then Jennifer rose, pulled on a jacket, and gave Audrey a look that was mostly still daggers, but might have been the trick kind that slid back into the hilt when you stabbed somebody with them.

"Well," she said. "Back to Kansas with you, sunshine." And then after a moment's pause she added, "Thanks for your help."

Audrey stared at her. "Did you just thank me for my help?

"Clearly having your cunt on my face made me a better person."

"Clearly it didn't."

"You're right. Fuck off."

And, for some reason, Audrey was laughing as she left.

WEEK FIVE

Patisserie

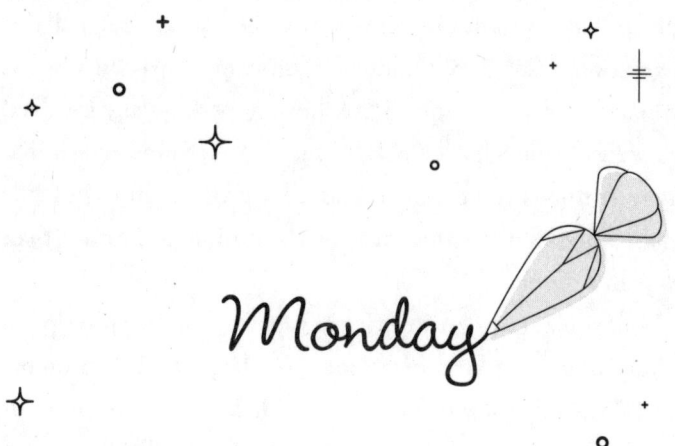

Monday

"THE PROBLEM IS," Ms. Waverly, the custodian of the @bagleybrooktrolleys Instagram account was saying, "that we're at a nexus."

Hoping that she'd explain what that meant without being asked verbally, Audrey gave an encouraging nod and a tell-me-more handwave.

"There's a Spar, a Tesco Express, and a Morrisons in a triangle around us, and for some reason people like to take trolleys from all of them and leave them right in the brook. And I swear I don't know what they're doing with them. Because I'm sure it's nobody that lives nearby, so if the trolleys are full then where are they putting the shopping, and if they're not full then what do they want them for?"

"Probably kids," suggested Eddie, forgetting as usual that the role of the cameraman was to remain silent.

"It probably is kids," Ms. Waverly agreed.

A tiny, ever-so-slightly traitorous part of Audrey couldn't help but feel that a truly excellent journalist wouldn't be running stories to which "kids" was the ultimate solution. Of course, she'd had this conversation with herself hundreds of times in the past. It was just that being on the show, or off the show, or peripherally involved in *Bake Expectations* however she was now, was reminding her that there were things you could do under the broad umbrella of "the media," which felt a whole lot bigger and more important than trolleys in a brook.

"And you've been getting a lot of support," Audrey prompted.

Very much the kind of person to respond well to prompting, Ms. Waverly took it from there. "There's been real community uptake," she said. "I've got over two thousand followers on Instagram now, and there's people submitting pictures from all over Shrewsbury. And further. We got one from Pontesbury the other day."

"And what do you do with the trolleys, once you've found out about them?" asked Audrey.

"Well there's a little band of us now because there's me, and Mr. Waverly—no relation—and Donna that works down the pub. And when we get a message in, one of us will usually head down and see if the trolley is still there, and if it is we'll take it back where it's meant to be."

Audrey nodded again. People liked it when you nodded. It made it seem like you were agreeing with them. "And how many trolleys have you returned since you started?"

Ms. Waverly fell silent a moment. "It's tricky because we've been going since January and we've not kept detailed records, but if I had to put a number on it, I'd say"—she began counting on her fingers—"about six."

Congratulating Ms. Waverly on her triumph against a half dozen inconveniently situated shopping trolleys, Audrey and

Eddie made their way back to the car. As she settled into the driver's seat, Audrey caught herself unconsciously slipping her phone
out of her pocket and checking her messages. She had none. And
she'd expected none. If there was a woman on the face of the planet
who'd wait at a minimum of forty-eight hours after fucking you
before texting, it was Jennifer Hallet.

"Are you okay?" asked Eddie, and the fact that she'd apparently
been demonstrating sufficient not-okay-ness that even he could
spot it made her feel substantially less okay than she hitherto had.

"Yeah," she lied. "Fine."

"Still upset you got kicked off the baking thing?"

Was she going to actually have this conversation? And with
Eddie of all people? Apparently she was. "Honestly, that bit was
okay. But then—there's a whole big thing where some people were
upset because I'd sort of told them the thing was rigged and—"

"Wait, *Expectations* is rigged?"

She had to stop saying that to people. It was becoming clear
that it was the adult equivalent of walking into a primary school
playground and yelling, "Santa is just your parents."

"Not really."

"So why did you say it was?"

"Because it is. Sort of. And also not. Sort of. I mean all those
sorts of shows are."

Eddie seemed to be having a very small crisis. "What about
Strictly?"

"Less rigged, because there's rules about public votes."

"*MasterChef*? *Dragon's Den*?" His face fell still further. "Oh
my God, not *Drag Race*?"

Audrey nodded. "And *Drag Race UK*. Then again, I suppose
you could say—I mean what even counts as 'rigged' when the

whole system is that one person gets to decide who wins based on criteria they get to make up on the spot?"

As an alternative perspective, it didn't seem to be helping Eddie with his existential uncertainty. "It's not made up on the spot. It's based on Charisma, Uniqueness, Nerve and Talent."

"And who gets to decide what Charisma, Uniqueness, Nerve and Talent look like?"

Eddie's mouth worked helplessly for a moment. "I'm not sure I know who I am anymore."

"Anyway"—it seemed best to move the conversation on or back or somewhere that wasn't destroying Eddie's faith in humanity—"I told everybody this, and a couple of them freaked out that they stayed in while I didn't so I had to come back on Saturday and I'm still *sort of* interviewing Doris about the story we probably can't run—"

"The one with too much lesbian sex in it?"

"Yeah, that one. And there wasn't that much lesbian sex in it. Although probably thinking about it, *not that much* is still more than you'd expect in a story about baking and the blitz." Also, Audrey had to privately admit, there had been rather more in the most recent instalment. "Long story short, I sort of wound up banging the producer and now I'm waiting for her to text like I'm fifteen again."

Eddie was making a sympathetic face. "You could text her?"

"Maybe, but I'm worried that will make me seem desperate."

"That's very, *very* fifteen."

It was. Or it might have been. Either way, right *now* Audrey was technically at work. And although Gavin wasn't especially strict about conducting personal business on the *Echo*'s time, pretending he was let Audrey make a decision re: texting that she'd otherwise probably have prevaricated on for much longer. Instead, she put her phone away, started the car, and set off on the twenty-minute drive back to Telford.

Twenty minutes of light conversation with Eddie, it turned out, was not the best thing for Audrey's focus or for her commitment to the importance of local journalism. Eddie had many fine qualities—a surprising level of sensitivity to relationship issues apparently amongst them—but there was no denying that he was also very slightly…inane? Possibly one of the least *ane* people Audrey had ever met.

Which meant the whole trip back to the office, present-day-Eddie, who was very much the same as every other version of Eddie, was happily scrolling through the Instagram feed of @bagleybrooktrolleys and retweeting pictures of discarded supermarket furniture, present-day-Audrey was asking five-years-ago-Audrey to explain why she'd ever thought that this was a good career move.

Sitting at present-day-Audrey's desk cutting together the details of the rogue trolley article into something at least vaguely interesting, five-years-ago-Audrey tried to explain that working for a major outlet on stories that nine times out of ten were just glorified doomscrolling was an incredibly unhealthy place to be. And present-day-Audrey believed her. But she couldn't quite shake the conviction that there should be at least some middle ground between "the world sucks and everything's fucked" and "six trolleys in Bagley Brook."

A middle ground, Natalie asked, *between the nonsense you're doing now and actual journalism?* Gritting her teeth, Audrey got up, sauntered through to Gavin's office, and said as casually as she could manage: "I think we should run the *Expectations* story."

Gavin stared at her between his glasses and his eyebrows. "The story that the very angry, very litigious producer suggested you shouldn't run because it didn't fit with the way the show positions itself in the wider market?"

"The one with too much gay, yeah."

Tapping distractedly on his desk, Gavin frowned. "As I recall, that wasn't how she expressed it."

"It's never how people express these things, but it's how they are."

"However it is"—Gavin was never the kind to display strong emotions, but he was becoming cautiously agitated—"hasn't she made her position perfectly clear?"

"I was hoping I could persuade her to un-perfectly clear it."

Gavin's glasses slid an eighth of an inch down his nose. "And how might you do that?"

Anything for the story, Aur, said Natalie. *Although ideally the story wouldn't be a trite human interest piece.*

"Well the thing is," Audrey began, less confidently than she'd have liked. "You see—we're sort of—I think she likes me."

"Likes in the sense of considers you a valuable journalistic contact with whom she would be well advised to maintain a positive working relationship?" asked Gavin in a tone that anticipated a negative answer.

"No," answered Audrey, negatively.

"Likes in the sense of is sexually and/or romantically attracted to?" he followed up, in a tone which anticipated a response that may or may not be totally honest.

"Kind of," Audrey admitted.

"Is that not…ethically questionable?"

She really, really wished he hadn't gone there. "It's a grey area?" she ask-asserted.

"Is it, in fact?"

Gavin, in Audrey's experience, responded best if you took these kinds of concerns seriously. "I think so, actually?" She sounded less certain than she felt, and she didn't feel especially certain. "I really don't want to play the gender-reversal card, but if she was a man I think playing on the fact he fancied me would be pretty normal? Or at least pretty normalised."

You have him there, said Natalie, in a tone Audrey found worryingly approving.

"Isn't it also the kind of thing we're meant to *stop* normalising?"

Or does he have you? That's the problem with being a quitter—it makes it so hard to stick to your principles.

It was probably a bad idea to double down when you were beginning to regret betting in the first place. "What," Audrey suggested, "if I make it really clear that I intend to sleep with her whether she lets me do this or not?" It seemed like the wrong time to explain that she'd slept with her *already*.

Gavin blinked. "I think that creates a *different* ethical issue."

"Right, but a much, *much* less skeevy one. Like, imagine if she was my wife."

The expression on Gavin's face remained one of unalloyed doubt. "Imagining."

"If we were married, or she was, like, my cousin or something, then that would make it, you know, nepotism, which *I agree is bad*, but not as bad as just pimping myself out for access."

"I worry that's a low bar, speaking in pure journalistic standards terms."

It was. And invested as Audrey might have been in the story, and as convinced as she might have been that there were elements to it that were still worth telling, she wasn't quite sure she wanted "technically not much worse than nepotism" to be her professional legacy. So she quietly agreed that on the whole yes, that was a low bar, and yes, it probably was for the best she drop the whole thing.

She was just about to leave when Gavin looked up at her, readjusted his glasses, and said, "Audrey, I don't mean to pry but...are you happy here?"

There were certain people in your life that you didn't want to ask you if you were happy. Like your partner or your boss. Or your gynaecologist.

"Mostly," said Audrey, realising with a nanosecond's hindsight that *mostly* wasn't the answer a model employee would give.

Gavin motioned for her to sit, and she sat.

"When you started working with us," Gavin began, "I had my concerns that even with your Shropshire roots, a city big shot like yourself might chafe a little at the limitations of local journalism."

"I wasn't really a big shot," demurred Audrey. "Just a pretty run-of-the-mill hack."

Gavin's glasses seemed to be troubling him again. "This is the *Shropshire Echo*—you don't have to be very big around here to be a big shot. And this...this story you keep wanting to do. Well, it makes me worry you're not satisfied."

"I don't think it's that." It was at least a little bit that. "I just—I think I wish I was writing more about people and less about parking."

Gavin frowned. "Audrey, you know how I feel about gratuitous alliteration."

"Sorry."

Resting his chin on his hands, Gavin gave her a sympathetic look. "I do understand. It may shock you to realise this, but very few of us are passionate about covering tailbacks on the A5. And your ghost barge piece really had something."

"Thank you," replied Audrey, partly from instinct but partly out of genuine pride. Gavin, for all his faults, was short and sincere with praise, and if he said an article was good, it was because it was good.

"I'll try to give you your head a bit more," Gavin offered. "And see if we can't steer you towards stories with a bit more"—he waved a hand—"story. You're a fine journalist, Audrey, and I'd like to keep you."

Audrey hadn't felt she'd been sending un-keepy signals. Then again, she hadn't felt she was sending are-you-happy-here signals either, and apparently she had been. That was what happened when you went on TV. It brought things up that you didn't want brought up and made you think about things you were supposed to have stopped thinking about. Which unfortunately didn't leave her much clearer about what to say to Gavin. Because "Don't worry, I intend to work here until I die" was patently disingenuous. Whereas "Actually, you're right, I'm bored shitless" was just ungrateful.

Eventually she settled on "Thanks" and "Sorry I've been a bit off recently" before slinking back to her desk.

Where she sat, doggedly trying to focus on the Bagley Brook trolley story with limited success. Well, no success. And that made her feel even worse.

Good job, Aur, said Natalie.

Maybe if she just—

Quickly.

To get it out of her system.

Slyly, she alt-tabbed away the trolley copy—*"We're at a nexus," says disgruntled local*—and opened another window.

Her   working   theory-slash-excuse   was
that   maybe,   *maybe*   the   reason   this   whole

Doris-Emily-War-Domestic-Service-Sapphic-Romance narrative
had got so firmly stuck in her head was that she didn't know how
it ended. Her whole life Audrey had been a sucker for a serial and
finding out how the story went bit by bit as Doris felt ready to talk
about it was getting flatly torturous. And after all, what was the
point of being an investigative journalist if you couldn't journalis-
tically investigate, even if it was just for your own interest?

So she investigated.

Twenty minutes later, Audrey had a notebook full of leads on
the mysterious Emily Branningham. Or at least on possible Emily
Branninghams. Two were far too young and one was dead but—
and Audrey felt strangely relieved about this—also the wrong age
and from the wrong part of the country.

One, though, was more promising. Not just more promising,
but definitely the right woman. She showed up in two honest-to-
god newspaper articles from the 1960s and 1970s, one of which
had included pictures.

This Emily was older by some ten or twenty years than when
Doris had last spoken of her, and the stories hadn't focused on
detailed physical description, but there was something somehow
unmistakable about her. A no-fucks-given energy that had spoken
to a secret part of Doris more than seventy years ago and spoke to
a secret part of Audrey today.

She was a tall, sharp-eyed woman and, in the picture Audrey
was looking at, wore a pristine white suit and matching trilby as
she leaned on a wall and laughed at some long-forgotten joke with
a man in a loincloth. The photograph, according to the source,
was from a Halloween party at Studio 54 in 1977, and while neither Jennifer's nor Gavin's misgivings had made Audrey second-
guess the wisdom of continuing to dig, that caption did.

Because for all Audrey had a sentimental streak, the more grounded, more practical, more *experienced* part of her couldn't help but wonder how a woman who partied with Warhol and a woman who, as far as Audrey could make out, had lived all her life in either Stepney or Patchley, could possibly be anything but bad for each other.

After all, look at how things had worked out with Natalie.

Thursday

THE PROBLEM, AND this was a very *specific* problem—with being on a televised baking show was that it spilled into life in every possible direction. There were weeks of preparation before, weeks of actually doing it in the middle, and then weeks—well, a week and a half so far—of readjusting afterwards. It helped, of course, if you obsessively pursued something only tangentially baking show related that everyone around you kept telling you not to pursue.

But you still had evenings where you were suddenly a whole lot freer than you'd planned for. If she'd been in London, the hours would have filled up anyway. With work, with Natalie, or with the endless parade of going out that twentysomething Londoners needed to do to prove they existed. Here in Bridgnorth, though, the time was hers. To do whatever she wanted.

Which, Natalie reminded her, *is apparently nothing*.

Peering through the oven door at her lemon and blueberry cupcakes, Audrey was pleased to see that they'd risen nicely and were just the right shade of golden splodged with just the right shade of…blueberry. She slipped on her oven gloves, which because they'd been a not-so-secret Santa gift from Eddie a Christmas back, were printed with photorealistic manatees and was just mid-bend-down-door-open-tray-lift-don't-drop-anything-or-burn-yourself when the intercom buzzed. Then, as she was telling herself it was fine and she should put her cupcakes down carefully and close the oven properly because there was no rush, it buzzed again. And again.

Audrey did not get many urgently buzzing Thursday night visitors. Nor did she have anybody in her life who *would* be an urgently buzzing Thursday night visitor. If there'd been a family emergency her parents would have rung, texted, and emailed all at the same time and they'd done none of them. If it had been Natalie—and it wouldn't be, it couldn't be—but if it *had* been Natalie, suddenly contrite and coming to say, "I'm sorry, Audrey, I fucked up, what will it take to get you back?" she'd still have only buzzed once. She was the sort of person who wouldn't even press the call lift button if somebody else had already pressed it.

Balancing her cupcakes awkwardly, Audrey manatee-handled the intercom handset to her ear and got as far as "He—"

"Open the fucking door," said Jennifer Hallet.

"What? Why?"

"Because I don't want to stand on the fucking street in fucking Shropshire for the rest of the fucking evening."

"Why are you *on* the fucking street in fucking Shropshire?"

"Why do you fucking think?"

Honestly, Audrey had no idea. "You know," she said, "I'm rather enjoying being on the inside of the door for once."

"Yes, yes." Jennifer Hallet orally eye-rolled. "This is a terribly ironic role reversal. Now let me the fuck in."

The sensible thing to do—actually there probably wasn't a sensible thing to do. This wasn't a sensible situation. So Audrey did the thing she wanted instead and buzzed Jennifer up, taking advantage of the seventeen-second window between unlocking the front door and Jennifer Hallet bursting in to put down her cupcakes.

"What the fuck is wrong with your hands?" asked Jennifer.

"You make a baking show. You must know what oven gloves are."

"Why have they got ugly dolphins on them?"

"They're manatees," Audrey explained. "And they were a gift."

"Was it a gift from somebody who hates you?"

"Sorry, did you come here exclusively to swear at me and insult my cookwear?"

"No, I came to fuck you. But I got distracted by the vortex of quirk and cushions that is your life."

Militantly, Audrey stripped off her manatees. "So, what? We should just sit on spikes?"

"Whatever you're into, darling."

"Shall I tell you what I'm not into?" said Audrey, actually wagging an actual finger as she marched, newly de-manateed, from the kitchen to the living area. "I'm not into people showing up on my doorstep unannounced—at…whatever time of the evening this is—while I'm trying to make cupcakes and having a go at my soft furnishings less than a week after they doinked me then told me to fuck off, then gave me mixed signals, then told me to fuck off again."

Audrey's wagging and marching had brought her what would have been chest to chest with Jennifer Hallet had one of them been substantially shorter, the other substantially taller, or there'd been a box involved. As it was, they were more boobs to upper abdomen.

"Are you sure about that, Lane?" asked Jennifer Hallet.

And it turned out Audrey was not sure about it at all. Because while she was pretty certain it was Jennifer who started the kissing—mouths coming together in a hot, frantic whirlwind that felt on just the right side of angry—it was definitely Audrey who slammed into Jennifer so passionately that her satchel slipped from her shoulder, exploding papers everywhere. And then they were both on the floor, kissing and struggling in that reckless desperate way when you were so determined to get close to someone you kept bouncing off them.

"Jesus, woman." Jennifer Hallet sounded completely approving. "You're a fucking animal."

Audrey had both hands buried in Jennifer's hair. "And you're unreasonable, high-handed and…and…really annoying."

Jennifer just laughed, her face—and occasionally her teeth—against Audrey's neck. "You smell like lemons."

"That's because I've been cooking with lemons, you dick. Also…" Wriggling a hand up Jennifer's shirt, Audrey tried to do something sexy and sophisticated, and ended up palming Jennifer's left breast like a horny teenager. "What happened to not talking?"

"I'm not talking. I made one fucking observation."

Jennifer pushed Audrey aside for a brief moment neither of them had the patience for, tearing open her top and dragging Audrey back down on top of her. This did not help the horny teenager situation because Audrey found herself grinding as well as palming.

"Fuck," observed Jennifer, wrapping her legs—those long, long legs—around Audrey and arching up to meet her.

"Fuck," agreed Audrey.

It was probably the least dignified five to ten minutes of Audrey's life and, given how Audrey's life went in general, it was up against some stiff competition. Her glasses kept slipping down her nose. Jennifer's trousers were too tight. Somehow Audrey's apron ended up over her face. One of Jennifer's shoes flew off and did fortunately irreparable damage to the godawful Tiffany-style lamp Audrey had been given by an aunt and always hated. And, really, Jennifer should have been *grateful* for all Audrey's cushions. Because otherwise the whole enterprise would have been hell on elbows, knees, and both their backs.

But it was…it was also kind of amazing. Everything messy and slick and bitey and sweet. The sort of sex you spent your twenties thinking other people were having. Where it didn't matter what you looked like, or what you said, only that your fingers were *there* and her fingers were *there* and her tongue was *there* and now you both smelled of lemons and when you came it was almost defiant. Like you didn't need to be comfortable. Who cared if the angle was bad and your mouth was full of your own hair? It was perfect and lovely and *yours* and *hers*.

"You know something," said Jennifer Hallet when they were done. "I could really go for a cupcake."

Audrey's head was still resting on Jennifer's chest. Her hand was still down her pants. "They're not iced yet."

"Is this the face of a woman who gives a fuck?"

"It should be. You run a baking show."

"So what? The *Game of Thrones* guys didn't know how to sword fight." Jennifer's determination not to do anything even remotely resembling cuddling apparently got the best of her. Rising like a sweaty Venus, she strode into Audrey's kitchenette and ate three lemon and blueberry cupcakes.

"Make yourself at home," said Audrey. "Have something to eat if you like."

Jennifer swept up a fourth cupcake and propped herself louchely in the doorway. "These are good. They'd get you to at least week three."

"Fuck off." Audrey's attempt to throw a cushion across the room was stymied by post-orgasmic weakness and a general lack of coordination.

Apparently, Jennifer Hallet could actually mellow. But only immediately after sex. Only if you fed her cakes. Only for about thirty seconds. And only about two percent. "No, really." She sounded oddly sincere. "They're all right."

"But?"

"But nothing. They're all right."

For some reason, the words weren't quite going in. "Huh," said Audrey.

"Help me out, Lane. Which line of bullshit is this? Is it *Big, bad Jennifer never says anything nice*? Or *Poor ickle Audrey can't believe she made a decent cake?*"

"Neither actually, thanks." Audrey rotated her apron back into its non-fucking position and sat up, with her legs tucked under her. "It's just been a while since I've baked for someone. Not that I technically baked for you. I was baking for the office, and you ran interference."

"Oh, come on. You must do this sort of thing all the time. I bet you show up on dates with a tin of muffins and a dildo."

"I do not show up on dates with a tin of muffins and a dildo."

"Okay, but I bet you made welcome cookies for your neighbours."

She'd thought about it, and then wussed out, and she wasn't

sure whether the thinking or the wussing reflected worse on her. "I probably would have at some point in my life—"

"Hah," said Jennifer. "Knew it."

"But I kind of got out the habit."

"What happened? Did you move to London and decide you'd rather be snorting cocaine off an art student's taint with some prick who works for Morgan Stanley?"

Audrey boggled and goggled at the contortions required to do any of those things. "How would you even do that? Like, logistically?"

"It's easy." Jennifer shrugged. "London's full of investment bankers."

"Well, no." Probably best to leave the taints and bankers in the city where they belonged. "None of that really. I mean, I did cocaine once because it seemed rude not to. But just off, you know, a table?"

"Audrey Lane, are you really telling me you did a Class A drug out of politeness?"

"I think politeness and wanting to fit in?"

Jennifer was laughing. "Oh my God, you got peer pressured like you're a needlessly didactic subplot in *Grange Hill*."

"Shut up. I'm sorry my cocaine use wasn't cool enough for you."

"And that's why you stopped baking for people?"

"What?" Audrey's head was spinning slightly. Too much sex and too much Jennifer. "Because I did cocaine once?"

"Wanting to fit in."

"Mmm…a little bit. But more…" It was surprisingly difficult to talk about. Maybe because Audrey hadn't realised there was something *to* talk about. She hugged her knees. "My girlfriend wasn't into it."

"And she made you stop?"

"She didn't *make* me. We were just very busy. And it didn't feel very productive. And it wasn't worth the—the…" Audrey ran aground, trying to describe the quiet wasteland that was Natalie's disapproval. "The hassle?"

There was a long silence. Jennifer looked typically glowery but atypically solemn. And, for once, she seemed to be glowering at something that wasn't Audrey. "So you stopped baking because of your ex. And then you decided the best way to get back into baking was to go on the nation's biggest, most successful, and most competitive amateur baking programme?"

Put like that, it sounded bonkers. "I mean I *was* drunk when I applied."

There was another long silence. Then Jennifer crossed the room in two long steps, dropped to her knees on the cushions, and kissed Audrey's very surprised mouth. "You are a bizarrely impressive woman, Audrey Lane."

"Thanks?" said Audrey.

"Anyway," continued Jennifer, setting some kind of kissing to dismissing speed record. "I should be off."

"You could…not," suggested Audrey.

"Aye. But I'm going to." Jennifer was already stuffing her thoroughly scattered and somewhat rolled on papers back into her bag. "And we should really stop doing this."

"We won't though, will we?"

"No. Probably not." Throwing her satchel over her shoulder, Jennifer retrieved her shoes and snatched one last cake from the kitchen. "See you around, Lane."

Then she vanished into the night like hot, sweary mist.

Friday

IN THEORY, THE most important thing Audrey had to do that Friday, apart from distributing what remained of her lemon and blueberry cupcakes to a gratifyingly enthusiastic office, was write a short piece about a product recall on lasagne sauce at a local supermarket.

In practice, she had to do that, decide how much deeper she wanted to dive into Emily Branningham, and work out what the fuck it meant that Jennifer Hallet showing up at her flat for sex was just a thing that could happen now.

Half-past-ten-Audrey was pretty delighted about it. Because having cool no-strings hookups with an awesome sexy TV lady who said nice things about you made you a cool and awesome person.

Quarter-to-twelve-Audrey hated herself. Because while she was very much in favour of people's right to have casual sex if they wanted to, being in the particular kind of casual sex relationship where it all happened on somebody else's terms was not something she wanted to be okay with.

Five-past-one-Audrey was mostly concerned with whether "Local Supermarket Recalls Lasagne Sauce" would read as too vague to a general audience and/or if "Lasagne Sauce Recalled Over Contamination Risk" would read as too sensationalist to Gavin.

Two-thirty-Audrey had been through the options with Gavin (he *had* thought it was sensationalist but eventually accepted that the public health concern justified the stronger language) and was back to feeling smug about getting laid and idly seeing if she could get any more information about the mysterious Emily.

Four-o'clock-Audrey was relatively sure that she'd found as much out about Emily as she'd be able to without taking the bigger, scarier step of contacting actual living women to see if they were the right person, and was sliding back into feeling taken for granted, sex-wise.

Five-thirty-Audrey was far more exhausted than she usually was at that time in the afternoon.

Quarter-past-six-Audrey returned to her still fuck-ravaged flat and realised that as well as the lasagne sauce and the elusive aristocrat and her suddenly complicated love life, she also had a bunch of cleaning up to do.

It was gratifying, in a way. To know that even in her (whisper it) early thirties she could still have the kind of sex that overturned furniture and did away with ugly lamps. At least it *should* have been gratifying. Audrey tried very hard to be gratified. But as she swept up little bits of coloured glass and transferred them to the recycling bin, she was conscious of a growing sense of ungratifiedness.

If there had been one thing that had drawn Audrey to journalism more than any other—well, more than any other except the fact that the then love of her then life had decided on the career for both of them when she was about twelve—it had been the lure of the follow-up question. Natalie had been different. For her, it had always been about *Truth* with a capital *T*. Where are the bodies buried and who buried them and who paid for the shovels? But all Audrey had ever really wanted to do was to ask what happened next?

And on that score, both Doris and Emily's home front romance and what she was increasingly thinking of as "the Jennifer situation" were leaving her profoundly frustrated.

Of course, both of those frustrations had, on some level, a common remedy. She could get in her car, drive to Patchley, ask Doris to tell the next part of her story, and demand that Jennifer at least have a conversation re: what the fuck was going on between them.

She could also stick her face in a beehive, and it would be about as likely to end well.

With the wreckage of the Tiffany-style lamp dealt with and Lion the tortoise returned to his proper place on the armchair, Audrey was just ready to declare the tidying done when she noticed a little box half-slid under the coffee table.

It was small, red, rectangular, and had Jennifer Hallet's name printed quite plainly on the side.

Not being a pharmacist, Audrey couldn't say exactly what it was for—and googling felt way, *way* too intrusive—but she did suspect that leaving your medication at somebody else's house was a problem, and that if you knew that a hypothetical somebody had found the hypothetical medication you had left at their hypothetical house, you would probably, hypothetically, want them to bring it back.

She's a highly successful woman, Natalie pointed out, *with an enormous staff working for her. She doesn't need you running her errands. She doesn't need anything from you at all.*

A tiny, self-loathing part of Audrey agreed. On a rational level it was completely impossible that Jennifer would feel less inconvenienced by Audrey showing up unannounced than she would by having to send a minion to pick something up. If Audrey *did* decide to make the long drive to Surrey, that part of her continued, she'd be doing it for purely selfish reasons and shouldn't pretend otherwise.

Nevertheless, despite its protestations, that part of Audrey was carried along with the rest of Audrey when she grabbed the box, stuffed it into her bag, and set out for Patchley House.

She arrived somewhat earlier than last time and found that nobody challenged her as she parked, de-carred, and set out once more for Jennifer's trailer. Having been to Patchley three times as a contestant and once as an invited-if-sworn-at guest, Audrey felt a bit odd showing up now as—technically, at least—an intruder.

It felt even odder when she banged on Jennifer's door and wasn't immediately told to fuck off.

"What is it Co—hang on, I know that knock."

"Hi," offered Audrey, a little weakly.

There was a longer beat than usual before Jennifer came back with, "What the fuck are you doing here?"

"You, um, you left something at my place."

"If it's my pants you can call it a swap."

Ah yes, she'd never actually got those back, had she? "No. It's more sort of—I'd rather not say outside because it's a little bit sensitive."

"Oh, right," Jennifer's voice was beginning to skew sarcastic again. "You mean it's my prescription antidepressants."

Audrey nodded, then realised nodding was a purely visual form of communication and said, "Yes."

"Grand. I've been looking for those. Come in."

So Audrey came in. It was a bit disorienting to actually be invited instead of ordered or ignored. Inside, she found Jennifer sitting at her desk as usual, in the middle of doing something complex to footage.

Without further comment, Jennifer held out a hand, and Audrey fished in her bag for the little red box.

"Thanks," said Jennifer, taking it. And then after she'd left Audrey to stand in silence for three seconds, she continued, "You going to ask?"

Normally when Jennifer was gnomic, Audrey didn't have much patience for it. But she tried to be patient this time. "If you mean, *am I going to ask what specific condition you're medicating for* then no. I don't think so, actually."

"Suit yourself." Jennifer returned her attention to her monitors. "But since you're probably wondering anyway—"

"I'm really not."

"—I'm on a low-dose SSRI for anxiety. No idea if it helps, but I'm used to it. Up to you if you think that explains why I'm such a bitch."

"Again, could have expressed that without using a gendered insult," replied Audrey, feeling that they'd both be more comfortable if the conversation went back to more familiar ground.

"Fuck off."

Audrey hovered. In a way, fucking off was probably what she should be doing. Except since she'd tacitly admitted to herself that bringing Jennifer her pills had been a thinly disguised excuse to see her and maybe talk and/or bang, it seemed cowardly to back out now.

"While I'm here…" she began.

Jennifer looked around, a deep suspicion settling onto every part of her face that suspicion could reasonably settle on. "Yes?"

"Well—the thing is—you know how I sort of quit baking for a while because…"

"Because of your ex?" Jennifer rolled her eyes. "Fuck, is this because I called you impressive? If so, I fucking take it back."

This was going less badly than Audrey had feared. Actually now she thought about it, it had been going less badly than she'd feared for a while. She'd even been let into the trailer without the usual twenty minutes of sexually charged hostility. "No, it's not that. It's just…one of the things about that particular ex was that she wound up making me feel like I was the junior partner in the relationship. And I really don't want to be going there again."

"Hold it, Lane"—Jennifer had swivelled fully around to face Audrey and extended an admonishing finger—"we do not have a *relationship*. We just…we sometimes fail to not fuck."

There was a framing issue there that Audrey felt could be revisited at a later date. "Right, but at the moment it feels a bit like it's more that you fail to not fuck me, and I think I'd quite like to be able to fail to not fuck you at some point."

Jennifer checked an imaginary watch. "I've got ten minutes if you have."

Even though she'd been expecting Jennifer to try to shock her, Audrey was still a little bit shocked. Not by the suggestion, so much as by how little swearing or telling her to leave had gone with it. "I mean in general."

"I mean in particular. We're both busy women—we need to line up our windows where we can."

An unhelpfully easily distracted part of Audrey's brain suggested that there wasn't anything she needed to say now that she *couldn't* also say after a short sex break. But she tried her best to ignore it. "I'm serious."

"So am I."

Suspecting that she might need to conserve energy for an argument, Audrey leaned against the wall in a way she hoped looked casual. "Really, though. I need to know that this isn't going to consist entirely of you showing up on my doorstep and saying, 'I'm horny, let's bone.'"

Jennifer looked Audrey up and down, then made a show of examining her immediate surroundings. "Sorry, who is in whose workplace right now?"

"That's different," Audrey replied, only afterwards realising that she couldn't quite articulate why.

"Is it?"

"I was doing you a good turn. I wasn't just showing up to—"

"To say, 'I'm horny let's bone'?" asked Jennifer in a tone that suggested she'd rather never hear or speak that particular combination of words ever again.

"Exactly."

Jennifer shrugged. "You could have done that, though."

"Sorry. What?" This was veering further and further off-script as they went. Audrey had come in expecting to be told to leave, repeatedly. Not to be told that she could come back any time for a casual hookup.

"I mean, I never said this had to be one way. There is absolutely nothing stopping you showing up at my office and saying,

Hi, I'm at a bit of a loose end, do you fancy bending me over and fucking me so hard I piss myself'?"

"I'm not sure I'd put it quite like that."

"Well"—Jennifer gave a you-do-you gesture—"you can always take your pants off again."

"That was once. And there was context. And, for the record, I'm not super into the hard fucking thing?"

"Oh? Good to know."

"I mean," Audrey babbled, "a finger's fine. But…I don't really like. Anything more. Or hard. In there. It just feels weird."

"Then say, 'I'm at a bit of a loose end, do you fancy bending over and I'll fuck you so hard you'll piss yourself'?"

Okay, off-script no longer covered it. "Must there be piss involved?"

"No, Audrey." It was Jennifer's most sardonic voice and most sardonic face, both of which were extremely sardonic. "The piss is optional."

"Okay, good." And then the traitorous part of Audrey that hated her and didn't want her to have nice things seized control of her vocal chords and added, "But you don't actually mean it, though?"

"You're really hung up on this piss thing aren't you?"

"Not the piss," Audrey kind of yelled. Realising a fraction too late that Jennifer was taking the—well, taking the mickey. "You wouldn't really be okay if I showed up at your workplace and was like, 'Do you want to have sex now?'"

"Try me," suggested Jennifer.

"Now?"

"Well isn't that what all this is about?"

"But what if you're busy or…or not in the mood or…"

"Then I'll say, 'I'm busy,' or, 'Not in the mood.' This isn't complicated. Don't make it complicated."

Jennifer was right. There was no need to make this complicated. And while Audrey wasn't keen on being used for sex, having a mutual using-for-sex agreement felt a lot more equitable.

Also hot.

"Okay," she said. "I'm at a loose end."

After what wound up being slightly more than ten minutes of disarranging Jennifer's sheets (although this time they had at least removed the quilt to a safer distance), Audrey got up, smoothed out her dress, and made polite I-should-be-going noises.

"Will you be around for the weekend?" asked Jennifer with way more casualness than she'd earned.

"Isn't that your call?"

Jennifer gave her a look of infuriating nonchalance. "The Lodge is booked for the whole run. You can have your room if you want it."

Chances were, this was as close to an invitation as Audrey was going to get. "Yeah," she said, "okay."

"Besides, I assume you'll want to catch up with the granny."

Okay, maybe *that* was as close to an invitation as she was going to get. "I thought you told me to stop doing that."

Jennifer was still radiating a studied apathy. "Where you're concerned, Lane, I've learned that telling you not to do things doesn't get me very far."

Studied apathy was not in Audrey's repertoire. She stared at Jennifer so hard it was practically a gawp. "Seriously? You're letting me do this?"

"I'm admitting I can't be fucked to stop you."

"Jennifer," Audrey exclaimed, a little embarrassed at how glee-ful she sounded. "I would hug you but—"

"But I'd bite your fucking nose off."

Audrey touched her nose protectively. "I mean, I wasn't going to say that specifically. But basically yes."

"I do get it." Postcoital-Jennifer was definitely the most rea-sonable Jennifer. "I know there's a story here and I know you want to follow it. I can't let you publish it, though."

This was more than Audrey had ever expected and was begin-ning to sound almost disturbingly out of character. "Who are you and what have you done with Jennifer Hallet?"

"What can I say, you wore me down. Blame the sex."

All things considered, Audrey would rather *not* have blamed the sex. That—as she and Gavin had discussed at length—went to some bad places integrity-wise. "Can I blame something else instead?" she asked. "Like my infuriating but secretly charming persistence?"

Jennifer Hallet hauled herself out of bed, made rather less effort to tidy herself up than Audrey had made, and went back to her desk. "If you like. Just keep me in the loop."

Deciding that it was best to quit while she actually *was* ahead for once, Audrey left Jennifer to whatever important producer work she had to do and returned to her room for a shower. If she was going to talk to Doris, and since it was actually still pretty early in the evening, there wasn't really much reason *not* to talk to Doris, it would be polite to do so while not smelling intensely of fuck.

"Is everything all right?" asked Doris when Audrey knocked on her door.

"Yes," said Audrey, and then feeling at least some need to explain she added, "it's Audrey."

The door creaked open an inch. "Still around then?"

"Yeah. I think Jennifer sees me as some kind of lucky charm."

"I think it's simpler than that dear," replied Doris. "I think she just likes you. Now, what do you want?"

That was probably more of an essay question than it had been intended to be. "Lots of things, but mostly I...I guess I just want to hear more about your life. If there's any more to tell."

"I'm nearly a hundred," Doris pointed out. "There's always more to tell."

Which made Audrey feel awful, because as fully-rounded a person as she knew Doris was, there was a very specific more she was interested in. "I was actually wondering..."

"If there was more to tell about Her?" asked Doris, with audible capitalisation.

And Audrey just nodded, a little abashed.

The door closed. And for a moment Audrey worried that she'd blown it. Or perhaps not even blown it, just unnecessarily upset a nice old lady who'd done nothing to really deserve upsetting. Not that anybody deserved upsetting, really.

After a moment, though, it opened again and Doris stood there looking—not quite grave, but serious. "You'd better come in."

So Audrey came in. Much like in Jennifer's trailer there was nowhere to sit but the bed, so that's where Audrey sat, with Doris next to her looking straight ahead. And for a while they remained quiet, Audrey not wanting to speak and Doris looking for words.

"I know how you feel," said Doris. "Because it gets you like that. *She* gets you like that. I've not thought about her—no, that's a lie—I've not *talked* about her in years, but now I have, she's everywhere all over again."

"I'm sorry," replied Audrey. And she was. Although not so sorry that she didn't also want to hear whatever it was Doris was going to tell her next.

"Don't be. It's been good in a way, remembering. And as it happens I did see her again, after I left Patchley. Just a couple of times."

And Audrey sat quietly and listened.

JUNE 1953

I'D KNOWN BOBBY Rice for years. Grown up together. And when I come back from Patchley and I still weren't married and he still weren't married, it got to be what you might call inevitable. I liked him well enough, and he liked me well enough and all, and in them days there come a point where if you wasn't married folks wanted to know why, especially for a girl.

Happiest day of your life is what they say, isn't it? Always struck me as funny, that did. Because if your wedding's the happiest you ever get, then, well, don't that mean it's all downhill from there? And maybe that's how it is for some, but it weren't like that for me. I was all nerves that morning with my stomach going in knots like I'd ate a bad eel and my mum and aunties telling me it would all be okay and me not really believing them.

It was, of course, in the end. Most things are.

I don't remember much of the service. We got married in church because everybody did, though I'm not sure if either of us believed in very much of anything, and we had pictures took outside. I've still got them on my mantelpiece at home, and one of my granddaughters come to me a few years ago for a copy because she wanted to have a set going as far back as she could go. So I had some run up for her and all.

Most days I don't notice they're there, the pictures. But when I do see them, really see them, I get all caught up and stopped short and feeling like—well, like nothing, really. That's what's odd about it. I look at that picture and it's like a girl I never was.

She looks happy, though, and I'm glad for her. And I know she'll go on to have a good life.

I don't want to—I'm making this sound like there was something wrong with Bobby, and there weren't. He was a good husband, a good dad, a good granddad. He never got to see the great-grandkids, but if there is a heaven or whatever, I'm sure he's looking down and proud of them. Though if he's looking down at me—at me right here right now talking to you—I don't know what he'll be thinking.

Because the thing is—the girl in them pictures—she feels like a different girl because she *is* a different girl. Not because of how long ago it was, least not just because of that. But because who I was with Bobby and who I am now, talking to you. Who I was with Emily back when. They're different.

And thinking about it, I don't know if I made that as clear as I should've. 'Cause the thing is, I've not ever said nothing about this. Not to nobody. Especially not to my husband. I mean, what would I say? That I'd never love him the way I loved her? What'd be the point of that? It'd be cruel. So if you're listening, Bobby, if you are up there or out there or something, I'm sorry you had to hear it. Least I saved it until after you was gone.

But I'm getting away from myself, ain't I? I'm just trying to explain that this isn't about Bobby, not at all really. He was a good man and we had a good life together and when I look back I'd have not chosen another but—well—I suppose that's where we came in.

It was my wedding day, and I was all twists and fidgets and I'd come to think that I was losing my mind a bit or at least that my eyes was playing tricks on me, because I kept thinking I saw her. Just on the street, in the crowd, on the telly sometimes if they was doing a bit about Ascot or one of them other things that the gentry likes to get in on. And I don't know if it'd been fear or hope or regret but as we got closer and closer to the moment, I kept wanting to see her so badly.

And then I did.

I was walking down the aisle, proper done up for the day, sixpence in my shoe and all, which were a bit uncomfortable, but tradition is tradition and I reckoned we'd need a bit of luck what with everything, and I caught a glimpse of her face out the corner of my eye.

Well, for the moment I figured it was just my imagination, like it had been every other time so far, but when I got back to the altar I looked again, really looked, glad the veil meant nobody could see my face.

It was her. I knew it was real because she didn't look like I'd expected her to look. It'd only been a couple of years since I'd last seen her but that was the thing with Emily—there were worlds inside her. And you never knew what she was going to be next.

I think maybe, her being there, that might have been why I didn't remember much about the ceremony. The vicar said some things and Bobby said some things and I said some things and then we was outside getting our pictures done and all I could think of was her face. How she'd been watching me like I was—it's hard to describe—like I was letting her down somehow.

We had the reception in a pub down the end of the road. It was back before everything was chains and my old man knew the landlord so we'd got a good rate on the whole do, and I was trying to just be happy, but now I'd seen her—and I knew I had, that it weren't just my head like—I couldn't stop thinking about her.

So there I was in my white dress, standing around while everybody said how lovely I looked and how happy I must be and everything folk say at weddings, and all as I really wanted to do was find her. 'Cept I didn't know where to look, or even if she were still around.

A bit after sunset I slipped outside for a smoke—I know, I know, but it was 1953 and things was different—and she was there. I remember it had been a hot day so the cool of the pub wall behind me was a welcome change and I was just leaning there trying to enjoy it when I saw her, standing a little way back and watching me with them bright-as-onyx eyes she had.

And she said, "Hello, nymph," like nothing had happened and no time had passed.

Fool that I was I nodded and said, "Milady," like that was still who we were to each other. Like she was still my mistress, or still my...my whatever she'd been.

Then she said—and you'll forgive my language but it's what she said and while I don't remember much else I remember this part clear as day—"What the fuck do you think you're doing?"

"What do you mean?" I asked. And looking back I wish I'd asked all defiant-like, that I'd said it forceful and proud. But I didn't. I talked like a servant.

"This," she said, waving a hand at me and my dress and the pub as if it explained everything. "What are you doing with...all of *this*?"

"I'm getting married," I told her. "I've just *got* married. You was there."

"Just because I saw it"—she was smiling at me, the way she did when she thought I was being an idiot—"doesn't mean I believed it. I *know* you, nymph. I know this isn't what you want."

The bitter thing was that she weren't wrong. Because what I wanted—what I'd always wanted since I were a little girl—was *her*. But I couldn't tell her that, so I lied and said, "It is."

She stepped closer to me then, and even though I was only an hour and a bit out from my wedding, my whole body was screaming for her to touch me. So I didn't move when she reached up and started undoing my hair from how it'd been put up for the church. "This," she said as she smoothed it out over my shoulders, "this is you."

I was trembling all over, wanting to go back in to my family and my husband, or wanting to run away and hide, or wanting to just take her and kiss her there and then, and not knowing which wanting to listen to. "You just let me go," I told her. And I think I sounded stronger, then, than I had. Though maybe that's just memory being kind to me.

And that did stop her, because—and I'm not proud of this—I didn't often stand up to Emily, and when I did, she was, well, she didn't always take it the same way. And the way she took it this time was to ask, "What choice did I have?"

"You could have said something. You could have told Sir Arthur that…I don't know, that it was okay, that you wanted me to stay."

"And how do you think that would have gone?" She had that you-bloody-idiot look again. "You think my father would have said, 'Oh well then, you can carry on fucking my daughter'?"

"Don't talk like that," I said at once, but she only laughed.

"Does it not strike you as odd that *talking* is the one thing I do with my tongue that you object to?"

"Don't be dirty."

She raised an eyebrow. It was something she'd learned to do young—I reckon she'd seen it in movies. "I think you rather like it when I'm dirty."

And now she was standing close to me again, and my heart was going like the clappers. "You ain't being fair."

"Fair is for small people, and you, my nymph, have never been a small person."

It was getting hard to breathe now. In what I'd have thought once was a good way, would still have said was a good way if I'd not been in a wedding dress with my husband on the other side of a pub wall. "Small's all I've ever wanted to be. You was the one wanted—"

"Everything?" There was something about the way she said it that made it sound…well…like everything. Like a promise and a secret and a dream all wrapped up together. "Come *on*, nymph, what sounds better to you, really? What's in there"—she put her hand on the wall beside my head, which I took as her way of talking about Bobby and the reception and the life it all meant—"or what's out here?" And now her hand came down, brushed the side of my jaw, and turned my chin towards her, and she kissed me.

It must seem such a little thing to you, your generation being your generation and mine being mine, but you need to understand that them words—*and she kissed me*—they weren't words I'd ever said until I met you, until you got me to talk about this. It's something I've not even wanted to think of most days. How it was and what it meant. Looking back at it now, I feel like, you know,

that poem about that bloke what's getting old and there's this girl
he kissed he's still thinking of and it's this whole important thing
for him? It's like that.

"I'm married," I said when I could manage to say anything.

"Most of the best lovers are."

"That's a terrible thing to say."

I felt her smiling against my lips. "Is it, or does it tempt you
just a little?"

"Tempt me to do what?"

Her hand strayed to my waist. "Come with me."

For an instant, I let her fill my head with possibilities. For a
little bag of moments it was a fairy tale and she'd come to whisk me
away on her white horse, or at least in a car that she stole from her
dad. Except it weren't, it were just me and her out back of a pub in
Stepney. "I can't."

"You can. You can do anything you want."

"I'm married," I told her for what must have been the third
time, though I wasn't counting.

"Married people do things like this all the time, and if it really
bothers you, that's what annulments are for." She ran her fingers
through my hair and I shivered. "I'm rich, nymph. Honestly I'm
quite *disgustingly* rich. Which means I can do what I like, and it
turns out I want to do it with you beside me."

It was wonderful to hear, and terrible, and a little tiny bit of
me was angry. "Where was this two years ago?"

She looked—not sorry, not really, Emily never looked sorry,
but regretful. "I'm not saying I didn't make mistakes."

"Then what are you saying?" And I was challenging her now,
more than I ever had.

"I'm saying that he can't offer you anything."

I'll always stand up for them as I care about, and whatever Emily may have thought, I cared for Bobby. "He can offer me safety. He can offer me family. And he loves me."

She kissed me again then, quick and soft, just a peck on the lips. "But do you love him?"

"I do," I told her. It were the second time I'd said those words that day, but they meant more then, in a way.

Pressing herself closer against me, she dropped her voice almost to a whisper. "Does he make you feel the way I make you feel?"

I couldn't get the words out, but I couldn't lie neither, so I shook my head.

"Then *come with me*."

My mouth was dry and my head was aching, and I could still taste Emily on my lips and my wedding dress felt like a prison all of a sudden. I felt myself nodding, heard my own voice—not much more than a breath—saying *yes*.

And then I heard myself say "If…"

And I heard her say, "Anything."

And I said, "Tell me you love me."

And she said—she said nothing.

So I had my answer.

There were tears in my eyes when I turned away from her. And when I ran back inside, Bobby asked me what was wrong, and I said I was afraid. And he said so was he.

I never loved him the way I did her, but I loved him for that.

Saturday

IT WAS STRANGE to Audrey, in a way, how quickly she'd settled into a new pattern. Rather than eating with the contestants, she'd got up and gone straight to Jennifer's trailer where they'd shared a breakfast of coffee and bacon rolls, brought to them by an unquestioning Colin Thrimp. And then instead of being herded into the ballroom to watch Grace Forsythe's introduction from an uncomfortable stool upholstered with stress, she watched it over a closed-circuit feed.

"Welcome back, welcome back," Grace Forsythe was saying to the remaining six competitors. "This is the fifth week of the eighth season of *Bake Expectations* and in keeping with our back-to-basics theme, our ever-wise production team has chosen to dedicate it to a style of baking that is famously complex and technically demanding. But don't worry, I'm sure they know what they're doing."

Jennifer pushed a button. "Knock it off, Grace."

And in the ballroom, Colin Thrimp echoed that *knock it off* to the talent, who promptly ignored him.

The blind bake for the fifth week of the eighth season of *Bake*

Expectations was custard slices. Which to be fair to the production crew *was* about as close to back to basics as you could get while still keeping a patisserie theme.

It still felt distancing to be watching from, well, from a distance, but now that the initial shock of elimination was a fortnight behind her, Audrey was beginning to find she preferred it. As a way of forcing herself to get back into baking post-Natalie, the show had been great. But now it was behind her she could admit she didn't miss the stress or the waiting around or the judging or the competitiveness or constantly feeling like she was letting herself down because she had this great opportunity she wasn't super focused on.

By contrast watching the footage as it came in was almost soothing. If there was one thing that had attracted Audrey to journalism more than anything else, it was that it let her elevate her love of people watching to the status of a career. But in some ways having a producer's-eye-view of a reality TV show was even better. Something she'd always admired about *Expectations*, about the whole genre really, was the way it created a narrative from whatever footage its still-mostly-unscripted subjects managed to produce.

And, from here, even more than in the ballroom, she could see the stories coming together. There was Alanis tackling every challenge like it was her GCSEs, and Reggie, tackling every challenge like it was a prototype rocket engine, and Joshua, tackling every challenge like it wasn't a challenge at all. There was Linda, already beginning to panic. And Meera who never panicked about anything. And Doris, of course, who the nation would love but never know.

Every so often Audrey would glance away from the monitors and look over at Jennifer, only to see her watching, totally focused, breaking her silence periodically to issue an instruction or—because even in her element she was still Jennifer Hallet—an insult.

From some quiet, almost domestic impulse, Audrey rolled her chair sideways and leaned her head against Jennifer's shoulder.

"What are you doing?" Jennifer asked with, in the circumstances, much less hostility than she could have.

Audrey took a deep, relaxing breath. "Just enjoying the company."

"You're the fucking worst, Lane."

But despite how much the worst Audrey was, Jennifer let her stay where she was. And they remained that way until filming broke that evening.

"Right," said Jennifer with grim professional finality. "That's that." She pressed another button and spoke into another microphone. "Colin, Audrey'll be needing food as well—sort something."

Audrey wasn't quite sure how she felt about getting her evening meal delivered by an underling or, more pertinently, how she felt about her evening meal being delivered by an underling without her really being consulted about it. "Actually…" she began.

"Hold on, Colin." Jennifer swivelled around to face Audrey. "Are you rushing off?"

"No, not exactly. I just—how about if…as well as failing to not fuck we also sort of failed to not have dinner together?"

Jennifer's eyes narrowed. "You'd better not be trying to date me, Lane. That's not the arrangement."

"No, no." Audrey shook her head perhaps a touch too exaggeratedly. "Just thought maybe eating somewhere that wasn't a dingy trailer might make a nice change?"

"Excuse me, this isn't dingy. It's practical."

"It's practical for being the supreme overlord of a reality TV show," Audrey pointed out. "It's not very practical for, y'know, eating in. You don't even have a table that isn't covered in…in telly stuff."

"I'm busy. I eat at my desk."

"And I ate at your desk this morning. But we can't live on bacon rolls and stress."

"Can. Have. Do."

This needed a different approach. "Okay then. *I* can't live on bacon rolls and stress, so I'm going into the village, and I'm going to eat somewhere that's actually nice. You're welcome to join me."

And while Jennifer didn't say yes, she did get up, grab her bag, and follow.

It was late enough in the day that the eateries of Crinkley Furze had opened, traded, and then closed again, which meant that Audrey and Jennifer's choices for dinner were restricted to the village's two pubs, the Duke's Arms and the Rusty Badger.

"Overpriced crap?" asked Jennifer, indicating the Badger. "Or just regular crap?" She indicated the Duke's Arms.

Audrey gave a smile that was just shy of a smirk. "You make them both sound so tempting. Let's go overpriced, I'm sure we can afford it."

The Rusty Badger was the studied kind of rustic, the sort of place that had tables where you could still count the rings from the tree and chairs that felt hand-carved but almost certainly weren't. Running her eyes down the menu, Audrey was pleased to see it fell on the acceptable side of rip-off, which meant her only problem now was working out how to navigate dinner with a foulmouthed, habitually confrontational workaholic she'd spent more time fucking than talking to.

"So," tried Audrey, "this is nice."

"I'm beginning to think I should have stuck with the bacon."

"Just trying to get the ball rolling."

Jennifer's gaze was momentarily withering. "And you decided to start with 'This is nice'?"

"It worked, didn't it?" Audrey pointed out, determinedly unwitherable.

"It did not. It was shit."

"But you are actually speaking to me."

"Only about how shit your opening line was."

Under normal circumstances if you went on a date—not that this was a date—and it started with the woman you were not-on-a-date with telling you that you were shit at mouth words, it would be a bad sign. Of course, maybe the fact Audrey wasn't seeing it as a bad sign was, in fact, a bad sign. "And how would you have started?" she asked.

"I'd have said"—Jennifer withered harder—"'Given the myriad challenges facing the world today and the existential absurdity of living a finite life in an endless cosmos, how about we shut the fuck up and eat?'"

"Is 'shut the fuck up' and verb your rule for all interactions?"

"Yes," said Jennifer Hallet.

"Okay." Audrey glanced at the menu. "Do you want to split the cassoulet?"

"Do I want to what?"

"They do a cassoulet that serves two. Do you want to split it?"

"Sure." Jennifer made a subtle but unmistakably commanding gesture towards a waiter and, when he hurried over, immediately said, "We'll have the cassoulet, a coffee, and…" She gave Audrey a pointed look.

"Glass of the house red," said Audrey. And then when the waiter had gone added, "Well that was very take-charge of you."

"You're the one who said get the cassoulet."

Audrey looked at Jennifer coyly over her glasses. "Not complaining. It was very sexy and domineering."

"Oh fuck off."

"Really, I'm feeling very into you right now."

"Can it, Lane."

And because there was something in Jennifer's voice—something that wasn't quite her usual snarling confidence—Audrey canned it. "Jennifer, are you okay?"

"I'm fine. Why wouldn't I be? I'm having glorified bean soup in a second-rate gastropub with the most frustrating woman I've met in my entire life. And, may I remind you, I work with Grace Forsythe."

"All of which you've chosen to do."

"Chosen's a strong word. We had a limited budget for season one and Grace is so desperate to stay relevant she'll work for gin and peanuts."

This was pretty typical Jennifer evasion. But she didn't normally seem this uncomfortable. And that was complicated, because Audrey didn't want to be viewing every interaction she had with Jennifer through the lens of a low-dose SSRI. But also, you shouldn't ignore people's context. And Jennifer's context was that she preferred standing behind a camera being inventively rude to people to, for example, talking about her feelings. Or about anything. At least anything she couldn't control. Which made the show a pretty safe topic. And Audrey, sap that she was, wanted Jennifer to feel safe.

"Oh, come on," she said. "*Expectations* is too well put together for me to believe that you didn't pick Grace for a reason."

"I told you. She was cheap."

"And?"

"And"—Jennifer sighed—"she tests well. She's got a good relationship with the BBC. The public loves her. The contestants love her. And for all she's a washed up, pretentious, overrated, pseudo-intellectual luvvieish fame junkie, she's got strong instincts. The *three darlings* thing is pap but it works."

It's pap but it works seemed to be how Jennifer saw the show in general. Which was something Audrey had always found odd. "You keep saying things like that," she tried. "But if you feel that way, why make a show like *Bake Expectations* in the first place?"

Jennifer had a range of scornful expressions, and the one she reached for now was number seventeen, the one that said quite specifically *I am disappointed that I have to explain this to you, but I shouldn't have expected better.* "You understand that the TV industry is an *industry*, right? It's not about your heart's secret truth. It's about selling shit to pricks in suits by convincing them they can sell it to pricks in suburbs."

"To an extent," Audrey admitted. "Maybe. But you've poured your whole life into this show. It must mean *something* to you."

"It means I made a lot of money and a lot of powerful friends."

While Audrey was making her sceptical face, the waiter circled back around with the drinks.

"There must be more to it than that."

Jennifer wrapped her hands around her cup like she was trying to stop crows from stealing it. "Sorry, if you're hoping I've got some saccharine story about how I used to bake every Sunday with my dear old grandmama and I wanted to share that feeling with the nation, then you're out of luck. I don't."

"So, what?" It wasn't clear to Audrey whether it would be more naïve to accept that Jennifer was really that cynical, or naïve to assume she wasn't. "You just thought, *What do people I have complete contempt for like? I know, baking!*"

"You missed a couple of steps and a whole lot of workshopping, but basically."

"I don't believe you."

Jennifer shrugged. "Suit yourself."

Audrey could have left it there. But she was a compulsive not-leave-it-there-er. "What about the workshopping?"

"What about it?"

This was going out on a limb and Audrey knew it. She was familiar enough with the mechanisms of broadcast media that she could make overconfident statements to the other contestants, but Jennifer was an actual pro, so there was a good chance Audrey was about to talk largely out of her arse. "Well, my industry's different, but getting something all the way from pitch to finished product takes—I mean it takes *some* kind of motivation. Faking it 'til you make it is one thing, but if you really gave as few shits as you say you do, I think you'd be even more miserable than you're currently pretending to be."

"What makes you think I'm pretending?"

That was a good question. And Audrey hoped she had a good answer. Or else she was just making a fool of herself over another ambitious, emotionally unavailable woman who would always see her soft, sentimental, and lacking.

You do so love to blame me for things, don't you Aur? sighed Natalie.

"Because," Audrey went on doggedly, "if you really didn't give a damn about anybody or anything, Grace wouldn't like you enough to interfere in your love life, and you wouldn't like her enough to let her."

"Is that what you think happened?" Jennifer was sounding more guarded than usual. Or perhaps guarded in a different way—shutting off rather than pushing back.

"You could very easily have never seen me again. But you did. And you still are."

For a long moment, Jennifer said nothing. Then she just rolled her eyes. "You know, Lane, I think I'm going to *profoundly* regret meeting you."

Which was another one of those Jennifer Hallet compliments that Audrey was secretly beginning to treasure.

It was a beautiful evening to be walking home with a beautiful woman. Not that *beautiful* was an adjective that Jennifer Hallet seemed like she'd appreciate. Besides, it was too simple a word for her. Because while she certainly *could* be beautiful, in the same way that a shark or a cyclone could be beautiful, it wasn't the thing that drew you in. And it certainly wasn't the thing that kept you drawn. At least if you were Audrey. It was as if some mischievous imp had appeared in a dream and said, "I bet I can find a way to keep you fascinated and annoyed for the rest of your life. Also she'll be really hot." And—fool that she was—dream-Audrey had said, "bring it."

At the edge of Crinkley Furze, a little sign pointed temptingly towards a public footpath.

"How about," suggested Audrey, "we go that way?"

Jennifer Hallet looked at her like she'd rather deepthroat a walrus. "Why?"

"Because it'll be fun?"

"It'll be fun to walk across a muddy field in the dark?"

"By starlight. And it's not going to be that muddy. It's summer."

"It's the countryside. It's made of mud."

"You really hate rural England, don't you?"

"I hate everything. Have you not been paying attention?"

And taking a leaf out of Jennifer's very well-worn book, Audrey responded with an eloquent, well-thought-out, "Oh fuck off."

Which only made Jennifer laugh.

They did, however, turn onto the footpath and stroll between the hedgerows, the fields stretching out on either side of them in great dark lakes.

"I'm still waiting," said Jennifer, after a minute or two.

This wasn't even a trap. It was a call and response. "You want me to say, 'waiting for what?' don't you? So you can say something devastatingly cynical."

"I'm waiting for whatever experience you expect me to have that's going to make *this* better than the shorter, easier walk up the road we could have been having."

"Does this help?" The part of Audrey that, despite Natalie's best efforts to kill it with self-consciousness, was having a serious crack at living its best life took Jennifer's hand.

"You could do that anywhere," Jennifer pointed out. Although she didn't pull away.

"Yes, but it's less…" Audrey stopped herself from saying *romantic* at the last minute. "Nice?"

"Have I told you today," said Jennifer, still holding Audrey's hand, "how much I don't like you?"

"You tell me that pretty much every time I meet you."

"And it still doesn't fucking stick."

"I must think you lack conviction."

"I have conviction," retorted Jennifer Hallet, going full Jennifer Hallet. "I have so much conviction that—oh, forget it."

This brought out Audrey's helpful side. "You have so much conviction that you're currently serving six concurrent sentences?"

"Stop it, Lane."

"You have so much conviction that they're putting you on a ship to Australia."

"Lane."

"You have so much conviction that you've been removed from the bench for—"

She got no further because Jennifer kissed her with the ambiguous ferocity of someone who either found her utterly irresistible or just really wanted her to be quiet. Which seemed the ideal reward for deliberately riling up an easily rilable person.

"See," said Audrey, post-kiss giddy in a way that fifteen-years-ago-Audrey had taken for granted. Had assumed she would always feel. "We're having a lovely walk."

Jennifer just growled.

"There's trees and grass and the moon."

"Literally all things you can see everywhere."

"What about that"—Audrey cast about for something more iconically countryish—"that tractor."

"That's a combine harvester."

Audrey strongly suspected that Jennifer couldn't tell a combine harvester from a cheese sandwich. But contrary for no reason seemed to be her love language. "That sweet little goat?"

"Are you sure," murmured Jennifer Hallet, with a private smile, "it's not a bull?"

"No. How could you possibly mistake a tiny goat for a bull?"

"To this day, I have no fucking clue."

"Should I ask?"

"No."

"But I'm curious now," Audrey definitely did not whine.

"God you're cute when you're needy."

"I'm not needy," Audrey protested exactly the right amount. "I just like to know stuff. That's a good trait for a human being to have. Otherwise, we'd still be eating raw mammoths and pooing in holes."

"Are you implying that all human progress has been caused by slightly annoying people asking intrusive questions?"

That one glass of wine, or that one kiss, must have packed a hell of a wallop. Because Audrey was still feeling weirdly…bubbly? Hopeful? Happy? "Ooh," she said, "I'm only slightly annoying now."

"Stick around," Jennifer told her, "and I might upgrade you to mildly vexatious."

"*And* you want me to stick around."

"Oh fuck off."

Before Audrey could challenge Jennifer on her mixed messages re: around-sticking versus off-fucking, they crested a low rise, and the gabled roofs of Patchley pierced the skyline. Exterior lighting brushed the facade with gold and, although that was probably a recent addition, it made it easy to imagine a time when a house like that was its own fairy tale. Albeit one where the princess ran off to New York and Cinderella went back to Stepney.

You're pathetic, said Natalie in tones that Audrey had once read as affectionate. *Getting so worked up over something so… pedestrian.*

And for once, Audrey let herself disagree. It wasn't pedestrian, it was…it was complex. It wasn't just complex, it was fucked. She'd been drawn to Doris because she'd wanted so badly to know that people like her had been at that house and walked on those floors and lived and loved in those rooms. To feel connected to the past as the whole of herself, not just the parts of herself that fit into the visible bits of history.

And you got it, said Natalie. *So what are you complaining about?*

Like her, Doris had fallen in love with a woman. Which was affirming. But like her, Doris had fallen in love with a woman who could never, ever love her back. And that was something else entirely.

Audrey sighed the messiest sigh she'd sighed in her life.

"What's that about?" asked Jennifer, with an air of warranted suspicion.

"I was just thinking what it must have been like. For Doris."

"It was shit. The whole system was shit. The whole system is still shit. It's just slightly less shit."

Two minutes ago, a bunch of swearing with a covertly anti-establishment worldview would have been all Audrey needed from Jennifer. But now she'd got herself turned around and somewhere in the distance, alarms were starting to clamour. "Okay, but, I'm not doing social commentary here. I just mean…how she must have felt. Even if she was trapped by an unjust system, she still loves this place. She still loved somebody who lived here. Maybe still loves her."

And perhaps it was the light, but Audrey saw a coldness in

Jennifer's eyes that she hadn't before. "Right. Because loving some-thing means it can't possibly be bad for you."

Audrey's breath caught. She wanted to say nine different things at once—*That's not what I was saying* and *Of course it doesn't* and *This wasn't supposed to be an argument* and *Please, please hear me*—but she managed to say exactly none of them.

Jennifer half-turned to look at her, and Audrey tried so hard to see understanding in her expression and she couldn't. "Something wrong?"

"Not really." Staring past Jennifer, at the distant light of Patchley, Audrey tried to lose herself and come back to herself all at once. "I'm just…processing some things I suppose."

"And?"

Something about that *and* made a little string inside Audrey's heart that had been fraying for a long time now snap all at once. "Wow. You're so easy to talk to."

"You seem to have managed so far."

"And you don't want to say, I don't know, 'What sort of things are you processing, Audrey?'"

"I could," conceded Jennifer, in the fashion of someone con-ceding absolutely nothing. "But I'm not sure I can be fucked."

Audrey threw her hands in the air. "Great. Nice to know. And fuck you."

She stomped off towards the house, not sure whether she wanted to cry or set Jennifer's trailer on fire. Or both. Both could be good.

"I'm not going to chase after you, Lane," said Jennifer, chasing after her.

"Good," yelled Audrey. "Because I don't want you to."

Jennifer caught her by the elbow and spun her round. "Let

me guess. You only went to London because you'd fallen for some judgmental journo bitch—"

"Natalie wasn't—"

"She blatantly was. And either way she broke your heart or fucked you up so you moved back to pigfuck nowhere and now you're looking for meaning in someone else's memories and making the same mistakes all over again with a slightly different flavour of terrible woman."

It was nothing Audrey hadn't thought for herself. But having it said out loud, and put so bluntly, made her feel cheap and obvious. "It's…I'm…it's more complicated than that."

"Are you sure? Because, if you haven't noticed, I'm a complete piece of shit."

Audrey stared up at her. Jennifer's face looked especially harsh in the moonlight, all angles and ferocity. Weirdly, seeing her like this, it made it harder to be angry at her. Especially because, for once, she was directing her venom at herself. "I don't think you're—"

"Oh, come on, I just upset you so much you stormed off down an unfamiliar hill in the dark despite being way too countryside not to know that's a lousy fucking idea. You can tell me I'm not a nice person, I'm big enough to take it."

If this had been a trick to get Audrey to calm down, it was kind of working. Although that, in its own way, was also annoying.

Oh come on, said Natalie, *I'm nothing like this woman. I cared about you. I tried to help you. I wanted you to be better.*

"I…" Audrey tried and when that didn't work she had a go at, "You…"

"*I, you?* Is that all you've got?" asked Jennifer, folding her arms.

Audrey folded her arms back. "Okay."

Finally, said Natalie. *Tell her—*

"If that's the way you want it," said Audrey, "you're a piece of shit. You fucking suck. You drive me round the bend and up the wall and yes you do make me want to cry sometimes but…" Natalie had a lot to say about this. She might even have been right. But Audrey wasn't listening and didn't care. "You're not *like* her, because…because when you've hurt me or upset me or pissed me off—and you've mostly just pissed me off—I've never once blamed myself."

To Audrey's strange, cathartic relief, Jennifer Hallet raised an eyebrow. "That's ironic, because I think you'll find I've been completely in the right every time we've disagreed about anything."

"I think you'll find you haven't. But the point is, it doesn't matter."

"I think you'll find it fucking does."

"Look." Audrey brushed an emotion-displaced hank of hair from her forehead. "When I was with Natalie, we never fought because we both took as it read that what she wanted was best and what I wanted was what she wanted. And because we never fought, I thought that was a healthy relationship."

"And you don't think I'm a bit of an overcorrection?"

"You might be. Or I might just like you."

Jennifer shook her head wearily. "You think that now, Lane. But I know how this goes. At the moment, I'm sure this is fun. But it won't take long before you realise I don't fit in your world."

"And what's my world exactly?" asked Audrey.

"A cosy little flat in Shropshire with hand-stitched quilts and a special place on the chair for a cuddly tortoise. Cupcakes in the oven and walks in the countryside. All that lovely bullshit."

Maybe Jennifer was rubbing off on her, but Audrey snorted.

"You know I'm a lot more than lovely bullshit, right? Remember, I threatened to embroil you in a nightmare storm of litigation to get what I wanted."

"I'm not saying you can't hack it. I'm saying you'll get sick of it. The late nights staring at audience metrics. The constant carousel of focus groups. The endless fucking meetings about BBC neutrality. Screaming down the phone at Americans about syndication rights. And one compromise after another after another until all you can think about when you look at me is how disappointing I turned out to be."

"That seems highly specific."

"You don't have a monopoly on shitty relationships, Lane."

It was weird as hell hearing Jennifer Hallet say the *R* word. Especially since she'd made it so abundantly clear that they weren't dating. "What if I make you a deal," said Audrey into the crisp silence of the night. "I won't turn into your toxic ex if you don't turn into mine."

"She wasn't the toxic one. That was the problem."

"I think making your partner feel that they're disappointing you is pretty toxic."

Stuffing her hands in her jacket pockets, Jennifer let out a defeated huff. "She just wanted a nice fucking life. In some ways, so do I. But I don't want it to be something someone does for me. I want it to be something someone builds with me."

"So you *are* a romantic?"

"Oh fuck off."

If it had been anyone else, Audrey would have considered this a poor end to a discussion. With Jennifer Hallet it felt like peace.

"Did we just have our first fight?" asked Audrey, after they'd tromped a bit further down the hill.

"No." Jennifer sneered at the darkness. "We had our first fight when you waltzed into my trailer and asked me not to call you a spunkstain."

"Excuse me. I didn't waltz. You invited me."

"Aye, for the express purpose of calling you a spunkstain."

"Those fights don't count," Audrey protested. "They were about things. This was about…us."

"Stop being a spunkstain."

As they walked, Jennifer radiating slightly less hostility than usual and Audrey smiling to herself for reasons she didn't want to name in case they went away, Patchley House only grew closer, and bigger, and more golden.

"You're going to start sighing again, aren't you?" said Jennifer.

Audrey sighed. "Well, it's beautiful. You have to admit, it's beautiful."

"It's all right."

And then, because Audrey was always going to Audrey, "I found her, you know."

"The posh bitch?"

"Well, personally I think of her as Emily. And I've not *found her* found her. But I've got some pretty promising leads."

This time Jennifer sighed. It was quite a different sigh to Audrey's sighing. "Of course you fucking have."

"What's that supposed to mean?"

"It means you never give up anything and you're clearly obsessed."

"I'm not obsessed. I'm *interested*."

"Listening to an old lady talk about her girlfriend is interested. Tracking the girlfriend down when she hasn't been seen for fifty years is obsessed."

This was fair. This was worryingly fair. "I don't like loose threads. It's a quilting thing. Or a journalist thing. Or both."

"And you're sure you're not trying to get closure on your ex-girlfriend by tracking down someone else's ex-girlfriend?"

"No," said Audrey, too quickly. "Well. I don't know. But even if it's true, is that bad?"

"Yes. Obviously. You can't go around confusing other people's shit for your shit."

"Says the woman who just gave me a huge speech about how we could never have anything nice together because of something that happened with a completely different person."

"This isn't about me. And Doris isn't about you."

"But doesn't Doris deserve—"

"Don't give me bollocks and tell me it's a delightful lychee salad, Lane. You want to do this because you're curious or you've got your own baggage or because you've read so many Sarah Waters novels you want to live in one."

"I…" Audrey would have debated the accuracy of that characterisation except there wasn't a lot to debate. "This will probably end better than the average Sarah Waters novel."

"So you're saying it might end in betrayal *or* misery instead of betrayal *and* misery."

"Not all Sarah Waters novels end in betrayal and misery."

"Name three where they don't."

"They're together at the end of *Fingersmith*."

"Yeah, after betrayal and misery."

"And technically there is a happy successful lesbian couple in *Affinity*."

"Neither of whom are the protagonist, who suffers betrayal and misery."

"Okay, but *Tipping the*—"

"Is the worst one because she winds up with a boring woman named Florence."

"All right." This was clearly the wrong tack to have taken. "You've made your point. But look at it this way: if I can find Emily and it doesn't end with betrayal and/or misery, it would make amazing TV."

"Fuck," said Jennifer Hallet. "I keep forgetting that underneath the polka dots and the cupcakes you're as cynical as I am."

"I do also think it would be good for Doris," added Audrey, only slightly guiltily.

Jennifer gave another deep, *deep* sigh and turned her face to the stars like she was seeking patience among their number. "You better not balls this up for me, Lane."

"I'm not going to hurt your show."

"I mean it. This one matters."

There was something in the way she said it that brought Audrey up short. "What do you mean, 'This one matters'?"

"I'm in talks," non-explained Jennifer.

"What sort of talks?"

"Don't be obtuse. Talks about selling the show."

It shouldn't have been shocking—TV franchises changed hands all the time—but Audrey was shocked anyway. "Selling to who?"

"There's a couple of offers on the table. But how much I get and what I do next depends on how well this series lands. If I nail it, I can do what I fucking like. And I enjoy doing what I fucking like."

"Still," Audrey tried. "It must be hard."

"Hard?"

"Giving something up after you've put so much of yourself into it."

Jennifer glared. "I told you, I haven't—"

It was dark enough that Audrey didn't think an eye-roll would be effective, so she just groaned theatrically. "Yes, yes, you haven't actually put any of yourself into the show at all. It's just mindless tat you hate aimed at people you despise. Except if that was true, you'd have bailed long ago."

"Would I now?"

"*Expectations* has been one of the biggest things on television for years. If you'd wanted a buyer, you'd have found one. If this was just a stepping stone for you, you'd have stepped."

"Perhaps I was being lazy."

"Oh, right." Audrey made the most sceptical face she could. "Because a lack of energy and ambition is one of your most noticeable character traits. It's right up there with tact and fear of conflict."

Jennifer didn't have a reply to that. She just stood there in the starlight looking miserable and wounded.

"You *are* allowed to care about things," Audrey told her. "It's not a personality flaw. Or, if you prefer, it's not incompatible with the personality flaws you're so damned proud to have."

"Maybe." Jennifer made a surprisingly wistful sound. "But the thing is, this was never my idea in the first place."

There were times to ask follow-up questions and times to give people space. This felt very much like a space-giving time.

"You know how…" For perhaps the first time since Audrey had met her, Jennifer hesitated. "You know how I said things hadn't worked out with my ex because she wanted…all the lovely bullshit?"

Audrey made a valiant attempt to stop her brain filling in all the blanks at once. To respect the fact that this was Jennifer's story and not hers. And she nearly succeeded. "The show was her idea?"

Jennfier nodded. "Turns out founding a production company together is a fucking stupid way to fix a relationship. Almost as bad as getting married. She left just as the series got picked up, and once she was gone, well—I mean I had to make something out of it, didn't I? Otherwise, what would I have had to show for all those years and all that work?"

While Jennifer didn't seem the sort to respond well to comfort, Audrey reached out anyway and laid a hand on her arm. And while she could still feel the tension through her sleeve, she thought it was easing.

"But you're right," Jennifer went on. "I could have got out years ago. Just—nostalgia, I suppose."

They walked a little further, each in her own thoughts.

"You know what?" Jennifer made a visible attempt to pull herself together. "Fucking do it."

The last time Jennifer had agreed to something, Audrey had made a who-are-you-right-now joke. But this seemed like a bad moment for it. Especially because this felt like she was seeing more of Jennifer Hallet than she'd ever been allowed to before. "Find Emily?"

"Why not? If it works, it'll be a *banger* of a finale."

"And maybe we'll have done a nice thing for two old ladies?" suggested Audrey, clinging to the idea that she wasn't driven totally by ruthless pragmatism.

"Of course," Jennifer went on, "if it goes to shit it could ruin the whole series and both their lives." She paused. "Then again, their lives are going to be quite short."

Audrey squeaked. "Jennifer."

"I'm sorry, was that uncharacteristically insensitive of me?"

"No…no, you're right. It's worth considering. I mean, the possibility of a bad outcome is worth considering. I don't think we need to be speculating about life expectancy."

Jennifer gave a sort of sardonic chuckle. "You do you, Lane. Just don't start anything until you've got actual formal consent, preferably in writing. Ethically, this should be up to the granny. Aesthetically, I don't do ambush bullshit. And practically, I don't want to get myself fucking sued."

"Look at us." Audrey nudged her arm against Jennifer's. "Talking through our differences. Working as a team. Coming up with a plan."

Pausing, Jennifer looked down at her. The look on her face was abstract and unreadable. Then the corner of her mouth kicked up very slightly. "Oh fuck off."

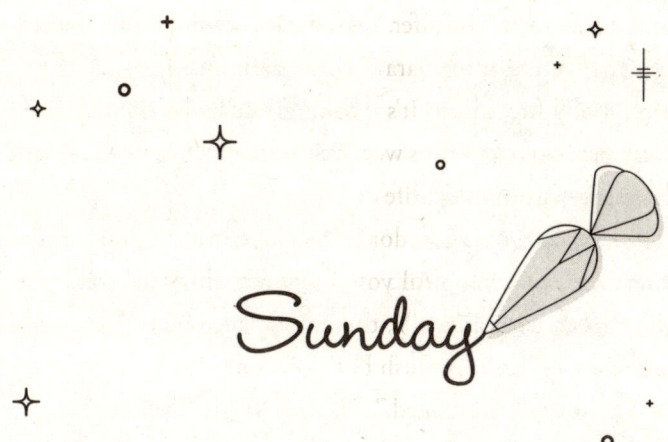

Sunday

JENNIFER, IT SEEMED, had the same breakfast every day, which didn't surprise Audrey at all because for a woman who worked in a creative industry, Jennifer seemed very much to be a creature of habit. And so now, she and Audrey were sitting side by side, their bacon rolls half-eaten alongside smears of ketchup, while through their headsets Grace Forsythe was pouring out another of her mellifluous introductions.

"*Bonjour,*" she was saying to the half dozen remaining contestants. "And the bonnest of jours it is because today we are asking you to focus on a French classic. We want you to demonstrate your mastery of meringue and your finesse with flavours as you make us no fewer than forty-eight perfectly formed, identically sized, beautifully presented macarons. We're asking for two dozen sweet and, in a move I frankly consider slightly too trendy—"

"As do I," added Wilfred Honey.

"—two dozen savoury. You have four hours starting on three." Grace Forsythe paused for—now Audrey was watching timestamps—exactly the same amount of time she always paused. It was actually quite impressive. "*Three*, darlings."

Everybody started furiously baking. Well, everybody started furiously baking except for the people who had been collared for the mandatory banter segments.

They began with Meera, who was blitzing almond powder together with something Audrey didn't recognise. Which inevitably meant that Marianne Wolvercote opened with, "Well, this looks interesting."

"Freeze-dried beetroot," Meera explained. "It's a bit hard to get hold of, but you need the flavour without the moisture."

"Clever," Marianne Wolvercote conceded. "And for the filling?"

Meera nodded at a little pile of goat cheese, cream cheese, and dill.

"So what's the cardamom for?" asked Wilfred Honey.

"That's for the mango and cardamom sweet," Meera told him. Then she immediately gave the blender another pulse.

Audrey gave a little preemptive wince. Wilfred may have been the nation's grandfather, but, like many grandfathers, he sometimes made some very culturally specific assumptions about food.

"Is that not more suitable for a savoury?" he asked.

"It pairs well with mango," Marianne Wolvercote put in, "which I notice you're also using."

Meera nodded. "That's right. It does mean that I'll have a tray that's all purple and orange, though."

Jennifer had been right about Grace. She had a tremendous instinct for how to deflect an awkward line of questioning onto something frivolous. "Fabulous. Reminds me of a suit I used to wear in the eighties." She turned to the judges. "Shall we?"

So the three of them continued their circuit, leaving Meera to continue grinding her freeze-dried beetroot into a fine powder. And when the camera operator judged that they'd got all the footage they needed from her, that feed moved away, and Audrey switched her attention to another contestant.

Towards the back of the ballroom, Linda seemed to be having a rough time of it. There was no sound, but she was staring into her bowl of macaron mix looking like she was worried it was going to explode.

Jennifer was occupied elsewhere—issuing a series of instructions through Colin to the camera operators—but, as Audrey watched, the image on the screen in front of her evolved from bit-of-a-bad-day to definite-freakout. The initial stage of the macaron-making process wasn't exactly frenetic, but it definitely involved doing more than just staring at a bowl of rapidly settling egg whites with a panicked expression on your face.

"Should somebody check on her?" Audrey asked, leaning over a little closer to Jennifer.

"The nervy one?" Jennifer hadn't so much as glanced at Linda's feed, but she knew at once who Audrey had meant. "No, she'll be fine."

"Are you sure? She doesn't *look* especially fine."

Jennifer's eyes flicked for half a second to Linda's screen. "Not looking exactly fine is what she's here for."

"That seems cruel."

"It's a cruel business. You want to complain, complain to the viewers."

"You know there's not actually an award for needless cynicism?"

Glancing briefly away from the monitors, Jennifer smirked. "What do you think BAFTAs are?"

On the live feed, Audrey watched as Alanis wandered away from her station and back towards Linda. And the fact that Linda had barely started while other contestants were in the taking-a-break-to-talk-to-other-people stage did not bode well for her. Audrey was about to ask Jennifer for audio, so that she could hear what the two were saying to each other, but she only got as far as "Could we" before a squicky, intrusive feeling shut her down.

Jennifer, however, was thoroughly unsquickable and flicked over to their channel anyway. "Monitor the child and the flake, Colin," she said into her headset. "And make sure it stays wholesome."

And it *was* incredibly wholesome, from the little Audrey managed to hear before she removed her headset out of a perhaps overzealous respect for Linda's privacy. Alanis came in quiet and confident and supportive, and Linda looked at her with real gratitude when she said everything was going to be okay.

"Are you going to broadcast this?" Audrey asked.

"Of course. If it edits right, it'll come out incredibly heartwarming."

"Okay, but, is it not also a bit personal?"

Swivelling her chair around, Jennifer gave Audrey a flatly disappointed look. "They both know they're on television. They both signed the exact same bits of paper you did."

"Okay, but they're still *people*."

Jennifer nodded. "And so is every other prick you've seen a meme about. It feels different now because you've met them."

It would have been hypocritical for Audrey to disagree. Because while she wanted to believe that she was the kind of viewer who watched a reality television show with an eye to what was best for the mental health of the contestants, she strongly suspected that she, like a whole lot of other people, cared mostly about what made good drama. It just felt bad to say it out loud.

On the other hand, disagreeing seemed mandatory. "Okay, suppose you're right. That doesn't change the fact that I *have* met them and so I *do* feel differently. Like"—searching for inspiration, Audrey picked up the cold remains of the bacon roll from the desk in front of her—"I'll happily eat this, but I'd probably hesitate to stab a pig in the neck."

"And there's me thinking you were a farm girl."

"You know there are people in Shropshire who aren't farmers?"

Instead of replying, Jennifer just said, "She's moving; Colin, keep eyes on her."

Looking up at the screen, Audrey saw Linda step away from her workstation and head out the doors. Feeling weirdly responsible for the whole situation, she stood up herself. "Should I…?"

Jennifer shrugged. "Can if you want to. Colin's following her, but you *might* do a better job than him. Then again so would my grandmother."

"And she's been dead for six years?" added Audrey.

"Actually she's a fully qualified workplace psychotherapist. Also, she's completely hypothetical. Now go out there and stick your oar in."

Audrey wasn't especially fond of being told what to do, especially not in such dismissive terms, but she'd also finally got to the point where she was emotionally mature enough that she wouldn't let being told to do something she wanted to do anyway put her off doing it. "Is this your way of looking after people?"

"It's my way of saying, 'I've given up trying to stop you so I might as well get something out of it.' Go talk to Linda. If you want to tell her what a sinister mastermind I am for filming her with the cameras I cleverly hid by disguising them as a film set, you can. Let me know when you're done."

Given that arguing with Jennifer Hallet could distract Audrey indefinitely, she just nodded her agreement and headed out.

Linda was sitting glumly on the sitting-down log and Audrey approached in the most definitely-haven't-just-been-watching-your-emotional-crisis-on-screen way she could manage.

"Hi," she tried.

Linda "Hi"ed back.

"Not in the ballroom?" was Audrey's next gambit.

"No."

Now Audrey was closer, she could see that Linda had tears in her eyes. "Rough week?"

Linda nodded.

And Audrey, still not completely certain she wasn't being either invasive, manipulative, or both, sat down next to her. "I—umm—I should probably say that I've been watching you from Jennifer's trailer."

"How'd I look?" asked Linda. There was a kind of hollow irony in her voice, a trying-to-have-a-sense-of-humour-about-things tone that Audrey recognised.

"Like you'd had a rough week."

"I've completely blanked on macaron." It was an absurd sentence to be saying. In some ways even more absurd now she was off camera.

Audrey did her best to radiate sympathy. "Yeah. You did freeze up a bit."

"I just"—Linda made a swirling motion next to her head—"I just got stuck in a loop because I know meringue is really finnicky and if you don't fold it exactly right it doesn't foot properly—"

"Foot properly?"

"A macaron should have a little"—she made a sort of very broad hourglass shape with her hands—"foot at the bottom of each half."

That wasn't something Audrey had ever noticed, which suggested she'd probably been eliminated at about the right time. "And that made you get…stuck in a loop?"

"Short version: I couldn't decide what to do because I was getting too worried about how little time I had left to decide what to do."

It wasn't *quite* a problem Audrey could say she'd shared. Her brain tended to play different kinds of tricks. But she could understand the heart of it. "So how do you want to play this?"

As soon as the words were out of her mouth, Audrey was wondering at the shape of them. They did and didn't sound like her. But they also felt like the right thing to say. Because Jennifer had— once again and fuck her—been right. Linda knew she was on TV and needed to act like it.

Linda looked down dolefully. "I'm not sure. I could go back in, but honestly I don't think there's any way I can make forty-eight macarons in the time left. And then I'll have to stand in front of Wilfred and Marianne and hear them trying to be nice about my total failure. I'm almost—would it be really shitty of me if I just, like, quit?"

There was a pause while Audrey thought about it. If she'd just been a contestant on the show, she wouldn't have hesitated to say, "Do it." But now she was…she was something else? And it was hard for her not to look at the show from Jennifer's perspective; to think not only about the stories, but how to frame them. What the numbers would do and what people would say and how it would play in the East Midlands and the U.S. syndication.

Except she was still Audrey Lane. And, while she'd kind of lost track of who that was for a time, she was starting to remember what it meant. That although Audrey Lane could be as hard-arsed as she needed to be, she also baked cupcakes. And made terrible quilts. And gave a shit about people.

"You know," she said, "you're here for yourself at the end of the day. If the show's messing with your head, it's fine to just say fuck it."

Linda blinked. "Are you sure?"

"Completely."

"But won't I—I don't know—be letting people down?"

There were a bunch of ways to go here. So Audrey decided fuck it and went with the simplest. "No. You absolutely aren't. I know it feels like a big deal, but it's just a TV show. It's not worth making yourself unhappy over."

"But what if I'm more unhappy if I leave?" wondered Linda, perhaps predictably given the role she was being edited into.

"Don't overthink it." Audrey laid a partly reassuring, partly restraining hand on Linda's shoulder. "One, you are your own priority. Two, I guarantee Jennifer has gamed this out."

"Is this the wires and the mirrors again?"

"Kind of. But it works for you this time."

"How?"

"Because you're here to be the one who takes everything really to heart."

"Okay," said Linda, with an air of unreassuredness. "But none of the other ones who took everything to heart bailed before the end."

"Which is why," Audrey told her, "it'll make a good story beat. This is best for you. And it's probably best for the show as well."

Linda had televisually large eyes when distressed. "Really?"

"Yes." Audrey stood up. "Now come on, let's go tell Jennifer you're walking."

"…the saddest part of the show," Grace was saying. "Although this week, perhaps mercifully, Wilfred and Marianne have been spared the task of deciding which of our wonderful contestants won't be coming with us into next week. Our darling Linda, with the full support of the *Bake Expectations* family, has chosen not to progress in the competition—"

Audrey took off her headset and turned to look at Jennifer Hallet, who was smiling to herself. A queasy sensation stirred quietly in Audrey's stomach.

"Did I just play her for you?" she asked.

"Paranoia doesn't suit you, Lane."

Across the various screens, Linda was being hugged. Audrey had been expecting tears but, while the cameras were making sure to capture looks of affection on everyone's faces, the atmosphere was surprisingly upbeat for an elimination. Even if it was a self-elimination.

"No, but—was this the plan? Did you know I'd help her do this?"

"I knew you'd do the right thing."

"The right thing for your show, you mean." Audrey's head was spinning. And she was beginning to worry she'd set it to the Jennifer cycle.

Jennifer made a noise of annoyance that Audrey was beginning to feel increasingly familiar with. "If I wanted someone to only think about the show or about what I wanted, I'd do it myself or send Colin. There's a fucking balance."

"But"—the contestants were being shepherded out the ballroom for interviews—"what if I made the wrong call? Maybe Linda would have been fine. Maybe I've taken an opportunity from her. Maybe—"

"Linda was not fine. She was definitely going out. The only question was whether she went out on her terms or on the judges'."

"And you just happen to get an amazing watercooler moment out of it."

"Oh, please, I can make a watercooler moment out of a slightly limp baguette. Look"— Jennifer swung back on her villain chair with the air of someone about to tell an international superspy why they couldn't possibly thwart her evil plan—"the story was going to go one of three ways. Either she soldiered on to a valiant defeat. Or she flounced out in a huff. Or she walked out with her head held high. I'd have been fine with any of them. She'd have been fine with one or three. You pushed it towards three."

It felt weird to hear Jennifer trying to be reassuring. And it felt uncomfortable to be reassured by it. "She's still a person, Jennifer. Not a chess piece."

Leaning forward again, Jennifer pressed a button. "Colin, send in the bishop." There was a pause. "No, no, not literally. I'm doing a chess thing with Audrey. I mean send in the whiny one."

The response wasn't quite instantaneous. As much as Jennifer would probably have liked everybody to spend all day standing outside her trailer waiting for her to yell for them, Colin and Linda were still on the terrace outside the ballroom doing postshow interviews, and so it took a couple of minutes for the door to swing open and Linda to creep sheepishly in.

"Sorry," she said. Which was pretty much what she'd said when she first told Jennifer she was bowing out as well.

"Don't be, you did me a favour. Always good to have something to shake up a mid-season episode."

Linda was still looking doubtful.

"On your way out, Colin will give you the details of our in-house counsellor. You don't have to use them, you can find somebody else if you want, but you do need to speak to *somebody*."

"I don't want to make—"

"A fuss, I know. But look at me, Linda." Jennifer fixed Linda with her most no-nonsense stare, which was very, very no-nonsense, indeed. "Do I look like somebody who lets people make fusses?"

"No," Linda admitted.

"You made the right call. It's intense while you're here, but this is just a TV show. Say goodbye to the cast, go home, put your feet up, and remember it's not really important."

Linda just nodded, murmured something vaguely in the direction of *thanks*, and went back out to liaise with Colin.

When she was gone, Audrey gave Jennifer a distinctly unimpressed look.

"Was that supposed to prove something?"

"Yeah," said Jennifer. "It proves she'll be fine. And it proves that you're good at this. And it proves you don't have to tie yourself in fucking knots just because you did something with slightly higher stakes than reporting on a teenager stuck in a swing."

Audrey didn't know whether to be flattered or freaked out that Jennifer still seemed to be reading her articles, even though she'd been off the show for a fortnight. "Hey, that was the second time it had happened to the same kid, which is why it was newsworthy."

"Because *teenager makes bad decision twice* is such a rare event."

"Yeah…" Standing, Audrey de-cricked her neck from an afternoon hunched over footage. "I'm not sure low-key manipulating reality TV contestants is exactly my calling either."

"Doesn't have to be. I'm just saying that your options aren't limited to working yourself to death on Fleet Street or boring yourself to death in Felton Butler."

Jennifer was trending pointwards and Audrey didn't like it. "Frankly, I'm just impressed you know where Felton Butler is."

"Well, I'm a very impressive woman. And right now, I'm an impressive woman with a job to do, so you can either shut up and let me get on with it. Or piss off back to Shropshire and cuddle your tortoise."

This was definitely new. This whole being offered a choice whether you pissed off or not. In Jennifer Hallet world it was practically a candlelit dinner. And, on a different day, Audrey would have stuck around. But she also had things to do because she was—as Jennifer had reminded her—in her own way also a very impressive woman.

Audrey managed to catch Doris in the carpark, where she was waiting for a taxi to take her to the nearest train station.

"Hi," she began, a little self-consciously.

"Hello." Doris shuffled over on the bench to make room, and Audrey sat down next to her.

Probably it was best not to jump straight into *Can I try to locate the woman who broke your heart half a century ago?* so Audrey went for a more neutral opener. "What a week."

"Yeah," agreed Doris. "All excitement here on *Bake Expectations*. I think Linda made the right call, though. No sense in the poor thing staying if it was going to be tough on her."

"And I think it was brave of her, in a way," added Audrey, not quite sure who she was trying to convince.

Doris nodded. "S'pose so, s'pose so. And young Reggie deserved the win."

Audrey hadn't even paid attention to that part of the competition, but it seemed rude to admit it. "Patisserie was always going to be his week," she said. "He's so precise."

"Oh yeah, Marianne loved how identical his macarons was."

If there was ever a man who could make four dozen identically shaped and sized macarons it would be Reggie. And while Audrey didn't think he was making the final, patisserie week was a prestigious one to win.

"Beginning to think you're wrong about the final, actually," Doris went on. "I've not won one yet, and I don't see as how they can let me through without at least one win under my belt."

"Maybe. Like I say, I'm not an expert. But they *do* pay attention to story. And I think your story's pretty compelling."

Doris gave her an almost melancholy look. "Maybe. But if you mean about, you know, about me and her, then that's not what the show's about and there's not that much more to tell."

"Actually"—this seemed like too good an opportunity to pass up—"there was something I wanted to ask you about that."

Doris nodded. It wasn't quite a wary nod, but it was the nod of a woman who knew there was another shoe to drop.

"How would you feel if hypothetically I…I'm sort of thinking I could maybe find Emily. If you wanted."

For a long while there was no reply. Doris just sat there,

processing and looking for words. And Audrey let her sit because if bringing this up in the first place had been borderline unfair, pushing the issue now would be flat-out mean.

"I reckon," said Doris at last, "that I'd always figured she was dead. Not always, I mean, but eventually. Most everybody else is."

Audrey didn't want to interrupt, but she told herself that there was nothing wrong with sharing information. "I've not found a death certificate. And I've looked."

"Oh." There was a long pause, followed by, "Well that's a thing."

"I can stop," Audrey volunteered, perhaps more urgently than she meant to.

Doris didn't immediately say no, which made Audrey uneasy. And not just because she might say *no* but because if somebody took too long to get to *yes*, Audrey always felt like she'd twisted their arm.

"I think"—Doris wasn't normally hesitant, and that wasn't doing wonders for Audrey's confidence—"I think I'd like to at least know where she is. What happened to her and everything."

"Are you sure?" asked Audrey, more out of conscience than strategy.

"No," admitted Doris. "But—well—can't be no harm in looking, can there?"

It was all Audrey needed, in theory. Although privately she wondered if maybe there could be.

But aloud she just said, "No. No there can't."

WEEK SIX

Chocolate

JANUARY 1962

I ONLY SAW her once again (Doris was explaining the following week), the last time I went back to Patchley. Must be—must be sixty years ago now, and ain't that a thing. Me and Bobby, we'd been married a bit less than ten years and we'd had all our little 'uns so we was as you might say settled. But over New Year's I'd got word from Tom—you remember Tom, we was evacuated together and stayed in touch—as how Sir Arthur had died and how a lot of us as had stayed with him was going back to pay our respects and would I like to come along.

I told him I would but as it'd be difficult what with Bobby and the kids and he told me it'd be all right. He'd done well for himself since Patchley. Things was tough after the war, but there was opportunities for them as knew where to look, and Tom had always been canny.

He showed up day of the funeral in a Mark II Jaguar that couldn't have been more'n a year old and shipped the lot of us down to Surrey in style. Well, sort of in style. Him and Bobby was up front while I was squeezed in the back seat with three kids.

It weren't the best road safety, but it was the sixties and we didn't think so much about it back then.

It weren't at the house—the funeral, I mean. You'd have noticed a graveyard and there's not one, and though the Branninghams is an old family, they're not so old as they've got some ancient crypt in the cellar full of big stone coffins. No, for all they was rich, they got buried in a churchyard in Taplow same as a lot of poorer folks. Swankier graves of course, but I don't think that makes much difference to the worms.

Though the car was nice, the trip down was a bit of a bugger if you'll pardon my French. It was crowded in the back and young Robert wouldn't sit still and little Maggie didn't want to go and said so every six minutes. Susan fell asleep nicely enough, but she fell asleep on my lap, which meant I had the weight of her the whole way, so by the time we got there my legs was asleep and I half staggered out the car.

Tom had tried to get all ten of us together for the funeral— sort of a reunion if a bit of a morbid one—and it had half worked. Well, more than half by the numbers because he'd managed to get eight. We was all alive still, back then—Tom was actually one of the first to go what with being older and not making it to seventy, but two of us was overseas, one in Australia and one in the States and though they'd sent their thoughts and all that, it was a hell of a long way to come for a man they'd not seen in fifteen years or more.

We made quite the crowd in the end, because I weren't the only one had brought family. All the girls and most of the lads had wound up married, and most of those who'd married had brung kids, so when we showed up at the church we near outnumbered the actual relatives. Not that actual relatives was that big a part of the group anyway, what with friends and business associates and all the layers and layers of people that gather around money over the years. I'd been to a couple of funerals in my time—lot more since, of course—and this had more folk at it than all the rest put together.

Some I thought I recognised from my days in service, old staff and old guests both. The guests didn't recognise me because back then it'd been my job to be invisible, but Mrs. Loris did. It's funny, thinking back on it now. Every time I met her, I thought she was old, though she couldn't have been much older when we first met than I was when I met her again at the funeral, and when I met her again then, she would have been far younger than I am now. Still somehow she's old in my head and always will be.

"Cooper," I remember her saying. Just "Cooper."

Out of habit I wanted to look down and just say "Mrs. Loris," back, but I weren't Cooper no more and so I told her as much.

"Ah," she said, and she looked at Bobby and the kids with a kind of approving expression. Then, "Congratulations," and, "Are you, that is, I'm sure you're very happy."

I told her I was, because I was—least no less happy than most because life is what it is at the end of the day—and she looked relieved. I didn't know how to take that. It was almost insulting.

After Mrs. Loris had said her piece, we was all ushered in for the service—us evacuees was at the back because there wasn't room for a bunch of unwashed oiks from Stepney at the front of the big swanky church Sir Arthur was getting buried in, but we got a shout-out about halfway through when they was listing all the good things what Sir Arthur had done in his time. And after that, we was brought back up Patchley House for the wake.

That weren't normal neither.

A wake, the ones I'd been used to, was a couple of drinks in whatever pub was nearest the church and a couple of toasts from friends or family. But for Sir Arthur it was—well, you remember how they used to open up the house at Christmas? It was that, but for death. Catering for hundreds, a book of condolences with messages from folk as I'm sure never met Sir Arthur in their lives. Crowds and crowds and crowds and crowds and crowds. But that's the gentry for you, isn't it? They don't live like us so why should they die like us?

Now we was at the house, I was feeling that neither here nor there sort of way that you get when you go back somewhere after a long time. Like I'd never left but also like I'd never been there before. And Bobby must have known something was up because he looked at me quiet like and said as I could take a minute if I needed to. And I did.

I let my feet take me down the hill—I told you I've been up and down it a lot and that I'd no need to get moved on account of it—and to the river and to the spot where I'd found her all them years ago. Where she'd been throwing rocks at frogs.

Where I found her again. Where a silly little part of me thought I might always find her.

"Why are you here, nymph?"

"Come to pay my respects." It was only half the answer and she knew it.

"There's a book for that in the house. I think they have it laid out in the ballroom." She weren't looking at me. She was staring at the water like it'd done something cruel and personal to her. And though it'd been nearly ten years she still looked like a furious angel. "I wanted to have a think," I told her.

Almost dreamy, she picked up a rock, weighed it into her hand

and then flung it into the river like she was trying to kill something. "About a man you barely knew? That seems melodramatic."

"We didn't talk much, but he was good to me."

"He fucking well was not."

"He took us in when he didn't have to."

Emily threw another stone. "Please, it was wartime. Everybody was doing it. Patriotic duty and all that."

"All the same"—I began, but she weren't in a mood to listen.

"All the same what? You think he'd have come to bury *you*? You think he'd have descended from the big house on the hill to whatever grubby little churchyard in Stepney they'll throw you in when you go and told your unwashed children how great a loss you were?"

"Don't matter what he'd do. It was right for me to come here for him. And my kids ain't unwashed."

She didn't say nothing more about the children, she just turned and looked up at me, all spite and challenge. "So will you come back for me, too?"

"What do you mean?" I knew, but either I didn't want to say it or I wanted her to.

"When I die, nymph. When I am dead and in the ground, will you come and stand in the church and weep for me?"

Even then, somehow, I didn't like to think of it. Though I'd not seen her in going on a decade, the idea of her being dead cut my heart like a fish knife. "Don't talk like that."

She stood up then and walked very close to the river, staring down into it like it was the edge of everything. "I shall talk," she said to the water, "as I please. As I always have."

I didn't really think she meant to drown herself—there'd always been a dark edge to Emily, even when she was young—but I went towards her anyway so as I could catch her if she fell. Because it's not always the things we means as hurts us.

"Would you speak?" she went on. "Would you stand up at my funeral and tell the world what you thought of me?"

"If I had to," I said, and only then realised I'd fallen into her trap.

"And what would you say?"

I'd never had the same fire as Emily, but time to time I'd known how to borrow it. "Same as you'd say about anybody—that you was a good person, even if you wasn't."

"And am I?"

"You know," I said, "I think maybe you ain't."

"That's a bold thing to say to a woman at her father's funeral."

"No bolder than what you said to me at my wedding."

That shut her up, but only for a couple of seconds. She turned to face me—she was wearing this narrow-fitted jacket and men's trousers; all black but on her it didn't look like mourning, it looked like armour. "I meant every word."

"And if you'd said 'em a year earlier, I'd maybe have listened. But you waited."

"I was young. I'd spent so long trying to forget you and—"

"And you think I hadn't tried the same?" I weren't angry with her, not really. But I also didn't believe her entirely.

She smiled all cruel and wounded. "You seemed to have moved on from where I was standing."

"Then why didn't you just let me?" I asked. Though even then, even at the time, even now, I'm not sure I'd wanted her to.

Still, whatever I wanted, she gave half a laugh back. "I suppose you're right. I'm *not* a good person."

I looked down, partly from habit because even in my thirties a bit of me still thought of her as the mistress, partly because looking at her was just getting hard. "Was it even about me?" I asked. "I mean really? Or did you just not like the idea of somebody else touching your things?"

Sometimes, no answer is all the answer you need.

"Maybe I shouldn't have come back," I agreed, a little late.

When I looked up again, she was staring at me. "You had a right," she conceded. "And—I won't say it's been good to see you, nymph, because it profoundly has not. But it might have been bad in a positive way."

Of course I didn't know what to say to that. She always could talk me in circles. "I should go back to my family," I told her.

She didn't say anything. She just nodded and let me go.

Up at the big house I met up with Bobby and the kids. Honestly the little 'uns was pretty bored by then on account of not knowing anybody and Maggie being shy around strangers. I felt a little bit bad about sticking Bobby with them while I went off alone, but he was a good dad and he didn't mind overmuch. Least he didn't mind taking care of 'em—he minded that they wasn't happy.

"We should be thinking about going," he said to me when I got back. "I've signed the book, and I don't think it's right to bother the family. There's a lot of people here and we should—"

"You must be Doris's husband," said Emily's voice behind me. It had that so-fake-it's-real tone that the fancy folks use when they're talking to us commoners, without a trace of warm or cold or happy or sad or of knowing me from Adam. "It's so good to see the evacuees again."

"She's been back before," Bobby told her, just like you would if you didn't know that she already knew, that she was the cause of so much of it. "She worked here for a while in the fifties, didn't you, love?"

"Yes," I said, weak as anything.

Emily grinned. "You don't say? You must have some stories."

"Some." There weren't no other reply. Saying *none* would seem like an insult, but I couldn't exactly come back with *Yes, we used to be lovers*. Though part of me wanted to, if only because I knew she wouldn't expect it. "I remember Sir Arthur used to hold a lovely fair at Christmas."

That caught her, at least, because though Bobby and the kids didn't know what that meant, Emily did but also couldn't let on that she did. "Oh yes," she replied, "that was such a highlight of the year. I do miss it." Then she looked me hard in the eyes. "All of it."

I had no answer, but Maggie chose that moment to come in with a, "Mummy I'm tired."

"I'm not," replied young Robert. "I could stay up *all night*."

And before I knew it Emily was crouching down and talking to the children. To *my* children. A rush of hot ice ran through my heart and my brain all at once because seeing *her* and *them* together was more than I could take because they was different worlds, different lives, different possibilities. And I'd chosen. But I'd chosen without knowing how or what or if there was ever really another option.

"And what are your names?" she asked, and in my head I was wondering if there'd ever been a way I could have had both—Emily and Robert and Maggie and Little Susan all together. But there wasn't.

"I'm Maggie," said Maggie to the woman who I so badly wished could have been her mother.

"And I'm Robert," added Robert. And then, "After my father. And that's Susan."

Susan—Susan who would never have been if I'd taken a different path—was still asleep in Bobby's arms.

"How delightful to meet you," Emily was saying. "Tell me, is Doris a good mother?"

And to that Robert said *yes* and Maggie said *no* and Bobby said, "If you don't mind, Miss, I'm not sure that's the sort of thing I want you asking my kids."

So Emily stood back up and turned to me. "Quite right," she said, "my sincerest apologies. You have a lovely family, Doris." Her lip curled into a private smile. "I'm almost jealous."

"Not got a man in your life then?" asked Bobby.

"No." Emily was still smiling. "Sadly not. Would that I were as fortunate as Doris here."

She was saying my name a lot, and I didn't like it.

"We should probably be going," I said, louder than I should have. "I think it's a bit much for the children."

And Maggie said *yes* and Robert said *no*.

"So soon?" Emily asked, all fake-disappointed. "Well it was good of you to come. I'm sure Father would have appreciated it."

I could feel myself beginning to tear up, which was natural enough at a funeral, but I didn't want to give her the satisfaction of seeing it. "You must have loved him very much."

Of everything I'd said to her that day, that was the thing that silenced her. She looked at me, blinking like I'd said something strange or impossible. "He was a good father."

Before anybody could say anything else, she'd turned away, seeing or pretending to see somebody across the crowd who was much richer or more important than we were. When she was gone, me and Bobby rounded up the kids and went to ask Tom if he'd be okay to take us back. Which he was, because Tom was a love.

So we piled into the car, and I held Susan on my lap while Robert and Maggie sat next to me. And when I started crying for real, because I was always going to, Maggie reached out and put her hand on my arm and said, "It's all right, Mummy. He was probably very old."

I couldn't help but laugh. Because even though walking away from Emily that day had half broke my heart, I knew it'd broke before, and I was pretty sure it'd break again. But right there and then I knew it didn't matter. That it had been right to love her and right to leave her and right to get back in the car and go home for the last time.

I won't say I never thought of her again, because I did. But as the years went by it got less and less until—well—until you come along and started asking questions, no offence. But maybe now's the time it was right to talk and all, because I think—I don't know, maybe I'm just an old lady who likes to ramble, but I reckon it was a story worth telling, for all it don't really have a proper ending.

Friday

AFTER DORIS HAD gone, Audrey stayed sitting by the river for a while. The evening was a balmy one, so it was easy enough for her to linger with her thoughts as the light waned and the first pale stars started glinting through the still blue sky. Every so often she'd pick up a stone, weigh it in her hand, and then set it down again. There were no frogs to throw them at, and anyway, Audrey—like Doris—wasn't a throwing-rocks-at-frogs sort of person. Maybe she was just—like Doris—drawn to throwing-rocks-at-frogs people. Maybe, in fact, all relationships consisted of the one who threw rocks at frogs and the one who didn't.

Except no. Even as the thought assembled in her mind, she dismissed it. It was cerebral clickbait: superficially insightful but utterly meaningless. Jennifer Hallet was arrogant, high-handed, and performatively offensive, but it was hard to imagine her indulging in casual cruelty. If only because it was hard to imagine her indulging in casual anything. *Why the fuck*, Audrey could imagine her saying, *would I want to throw a rock at a frog? Who's got the fucking time?*

And as for Natalie… While Audrey didn't condone throwing rocks at frogs, it had a kind of cheerful nihilism to it, and Natalie was neither. Even so, it had been far too easy for six-weeks-ago-Audrey to convince herself, at the time unconsciously, that Natalie was basically her Emily Branningham—a woman she'd spend her life reaching out to hoping in vain that she'd reach back. Now, though, all of that felt abstract and disconnected. Something that belonged in the past.

Which might have been where Emily belonged as well. And, if it was, then this story that Audrey had so desperately been trying to find an ending for was never meant to have one. It was just two women hurting each other over decades and then eventually maybe one or both of them partly getting over their otherwise doomed relationship. Until Audrey stumbled in with her actually fairly small feet and stomped all over everything.

"Lane?"

She'd been so absorbed in her thoughts that she hadn't heard anybody approaching, but she tried not to look too startled as she twisted around to face Jennifer Hallet, who had appeared from out of the dark like a sexy banshee in a shabby leather jacket.

"You've been a really fucking long time."

"Sorry." Not wanting to keep craning her neck, Audrey swivelled and found herself kneeling on the riverbank staring up at a woman who seemed to naturally default to being stared up at. "I was just having a think."

To Audrey's very mild surprise, Jennifer lowered herself to the ground and sat opposite her, one leg tucked underneath her, one knee up. "Thinking about what?"

"All of it."

"Oh, nice," replied Jennifer with reassuring sarcasm. "Very specific. What *bits* of all of it?"

Audrey wasn't sure where to look. Jennifer was sitting closer than she usually did, at least in nonsexual contexts, but she still wasn't a stare-soulfully-into-my-eyes type of person. Which was awkward because Audrey was in the mood to stare soulfully into something. She cast her gaze slightly downwards, which had the unfortunate consequence of leaving her staring soulfully into Jennifer's breasts.

"The bit where I'm still not sure I'm doing the right thing, but where I know I want to do it anyway even if it isn't, and where I'm worried that makes me a terrible person, and—"

Jennifer laid a finger over Audrey's lips. "Calm down. This is a shitty fucking world full of shitty fucking people who spend more than half their time making other people's lives shittier. But you won't make it a better place by beating yourself up about questions you can't answer."

"I might," replied Audrey, a lightly laid finger proving little to no impediment to speech.

Jennifer looked unimpressed. "Doris chose to talk to you. She chose to let you look for Emily. If you find her, they'll both get to choose if they want to meet again. There really does come a point where it's fucking hubristic to pretend you're the one calling the shots."

It was comforting logic. Sufficiently comforting that Audrey was inclined to mistrust it on principle. "Okay, but—"

"No buts. All this *what if* pap is helping nobody. Now, how's the search going?"

For a moment, Audrey didn't know how to answer. Not because she didn't *have* an answer but because she still wasn't quite used to Jennifer being on her side. It was a weird sense of power and danger, like having a pet tiger.

"Badly?" she said. "Or possibly fine? The problem with this kind of thing is that you don't really know. I've got some leads I'm following up, but they could all turn out to be dead ends. Or, y'know, I could have Emily's home address and phone number by this time tomorrow."

Jennifer gave a sly smile. "You're enjoying the chase though, aren't you?"

That was another place Audrey had been trying not to let her mind go. While there was a lot about her old, higher-stakes, higher-stress career she didn't miss at all, she *had* missed that. "A bit," she admitted.

Jennifer's smile grew even slyer. "We'll make a ruthless corporate husk out of you yet."

"Looking forward to it."

The sky was fully dark now and the air fully chill. Jennifer rose to her feet, shook herself against the cold, and then said, "I should be heading back. Work to do, you know. If you wanted to—I mean, you'd be welcome to join me."

And that, more than permission to search for an enigmatic aristocrat, more even than the final chapter of a story she was still trying to process, was the best offer Audrey'd had all evening.

Saturday

IT HAD BEEN an incredibly long time since Audrey had tried to actually spend the night sharing a single bed with another adult, so when she and Jennifer were awoken by a hammering on the trailer door she was feeling like a badly braided loaf.

Jennifer slid out from under the covers, wrapped herself in Audrey's quilt, and went to see what was up. Or rather, to hear what was up by shouting to whoever was outside from the comfort of her supervillain chair.

"What is it?"

"Alanis isn't coming on set," replied Colin Thrimp's trembling voice. "I don't know why but she's refusing to come out of her room and they'll be needing her in makeup soon, and if she throws off the schedule—"

Jennifer was already dressing, as was Audrey. Although Audrey was managing to do it without also saying *fuck* repeatedly under her breath like it was the opening scene of *Four Weddings and a Funeral*.

Once they were both presentable, Jennifer yanked the door open and Colin came stumbling in like a surprised Labrador.

"I've tried everything," he explained, "but she seems quite inconsolable."

Jennifer looked over at Audrey. "Well?"

"Well, what?"

"Well, go on. Get out there and hold her hand and tell her everything is going to be fine."

That put Audrey in a bit of a spot because she hadn't *not* been going to do that, but she didn't really want to be taking instructions from somebody she was sleeping with. "Can I remind you I'm not an employee?"

Jennifer made a strangled noise of frustration. "I'm so sorry. Audrey, my dear friend, will you please as a personal favour and out of the goodness of your heart get the fuck up and sort this fucking mess the fuck out?"

Adjusting the line of her dress to something slightly more face-the-world-worthy, Audrey smiled. "Glad to."

With Colin Thrimp scampering in her wake, Audrey made her way down to the Lodge and, from there, up to Alanis's room. And it was only when she was knocking on the door that it struck her she wasn't actually the best person on set to be doing this, since Meera had kids of her own, Doris had kids and grandkids, and Joshua was way closer to Alanis's age. On the other hand, all three of those people were still in the middle of a high-stakes baking competition.

"Go away," said Alanis. "I've already said I don't want to talk to you."

"I'm not Colin," Audrey told the door. "I'm, um, me."

"Audrey?"

"Yes."

"You know"—Alanis made a sniffling noise from inside—"for

someone who's not on the show anymore, you're on the show a lot."

"Yeah, it's a long story. Can I come in?"

For a moment, there was no reply. But eventually Alanis opened the door, looking as miserable as Audrey had ever seen her, even worse than she'd been after a bad week's baking. Then she went and perched on the edge of the bed, still in her self-consciously retro nightdress, her eyes tearstained.

"Want to talk about it?" asked Audrey. Which wasn't a great opener, especially since she had no idea what *it* was.

Alanis just shook her head. And Audrey—still not completely certain what to say—sat down beside her. Maybe if she was lucky, this would be one of those situations where silence was stronger than words.

It wasn't.

After a few minutes in which the only sounds were intermittent sniffing from Alanis and the muffled tapping of Colin Thrimp pacing outside, Alanis leaned her head against Audrey's shoulder and started full-on crying again.

"Is it all getting a bit much?" Audrey tried, getting an unwelcome insight into how her own parents must have felt when twenty-years-ago-Audrey would come home from school sad about friends, a girl, or homework and totally unable to communicate about it.

She felt Alanis's head shake, but there was otherwise no answer.

"Whatever it is," she tried again—hoping a more open approach might work better—"it'll be okay."

Alanis's breathing deepened and, after a couple of moments steeling herself, she finally said, "You can't possibly know that. You don't even know what it is."

"I mean, you could tell me. If you wanted."

"I don't want to talk about it."

"And you don't have to. But…actually." Audrey paused. "I don't really have a good but. You don't have to."

"Don't shame your butt," said Alanis, with an echo of her usual spirit. "You've got a great butt."

"Aren't you a bit young for dad jokes?"

Somehow Audrey sensed she was getting a look, even though they weren't looking at each other. "No. Millennials don't own irony."

It was the first time Audrey had heard someone use the world *millennials* to describe an older generation, and she wasn't sure she liked it. "I'm sorry. I stand corrected. Sit corrected."

"Oh, Audrey," replied Alanis, with indulgent teenage pity. "And…it's Joshua."

Sudden shifts in topic were something Audrey was very much used to. Unfortunately, the topic to which they'd shifted meant her immediate instinct was to say, *Fuck, what did that hipster piece of shit do?* Except that would have been unhelpful on many levels. Especially if the hipster piece of shit had, in fact, done something. "What happened with Joshua?" she asked carefully.

"I—" Alanis was still very much mid-sniffle. "I asked him if he wanted to…" She didn't specify exactly what she'd asked him if he'd wanted, which meant Audrey's imagination went to a whole lot of different places. "And he said I was too young."

The sheer relief almost made Audrey burst out laughing. She didn't, because that would have been an unbelievably awful response to have to an upset teenager. But now the moment had passed, she was realising quite how prepared for the worst she'd been.

"Okay," she offered, trying to strike a balance between reassuring and minimising. "Well, that's—"

"I'm *sixteen*," Alanis went on. "I'm old enough to make my own decisions."

They were already on sensitive ground and it was only getting sensitiver. "You are," Audrey agreed, because there was no point disagreeing. "But so is he. And I guess maybe he didn't want to think you'd look back in a few years' time and decide he was a prick?"

Alanis looked up, wide-eyed. "That's what he said."

"Is it?" Audrey was genuinely surprised. Joshua didn't seem like the kind of guy who would have a sense of his own prickishness.

"Pretty much. He said, 'I don't want to be something you look back and regret,' but basically."

That seemed more like him.

Alanis was crying again. "I'm just so humiliated. I humiliated myself."

Having, not too recently, removed her own underwear in public to score a point in an argument with a scary woman, Audrey wasn't quite sure she was the best person to be giving advice on humiliation. Or perhaps she was absolutely the best person. "That's not how it seems to me," she said. "How it seems to me is that you put yourself out there, even though you knew you might not succeed. And it didn't work out because not everything does, but that's okay."

With an ability to leap around different reasons to feel bad about herself that Audrey found deeply familiar, Alanis segued. "I just really thought he liked me."

"I think he really does. I just also think he…"

"Doesn't want to be something I'll regret?"

Audrey nodded.

"Well, I hate it."

Privately, Audrey hated it a whole lot less than the alternative. But she didn't say that because at the end of the day Alanis *was* entitled to her agency. So she just said, "Yeah, but you might hate it less tomorrow."

"That's tomorrow. Today I have to be on TV with him."

"Which will suck. But you'll get through it."

Alanis made a small want-to-believe-it noise. "Promise?"

"Promise," replied Audrey, trying to project confidence and certainty and, she thought, mostly succeeding.

"Not gonna lie, it doesn't *feel* like I'll get through it."

Here, Audrey was on firmer ground. "It never does. Like if I'd actually not got through all the things I felt I'd never get through, I'd…"

With an instinct for kindness that Audrey couldn't help admiring, Alanis waited until it was clear that no, Audrey really had run that sentence off a cliff. "You'd be…not through any of them?"

"Yes," Audrey finished with a grateful nod.

"Thank you for your wisdom."

"Anytime."

For about half a second, Alanis looked at least partially reassured. Then she glanced up at Audrey with visible concern. "Shit, do I look really cry-face?"

"A bit," Audrey conceded, "but they can do a lot with makeup."

They both got up and stood facing each other, which meant Audrey was left trying to be all sage and comforting at somebody who stood about an inch taller than her.

"Don't worry," she said. "You're going to"—Audrey excavated her reserves of synonyms for *do well*—"rock this or nail this or kick arse or eat and leave no crumbs or whatever means you've got this."

Alanis was looking at her with faint concern. "Are you having a stroke?"

"No, I'm being encouraging."

"Okay." She patted Audrey's shoulder reassuringly. "I'm encouraged. But please stop."

For the rest of the day, Audrey sat in Jennifer's trailer, watching whichever camera feed was following Alanis. Although it was hard to tell without sound, she seemed, as far as Audrey could tell, fine. It made her retrospectively resentful of her teenage self who had been significantly less fine about almost everything.

The blind bake for this episode was brownies and, unusually for the doing-simple-things-well season, it actually *was* about doing simple things well. There were no tricks or hidden gimmicks, but there was a whole lot of talk about texture and evenness of bake and crumb density. What with it being the week before the semifinal, everybody left in the competition categorically belonged in the competition, and so the judging for that week was achingly close, with Joshua just taking it, Meera coming an unexpected bottom, and the rest clustered in the middle for a variety of highly technical reasons.

"Well, that seems to have shaken out okay," Jennifer told her when they'd done. "You could barely tell she started the day with a tantrum."

"It wasn't a tantrum, Jennifer. She was really hurt."

When she turned her chair to face Audrey, Jennifer was smiling a more sardonic, less malicious smile than she usually gave.

"Yes, yes, people have feelings, children should be protected, I'm terrible. Now how about you take the win and kiss me?"

And on this occasion at least, Audrey was happy to follow instructions.

Sunday

"WELCOME," GRACE FORSYTHE was saying over the live feed, "to the *last* challenge before the *semi*final of this the *eighth* season of *Bake—*"

"Colin, ask Grace what the fuck she thinks she's doing with her stress patterns."

In the ballroom, Colin Thrimp relayed the question and Grace Forsythe, speaking into open air, explained that if Jennifer had to ask, she'd never know.

"The *eighth* season," Grace Forsythe repeated, "of *Bake Expectations*. And because this is chocolate week, you are to be set a challenge worthy of Willy Wonka himself—before you say anything, Colin, that is *not* advertising; it is a *literary* reference. You are to craft the most spectacular, most elaborate, freestanding chocolate centrepiece you can possibly imagine. The judges have asked me to remind you that this is a *baking* show and so it should have a *baked* element, but that otherwise not even the sky is the limit. We expect to see chocolate work, we expect to see spun sugar, we expect to see something that the *Daily Mail* can say was 'extremely graphic' even though it really didn't look very phallic at all. You have four hours starting on three"—she paused, as always, for effect. "*Three*, darlings."

Monitoring by video, Audrey was glad that she was already out of the running. Chocolate work had never been her strong suit, and as she watched the other contestants bring their remarkable constructions together, she felt very, very sure that she'd have just embarrassed herself. The other thing she was glad about was that Alanis appeared to be continuing in her earlier fine-ness. Grace Forsythe was with her now, as she happily whipped up a cake base while chatting to the camera.

"So since I did chilli chocolate in the first week and it didn't work," she was explaining, "I thought I'd do it again. Which will either be my shot at redemption or"—she made a kind of exaggerated wince that would play great on TV—"a really bad idea."

"All the best ideas are," replied Grace Forsythe with a smile. "But tell me, do you think a week one bake will be enough for the semi-demi-final?"

To Audrey's relief, Alanis was back to her trademark confidence. "I'm doing a mirror glaze, and I'll be putting tempered chocolate decorations on the top in a sort of forest scene."

"Wonderf—" the sound cut off as Jennifer switched feeds.

"Colin," she was saying, "nudge Marianne and Wilfred over to the granny and make sure they push the *execution* angle because it's looking like she's gone underambitious this week, and I don't want to lose her."

Her eyes flicking from monitor to monitor, Audrey followed the darting figure of Colin Thrimp as he crossed the ballroom to find the judges and convey Jennifer's instructions. And then the sound cut back in as they appeared, seemingly spontaneously, at the end of Doris's workbench.

"Cherries," Marianne Wolvercote said, inspecting the arrayed ingredients, "and kirsch—I have a feeling I know where you're going here and, well, there are very much two ways it could end."

"Nowt wrong with a black forest gateau, Marianne," insisted Wilfred. "Just because they were big in the seventies don't mean we're never allowed to eat them again."

Doris nodded. "And you said centrepiece, and when we used to have family dinners, our centrepiece was always a black forest gateau."

Jennifer slid her headset down for a moment. "Lane, if the old lady fucks this because she doesn't know what the word *centrepiece* means to a TV audience, I'll be very mildly peeved."

"She'll be okay," Audrey reassured her, not actually especially certain. "She knows what she's doing."

On screen, Marianne was peering inquisitorially at Doris's bench. "These aren't all black forest ingredients, are they?"

"Got to have some decorations. I'm not just serving up a cake and nothing else."

Wilfred Honey looked sage. "So what's the story?"

"When I was young," Doris explained, "and not so young, come to think of it, there was this bomb site near where I lived—it's a city farm now, which I reckon is good—and what with it being just waste ground and all, we used to use it for fetes and things. And that felt—I don't know—that felt nice to me. Because me and my Bobby and the kids, we could get together and we could go and be happy somewhere what was all ruins." She stopped and looked down, almost wistfully. "Felt like hope."

With palpable relief, Jennifer turned to Audrey. "Okay, you're right. She fucking nailed it."

Filming proceeded well after that, and Audrey's increasingly producer's eye view allowed her to better appreciate the artistry with which the whole thing was assembled. The way Grace and the judges teased camera-ready segments from everybody they spoke to. The way the crew flickered invisible behind everything that happened. The sheer volume of footage that was being generated and processed and would eventually make its way onto television screens as a little capsule of magic. All the mirrors and wires carefully hidden away.

Once the contestants had finished their bakes, they were ushered outside for interviews while the camera crew swarmed around their various offerings to film them from televisually appropriate angles. When they were brought back in again, Doris was the first up.

Her finished bake was, by the standards of the show, highly unusual. She had started out by making a perfectly ordinary if well-executed black forest gateau, with a series of ominous rectangular blocks of chocolate shortbread and chocolate brownie that she'd arranged around the outside like ruins. Then, in a fit of something Audrey felt could have been either boldness or pure whimsy, she'd smashed half the gateau to pieces.

Or rather not smashed. It *looked* smashed, but she'd actually deconstructed it very carefully.

"Well," Marianne Wolvercote observed as it was laid in front of her. "It's definitely not just a black forest gateau."

"Although," added Wilfred Honey, "I do think smashing it up might have been taking things a touch too far."

Doris smiled. "In for a penny, in for a pound."

Marianne Wolvercote had started tasting. "It's baked exceptionally well. It has all the flavours you'd expect, and while I know Wilfred has his misgivings, I think the presentation is completely on point."

While Marianne had been sampling the gateau itself, Wilfred had been trying the brownies and biscuits, and was now expressing his approval. "It'd have been very easy to cut corners here," he explained, "but you've done a good job on each of them. I think we can safely say we're impressed."

They were slightly less impressed with Meera's and Joshua's offerings. Meera had made a chocolate Eiffel Tower in memory of a family holiday to Paris, but the judges felt it included too few elements, while Joshua had presented a pretty straightforward chocolate cake decorated with chocolate work that was clearly intended to be intricate but that in practice had come out just looking a bit messy.

That left Reggie and Alanis, with Reggie up first. As the engineer of the season, he'd taken the large, freestanding structure mandate to heart, creating a three-tiered cake with each tier held above the last by a latticework of pure chocolate.

As the camera zoomed in on the towering edifice, Audrey's general respect for Reggie's engineering knowhow found itself in a low-key argument with her finely honed sense of dramatic necessity and inevitable doom.

It was a very impressive piece of baking. But what made it impressive was that when you looked at it, your first thought was, *I can't believe that actually stays up.*

So Audrey wasn't entirely surprised when it didn't.

The moment it started to topple, Jennifer was barking instructions into her headset faster than Audrey could keep up, directing every camera and every member of the crew to make sure the event was chronicled as completely and as cinematically as possible.

"Fantastic," she was saying, "two and three, keep on the cake; five and nine, I want reaction shots. Faces, people, show me faces."

And faces she got. Expressions of shock and empathy from other contestants and pure mortification from Reggie. And somewhere off-camera, Grace Forsythe was coming forward and making yes-isn't-this-exciting-but-we-have-a-show-to-shoot noises.

Once the footage was collected and the floors were cleaned, Reggie—encouraged by Grace—made his way up to the front of the ballroom.

The judges were very nice about it, explaining that they'd only be able to judge based on what they'd been served, but that his ambition had been commendable.

"What remains," said Marianne Wolvercote as gently as she could manage without harming her brand, "is nicely baked. And if the structural integrity of the piece had held, you might have had something first-rate."

Wilfred Honey gave one of his trademark grandfatherly nods. "You've had a bad week, lad. And that can happen to anyone."

That left Alanis, who approached the judges with the perfect mix of confidence and humility, laying down her chilli-chocolate-mirror-glaze-cake-with-forest-scene with just that little bit of extra care in the wake of the great entoppling.

"Now, this *looks* beautiful," Marianne Wolvercote began. And it did. It was recognisably the same cake as week one, but elevated as only two months of intense competitive training could elevate. The glaze was bright and reflective, and it was decorated on top with a dense, three-dimensional forest rendered in tempered chocolate.

As the cameras panned around, Audrey could see that

amongst the trees walked a girl—or the silhouette of a girl—in a flowing dress, the path beneath her feet picked out with a dusting of chilli flakes. It looked like an edible fairy tale, or perhaps an edible self-portrait.

"The presentation is just lovely," Wilfred Honey agreed. "It's so good it almost feels bad to cut it."

Marianne cut it. She levered out a slice and subjected it to the autopsy-level scrutiny she applied to every bake that wasn't an obvious dud. "Good texture," she said. "Even layers."

While Marianne was analysing, Wilfred Honey took a forkful. "Aye," he said, "you've done well there. No complaints."

"Is the chilli coming through?" asked Alanis, almost shyly.

"It is," confirmed Wilfred Honey.

Marianne Wolvercote had just finished her own sample and was looking a little more reserved. "Ordinarily, I'd suggest that *Bake Expectations* isn't a show that allows do-overs, but I think you've been clever here. It's definitely more of a reimagining than a simple repetition, and on this occasion it was a good opportunity to show us what you're capable of." She nodded, as if agreeing with herself. "Well timed."

With that the judges retired, and Audrey followed Jennifer out to the gazebo where both the actual decision and the for-the-cameras fake decision would be made.

Having seen this side of the curtain, it was beginning to feel a little anticlimactic. While the tension of Grace Forsythe needlessly stretching out the reveal of that week's winner and loser was clearly artificial, artificial things did tend to work a lot of the time. Being in the room with everybody else, each of you wondering, *Will it be me?* in one direction or the other created something real from something that wasn't.

By contrast the flat, matter-of-fact discussion in which Grace, Wilfred, Marianne, and Jennifer decided in less than seventy seconds that clearly Reggie was out and that on balance Alanis looked better for the win was almost the opposite. It took something real—the final decision over who would be going forward in the series—and made it feel like nothing at all.

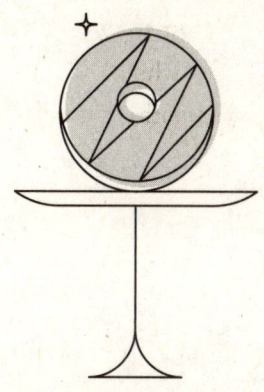

WEEK SEVEN

Childhood

Monday

"AUDREEEY," **SAID THE** voice down the phone. The voice that belonged to Andrew Spencer-Johns, one of Audrey's erstwhile colleagues from her London days. "Dreedree, the Dreester."

"Hi Andrew," Audrey replied, newly weary despite not having heard this particular introduction in more than two years.

"So that chick you emailed about?"

"You mean that nearly a-hundred-year-old woman?"

"That's the one. Think I've got a lead."

Audrey grabbed a notepad. "Fantastic, where?"

"Monaco."

Of course. Emily Branningham couldn't be somewhere nice and accessible like Dagenham or Cleethorpes. "Care to narrow that down a bit?"

"Hold on Dreebedee, it's been *yonks*. What's with all this straight-to-business tosh?"

What it mostly was, was that Audrey and Andrew Spencer-Johns had never actually been anything even close to friends. They'd worked together, he'd been vaguely in the room that one time she'd tried cocaine, and he'd made fewer awful comments about her sexuality than most of the other guys she'd worked with. But that didn't exactly make them mates.

"Sorry, just on a bit of a clock here."

"Really? I was talking to N the other day and she said that you were working for some nowheresville shitrag and trying to get on *The Apprentice*."

It was, a cynical part of Audrey observed, very typical of Natalie to be paying enough attention to know that she was going to be on TV but to performatively misidentify the show so that everybody could see that she was terribly above it all. "Shropshire's second largest regional newspaper," she clarified. "And I'm on *Bake Expectations*."

"Right, right." Andrew seemed only to be half listening. "But what's Shropshire got to do with a jet-set society rando?"

There was a limited amount Audrey could say here without massively pissing off—and for that matter actively betraying—Jennifer. "She had a kind of a thing with a local back in the forties and it didn't work out so there's this whole human-interest-forbidden-romance piece I'm working on."

"And it's suddenly on a clock despite the fact that it's waited more than seventy years already?"

Audrey didn't like playing the mocking-the-elderly card, but there were times you had to do what it took to get the outcome you wanted. "Well, yeah. Because either one of them could drop dead any moment."

It got a laugh, which had been the whole point. People thought less critically when they were congratulating themselves for how clever and detached they were being. "Touché, Audie, touché. But very well. I've had a bit of a word with Seb—you remember

Seb, works for *Milieu* now—and he was saying that she's actually a touch infamous in the right circles."

"A *touch infamous*?"

Andrew gave a kind of verbal shrug. "You know: old, rich, doesn't give a shit. Bit of a nightmare by all accounts but something of a fixture."

"Great." Audrey readied a pen. "So where can I find her *exactly*?"

"Hotel Metropole. But"—a note of embarrassed condescension crept into Andrew's voice—"not wanting to be too dismissive, you might not want to *over*emphasise the regional newspaper angle. I can't imagine it'll go over well."

The sad thing was, it wasn't too dismissive. It was just kind of a fact. *Let me through, I'm with Shropshire's second largest regional newspaper* didn't exactly open a lot of doors. So Audrey just said, "Cheers," and left it at that.

"Oh, by the way, Aubore. What would you say to cocktails sometime in the next few? I know the lads here would *love* to catch up."

Knowing full well that they wouldn't at all, Audrey replied with a sincere-sounding, "Yeah, that'd be great." Then because it was how you played the game, she added a, "Let's work something out."

They made mutually polite goodbye noises and Audrey was left alone to decide how to convert *This woman is probably in this one hotel in Monte Carlo* to *This woman is talking to me face-to-face right now.*

Hotels, as a rule—and especially rich people hotels—did a pretty good job of screening out irritating journalists, especially irritating journalists whose credentials the wider industry tended to see as one step up from a school newspaper. Of course, if Emily was as infamous as Andrew had suggested, she might not be too hard to at least get a message to, even if she wouldn't take a call. And then the trick would just be making sure she'd call back.

Two hours later, having spent most of the afternoon gaming out scenarios in her mind, Audrey decided that she might, *might* be stalling.

Besides, she had a pretty good idea of which approach would work best. If any would work at all.

So she called the Hotel Metropole and asked if she could leave a message for Emily Branningham. And when the whatever-you-called-the-person-who-answered-phones-in-an-expensive-hotel answered that she could, Audrey left her number and seven words: *I want to talk about the nymph.*

Wednesday

AUDREY'S PHONE STARTED ringing at four in the morning and she rolled sideways on the bed to answer it.

"Who is this?" asked a silken, upper-class voice from the other end of the line.

Had she been very slightly more conscious, Audrey would have identified the caller at once, but she wasn't so she didn't. "You're the one who called me."

"You left a message."

With an internal *fuck*, Audrey swivelled herself into a sitting position. "You're Emily Branningham."

"And you still have the advantage of me."

Audrey really wished she'd had the foresight to leave coffee by the bed, because if there was anybody who'd call back at the exact least opportune time, it was Emily. Still, she tried to come across as confident, assured, and professional instead of, for example, somebody whose mouth still tasted like midnight.

"I'm Audrey," she said. "Audrey Lane. I work for"—she hesitated for a heartbeat, but decided to err on the side of fuck it—"I actually work for a tiny local paper you'll never have heard of, but I've recently met a woman called Doris Rice, and I want to tell her story, and I think you're part of it."

The other end of the phone was dead silent for a few agonising moments. Then Emily replied with a cautious, "Part of it in what way?"

There was a time for circumspection, and a time for very much not circumspection. "She said you fucked."

And then Audrey heard Emily Branningham laugh. And it was everything Doris had described it as; an audible chiaroscuro, an angel who you'd just this second realised picked the *other* side. "My dear sweet thing, I don't believe she used any such words."

"No, but that was very much the gist."

"And what do you want to talk to me about? Do you want me to confirm her story? Because if so, I'm sure my lawyer would suggest I offer you a polite *no comment*."

"I think," Audrey replied, only really articulating it to herself as she was saying it, "that I just wanted to meet you. Because, well, I think I can't understand her unless I do."

In the brief silence that followed, Audrey could see Emily's smile as clearly as if she'd been in front of her. "Well, you know where I am."

"And you'll still be there?" Audrey confirmed, because it was a whole lot safer than not confirming. "If I get on a plane to Monaco and rock up at the Metropole and say, 'I'm here for Emily Branningham,' they won't just tell me to go do something humiliating with something it would be humiliating to do it with?"

"Well I can't *absolutely* guarantee it," admitted Emily. "But don't you think it would be fun to take the risk?"

Fun wasn't quite the word Audrey would have used. But *exhilarating* might have been. "I'll be there tomorrow."

On the other end of the line, Emily Branningham made a little putting-things-together sound. "You'd already booked tickets, hadn't you?"

"I had a feeling this would work out," Audrey lied. But it seemed cooler and more confident than, "I had no clue if this was going to work out, but I needed to be sure I could get there and back before Friday, and I was already cutting things really fine."

"I do admire a woman who takes risks," replied Emily Branningham and, without giving Audrey room to respond, she hung up.

Flopping back on the bed and not quite sure she could believe that this was actually happening, Audrey fired off a text to Jennifer. It just read: She called.

It didn't really surprise Audrey that a reply came back near instantly. Jennifer was the up-at-all-hours sort. The reply in question being: I'll come with you..

She's in Monte Carlo.

The three dots hovered for a while as Jennifer composed her response, which eventually landed as: I'm a TV executive. I travel. And I'm not letting some mad posh tart on my show without meeting her first.

A fortnight ago, even a week ago, Audrey would have assumed that the probability of Emily actually being allowed on camera was something around the square root of zero. If you think you can swing it. I got a ticket for Thursday.

Another dance of the three dots. Then: So did I.

Because of course she had. We could have booked together. We probably won't be on the same flight.

Oh no. However will I survive three hours on a plane without you.

Barely even thinking, Audrey texted back: Fuck off.

And Jennifer responded with: Fuck off to you too.

Thursday

AS SOMEBODY WHO resolutely considered herself a country girl, Audrey was weirdly more comfortable with Monte Carlo than with London, possibly because she knew she would in no way be required to live in it.

The hotel was opulent without being extravagant and, had Audrey not seen her fair share of lifestyles-of-the-rich-and-famous nonsense in her years as a ver srs journalist doing ver srs journalisting, she might have been slightly staggered by it. Jennifer, of course, seemed like she'd never been staggered by anything in her life. She approached the exquisitely tasteful concierge's desk with the unwavering resolve of a woman who saw desire and action as the same side of the same coin.

"We're the hacks," she said. "Here for Branningham."

Although neither politeness nor patience were Jennifer's strong points, she did at least manage to wait politely and patiently while the concierge called up to Emily's room, explained that her guests had arrived, and that yes they were guests *plural* and that he trusted this would be acceptable. Then he gave them a room number and directions to the lifts.

It came as no surprise whatsoever to Audrey that Emily Branningham had taken a suite on the top floor, which meant it was rather a long lift ride to meet her. A long lift ride in which she valiantly suppressed all of the voices that were telling her that this was a spectacularly bad idea.

"It'll be fine," Jennifer reassured her. "After all, she's not the love of *your* life."

"I'm not sure that helps as much as you think it does."

"Worst-case scenario, it's a 'Thanks but no thanks' from us or from her."

Audrey tried to accept this as fact and failed. "I don't think it is. I think the worst-case scenario is that talking to her stirs up all kinds of things we should have just left alone and makes her life and Doris's life and possibly *my* life materially worse."

The expression on Jennifer's face wouldn't have been comforting to anybody who didn't know her very well indeed, because it was an expression that said, *Your concerns are trivial and I cannot be fucked with them.* It was only if you'd got closer to her than most people dared that you could see it was also saying, *Therefore you shouldn't be fucked with them either and I'll have your back if they try to be fucked with you.*

"Emily's life is"—she gestured at their surroundings—"like this, so she'll either be fine, or if she's not fine it'll be her own fucking fault. And Doris made her choices a long time ago and you don't get to take that away from her. As for you"—Jennifer gave that twist of the lips that wasn't quite a smile but was better in so many ways—"clearly you can take care of yourself."

The door to the suite was opened not by its resident but by a member of the hotel staff, and Audrey couldn't quite help but suspect that it had been arranged that way deliberately. Because it meant that when Audrey first saw Emily Branningham she was framed in a window, sitting in a wicker chair on a private terrace overlooking the Mediterranean. The little girl who wanted to grow up to be Rebecca de Winter had got her wish and then some.

With a studied, casual slowness, she turned her head to acknowledge her guests. Her hair was silver now, beneath her sunhat, her face lined with age. But her eyes, peering over the top of dark glasses that Audrey's personal taste for the retro aesthetic couldn't help but approve of, still shone like flakes of obsidian.

"Would it be unforgivably cliché of me," she asked, "to begin, *Audrey Lane, I presume.*"

"Classic for a reason," replied Audrey, crossing the floor of the suite without waiting for further invitation.

Emily Branningham's gaze flicked to Jennifer. "And who's this? Your assistant?"

To which Jennifer replied with an inevitable, "Fuck off."

"She's a TV producer," Audrey explained. "Of—I assume you know about *Bake Expectations*?"

"Not really the TV sort." Emily Branningham waved a hand in the direction of the one free chair on the terrace. "Do feel free to sit, though you'll have to fight over it."

With pointed apathy, Jennifer propped herself in the arch of the French window, leaving the seat for Audrey.

"I don't mean to pry," asked Emily Branningham as Audrey was sitting down, "but are you two fucking? I get a vibe."

Audrey was about to say something evasive, but Jennifer cut in with a sharp, "Yes; next question."

And Emily Branningham smiled that smile Audrey had seen so often in her mind's eye. "You know," she said, "I think I might approve of you."

Slightly concerned that things were getting offtrack and irrationally peeved that Emily Branningham seemed to be sort of flirting with her sort of girlfriend, Audrey attempted to bring things back around to the topic at hand. "TV aside," she tried, "the reason you might have heard of *Bake*—"

"Oh, of course." An expression of amused realisation blossomed across Emily's face. "You must be in charge of that show they're making in the bones of my family's legacy. How interesting."

"It pays the bills," replied Jennifer.

A conclusion was forming rapidly behind Emily Branningham's quick, dark eyes. "Well, well, well, so the nymph's come back to Patchley."

Audrey nodded.

"Now isn't that a thing. I always thought she might. That's the trouble with those old, dead houses. They reach out from beyond the grave and drag you down with them."

Sensing that she might be getting somewhere, Audrey slipped her phone from out of her bag. "Sorry, do you mind if I record this?"

Emily Branningham gave her the kind of insouciant look you could only give after a near century of making a positive virtue out of carelessness. "As it suits. Now where was I?"

And after taking a moment to gather her thoughts, she continued.

JUNE 1987

JIMMY LEFT IT to me to shut the old place down. He'd always been weak like that, sentimental. I think it was the shame that got to him in the end—the shame of losing it all. And he bloody well *should* have been ashamed because if you're going to lose a fortune you should at least have the decency to lose it on something interesting. Gamble it or snort it or go off your head and spend it all building a starship out of Norwegian spruce or something.

Not Jimmy. Jimmy was just a Lloyd's name. But that was all it took, in the end. Asbestosis hit and Lloyd's of London was paying out hand over fist, and poor bastards like Jimmy were on the hook for more than even we could afford, and the Branninghams had never been short of a bob or two, as I'm sure you've worked out by now.

I had my own inheritance, of course, but they couldn't touch that. He actually asked me if I could bail him out, and I'm not ashamed to say I laughed in his face. Even if I could afford it—which I couldn't, Lloyd's liabilities were uncapped and I wasn't about to write him a literal blank cheque—I wouldn't have. He was the man of the house, after all, the golden boy, the heir to the name and the estate. It had never been mine, not really. Nothing in the whole fucking house had ever been mine.

Don't look at me like that, it spoils the flow of the story. That was a deliberate setup.

Although actually, maybe you've done me a favour. If this does end up in your little paper, I don't want to come across as some godawful cliché. No, I really don't think that's how I want to be remembered. *Nothing in this house had ever been mine…dot, dot, dot, pause for effect…except her.* Gah, no, I can't believe I even considered going there. It's like something you'd read on the back of a cheap paperback you buy in an airport.

I am choosing, for what it's worth, to assume that the nymph is fine. If she was dead, I expect you'd have told me. And besides, I'd have known—I keep an eye on obituaries and these days I have a Google alert as well, which I'm sure will get *deeply* wearing once she starts appearing on television.

Well she always was a handy little cook, although if you don't mind my saying, that wasn't the skill I most valued in her.

Where were we?

Oh yes, Jimmy. Didn't even have the balls to shoot himself, you know. That's what I'd have done—at least it's what I'd have done if I'd been in his situation, which as I think we've established is a situation I would never have been in to begin with. That's the done thing, you see, in our set. You let your family down like that and you quietly dig out your father's pistol or the groundskeeper's shotgun or whatever and you blow your brains all over the Axminster.

Jimmy just got sad and resentful for a few years. At the very least you'd think he'd drink himself to death, but no. It was cancer in the end. And not one of the glamorous cancers. I think it was his bowels although I was in Paris at the time.

Anyway, back in eighty-seven, when he'd lost everything in the most flatly pathetic way you could lose everything, he called me up and said, "Emmy, I need you to sort out the house, you never liked it anyway"—that much was true; Patchley was pretty enough but a big shiny prison is still a prison—"so you'll have an easier time of it."

Well, I told him I wasn't a fucking accountant and he could get the solicitors to do it, but he said it had to be family.

"Family," I remember saying to him, "can go fuck itself."

And he said, "Emmy, please," and he sounded so wretched I agreed just to shut him up.

So there I was. I'd already done the dark business of telling the staff that they'd no longer be needed, which they didn't take well but they'd not exactly had much choice in the matter. And with the people gone, all that was left was the *stuff*.

After all, isn't that what a legacy is when you think about it? Nothing but *stuff*. Old wood and brittle porcelain and ink on paper and paint on canvas. We pretend it's history, we pretend it's memory, but it's nothing of the sort.

Still, on the day the hotel people came around to decide what pieces they wanted to keep and what pieces they were going to sell off to the public like some grotesquely over-glorified garage sale, a little of Jimmy's sentimentality must have rubbed off on me, because I found myself wandering the house looking at rooms I hadn't really looked at in decades, just trying desperately to *feel* something.

I don't like to, as a rule. Emotions are such sticky, unhelpful things. But there was an end-of-an-era sense about the selling of Patchley that made me want to indulge, if only a little, in melancholy.

It wasn't very, in the end. Melancholy, that is. The more I walked the halls of that enormous, pointless house I'd grown up in, the more convinced I was that it had nothing to offer me or, for that matter, anybody else. A nicely assembled pile of rocks it may have been, but it was still just a pile of rocks.

Then I saw her.

At first I thought I was losing my mind or seeing ghosts, because this—let us not forget—was the year of our lord 1987 and we were all of us flirting dangerously with our sixties, but the woman I saw wandering the halls of Patchley House, staring at the décor like a tourist, was the image of the nymph as I'd known her all those years ago.

Fuck me she was beautiful.

I mean really. I'd called her *nymph* at first because a classical education does terrible things to a young girl, but by all the gods you might pray to, it suited her. I—and you'll forgive an old woman the indiscretion but this memory pleases me—I remember the first time I saw her naked. We'd actually been fucking for a while, but given the situation in the household it was hard to find time to properly *be* together. Once she became my lady's maid it was rather easier, and so it wasn't until fifty, fifty-one perhaps, that I got to know what she looked like as well as what she *felt* like.

And damn it all she was worth the wait. She stood there in the half-dark, her hair spilling lightly over her breasts, her eyes cast just slightly down. Titian could have painted her. And when I pressed my lips to her skin I felt closer to paradise than I ever have on this earth.

What she was doing now, this ghost out of time walking the halls of a dying stately home, I couldn't say.

So I asked her, "Can I help you?"

"Not really," she replied. And it wasn't her voice. Nor, now was I closer, was it her face. Like but not like. "I'm just looking around."

"The sale is tomorrow," I told her.

"I know. I just wanted to see the place, I suppose, before. I've always meant to visit but I've never really found the time."

A great many things about this woman were piquing my interest. In—I hope you understand—a strictly appropriate way. "Something particular about Patchley that stands out to you?"

"My mum used to work here. I think it might have been important to her."

As I say, I keep an eye on obituaries and I did then as well. But I am neither infallible nor incapable of reaching an obvious conclusion, so her use of *have been* made my breath catch and my throat close, like I'd had a bad reaction to a bee sting. "Is she…is she no longer with us?"

The woman laughed at that. "What? No, she'll see us all out, I've no doubt of that. I just mean—she'd talk about this place sometimes, and I got curious."

"What's your name?" I asked her—I suspected I knew but I wanted to be certain.

"Sue. Sue Rice. Going to be Sue Jones soon—that's another part of why I'm here, as well as the sale. It just feels…I don't know, there's sort of a chapter closing?"

"That makes sense," I told her, though I wasn't sure it did really. As I say, I've never been one for sentiment.

"So who're you?"

It was a reasonable thing to ask and to this day I'm not quite sure why I lied, but I did.

"Jane," I said. "Jane Loris. I used to be housekeeper here, and I'm helping the family put the place in order."

It was a silly deception, and honestly I think it speaks rather poorly of Susan that she didn't see through it. I neither talk nor dress like a housekeeper and I never have.

"When was your mother here?" I asked, as casually as I could, which, though I say it myself, was extremely casually. "I might remember her."

"The fifties, I think?" She couldn't be more specific. "Her name was Doris—it would have been Doris Cooper then."

My intent, I think, had been to say something cuttingly anodyne. *Oh yes, I recall, pleasant girl, good teeth* or similar. But hearing her name—even though I never really used it, she was always *the nymph* as far as I was concerned—silenced me and I stood there with my lips going dry and my eyes on the edge of betraying me. "She was a good girl," I said. Which was true. "Was there anything in particular she talked about?"

"Just that she'd been happy here," Susan said. "And that Sir Arthur had been a kind man. She took me to his funeral, I think, but I don't remember it."

I nodded, though I was fast losing interest. "Yes, he's much missed."

An awkward silence fell between us, and I was beginning to think that Mr. Jones was welcome to young Susan. She might have superficially resembled her mother, but she wasn't anything like as interesting.

"She mentioned you, too, I think," she added. "I forget the name, but she said the housekeeper had been good to her."

I confess that one burned. "How sweet." For a moment, it seemed she was about to go, and while I didn't think we would ever be bosom companions, I wasn't quite ready for her to leave just yet, so I asked her if she'd like a tour.

She said she would.

And so I led my nymph's youngest daughter around the house I'd grown up in. The house her mother, in many ways, had grown up in. Where she'd spent most of her girlhood. Where she'd made lifelong friends. Where she'd had her first kiss and, if you'll forgive my bluntness, her first orgasm. Hell, for all I know her last as well. Then again, maybe I'm flattering myself.

I showed her the public rooms, the ones anybody was allowed in because that was always part of the deal with places like Patchley, at least in the postwar years: families like mine got to live there and in return families like yours got to poke around and look at things and bother us. I'm not sure who got the better side of the bargain, if I'm honest.

But there were only so many parlours and galleries a person could pretend to care about. Then I showed her the family's rooms, including my own. Including, and I'm not too proud to admit that this thrilled me just a little, the bed where all those many years ago I had—to borrow a phrase that I believe is increasingly common these days—fucked her mother.

I elided that detail, of course. But I said it was the young mistress's room and asked idly if Doris had ever said anything about her. Which is to say, in case you're not keeping up with the complexities of the narrative, about me.

She hadn't.

At last I took Susan down to the servants' quarters. Honestly it wasn't somewhere I went much, the rooms were pokey and frankly the servants didn't much appreciate the family coming and nosing around their things. I opened a door more or less at random and Susan slipped inside like a thief through a window.

Fortunately, the maid who would have been living there had already gone, although she'd left a cassette copy of *True Blue* on the nightstand and a stray stocking on the floor. Susan sat down on the bed, picked up the abandoned tape, and stared at it like it held the secrets of the universe.

And maybe it did. They were the same age, I think, Susan and Madonna. Not exactly, but close enough. So here I am in my nineties thinking back thirty years to my sixties remembering a girl of twenty-eight staring at another girl of twenty-eight with her head thrown back on the cover of an album full of songs about true love inspired by a man she would later divorce.

Madonna, I mean. Not Susan. Although I confess I don't know how her marriage played out. Still it seems apposite somehow.

"So…would she have had a room like this?" she asked me.

"Very much like it, yes."

For some reason that seemed to strike her harder than anything else. She ran a hand over a mattress that was nowhere near old enough to have actually touched the nymph's skin, and gazed in something like wonder at the walls of a room her mother may never even have been inside.

Meaning, I think, is very much where we make it.

"You know," I told her, "they're selling the contents of this place in a couple of days. If there was anything your mother wanted she could"—and what was I doing, really? Trying to bait a girl I'd known thirty years ago back to watch the death of a house she'd been happy in?—"well, she might find something she liked."

Susan looked down at the cassette, then up at me. "Yeah," she said, "she might."

She left soon afterwards, and I didn't expect much to come of my little suggestion. And not much did.

But not much is not the same as nothing.

There wasn't, if I am honest, a great deal left in the house after the hotel had taken what they fancied. The drawing rooms, for example, they seemed to be planning to leave as they were, so that guests could get an authentic stately home experience during their stay, which meant none of those fixtures were up for sale. Even the beds they kept, although I'm sure they've replaced most of them since—it's been years after all, and hotel use isn't kind to furniture.

Most of what remained for the general public was knick-knacks, gewgaws, and tchotchkes. And portraits, of course, but I doubted that anybody was actually going to want a painting of somebody else's great-great-grandfather. At least not at the prices we were asking. I think most of them got bundled in with the house in the end.

In eighty-seven, though, they were still in the long gallery, all discreetly ticketed. I was there as well—in person and on canvas—and so, on that particular day, was she.

Age, I thought, had been kind to my nymph. I was under no illusions, of course, she was very much a woman in her sixties, her hair silvering and her skin lined, but I'd have known her anywhere—across years and continents.

I seldom weep—it was a habit I gave up in early childhood—but seeing her after all that time brought unfamiliar tears to my eyes. She was standing in front of my portrait, looking up at it with such an air of regret and melancholy that I froze.

Perhaps I should have spoken to her. I almost did, in fact. But then Susan came back through from the next room, a man beside her who I assumed was the elusive Mr. Jones. And when the nymph turned to her it was with such belonging and such easy intimacy, I could not quite bring myself to intrude.

Besides, I'd have needed to explain to the daughter that I wasn't really a housekeeper, and that would just have been awkward. And I have a hereditary aversion to awkwardness.

I don't know if she bought anything. Or what she said to her family when they asked her why she was staring at that one picture in particular or if they even asked her such a question.

They probably didn't. I've been alive a long time now and something I've gradually worked out is that while I have fought for decades to remain at the centre of my own world, it's a form of hubris to imagine oneself the centre of another person's. Secretly, I have always held, we are all of us solipsists.

So I left through the far door and retreated to my old room, half-stripped as it was, and sat on the window seat, crying like a fool or a child.

I never saw her again, and in the years since I have made my peace with the fact that I never shall. In my own way, you see, I'm just as great a coward as Jimmy was. I think perhaps I may have modelled myself after the wrong Mrs. de Winter. The money and the lovers were rather wonderful things in the moment, but looking back. Well. It's that silly nameless girl I envy. The one who took a chance and changed her life instead of spending the whole of it running away.

That's probably what I saw in the nymph, you know. What I lo—what I admired about her.

There, are you satisfied?

Thursday Evening

"I'M NOT FUCKING satisfied," said Audrey.

They'd retired to a corner of the lobby to lick their wounds. And if Audrey'd been less disappointed-slash-pissed-off she might have appreciated the fact that she had, at least momentarily, the kind of life where you sat in an intimate corner of a luxury hotel with your abrasively sexy not-exactly-girlfriend to bemoan your failure to persuade a jaded aristocrat to fly home from Monaco to be reunited with a woman she'd had an affair with in a stately home seventy years ago. Like, that was a whole mood.

Except it also sucked.

Jennifer was sitting sprawled in a plushly upholstered chair, looking like a twenty-first-century rakehell who'd had a hard night raking hell. "I mean, what did you expect?" she asked. "She spent her entire life bailing on the poor fucker. Did you really think she was going to turn around and say, 'Actually I'll make amends at the last moment'?"

"Um. No? But also…yes? Nice things do happen sometimes."

"Oh yes, because age and wealth are renowned for changing people for the better."

Tilting her head back, Audrey gazed at the intricate, multi-coloured glasswork that cascaded from the ceiling. "Can you stop being cynical for six seconds?"

"I could, but if I was going to, I'd pick a time when that cynicism wasn't completely justified."

"You came out here, too," Audrey pointed out.

"Due fucking diligence. That and not wanting you to spend an evening cranking into the Mediterranean because some haughty bint wouldn't give you the time of day."

"Doing what into the Mediterranean?"

"Cranking. You know, cry wanking."

Audrey bent her considerable journalistic instincts to assessing this from multiple angles. "Okay, I don't crank, and I'm not convinced that's a thing anybody does. But I'm glad you didn't want me to be upset."

By way of answer, Jennifer gave a low growl.

And, for a moment, they sat in marbled silence: Audrey still circling the whirlpool that was Emily Branningham and Jennifer presumably working out how to walk back the fact she'd done something a little bit lovely. Even if it had been obscured by a veil of cranking.

"I think," said Audrey finally, "what bothers me the most about all of this is that she clearly cares about Doris."

That earned a dark Jennifer Hallet laugh. "No, Lane. She's in love with her. And that's not the same thing."

"Isn't it?"

"Please, not even you are this naïve. Caring about someone means wanting what's best for them. Being in love just means wanting them."

"I want the best for people I'm in love with."

"I'm sure you do. But the fucking miserable thing about you, Audrey Lane, is that you're a good person. Most of us aren't."

"I think most of us are, actually?"

"Okay. But people like me and Emily Branningham aren't. Love to you is nice quilts, holding hands, and trying to make people happy. To us, it's just power you don't want to give away."

A couple of weeks ago, Audrey would have believed this little speech. "That might be what you tell yourself, Jennifer, and it might even be true of Emily. But you've still got that shitty quilt I made. And you've held my hand a bunch of times—"

"During sex doesn't count."

"Yes it does. *And*," Audrey went on triumphantly, "you came here because you didn't want me to be sad and alone."

"Oh fuck off."

"No, I will not fuck off." Audrey extended an accusatory finger. "This meaner-than-thou talk doesn't fool me anymore. You like me. You care about me. And…and I think we're both cool with that."

"I'm not fucking cool with it," retorted Jennifer Hallet at a hotel-lobby-inappropriate volume. "You snuck up on me like tertiary syphilis."

"And to think you keep telling me you're not romantic."

"Yes," said Audrey, as they wandered hand in hand across Larvotto Beach. "Not at all romantic."

Jennifer didn't even dignify this with a *fuck off*. "Well, it was this or go shag in a casino toilet, and I thought the beach would be more your speed."

"You realise there are more options than shag in a casino toilet or go take a walk by the sea."

"Not in Monte Carlo there aren't."

"Well, maybe we can fuck in a casino toilet later."

"I'm game if you are."

"Honestly," Audrey admitted, "I'm not particularly. I've never really got the whole…lavatorial-taboo-fetish thing."

"I don't think it's about being taboo. It's about having a door that locks."

"I'm so glad," said Audrey, "that we're on this golden beach beside the turquoise waters of the Mediterranean talking about toilets."

"You were talking about toilets. I was talking about sex."

"Sometimes I have no idea why I like you."

"Same. Now"—Jennifer had spotted something through a small forest of sunshades—"do you fancy a taco?"

"What?"

"There's a place over there called Sexy Tacos. Don't make me not eat at a place called Sexy Tacos."

"Are you seriously basing our dinner plans on the name of the restaurant?"

"No, I'm basing it on my detailed knowledge of Monte Carlo's dining scene. It's here, it's on a beach, it sells tacos—what more do you want?"

Put like that, Audrey couldn't name a single thing. And fifteen minutes later they were sitting on the sand, in the part not taken over by the militarised battery of sun loungers, Jennifer wolfing down a taco de cochinita pibil while Audrey tried to subtly check that she hadn't dropped guacamole down her bra.

"See something you like?" asked Jennifer.

"They're my own breasts, Jennifer. I see them every day."

"It's a topless beach, you know. You can whap them out if you want."

"I'm more concerned about spilling taco down myself."

"Let me check that for you." Before Audrey could stop her—not that she would have—Jennifer leaned over and made a brief performance of inspecting's Audrey's person for stray crumbs and dollops of sour cream. Finding none, she danced the tip of her tongue up Audrey's cleavage and across her collarbone. "Seems fine to me."

"Smooth moves," Audrey told her.

And Jennifer Hallet laughed.

"I suppose," she remarked, after a minute or two, "I could have taken you to some fancy restaurant."

Finishing the last of her taco, Audrey balled up the wrapping and popped it in her bag. "No, this is perfect."

"Never really liked restaurants. Full of sneering fuckers who judge you."

"I think, being a TV producer, you might be a sneering fucker yourself these days."

"Thanks. I've worked hard to get there. Still doesn't mean I want to pay two hundred and fifty quid for whatever Alain Ducasse deigns to serve up to me while the pricks at the next table try to earwig whatever the fuck I'm talking about."

There was a touch of…well, Jennifer didn't get vulnerable and didn't do uncertain. But, reading between the lines, Audrey almost felt like she was being asked a question. "I mean, I like the occasional restaurant. But it's not a deal-breaker."

"Didn't say I thought it was," said Jennifer, confirming she'd definitely thought it might be.

Audrey lay back on the oddly glinting sand and stared up at the cartoonishly blue sky. Beside her, Jennifer did the same, turning so she could rest her head against Audrey's side. Given the three-hour flight and the unsatisfying conversation with a disdainful lesbian, they were both hovering on the edge of exhausted. But with the heat mellowing as the sun dipped lower, and the contented feeling that arose from having had some really good tacos, it wasn't a bad exhaustion. It just turned the world a little hazy and swept its everyday concerns out to sea. Which was, perhaps, rare for both of them.

"How are the talks going?" asked Audrey.

Jennifer made a drowsy noise. "What talks?"

"Selling the show."

"Oh, those talks. All talks are the same. They want this, we want that. Grace'll probably go if it moves. She's BBC to the core."

"Will it still be *Bake Expectations* without her?"

"Some people will say it is, some people will say it isn't. But they'll carry on watching anyway."

"And what about you?"

"I probably won't. I think it went downhill after season three."

Lifting an indolent hand, Audrey batted in Jennifer's general direction. "I meant what will you do, like, career wise?"

"Technically I won't have to do anything. I'll be fucking rich."

Audrey's imp of the perverse fluttered its wings. "You could move into a suite in the Hotel Metropole and hang out with Emily."

"We could while away our twilight years consoling each other about what miserable fucks we both are. Well, her twilight years."

"I don't think you've ever whiled away anything in your entire life."

Jennifer made a not-disagreeing-with-you noise.

"But it's going to feel strange, isn't it?" asked Audrey Lane, investigative relationship journalist. "Not having *Expectations*."

"It's going to be a bloody relief," said Jennifer, with too much conviction. And then, "I suppose so."

"What were you doing before?"

"This and that. A couple of those be-angry-about-this-social-issue type documentaries that nobody fucking watches. A game-show called *The Box* where no one understood the fucking rules." Sitting upright, Jennifer scuffed at the sand with the toe of her boot. "And then Jemima was all like, let's do something nice and cosy, and it fucking worked and she fucking left me. And the BBC are already on at me to do a spinoff about sewing or pottery or hairdressing or something."

Audrey sat up, too. "I'm sure those would all be…great. But I don't know if trying to recapture what you did with *Expectations* is the right call."

"It's the right call financially. None of them will be as good or as big, but you can make a dozen of the fuckers."

"Yeah, but, like you say, you'll already be rich so why do spin-offs if they're not what you actually want to do?"

"Because I don't want to be rich and bored. And I also don't want to go off and make up-yourself vanity projects about dead fish and sad children. I want to make something people give a shit about." She turned so she was facing Audrey directly. "And they give a shit about *Expectations*. And I used to. And in an ideal world, those two would line up again."

"I'm sure they can," said Audrey.

"You can talk, Miss Shropshire's Second Largest Newspaper."

"Hey, I…" That brought Audrey up short for a moment. She felt nebulously defensive, but she wanted to make sure she was defending the right thing. "It's not about the size of the audience. It's about telling the stories I think matter."

"What? 'Parking Fees to Change in Much Wenlock'?"

Audrey sighed. "Yeah, and I'd like to do less of that. But that isn't because it's *small*, it's because I'm not particularly interested in parking. But then I'm not particularly interested in what the prime minister lied about this week either. I'm interested in—"

"Two sad lesbians in a house in the forties?"

"I mean, yes. Or, I don't know, Alanis's father's journey from Somalia. Or all the little stories that are going on all around us all the time. The ones we ignore or forget or pretend aren't part of our history and who we are."

"Careful, Lane." Jennifer gave her a sharp look. "It sounds like you're pitching a miniseries."

"You mean, the sort of dead-fish-and-sad-children, be-angry-about-this-social-issue show you've just told me nobody watches?"

Jennifer was quiet for a long moment, her expression unreadable. "Depends how you package it. If *Expectations* taught me anything, it taught me that. Well, that and don't stay on the same fucking show for eight years."

Six weeks ago Audrey would have made an obvious personal connection about the dangers of sticking with something that wasn't working for you for a very long time. But present-day-Audrey wasn't feeling it.

All present-day-Audrey felt was the last of the day's heat. Which—like Jennifer—stayed with her as the sun slipped away and the extravagant rainbow of the city lights streaked across the still waters of the bay, turning it into a fantastical slick of colour.

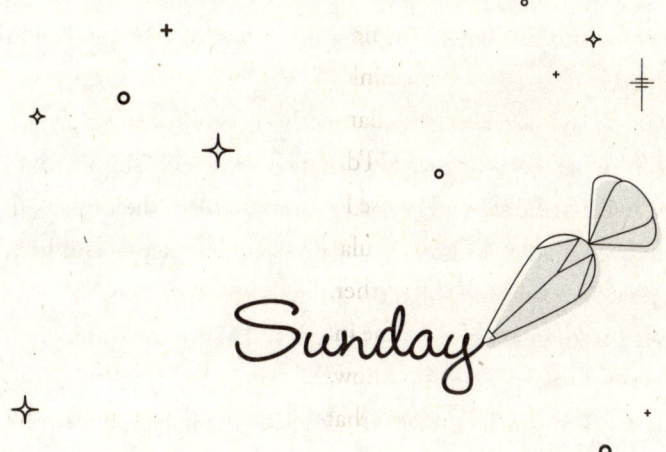

Sunday

NOT BEING QUITE as much of a workaholic as Jennifer and also suspecting that dropping the whole the-love-of-your-life-doesn't-want-to-see-you-again bomb on Doris right before filming would be kind of a dick move, Audrey took the Friday afternoon and the Saturday off, only returning to Patchley on the Sunday, arriving just in time to catch the judging.

The theme for that week's baketacular was simply "childhood favourites" with no instruction beyond—in Grace Forsythe's words—"blowing Wilfred and Marianne's little socks off." And while Audrey was sure Jennifer would characterise it as cheap, saccharine, and emotionally manipulative, she still appreciated the, for want of a better word, rightness of it.

Because it didn't only close the loop on episode one's *show us who you are* bake by asking the contestants to *show us who you were*, it grounded the penultimate episode of Jennifer's last series in reflection and retrospection. *How far we have come?* it seemed to be saying. And it was saying it in a room containing a woman who had lived in Patchley before it was even a hotel, and a girl who had been watching the show since she was eight years old.

Cheap and saccharine it may have been. But it was also *perfect*.

Meera had been first with a variety of extremely simple bakes of the make-at-home-with-mother variety, which, she explained, she enjoyed making at home right now with her actual children, plus a batch of laddoo, which the judges nitpicked.

"If I were in a mood to be technical," Marianne was saying, "these aren't baked."

It wasn't normally wise to talk back to the judges, but Meera did anyway, and Audrey could see why. "Neither are donuts, but you did those last series."

Jennifer pressed a button. "Colin, tell her the point's taken but to can the meta talk. We let the contestants go on like that and they'll be doing fourth wall shit all over the place."

While Colin was relaying this, Alanis raised a hand from the back of the room.

"What did the child say?" asked Jennifer.

"She's made sambusas," Colin relayed, "which aren't baked either."

Jennifer didn't quite headdesk, but her head moved in a desky direction. "Fuck it, tell Marianne to be less pedantic and we'll just accept that Disgusted of Tunbridge Wells will write us angry letters."

Next up was Alanis, who came forward and set her childhood-on-a-tray down in front of the judges. "So these are sambusas," she said, "which are really more from my dad's childhood, but I wanted to celebrate that as well. And this is unicorn toast, and I *did* bake the bread myself. And I made rainbow cupcakes to go with it."

Wilfred Honey and Marianne Wolvercote looked down at the riot of colour before them with the most kids-today looks on their faces that Audrey had ever seen.

"What I find really distressing about this"—Marianne Wolvercote picked up a multicoloured cupcake—"is realising that you would have been about ten years old during this particular trend."

Alanis nodded. "Yeah. When I was younger it was rainbow everything for days, and I wanted to get that feeling back."

While she'd been talking, Wilfred Honey had picked up a sambusa. "Now this," he said, "has a lovely golden-brown colour to it, which is exactly what I want from a pastry and—if I may say so—to me feels more like a proper food colour in general. And the flavours are *gradely*. The spices are coming through wonderful."

"This, on the other hand…"Marianne Wolvercote was poking at the unicorn toast. "Now as it happens, I do know how hard it is to get those swirls to look just right. But the problem is that, well, this was a trend that went away for a *reason*. Making something brightly coloured doesn't actually make it taste better, and while the bread itself is competently executed, I don't think the cream cheese and marshmallow fluff topping actually adds anything to it."

Alanis gave a fair enough kind of nod. "Yeah, it wasn't as good as I remembered."

Next up was Joshua, with his mix of homemade party rings and, for reasons Audrey wasn't at all privy to but which he'd presumably explained in an earlier to-camera segment, mini Cornish pasties. It being the semifinal, he received a base level of praise just because of the high standard of the competition, but unless Doris did extremely badly, Audrey was pretty confident that he'd done nowhere near enough to overcome the youngest contestant, oldest contestant, mum framing that Jennifer had as good as admitted she was going for.

That just left Doris. Like Joshua, she'd leaned heavily into keeping things simple. Like Alanis, she'd gone for recipes that unmistakably spoke to the exact time and place of her youth. They were all rationing-era—something called glory buns, a tray of jam tarts, and, in pride of place, a simple loaf of fresh-baked bread.

"I grew up round these parts," she explained to the judges. "Well, did some of my growing up round these parts at any rate. And it's food like this what I used to look forward to the most."

Marianne Wolvercote jabbed at a tart. "Simple," she said, "but excellently presented."

"And by 'eck it takes you back," added Wilfred Honey. "It's true not everything was better in the old days, but I can't fault a nice bun, nor a jam tart, and that bread is just wonderful."

The cynical part of her brain that Audrey sincerely wished she could switch off made her turn to Jennifer and ask, "Is that really what they think, or did you tell them the old lady needed a win?"

"Given the news you're about to give her," Jennifer replied, "would you say she doesn't?"

Doris did, in fact, get the win in the end. Audrey had skipped the gazebo talk, fearing that she'd find it too depressing, but that just meant she didn't know what had been said and had to assume the worst. She tried to tell herself it had been a clean victory. That everybody else had made some kind of crucial mistake, like not pushing themselves hard enough or serving something that looked better than it tasted. But she couldn't quite shake the feeling it should have gone to Meera.

Once the unsurprising news of Doris's victory had been delivered, Grace Forsythe moved on to the equally unsurprising news of Joshua's defeat. And since that would be the cue for the contestants to start going their separate ways, Audrey set out at once for the ballroom so that she could catch Doris on the way out.

She ran into Joshua first.

"Hi," she said, a little awkwardly. "Sorry to see you go."

He gave her an almost rueful smile back. "It's cool. I got all the way to the semifinal, and I was up against three amazing women who really deserved to go through."

There was the tiniest edge of rehearsal in his voice, which made Audrey suspect he'd used the same line for the cameras. "That's very chill of you."

Joshua nodded. Then just as Audrey was about to move on he said, "Alanis told me you spoke to her the other week. And, thanks, I suppose."

"I'm not sure what you have to thank me for," replied Audrey, who genuinely wasn't.

"Just for helping her out. It was—look don't take this the wrong way, but I know you think I'm a prick."

"I don't," Audrey protested, subconsciously kicking herself at the insincerity in her voice.

"Yeah you do. So do most people. And I get it. But this"—he indicated himself, but with particular emphasis on the trilby/goatee/slightly retro shirt combo—"isn't an act. People think I'm really tryhard because I'm really trying."

Not sure what to say to that, Audrey made a kind of encouraging *uh-huh?*

"So, yeah I guess I was glad that even though you don't like me you didn't, like, trash me to her or anything. But you still had her back. And, like, I know that's a tough line to walk so, thanks."

"Don't mention it?" Audrey tried. Partly because she was beginning to wish he hadn't.

Joshua nodded. "Bye, Audrey."

"Goodbye, Joshua." Then after a moment's pause she added, "Umm, do we hug?"

"Maybe not?"

"Yeah, good call."

She watched Joshua walk away, out of the competition and in all likelihood out of her life. And felt the mildest pang of guilt at the fact she still thought he was a prick.

Unable to put off telling Doris the bad news any longer, Audrey made her way over to the steps, where she was still giving her obligatory just-glad-to-have-a-win-at-last interview. In as little of a hurry as ever, Doris said a polite goodbye to the camera operator and ambled over to where Audrey was waiting.

"Congratulations," Audrey began, pushing aside any doubts she was still harbouring about the fairness of the whole arrangement. "It was about time you won a week."

"Because of the story, you mean?" asked Doris with a playful smile.

"Because you're good. You've done well every time, and this week you did best."

Doris gave Audrey an askance look. "You think? Or you think it was just my turn?"

The honest answer was that it was difficult for Audrey to judge. "The problem is I know why you went with the bread. And that makes me a bit biased."

"Bit pathetic really, isn't it," replied Doris. "Still thinking about that one day after all these years."

"It's not pathetic." Audrey's instinct would have been to say the nice thing anyway, but this time it really did have the virtue of being true. "We all have days like that, I think—ones we keep living in even when we shouldn't. And if you're going to have those sorts of days, better that they be the good ones than the ones that, well, that aren't so good."

Doris nodded a gentle agreement. "I've had a lot of good days."

"And you'll have a lot more."

That made Doris laugh. "Leave it out. I know I'm old. You don't have to pretend I ain't."

"I'm not pretending, I just mean—you know, life is still good. In general."

Doris had stopped laughing. "She's not coming, is she? You'd've said by now if she was."

"Sorry." Audrey tried not to squirm. On balance, she still thought going to see Emily had been the right thing to do. But it did mean she was now having to give shit news to a nice old lady. "And I would have told you sooner, but I'd had a long trip and I didn't want to ruin your weekend and it seemed really insensitive to just come straight out with it after you'd won and—"

With the impeccable instincts of somebody who'd been grand-mothering longer than Audrey had been alive, Doris came forward and folded her into a hug. "Hush now. It's no matter. You tried your best and—was she okay? Was she happy, like?"

And Audrey wasn't at all sure what to say to that either. "She was—she was exactly like you described her."

"Not sure that answers my question."

"Was she happy when you knew her?"

Breaking off the hug, Doris looked calm, almost contemplative. "Some days I thought she was," she said. "Some days I thought she wasn't. Some days I thought I was wasting my time trying to work it out."

Audrey nodded. "Yeah. She was a lot like that."

"I reckon," said Doris, with a deliberate slowness that suggested she only half trusted the notion, "I reckon that's good to hear. I'd not have wanted her to change. Not really."

Honestly, Audrey wasn't sure if she agreed. Then again she wasn't sure if Doris really agreed either. But you got through life by telling yourself what you had to tell yourself, and probably *The woman I love has always been a beautiful disaster and it comforts me that she still is* was the safest way to go.

Better than just admitting the whole thing was a miserable pissing letdown.

WEEK EIGHT

Final

Saturday

"WELCOME," **GRACE FORSYTHE** was saying over the feed, "to the last blind bake of the season. And *what* a *season* it has been. We've had ten wonderful contestants and we've lost the seven *least* wonderful, which leaves us here, now, with the *absolute* cream of the *absolute* crop. And at last we will crown our extremely deserving winner, who will walk away with a slightly underwhelming cash prize and lovely souvenir cake slice. And won't that have been worth it?"

"Tell her," Jennifer conveyed to Colin, "to stop running down the show on air."

"It's classic British self-deprecation," replied Grace Forsythe once the criticism had been passed on. "It plays wonderfully in the States."

"It fucking well does not. Tell her I've got metrics."

But Grace Forsythe, as ever, wasn't listening. "And without further ado, we shall launch directly into the final blind bake. And since this is our last back-to-basics challenge, we are asking you to go *right* back to basics. We aren't quite asking you to catch your own hare, but we *are* asking you to make your own jam, and your own marzipan as part of putting together your own, utterly from scratch, perfectly rectangular, Battenberg cake. You have four hours starting from three. *Three*, darlings."

And off they went. In a strange sort of way—and despite Grace's attempt to big-up the finality of the final—it was business as usual. Flipping over the recipe card, discovering it was inadequate, sorting through the ingredients, some of which were misleading, all of them in greater quantities than you actually needed, then making a valiant effort because what else could you do?

It had only been five weeks since Audrey had been standing there herself, but it felt impossibly distant. Like something from your childhood. Or an audiobook you'd fallen asleep listening to. She was conscious of a prick of nostalgia. Of being briefly part of something she loved. Something that was going away. And going away more completely than anyone in the ballroom could know.

To them, this was just another final. And maybe it would be the same to the audience, who probably wouldn't care what channel the show was on or who produced it. But it was Jennifer's *last* final. The only one she would ever share with Audrey.

On the screens, everyone was hard at work. Doris seemed to be taking the challenge the most in stride, but then she'd presumably been scratch-making jam since the war. Alanis, by contrast, was wobbling, her relative lack of experience showing through for the first time in weeks. But narratively, Audrey thought, she could afford the loss. That was the great thing about having a youngest-ever contestant. No matter how far she got, it was a win. She could have been eliminated in week one and she'd have done well to get through auditions. As runner-up, people would definitely remember her.

A glance at Jennifer proved, as ever, that she was hard to read.

It was business as usual in the supervillain chair. And whether that was because she genuinely didn't care about her legacy or because she knew doing her damn job the way she always did was the best way to secure it Audrey couldn't say. Actually. Strike that. She could completely say. It was the second one.

"Who's it going to be?" she asked.

It was oddly flattering that Jennifer didn't even pretend not to know what Audrey meant. "I'll tell you when I know."

"You haven't decided already? I'd have thought you'd planned it all out weeks ago."

Keeping her eyes fixed firmly on the monitors, Jennifer said, "I didn't say I've not thought about it. But you can only work with what you shoot. The old one or the young one will be easier to spin, obviously."

That was pretty much what Audrey had expected. But it still felt kind of bad. "So Meera's just filler? She's really talented."

Jennifer shrugged. "You want to know the dark secret of this show? People are exactly as talented as we make them look."

"And you're going to make Meera look worse than she is so you can give it to someone with a more interesting story?"

"Yes. Or no. Or maybe. It'll depend on how it comes out. If the granny drops a trifle or the foetus cracks under the pressure, then we'll give it to Meera and I'll find some way to make TV gold out of happy children saying how proud they are of mummy-slash-daddy for the third fucking time in a row."

"Is there not another story you can tell?"

"Yeah," said Jennifer. "There is. And it involves the granny or the foetus."

"I just…" Audrey felt naïve even as the words came out of her mouth. "I just think Meera might actually be the best baker?"

"And when the best dancer wins *Strictly*, I'll give a fuck."

Audrey would have said more but then Jennifer leaned forward and issued Colin an instruction so trivial that it was blatantly an excuse to end the conversation.

Ultimately it was a fairly quiet judging with no real surprises. It was close because despite their very different ages and levels of experience, the remaining contestants were all top-of-their-game baking persons. But Doris's years of getting by on one egg a week and darning her own stockings had paid off and put her just at the top of the Battenberg-from-scratch challenge, while Alanis's squares had been called out as being *slightly* uneven by Marianne Wolvercote, which—at this stage of the competition—was enough to consign her to the bottom of the pack.

Once the last interview had been concluded—something that happened a lot more quickly when there were only three people—Jennifer took off her headset and snapped her laptop closed. "Get your coat, Lane. You've pulled."

Audrey blinked at her. "Sorry. What?"

"It's our last night on set. I need to be top of my game tomorrow morning. A single bed fucking sucks. And I'm fucking horny."

"Okay? How do these all fit together?"

"I booked us into the main hotel."

The part of Audrey that was slightly on guard against deeply controlling women wasn't sure if she should be fine with this. The part of Audrey who had spent the past couple of weekends having fumbly, slightly elastic sex—and then trying to sleep—in a bed that was barely designed to fit one adult, let alone two, was very, *very* fine. "Great," said that part of Audrey. "Let's go."

Having not that long ago visited the Hotel Metropole in Monte Carlo, Audrey found Patchley House, despite its venerable history and excellent Tripadvisor ratings, a bit of a…if not a letdown, then at least a comedown. It didn't, for example, have a gargantuan glass sculpture hanging from its lobby ceiling or a dazzling view of the Mediterranean or a jaded aristocrat gazing enigmatically at the horizon. But it had one of those sweeping staircases so beloved of the rich and landed, and the décor was a well-chosen mixture of the modern and the traditional.

"Don't get too excited," said Jennifer, storming purposefully down a hallway. "I got this room because it was the only one that wasn't shit."

"It's not, like, a bridal suite or something is it?"

"Fuck no. But it's a bit…historicalish. And that kind of sentimental fuckbilge makes you all wet and gooey."

"Can you not?"

"I can not. I don't not."

Swiping the keycard, Jennifer pushed open a door and Audrey— neither wet nor gooey—followed her into a room that she couldn't help noticing was called the Branningham Suite. And it was, indeed, very historicalish. With a four-poster bed draped in red velvet, pan-elled walls of very dark wood, and oak, oak everywhere.

"Okay," said Jennifer, putting her laptop down on an old-fashioned writing desk and dropping her bag to the floor. "I'm going to give you two minutes to bask in the melancholy of a bygone age and two sad old women you're desperate to connect to. Then I'm going to pull the strap-on out my luggage and you're going to fuck me into seventeen sixty-four."

"Why," asked Audrey, still processing that entire speech. "Why seventeen sixty-four?"

"Is that really the detail you want to focus on?"

"Well, I don't want to overshoot. What if I accidentally end up fucking you into seventeen sixty-three? Or sixteen ninety-one?"

"It's fine. I'll use the safe word."

"We have a safe word?"

"Yeah, it's cut it the fuck out."

"You realise"—Audrey had now worked backwards into the two minutes basking part of the deal—"this was probably Arthur Branningham's room?"

"And probably the room where his son died with a leaky prostate. But I'm sure they've changed the sheets since."

"Jennifer, you're massively diminishing my desire to fuck you into any time period."

She gave a familiar frustrated-sounding *urghf.* "Look, Lane, it's an old house. It belonged to rich dead men. We can't get rid of them, but we can still fuck on their bones."

Put like that, Audrey was almost willing to consider it subversive rather than icky. Because actually there *was* something that felt…if not right, then at least the good sort of wrong, banging her girlfriend in Sir Arthur Branningham's private quarters. Not, of course, in the study where he'd sat Doris down and told her that his daughter loving her brought shame on the family. But where he'd probably slept easy afterwards.

Christ, no wonder Emily was so fucked up.

"Okay," Audrey said, "I'm in."

"Great." Jennifer rummaged in her bag and, like a much lewder Mary Poppins, produced a sexual aid of impressive length and girth, along with a complex arrangement of straps and panels.

These she tossed to Audrey, who completely failed to catch them. "When you said you were going to pull the strap-on out of your luggage, I thought you meant…metaphorically?"

"Who would a metaphorical strap-on get off?"

"I thought you just meant sex in general."

"I'm also up for sex in general, whatever that's a metaphor for. But I brought this because I thought we might like it."

Crouching nervously, Audrey retrieved the strap part, since Jennifer still had the on part firmly in her possession. "I mean, I might? But I've never actually—I mean, you know the whole…" Audrey tried to mime *being penetrated* with, she thought, remarkable success.

"Are you having some kind of breakdown?" asked Jennifer.

"No, I'm miming being penetrated."

"Well, no wonder you don't like it then."

"Very funny. The point is, I don't like it, my ex had political objections to—"

"Political objections to getting off?"

"Not to getting off," Audrey explained. "Just to getting off in what she felt was a phallocentric way."

Jennifer eyed the glittery blue-and-purpled swirled cylinder in her hand. "Whose phallus is this? A fucking unicorn's?"

It was not a good time to be thinking about Natalie. Then again, it never had been. So, instead, Audrey glared at Jennifer. "It's going to be mine if you stop stalling and hand it over."

Jennifer stopped stalling and handed it over. And, for the next five minutes, Audrey failed to put on a strap-on while insisting she didn't need any help.

"Look," said Jennifer. "I'd like to get laid sometime this election cycle."

"And this"—Audrey gestured at her partially adorned crotch—"hasn't dampened your ardour?"

"Not at all. You're being pointlessly stubborn, which is very adorable. And your tits are bouncing around and I'm a woman of simple tastes."

"You really are," agreed Audrey, finally letting Jennifer help. Which she did very efficiently. And that, in itself, was not completely unsexy. At last, Jennifer stepped away. And Audrey—feeling slightly self-conscious—put her hands on her hips and struck a pose. "Well, how do I look?"

Jennifer's mouth twitched. "Standing like that? Like the porn remake of *Captain Marvel*."

Still slightly self-conscious, Audrey raised one clenched fist over her head like she was about to burst into the stratosphere on an emergency sex mission.

"Audrey Lane, what is wrong with you?"

"I've never done this before. I don't know what I'm supposed to do."

"Not that," Jennifer told her.

"Seriously, though." Audrey withdrew her Carol Danvers fist. "What if I do this wrong?"

"It's not that hard. People have been doing it for centuries. Many of them straight men, and they fucking suck."

Deciding to leave the galaxy to solve its own problems, Audrey went and sat on the bed. And, shedding clothes with her usual unfuck-giveness, Jennifer joined her.

"Look," she said. "If it's not fun for you, we stop and we do the things we already know we like."

"But if I can't, what about in the future?"

"I'll do it my fucking self. Now do I need to remind you of the no talking rule?"

"I think we broke that rule a long time ago."

"Oh, shut up," said Jennifer Hallet, kissing her.

Which was definitely something Audrey already knew how to do and something they already knew they liked. And kissing flowed into caressing, which flowed from gentle into heated, with Audrey riding Jennifer's thigh, and Jennifer riding Audrey's fingers, and from there it seemed the most straightforward thing in the world to push Jennifer onto her back.

She looked especially good that way, at once fierce and surrendered, her hair snarled all over the pillow. And because Audrey couldn't feel what she was doing, she had to look as she guided herself inside—and that was way, way hotter than she could have imagined it would be. Getting to see someone's body open for you, red and slick and hungry.

"Fuck," said Jennifer. And they'd had enough sex—and for that matter enough conversations—that Audrey could read Jennifer's *fuck*s like music. This was one of her soft *fuck*s. One of her pleased *fuck*s. And Audrey, as ever, was filled with pride and triumph to have inspired it.

It took Audrey a while to get the rhythm—to learn how deep to go and how far to pull back, the best way to angle her hips to make Jennifer swear and groan—and it was fucking hard work. Nobody told you it was fucking hard work.

But in a strange way the hard work was part of the joy of it. Getting hot and sweaty and breathless with someone else. Sex turned into something you strove for. Worked for together.

And then, towards the end, Jennifer rose up in a carnal fury, flipped Audrey over, and rode her like a wave. One of those wild, white-topped waves that surfers spent their lives chasing. Dizzily Audrey clung to Jennifer's hips, pushing up into her until she came, her back arched with bliss, and her face as fleetingly still as the heart of a storm.

Afterwards they lay on the emperor-sized bed with the curtains half-drawn, perusing the menu for room service.

"You know what," said Jennifer, twirling one finger idly in Audrey's hair, "let's fucking do it."

Audrey looked up at her, wondering if there was a first half to this conversation that she'd blanked on. "Do what?"

"*Dead Fish and Sad Children.*"

For a moment Audrey had zero clues what she meant, not least because until about two minutes ago, she'd been in a situation in which dead fish and sad children were definitely the absolute last thing she wanted to be thinking about. "You want to make documentaries?"

"I want *us* to make documentaries. I think we'd fucking smash it. We could even start with *The Saga of Doris and Emily* if you wanted to."

This was a sufficiently unexpected twist that Audrey felt a strong need to play for time. "I'm not sure which name is worse: *The Saga of Doris and Emily* or *Dead Fish and Sad Children.*"

"One'd be for the series, one for the pilot episode. But don't worry. They're just working titles. *Expectations* was pitched as *Wholesome Baking Show TBC.*"

Thoughts of room service entirely banished, Audrey sat up. "Okay, but—what, do I just quit my job and come work at Inveterate?"

"Basically."

"So you'd be my boss?"

"We could structure around that. We can be co-showrunners with somebody else from the company in overall control."

That just about managed to fix the ethics problems. But there was another slightly elephantine issue still at least partly in the room. "Wasn't trying to make a TV show together what ruined your *last* serious relationship?"

For once, Jennifer looked more vulnerable than scornful. "No, being young, crap, and unable to communicate ruined my last serious relationship. Then we tried to fix it by making a TV show together, and for some reason that strategy failed. Who can say why?"

"I hate to point this out, Jennifer, but you're still not very good at communicating."

"Firstly, fuck off. Secondly, I've actually communicated my needs very effectively. Like, for example, when I said take two minutes basking time, then fuck me."

Audrey opened her mouth to dispute this. Then realised it was, in a very broad sense, correct. "And what about my needs?"

"Sweetheart, you've been doing nothing but communicating your needs since we fucking met."

Audrey also opened her mouth to dispute this. Then realised it was, in a very broad sense, also correct. And, perhaps more importantly, that Jennifer had—in her own way—fulfilled basically every need Audrey had communicated. Plus a fair few she hadn't. "I don't even know how to...make a documentary."

"Of course you do, it's just fucking quilting."

That seemed tenuous. "Pretty sure it's not."

"There's some technical bits around production, but I'll have that covered. What I want *you* to do is gather up scraps nobody else would look twice at, find how they fit together, and turn them into something beautiful. That's quilting. And it's what you do. I've watched you do it."

The key to Audrey's relationship with Jennifer remotely working was that she very seldom let Jennifer leave her speechless. But this time she'd managed it.

Because for the first time since…since forever—since before she'd met Natalie, or at least since before she'd let Natalie take over her life—she felt *seen*. Seen better than she saw herself.

The best gift, it turned out, was one you didn't even realise you'd been missing until you were given it.

It was almost too much. Almost too soon. Almost too good to be true. Which was probably why, when she could speak at last, Audrey went with, "I don't think we should be making serious decisions immediately after sex."

"Lane, when do you think I make all of my decisions?"

Privately Audrey still strongly suspected this was a terrible idea. But—and maybe it was the sex talking, or the whole wash of other feelings she was grappling with right then—she'd never wanted to act on a terrible idea more.

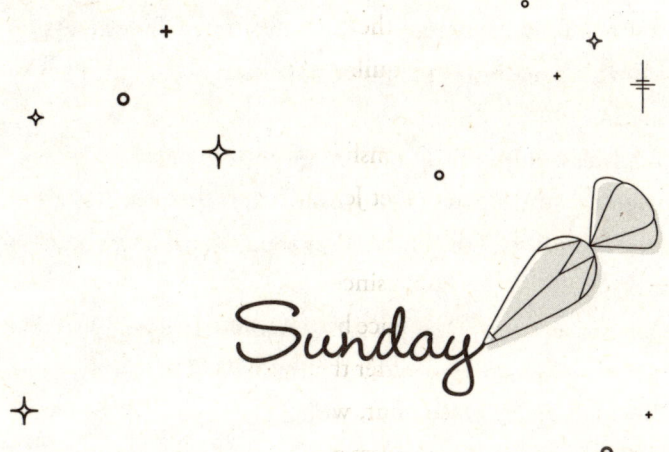

Sunday

FOR THE FIRST time since the beginning of the series, Audrey was regretting having been a contestant on *Bake Expectations*. Because it meant that the day of the final, instead of being able to watch the whole thing with Jennifer through every camera on the set, she was contractually obliged to wait outside on the grounds with all the other eliminated contestants and a huge crowd of friends, family, and well-wishers.

"I still think you deserved to win it," said Audrey's mum, loyally.

Grateful, or as grateful as you can be for something so utterly divorced from reality, Audrey patted her mother gently on the shoulder. "Thanks, but you know I really didn't."

"I think she might be right," agreed Audrey's dad. "These tea cakes are better than anything our Audrey's ever made, no offence."

Audrey's mum looked disapproving, and not—Audrey swiftly realised—because of her father's paternal disloyalty. "Those aren't tea cakes, dear, they're muffins."

"They're not," replied Audrey's dad with a conviction born

not so much from confidence as from a lifetime in a relationship whose love language was petty debates about nothing. "They've got fruit in."

"Muffins can have fruit in," Audrey pointed out.

Then she immediately wished she hadn't, because her mum took that as victory. "See. And Audrey should know. *She's* been on television."

"I'm not saying they *are* muffins," Audrey clarified. "Just that the fruit question isn't necessarily determinative."

"So what is determinative?" asked Audrey's dad, suddenly more interested in muffin definitions than in literally any topic in the universe.

"Well they're traditionally cooked on a griddle," Audrey replied, hoping against hope that something—anything—would come and interrupt them, "but they *can* be cooked on a baking tray and—"

Unusually, her hope was answered. A producer in a black T-shirt tapped her on the shoulder. "We'll be needing you in five."

Audrey had known going in that at some point over the course of the long day's filming, she'd be expected to give a thirty-second to-camera segment where she'd have to say who she was rooting for and to pretend she hadn't had that exact conversation with the producer only the day before. With the producer who she would also need to pretend she wasn't sleeping with.

It was going to be awkward. But right now it was probably less awkward than explaining the nuances of the tea cake/muffin distinction to her parents. So she made very quick, very sincere apologies to them, and dashed off to do her interview segment.

"If you could remember to answer as if you're not answering

a question," the producer reminded her, "and also as if you're not doinking our boss."

It was hard to be outraged at an essentially true accusation. "Hey, I am not—that isn't relevant to the current situation."

"So," the producer began, "how did you find your time on the show, and what's it like to be back?"

"It was so great to be here," Audrey replied enthusiastically, "and so great to be back to celebrate the finalists."

"Does it almost feel like you never left?" asked the producer, with a smirk.

"Honestly," Audrey parroted, only slightly resentfully, "it feels like I never left."

"And who are you rooting for?"

"Everybody in that ballroom is so talented," she said, "and they all really, really deserve it. I just"—she made a gesture she hoped indicated confused excitement rather than obfuscation—"ooh, don't make me choose."

"She's not told you then?" asked the producer dryly.

Audrey was about to make a disgruntled face, but realised just in time that it would be an incredibly bad idea when there was a camera pointed directly at her, so she smiled her just-pleased-to-be-here-est smile and walked away.

She should *probably* have gone back to her parents, but since the great muffin debate was likely still raging, she took the opportunity to people watch for a moment. The other returning contestants were gradually getting their own interviews, but the crew didn't seem to be in much of a hurry, or to be going in elimination order. Somebody was talking to Blue Collar Jim (out week four, Audrey's internal Rolodex noted) but they'd definitely not got around to Gerald (out week one) yet. Which was good, because it might give him time to realise he'd put his shirt on inside out.

"Do you want to tell him," asked a voice behind her, "or shall I?"

Turning, Audrey found Linda standing arm in arm with a thin, bespectacled man with an affable expression. "I think maybe we should leave it?" she suggested. "It's pretty on brand for him, and he didn't get long to make an impression."

"True." Linda paused a moment, then added, "Oh, by the way, Audrey, this is my husband Phil. Phil, this is Audrey. She's the one who told us the whole thing was rigged."

She was smiling as she said it, rather than looking like her world was falling down, which Audrey took as a good sign. "I didn't say it was *rigged*," she protested, "just…rigged adjacent?"

Phil looked perplexed, and although Audrey had only known him for eighteen seconds, she felt he had a good face for perplexity. "What does *rigged adjacent* look like exactly?"

"Like pretty much every reality TV show you've ever seen?" suggested Audrey apologetically.

"Oh. Mygod," said another voice just outside Audrey's field of vision. "*You're* the one who had Alanis all in her head about that."

Turning again—it was going to be a turny kind of day what with being surrounded on all sides—Audrey saw a girl about Alanis's age and about her own height. Like Alanis, she had a personal style that skewed rural, with a floral-pattern dress and a red scarf tied around her hair. She was holding two paper plates and fixing Audrey with a hard stare.

"Sorry," Audrey said. "Who are you?"

The hard stare only got harder. "I'm her *girlfriend*."

That was news to Audrey on several levels. "I…didn't realise she had one."

"Yeah, well." The girl made an extremely dismissive gesture. "There was this whole thing where there was a guy she was into and I was all, *Alanis, no seriously, get with me instead*, and she was all, *Oh but he's so mature and interesting*, and I was all, *I bet he isn't actually. I bet you just think that because you don't see him every day*, and she was all, *No, he totally is like, really, you'd like him*, and I was all, *Well maybe you could see if he's up for a poly thing then*, and she was all, *I'm not sure I'm into that*, and I was all—"

"But"—Audrey did her best to make it the polite sort of interruption—"she's with you now?"

The girl nodded. "Oh yeah. She asked him out and he was all, *Nah babe, you're too young*, and she was, like, *empirically* crushed and I was like, *I told you so*, and she was like, *It's too soon*, and I was like, *Okay*, but that was *weeks* ago."

Two weeks, by Audrey's reckoning. But time was different for the young. "Well, I'm glad I didn't get in her head too much," she said.

"Were you not listening? She was upset about that for *days*." Audrey was about to reply when her interlocutor spotted somebody across the field—an older woman in a bright yellow hijab sitting patiently at a picnic table—and seemed to remember that she had something more important to do than talk to a middle-aged rando. "Sorry," she said. "Love to stay and chat, but I was meant to be bringing cake to Alanis's grandmother."

Having heard at least a little about Alanis's grandparents, Audrey briefly considered going over to introduce herself, although having to start with, "Hi, I'm the one who really upset your granddaughter a few weeks ago," didn't make the idea a terribly appealing one.

While Audrey was weighing the pros and cons of cowardice,

she was interrupted by an announcement. Well, an attempt at an announcement. From across the lawn, Colin Thrimp was jumping up and down and waving. "Everybody," he was saying as loudly as his limited lung capacity and lack of a megaphone would allow. "We're about to bring the contestants out for the final scenes so please stand back, remember to look thrilled at the bakes, and do try to make way for friends and family."

There was an element of herding cats to the whole process, but eventually the crowd did resolve itself into an arrangement that would film well, and Grace Forsythe—always first in everything— emerged from the ballroom followed by Wilfred and Marianne and then, moments later, by Doris, Alanis, and Meera.

The bakes had already been examined by the judges in the more private and more easy-to-film location of the ballroom and so the versions that Audrey could see now were not all they would have been in their full glory, but they were still pretty damn glorious.

Since the contestants were told the weeks' themes in advance so they could start practising, Audrey already knew that the final challenge had been a cake that doesn't look like a cake— *Expectations* keeping up to the last its tradition of reflecting the latest in baking trends only a year or two after they came to mainstream attention.

None of the illusions were perfect, partly because amateur bakers under competition conditions couldn't be expected to achieve perfection, partly because making a cake totally indistinguishable from a non-cake object relied a lot on good lighting and friendly angles, and partly because they'd already had slices cut out of them. But even as imperfect illusions, they were impressive.

Alanis had made a bouquet of roses strewn on a bed of leaves, which, if Audrey was honest, probably looked the most cake-like of the cakes. Meera had gone for something more ambitious, a children's lunchbox complete with a sandwich whose crust really looked like bread, and crisps whose packaging really looked like something you wouldn't want to eat. Which Audrey supposed was a positive in this highly specific context.

And finally, there was Doris. She'd made a book. And although Audrey barely got close enough to see before the children, grand-children, and great-grandchildren flooded in, she managed to catch the title that had been painstakingly stencilled onto the leather-effect cover: *Rebecca*.

Once the cakes that didn't look like cakes had been thoroughly demolished and the contestants had been given time to get all the good luck and well wishes they needed from their assembled sup-porters, they were lined up in a row to wait for the final results.

The final, final results, Audrey recalled, with a twinge of regret for the past and excitement for the future.

"Friends," Grace Forsythe began, "Romans, countrypersons, lend me your ears. I come not to bury Caesar, nor to praise him. Actually, I've not come to say anything about Caesar at all. I have come, as I always do, to congratulate our marvellous, *marvellous* finalists. Three of the most exquisite human beings ever to be expected to bake on *Bake Expectations* and including, of course"— *Here it comes*, thought Audrey—"both our oldest"—camera hovers on Doris—"and our youngest"—camera hovers on Alanis—"ever contestant. But nevertheless the question remains, have age and treachery beaten youth and skill—"

"Jennifer says we're cutting that," interjected Colin.

Grace Forsythe gave a long-suffering sigh. "No sense of fun, no sense of nuance, that's her problem. Where were we?" She paused for a third of a heartbeat. "Ah yes, *the question remains*, who, at last, is our winner."

Silence reigned on the grounds. Or at least silence would reign once the birdsong, distant sounds of traffic, and muttering of unruly children had been edited out in post.

"Well," Grace Forsythe went on. "Without any more delay."

This phrase, naturally, preceded a delay of some seconds.

"I can announce."

She paused again.

"That the winner."

And again.

"Of the eighth."

Again.

"Season."

Again. And this time Colin Thrimp piped up. "Jennifer says you're just taking the piss now."

"Colin"—Grace Forsythe affected a tone of outrage—"there are *children* present."

"Jennifer says…" And here Colin Thrimp blushed and tripped a little on his words. "Um, that is, she says *eff the children*."

Grace Forsythe smiled. "I bet she doesn't. But do remind her that all she's doing is delaying things unnecessarily." Then she stopped, took a dramatically deep breath, and returned to her speech with the word "Of."

"Seriously Grace," Colin relayed.

"*Bake*."

"You are this close to being fired."

"*Expectations*." Pause. "Is."

"I mean it."

"None other."

"She says that's it, you're done. It's over. You're…well you can probably fill in the details for yourself."

"Than."

Still, Grace was pausing for effect.

"Meera."

The crowd burst into thunderous applause, Meera looked like she was about to faint, and Audrey, despite having deep down felt that Meera *deserved* the win, could scarcely believe that she'd actually *got* the win.

There was about a three-second window between Meera being handed her frankly tacky trophy-that-was-also-a-functioning-cake-slice and the whole group of finalists being mobbed by their various emotionally resonant guests, plus the occasional person who just wanted to take their last chance to get on telly. Audrey stood a little to one side, leaving the moment for the people who'd earned it. Besides, she was still processing.

"Some comments for the cameras," one of the interchangeable, black-T-shirted producers was saying to Meera.

With her adoring and, Audrey had to admit, adorable family gathered around her, Meera clutched her cake-slice-trophy like a sword and smiled at the viewing public. "I should probably say," she began, "that I'm just happy to be here, and everybody did so well and I wish we could all have been winners, and ladies—" she turned to Doris and Alanis who, Audrey was sure, would be at least briefly cut into the shot in post—"you were both brilliant. But I think what I really *want* to say"—she brandished the cake slice—"is: I earned this."

It wasn't the acceptance speech Audrey had expected, but she sneakily thought it had a good chance of becoming iconic.

As the production crew put the final, final touches on the

eighth season of *Bake Expectations*—exit interviews with the runners-up, texture shots of the lawn, the obligatory scenes of people hugging and being excited—Audrey let herself take a moment to just…be there. To savour having been part of something. Something that wasn't exactly going away but wasn't exactly sticking around either. Something that was ending and beginning and changing and staying exactly the same all at once. Something that, for a half of a half of a heartbeat was singularly, perfectly, *now*.

And then it was done. The celebratory noises had died away, the camera operators were putting down their cameras, the cleanup crew began thanklessly picking paper plates off the formerly pristine lawn, and Colin Thrimp came scampering over to where Audrey was standing. "Umm," he offered. "Jennifer says you were right. She was the best choice."

"Yeah," Audrey said, looking at where Meera had been before the crowd swallowed her. "She really was."

"She also says turn around."

Audrey turned around to see Jennifer Hallet, wireless mic still pinned to her lapel, sauntering across the grass towards them.

"That's a wrap, Lane."

She wasn't sure, but Audrey thought she heard a note of melancholy in Jennifer's voice. "And you're okay with that?"

"Always wanted to go out on a high note."

Cautiously, Audrey took Jennifer's hand. "So what now?"

"If you're up for it, I still say we have a go at *Dead Fish and Sad Children*."

There were a hundred reasons why they shouldn't. A thousand. Right then, Audrey couldn't bring herself to give a single solitary shit about any of them. "You know what," Audrey replied. "Let's fucking do it."

Jennifer actually looked shocked. "What, really?"

"Were you not serious?"

"I'm as serious as a brain tumour. But I thought you'd still be all, *Ooh no, it's too soon, what if*—"

"Oh, shut *up*, Jennifer. It's a risk. Of course it's a risk. But *life* is risks and I'm in the mood to take one."

"Even if—"

Audrey smiled a smile that somehow managed to be both aggressive and sappy. "Which part of 'Oh, shut *up*' didn't you understand?"

The intimate-ish moment of planning her entire future life and career with an annoying sweary woman was interrupted by a tap on her shoulder. Turning, Audrey saw a woman in maybe her sixties who, though her face was less lined and her hair closer to grey than white, was the absolute image of Doris.

"Excuse me," she said. "Are you—I don't mean to be weird, but are you Audrey Lane?"

"You'd better fucking believe she is," said Jennifer Hallet, helpfully.

"My mum's said a lot about you and I think—I mean I know—she didn't win, but I think it'd mean a lot to her if you were with us right now."

Audrey blinked in confusion. "Isn't this sort of a family time?"

Beside her, Jennifer was scowling. "Fuck me, Lane, you've been all over this woman's business for months. Go tell your friend she did well."

"I'm Susan, by the way," said Susan. Because of course she was. Who else would she have been?

And Audrey said, "I know," which thankfully Susan didn't think was odd and let herself be led over to where Doris and her family were waiting.

"This is my brother Robert," said Susan conversationally, "and my sister Maggie."

They both waved, although it seemed Maggie, all these years later, was still bad with strangers.

"This is my husband," Susan went on. And then she went on, and on, and on, introducing partners and children and children's partners and children's children until Audrey wanted to break down and cry. Because she'd barely thought about this side of Doris's life. The side that the rest of the world saw every day, the side that was, in its own way, just as much a monument to Doris's legacy as any story Audrey could tell. A side she wouldn't be complete without.

Doris's voice—a voice she'd heard so often over the last few weeks that she could hear it in her sleep—brought Audrey sharply back to the present. "Hello you. This is a nice surprise."

"We thought you'd want to see her," said Susan.

"She's not shut up about you," added one of the grandsons. A Tim, Audrey was pretty sure, although even her good-with-namesness had its limits.

"Don't you tell such tales Timothy Rice," replied Doris with grandmatriarchal authority.

Bobby Junior—Robert, he was actually called, a quiet, dapper man in his sixties with steel-grey hair and a glint in his eyes that Audrey suspected was hereditary—put his arms around his mother. "We're sorry you didn't win."

"I'm not," Doris replied. "I mean, I am but it's—you know when you watch the show and everyone's all, 'Ooh, I'm just glad I got to be here.'"

"And you're all, 'No you're fucking not, you're fucking gutted and you wish some other bastard had gone out instead,'" said Timothy Rice. "Yeah I know."

A murmur of assent from the extended family suggested that they all knew, and they all shared the same reading.

Doris gave a little shrug. "Turns out they ain't lying. I'd've liked to win. Course I would. But just *being* here was"—she locked eyes with Audrey—"it was special."

"Well, if that's good enough for you, Mum," said Robert, "it's good enough for—"

The sound of an engine cut him off. And since they were away from the carpark and the hotel had a strict no-driving-in-the-pretty-bits policy, which the *Expectations* crew enforced rigorously to minimise lost footage, the sound of an engine was extremely unexpected. Especially because it was so *loud*.

As everyone watched, a jet-black open-top Bugatti Veyron slid to a halt at a careless angle outside the ballroom. Colin Thrimp had already raced up to intercept it, but Audrey—knowing this could only be one person—did not at all fancy his chances.

Emily Branningham, her hair windswept from the drive, stepped down into the grounds of Patchley House. She was wearing wide-leg satin trousers and a navy-and-cream plaid jacket that was probably the most stylish thing Audrey had ever seen in real life. For a moment she paused, framed by the house she'd grown up in. And when Colin attempted to ask her why she was here and tell her why she couldn't be, she ignored him completely, stalking towards the crowd. Towards Doris. Towards Audrey.

"Gran," said a slightly balding man in his late thirties who Audrey was pretty sure was a William. "I think there's a strange woman coming for you."

The strange woman descended like the angel of death, and Doris stood waiting for her, either transfixed or defiant. Either way, Audrey couldn't help sidling closer.

Emily Branningham lowered yet another pair of fabulous, oversized sunglasses. "Nymph."

"Emily." It seemed Doris was choosing defiance. "This is my family."

"Charmed."

"Everybody," Doris continued, keeping way calmer than Audrey thought she'd have been able to in the circumstances. "This is Emily. She was—we was—look can we do this somewhere else?"

"It's all right, Mum," said Susan. "Whatever it is, it's all right."

Audrey held her breath just a little, half expecting—perhaps three-quarters expecting—Emily Branningham to say something callous, demeaning, or flat-out self-destructive.

She didn't. Yet.

"Your mother and I," she said instead, "we…"

"Hang on," said a woman in a chiffon blouse who Audrey was pretty sure was a Tiffany and one of Maggie's daughters. "Is this a coming-out speech?"

It could have been awkward, but Doris decided to own it. "Pretty much, yeah."

The part of Audrey's brain that Jennifer Hallet had both fallen for and taken up residence in really wished they were still filming this, because it really *would* have made a banger of a finale. The rest of Audrey, though, really didn't. While *in a garden surrounded by your entire family and quite a lot of other people's families* wasn't exactly a private setting, compared to a national TV broadcast, it was practically intimate.

Now that she'd done the hard part of explaining—or at least implying—to her family that this strange immaculately dressed woman who'd just gate-crashed a film set in a car worth north of a million pounds was something in the vicinity of her ex-girlfriend,

Doris could go back to defiance. She folded her arms, looked Emily Branningham squarely in the eye and said, "Well?"

Audrey didn't hear what Emily said next. She moved very close to Doris and murmured something in her ear. And when Audrey tried to imagine what that something might have been, all the options seemed wrong or trite or too much or not enough.

But whatever it was, it was what Doris needed. She nodded once. Then glanced towards her family. "You'll be all right here without me for a bit, won't you?"

"What's a bit?" asked one of them, but Susan said more confidently, "Course we will."

And then Emily Branningham led Doris Rice-nee-Cooper back up past Patchley House, helped her into the passenger seat of her irresponsibly dangerous vehicle, climbed in beside her, and the two of them sped away together.

Audrey watched them until they were gone.

Which didn't take long. Because Emily drove very, very fast, the afternoon sun catching upon the car like a starburst.

Since Leaving the Competition

Gerald has, in his own words, been up to "Oh, you know, all sorts of things, this and that, can't keep it straight."

John is still teaching his sons to bake; one of them is enjoying it. One of them isn't.

Audrey has left her job at Shropshire's second largest regional newspaper and is now pursuing other projects.

Jim is still making buns for the lads on his building site…but now they've stopped laughing at him about it.

Linda took six weeks off baking after filming, but is back on the horse now. She still avoids macarons, though.

Reggie has started a course in molecular gastronomy, and if it goes well, he hopes to see us on *Bake Expectations: The Professionals*.

Joshua has gone back to university, where his cupcakes are in extremely high demand, especially from his girlfriend.

Alanis has now finished her GCSEs. Between choosing her A-levels and cooking with her grandmother every Sunday, she's also writing a column for BBC Food. She says her schedule is "pretty intense."

Doris has sent us a postcard from St. Moritz. She is having a lovely time.

Meera has been inundated with requests for her cakes that don't look like cakes. So many, in fact, that a book of them will be out next year.

EPILOGUE

Episode One

Tuesday

"WELCOME," GRACE FORSYTHE was saying as she strode across the grounds of Patchley House, heading downhill now, towards the Lodge, "to my brand-*spanking*-new documentary series—"

"Can you emphasise *spanking* less?" asked Audrey from the sidelines.

Grace Forsythe stopped and gave her a hangdog look. "It's my *style,* Audrey. My *inimitable style*. Really, you're getting as bad as Jennifer."

"She is fucking not," Jennifer Hallet told her. "She's not threatened to fire you once."

"Although," added Audrey, "I'm beginning to see why you did."

Leaning her head back, Grace Forsythe pleaded with the heavens for mercy. "My God, I miss Colin. I knew where I was with Colin."

Jennifer Hallet gave half a shrug. "You could always go back to *Expectations*. It's his show now."

"After it went to commercial television?" Grace Forsythe gave a theatrical shudder. "No. No, I won't hear it. I have never been interrupted by advertisements and I never will be."

Aware that they were losing light, Audrey made an effort to get things back on track. "From the top?"

Grace Forsythe went begrudgingly back to her mark. "Welcome to my brand-spanking—sufficiently little spanking? Good—new documentary *We Are Britain*. Each week we will be travelling to a different part of the country and speaking to people about the parts of our little island story that maybe aren't told quite as often as they should be. And our first episode starts here"—she stopped and indicated the ground where she stood—"on a site eagle-eyed viewers might recognise from a show that BBC advertising regulations forbid me from naming. Patchley House, in fairest Surrey."

"She's fucking good, isn't she?" said Audrey to Jennifer, as quietly as she could manage.

"Infuriatingly," Jennifer agreed.

Grace Forsythe went on with her introductory spiel, explaining a little of the history of the house, of its part in the blitz, and evacuation, and the history of the family that had owned it and had sold it. And the unlikely love story that took place there.

"Is..." Audrey began, tentatively. "Is anybody going to watch this?"

Sliding an arm around Audrey's waist, Jennifer pulled her close. "They might. And if they don't, fuck 'em."

It was a sentiment that present-day-Audrey was getting used to. That two-years-ago-Audrey and ten-years-ago-Audrey were learning to live with, that fifteen-years-ago-Audrey might have understood all along.

"Yeah," she said, leaning against her hot, angry, TV-producing, definitely girlfriend. "Fuck 'em."

ACKNOWLEDGEMENTS

My special thank-yous to the usual suspects: my assistant, Mary; my editor, also, confusingly, Mary; and my fabulous agent, Courtney Miller-Callihan.

ABOUT THE AUTHOR

Alexis Hall lives in a little house in the southeast of England where he writes books about people who bake far better than he does. He can, however, whip up a passable brownie if pressed.